The Moon and Back

by USA TODAY bestselling author

GINGER SCOTT

For Kathleen.
Thank you for being an incredible friend.
You are an inspiration, and I'm so proud of you for standing tall.

Chapter 1
Present

I t hasn't rained like this in years. We've had rain, yes. Fire too. But not since I was a kid did the skies open up on the California desert the way they have the past seventeen hours. The coastal cities are already flooding. Mudslides destroying roads, sweeping away compact cars, and uprooting trees from front lawns. I tried to avoid the breaking news coverage, but my mom insisted I turn it on.

"Just look, Brynn!" she begged after I ignored her fifty text messages all begging me to cancel tonight's showcase music event and stay off the roads.

I'd love to cancel. I'd give anything to cancel. Anything except my job. And if I cancel, I *will* lose it. Because nobody blows off the Yucca Valley Music Showcase because they might get their hair wet.

Rain or shine. No matter what day of the week October fourteenth falls on. The showcase happens, and our desert valley's most promising young musicians stand up alongside local legends to get their chance at making it. My mom should know better than to ask me to cancel. Dad never did when he was music director at Yucca Valley North High. And I remember a few torrential downpours over the years that made the event a challenge.

My chandelier quivers, the crystal beads tinkling against one another seconds after a flash of light burns through every window in my home, illuminating the clutter left behind from my manic search for all things weatherproof and emergency centric. The thunder rolls on for several seconds, buzzing the metal-framed photos on my walls. My already pounding heart speeds up its beat a breath, and when my phone rings I leap a good foot in the air.

"Shit," I mutter, dumping the towels, plastic music-sheet covers, spare umbrellas, flashlights, and the sad, half-eaten granola bar I keep thinking I'll get to finish, on the dining room table. I grab my phone from my hip pocket and pause at the sight of my black slacks marred by tiny beads of cotton from my towels.

"Shit!"

I run my free hand down my thighs while I answer the call coming in from MaryAnn, my teaching assistant.

"Please tell me they have a generator." My out-of-breath plea goes unanswered, and I stand up straight, abandoning the dream of clean slacks for the evening. "How can they not have a generator?"

"No, Brynn . . . it's not that. It's . . ."

My chest tightens.

"Is it flooding?" It's probably flooding, which again, doesn't mean we cancel. The crazy people in this valley will endure anything for this showcase. It's not only the parents with musical prodigies, either. It's everyone who lives in this hidden dustbin of a county. This damn showcase is like life—like blood for veins, oxygen for lungs, a soul for the soulless. It's what makes this place feel special, and it's been that way for years.

Since way before I stood on the stage at Pappy & Harriet's and took my shot.

Since—

"Johnny's here," MaryAnn breaks in. I blink for a moment, wondering if I imagined her words just now as a way to finish my thought.

"He showed up maybe twenty minutes ago."

I did not imagine.

Since Johnny Bishop put the town on the map and went on to win every Grammy category he was nominated for the very next year.

"Why?" I nudge a nearby chair out from my table and flop down, my legs suddenly weak.

Since Johnny Bishop left town without as much as a goodbye.

"He's a mess, Brynn. And he's asking for you. Like, on the mic. He stood on one of the tables and cupped it as he shouted your name, making it squeal. He laughed, but George did not. People are videoing on their phones, and even though he's out of his mind, they all want their pictures taken with him."

My head throbs as MaryAnn paints the scene for me. George has owned Pappy & Harriet's for years. He doesn't find many things amusing, so no . . . I imagine an out-of-control celebrity scaring away customers isn't on his *funny* list. My eyes flutter shut as my mind builds the rest of the picture. Johnny has always been troubled. It's not entirely his fault, but at some point, on some level, he has to own his behavior. I knew things had gotten bad. As much as I try to avoid news about him, it's hard when his busted-up face is plastered on tabloid magazines in the grocery store. The latest headlines were all some combination of DRUG-FUELED FIGHT GETS POP STAR SENSATION JAIL TIME.

But if Johnny's here . . . if he's asking for me?

"I'll be right there. I'm bringing everything I can with me, and my car is packed. Can you ask a few of the students to watch for my car out front so they can carry in everything you'll need?" I form a fist on the tabletop and lower my head until my forehead rests on it.

"Yeah, but what do you mean by everything *I'll* need?" Panic vibrates her words. I swallow down the jagged lump in my throat. I wish I could send MaryAnn to take care of Johnny, but he isn't her promise. He's mine.

He has no right to collect now on oaths made when I was naïve and young. And I have every goddamn right to refuse. My gut twists harder on itself at the thought. I won't refuse. I don't think a lifetime of therapy will make me strong enough to renege on my promise to him.

"He's in serious trouble, MaryAnn. You know we're old friends." I've told her stories, though I've never shared much beyond the surface of our past. Class hijinks, a duet or two during the showcase, movie nights at my house. Johnny and I were friends, at least according to MaryAnn.

Since Johnny Bishop stole my dreams and broke my heart beyond repair.

"Yeah, I know, but it's the showcase. And this weather is nuts! And the parents who are already here—"

"Are nuts! I know!" I shouldn't yell at her. She's stressed. And I basically fed her to the wolves in the matter of a phone call.

I take in a deep breath and march to my pantry to get a fabric grocery bag for this last batch of emergency items.

"Look, I'll make an announcement and I promise that as soon as I am done with Johnny, I'll come back." Never mind that it's apocalypse-level raining for the next who-knows-how-many hours.

"The parents are going to hate me." Her meek confession tugs the corner of my mouth up.

"Yeah. But they hate everyone unless their kid wins, so don't worry about it." I scoop the pile from my table into my Charlie's Foods bag and tuck my phone between my shoulder and chin so I can lock up and rush to my car.

"I know this sucks, and I'm sorry. But I will write the review of a lifetime for you if you can manage that place for an hour. Two tops." We both know it's a lie. I'll be lucky to get back here in time to tally the judges' results. "I'm heading your way. Ask Jade and Malachi to wait by the door. They're the most responsible seniors." AKA their parents won't be hovering like the others will.

"Okay, drive safe." I end the call before I can answer her and instead chuckle to myself as I look at the smeared glass reflected in my rearview mirror.

"Safe," I echo with a punched out laugh.

I shift into reverse and glance back down at my black pants, now soaked and sporting flecks of terry cloth. My gray turtleneck is stifling, but there's no time to change. I wasn't expecting to spend the night weaving through the desert foothills back to Palm Springs so I can check my high school boyfriend into rehab. Maybe it's good that the world is ending all around me. It's a good distraction, and the only reason I'm not bawling my eyes out right now—or throwing up in the gravel alongside my driveway.

"What are you doing, Brynn?" I don't talk to myself often, and when I do, I rarely listen to the advice my better self—the voice inside me—gives. This time won't be any different, but I think if I don't yell at myself, at least a little, I run the risk of getting caught in Johnny's web.

I'm right. He doesn't deserve me. He hasn't earned the right for me to keep my promise. Besides, I was coerced into that promise a little—wooed by the cutest boy I'd ever seen staring into my eyes. I would have promised him the world. Instead, I promised if he ever really needed someone, needed me, I would answer his call.

So here I go, clocking a whole ten miles per hour down the highway toward Pioneertown, through Armageddon, to answer Johnny's call.

MaryAnn and a handful of students are waiting by the open door as I pull up. I park on the curb since in some places the water is creeping onto the sidewalks. The parking lot is full, and a part of me wonders how many of those cars will get stuck in the loose gravel after three hours of music. I have doubts as it is about my own off-road wagon.

Jade, my favorite student—because yeah, teachers have favorites—meets me first, taking the bag from my arm and hooking it across her body before holding out her arms for me to load up with a box.

"Is it true?" Her eyes are wide, and her lips play with a timid smile.

I'm not sure which *it* she's referring to, but I can guess.

"Yeah, I know Johnny Bishop. He's not well, so do me a favor and try to chill any rumors about me and him that might come up tonight, yeah?" I grab the box of ponchos from my passenger seat and twist around to hand them to Jade. Her expression is still childlike, star struck. I get it. I once saw Keanu Reeves surfing in Malibu and when he walked back up the beach and nodded, my face looked as frozen as hers.

"Jade." I snap her out of her trance.

"Yeah, umm, sure. No problem, Ms. Fisher."

I nod in thanks but cringe inwardly at how she said my name. It makes me sound like a schoolmarm. Such emphasis on that *Ms.* I'm twenty-eight. I have many prospects, as they say in the Austen novels I relish. I'm simply enjoying my independence. Granted, the black slacks, turtleneck, and slicked-back brown hair pulled into a tightly-bound bun don't exactly scream young and hip. But it's pouring, and I didn't want to spend hours doing my hair only to have it end up looking like a dirty mop. And I wasn't exactly planning to see such an important ghost from my past.

The rest of the students clear out my car quickly, leaving me to stand alongside MaryAnn underneath the portico as the door to the rugged western restaurant-slash-makeshift concert venue closes.

"He's in the back, by the stage—"

"*Shh*," I hush my coworker and friend, my finger to my lips. The weight in my chest is too much right now. I need a minute.

"I want to stand out here for a few seconds and pretend everything's going off without a hitch. It looks nice through the window, doesn't it?" I nod toward the blurred scene before us, framed by the black trim of the heavy wooden door, a warm glow of lights above and on tables flickering with the movement of bodies inside. Chaos ensues on the other side. Families are battling over the best seats in the house while the waitstaff is shorthanded and overworked. The usual scent of charred beef and burning wood and coals isn't here to lull everyone into submission, which means people are probably hungry and disappointed they won't be getting their favorite ribs or filet. Beyond the thick crowd is an older gentleman on a stage, wrestling a mic away from a man my age who has always thought he deserved the spotlight and attention. And as hard as I try to block out the sound emanating from inside, that mic makes it impossible not to hear him calling my name, or some variation of it.

"Brynnie Winnie Pooh!"

My shoulders hike up and my neck sinks into my spine.

"Like I said, he's really messed up." MaryAnn isn't

throwing an *I-told-you-so* at me, but rather offering me an excuse for feeling embarrassed right now. I'm not the one on the stage acting like a fool, but somehow, my skin is burning and the desire to bury my head in a hole is strong.

"I know he is. He came into this world that way. And here I am, taking him to get fixed." I turn to meet MaryAnn's eyes and blink once, my mouth a hard, resolute line. Johnny's been through rehab once before. He came out worse. At least, according to everything I've read. It's not like I've actually talked to him in years. With a sigh, I walk toward the door and yank it open. The barrage of shouting blasts my face.

I'm caught by needy parents within moments, but MaryAnn is quick to step in and handle concerns for me so I can stay on target. He's singing, and not well, which is weird to hear from his throat. His back is to me by the time I'm a dozen feet from the stage, but I swear to God he senses I'm close. The hand holding the mic drops to his side, and his head slumps forward, giving me a view of the crunchy curls peeking out of the back of his beanie and the long tag from his T-shirt flipped out from the collar. His hair isn't wet, but it was at one point. Which means he's been standing in here shouting for me long enough for it to dry.

Johnny twists his head a hint, finding me in his sideways glance, and as messed up as he is—as our history is—the slightest glimpse of his fucking perfect blue eyes, even when they're framed by red, stops my heart for more than a beat.

"Brynnie Winnie—" He trips over his own feet before he can croon the Pooh part into the microphone—*thank God!*

Johnny stumbles on the stage, losing this grip on the mic and sending it rolling in the opposite direction until it disappears off the edge. My only clue that someone finds it is the loud screeching sound it makes as they struggle to figure out how to turn it off. With a bloody lip thanks to the crash landing on the hardwood planks beneath him, Johnny lifts his weary head and stammers out my name one more time while dragging himself toward me in an army crawl.

"Brynn. I need you."

My gut sinks.

Shit.

This is why I came. Why he is asking for me. He knew I'd say yes. I have to. I promised.

"I know, Johnny. Come on, let's get you to my car." I hold my hand out toward him and he spends a few seconds staring at it. It's not that his eyes can't focus, though it's a shock that he can, given how wasted he is. This lingering stare is more painful than that. It's full of our past and what should have been.

Finally snapping out of his trip through our busted potential, Johnny drags his body to the edge of the stage and grips my hand while running the sleeve of his disheveled and dirty flannel along his bloody lip.

"Don't do that. You'll make it worse," I chastise, pulling his hand away from his face. Mothering him. Taking care of him.

Old habits.

Sitting on the edge of the stage with one hand clinging to mine, the other gripping the stage, probably to keep the room from spinning, Johnny's entire frame slumps as his bloodshot, broken eyes lock on mine. It hurts, seeing him this way.

"I'm sorry, Brynn. I'm so fucking sorry." He throws up on the floor between us, and my grip on his hand is the only thing keeping him from tumbling from the stage to land in his own mess. He smells awful. His vomit smells awful. This entire place is dank and probably populating tenfold with mold spores as the inches of rain stack up.

I don't have to survey the room to know that most of the parents are glaring at me with disgust. See, Johnny is this town's pride and joy. He's famous. The entire country—*no, world!*—adores him. He shot to stardom the minute he opened his mouth and sang in front of a few thousand screaming college girls all filming with their phones and instantly making his videos go viral. Nobody cares that he's an alcoholic drug addict with massive baggage he desperately needs to sort through. All they see is me, navigating him through this saloon and out into my car. It's my fault he's here. I mean, after all, he clearly came for me. And I know what assumption is in most of their minds.

It's probably her fault he's like this.

Chapter 2
11 years ago, age 17

T he cut grass remnants clump on the sides of my sneakers. The grounds crew keeps the football field nice and tidy. Nothing like the band practice field. Their hash marks are perfect, no trimmings left behind to clog up their cleats, or over-grown tufts around broken sprinkler heads. Who cares that our football team is mediocre and not a single person from this school has ever gone on to become a professional athlete. Mean-while, over here where the band practices, who knows how many of us will go on to score movie soundtracks, produce albums, write Grammy-winning songs.

Yucca Valley North High is an arts school. The cool kids don't like to talk about it, *but here?* It's the nerds who rule. Yeah, the typical cliques still win homecoming king and queen, and get elected class president. But the arts nerds? We're the ones full of potential. And I'm not simply being biased. There's an entire wall in the cafeteria covered with plaques and framed *Rolling Stone* issues and signed photos from famous actors and singers. We even have a few major mixed media artists who have come out of our little cove in the desert and gone on to have gallery showings in New York. But it's this music department that shines the brightest.

A lot of people around here think I have it easy—that being the music director's kid means I get a pass on rehearsals or easy access to whatever special project or club I want to lead. But my father's not like that. If anything, I have to work twice as hard. Ethics are big in our family, and sometimes I end up losing out even when I'm the best simply because my dad doesn't want it to look like I'm getting special treatment.

I'm determined not to let anything get in the way of becoming drum major for the Yucca Valley North Marching Howl. I grew up watching the band take the field and put on these massive displays of color and sound at halftime. Our brass blows every other band in California out of the water—or sand, in our case. And our drumline gets bigger cheers than our cheerleaders. But being the one with the whistle and the white gloves and that golden staff? That's it for me. I want to *lead*.

Josh Mezcal served as drum major for three years, and I spent every single one of them studying his moves. He trained me for this. And though he can't officially hand the staff down to me as a graduating senior, in a way he has just by giving me his time and attention. He's beautiful and perfect and so full of talent. And he can sing! It's not just drums and dance that shot him to the top of the podium on Friday nights—it's his charisma.

Charisma.

That's where I lack. And it's why I work so hard everywhere else to compensate for my wallflower tendencies. As confident as I am in my musical skills, my people skills score a big fat zero-point-zero. There isn't an instrument in this department I haven't mastered. We got a harp last year as part of a grant, and by spring, I was playing it for the end-of-year concert. I can sing, too. And even though my voice isn't the powerhouse that Josh's is, it's solid. My pitch is perfect. A mezzo-soprano, right in the middle. Flexible. Generic. Unremarkable.

That last word is the one that stings. It was written on my feedback sheet from the fall showcase. Being the drum major is only half of my mission. I plan on using everything I learn at the helm of our band to propel me into better results for the fall showcase.

Perfection and all the practice in the world aren't what wins hearts at that event. I know that now. And really? I knew better than to think I could win anything with a cutesy piano performance of "You've Got a Friend in Me." The students who win the fall showcase move people. They make the audience cry or do something that gets them on their feet. They own the room.

They're charismatic.

Which is what I'm going to master over the next seven months from the top of this podium during spring and summer practices and fall football games.

I knock my shoes against the curb at the edge of the field, clearing away the clippings so I can run through my audition one more time. I tap my earbud to play the drum count again and roll my feet along the grass, practically floating my way to the middle of the field before snapping into perfect posture and rotating around for my salute. Clean and simple—the way the judges like it—I extend my white-gloved right hand and bring it to my forehead in a single count, my left hand balled in red sequins at my side. I hold everything for a full breath then drop my salute and pull both of my hands into fists stretched out in front of me. My timing is perfect, as it has been for the last six dry runs, and the music begins with my direction, as if the band is literally in front of me on the field.

I complete the entire opening song, marching to the

podium on the fifty-yard line and scaling the five steps in sync with the music and the beats I'm counting out with my hands. I close the song out, push out a strong *hut hut* from my gut, and drop my hands to dismiss the invisible instruments held up in front of me. A bead of sweat slips from my brow and slides along my cheek, resting at my upper lip. I ignore it as long as I can, a test for myself to show I can handle distractions. But the sun is bright today, and this leather-brimmed feather-plumed black hat is baking my head. It's always miserably hot at the end of the school year. I finally relax and pull my earbuds out, stuffing them in their case and returning it to my pocket before taking a seat on the practice podium and resting my hat in my lap.

Leaning forward, I shake my hair out from its braid and run my fingers through the damp brown waves. I'm out of water, so it looks like that's it for today. I feel ready, though. The next time I step up here will be for my actual audition in front of the outgoing seniors, who all get a vote, our school principal, guest directors from other schools, and my father. A weekend break and then a truth test.

I sit back and rest my hands on the back edge of the podium and tilt my face to the sky. The afternoon sun kisses my cheeks, drying any sign of perspiration left along my hairline in seconds. I squint at the reflections on the few puffy clouds, then twist to catch the end of spring football practice on the good field behind me.

"Howl on three—one, two, three—Howl!"

I smirk, impressed that they can manage a four-four count. My friend Teddy knows me well enough to guess that I'm chuckling at them right now and he shakes his head at me as the huddle of players disperses. I wave him over and he holds up his green water bottle, shaking it in an offer. I fold my legs up as I face him directly and press my palms together as I shout, "Please!" Teddy nods and stops at the water cooler to refill his bottle before jogging toward me—my savior.

"Squirt it like they do on the sidelines," I call out as I push off from the podium and abandon my hat for cool water. I open my mouth like a guppy, tilting my head as I wait for my friend to hit me with a shot of water. The spray hits the back of my throat and teeth, misting my cheeks. I cough as I swallow what I can then back up a step or two in laughter.

"It's harder than it looks." I don't recognize the guy who stepped up behind my friend while I was busy embarrassing myself, and when he takes the water bottle in his hand and sprays water in his own mouth, I feel the weight of his comment—he didn't make that look very hard.

"Oh, hey. Brynnie, this is Johnny. He's new. And you won't believe this but he can actually throw a football." Teddy chuckles at his quip. Our quarterback last season could throw the ball too, only directly into the other team's hands.

"Nice to meet you." With his helmet tucked under one arm, the new guy reaches forward to shake my hand. He blows up at the lock of brown hair that's fallen over one eye and smiles with half his mouth. He's cute. Well, no . . . he's hot. My friend Teddy is cute, like one of those squishy stuffed toys at the gift shop cute. Teddy's a standard surfer-boy with curly blonde locks that he piles into a man-bun for football practice but otherwise lets flow freely from the back of a hat. This guy? He's got poster-boy good looks. Dark lashes. Perfect skin. A top lip that curls up a hint when he speaks. A few freckles along his cheeks and nose. Bronzed arms. And his exposed abs that I'm trying to avoid staring at with every ounce of will are like forbidden gold. He's unusual for this town. Polished. Definitely not the hippy-artsy type most of us fall into.

My mouth is a tight smile as I glance to Teddy while shaking Johnny's hand. I'm not used to people acting so formal. His grip is strong, like an interview handshake. And he holds on a little longer than seems customary, not that this is customary. Maybe it's that his hand is so much bigger than mine, or the way his fingers are callused, or the warmth engulfing my hand. My eyes bounce from our hands back to his face—again doing my best to avoid that glimpse of midriff under his jersey. His gaze drifts to the podium sitting behind me. He finally lets my hand drop as he steps toward it, hopping onto it in an impressive standing jump.

"This is pretty cool. What's it for?" Johnny takes a slow turn, shading his eyes from the setting sun when he faces it. It's as if he's memorizing the landscape, searching for something. He knocks my plume hat to the ground with his toe.

"Brynn's a band nerd," Teddy pipes in.

I squeeze Teddy's water bottle just as it hits his lips, spraying his face in retribution.

"What? You are!"

I grimace at his lame defense.

"What my friend isn't telling you is that this place is kinda known for music, dance, and theater. Not so much for football." I shrug. "Sorry." I twist my lips to show I'm teasing, but Johnny doesn't seem to be fazed. He's still finishing his turn on the podium, his gaze fixed on the few teammates still clearing out from practice. He squints, one eye closed more than the other, and lingers on the view until the only thing left to see is the empty field and a few stray water cups rolling down the fifty-yard line.

"Huh. That's cool. I didn't know there were schools for that stuff. How do you take those classes? You know, like band or whatever?" His gaze snaps to mine, and I hold my breath for a few seconds, waiting for his joke to land.

Holy shit, he's serious.

"Uh, I mean. You can talk to your counsellor. We only have

one more quarter before school lets out, but you can always try out for one of the clubs for next year." A few of the guys on the football team also work on the plays and musicals. Some of them are pretty great dancers, too. Our hip hop squad won state last year. And then there's glee.

"What are you trying out for?" He squats, still perched on top of the podium. He rests his helmet at his side under his palm for balance. He looks like a live-action trophy.

"Brynn wants to be the *head* band nerd."

I swing my arm to my right and land an open palm on Teddy's chest, knocking the breath from him. Asshole.

"Drum major tryouts." I leave it simple, expecting Johnny's interest to die immediately. Only, now he seems even more intrigued. He hops to the ground and picks up my discarded hat, dusting the grass bits from the black feathers before inspecting the inside.

"Is this like . . . one size fits all?"

He tugs the chin strap out to test its stretch before slipping my hat on his way-too-big-for-it skull. I glance to Teddy who simply chuckles and shakes his head.

"Kind of. I mean, there are two sizes, and I think you maybe need the bigger one." I reach my hand out in a grabby motion. He's stretching it out, and I don't like it.

Rather than give it back, Johnny slides the chin strap up so it's out of the way, then proceeds to climb the steps to the podium again. With his hands up and his head held perfectly still since my hat is merely balancing on his sweaty head, he moves his arms up and down in what I assume he thinks is drum majoring.

"Like this?" His grin is caught somewhere between euphoric and mocking, and I can't tell whether he wants my approval or is teasing me.

"Sure." I roll my eyes and decide he's probably being a jerk, and I really want my hat back.

His hands fall to his sides and his smile collapses as I walk to the front of the podium and hold my hand out once again for my plume. He dips his chin and catches my hat in his palms, then kneels to hand it to me.

"I didn't mean to belittle what you're trying out for. I swear." His half smile is only a third as big as it was when we shook hands, and my stomach drops with guilt. I was being defensive because as much as this place is where artists and hippies thrive, it also has its fair share of factions, and the football team and cheerleader crowd still has an air of superiority. Doesn't seem to matter that the bulk of them literally go nowhere after graduation.

"I'm sorry. I guess I'm a little stressed about it." I fidget with my hat in my hands, tugging on the strap to test the stretch—*to make sure he didn't ruin it.*

"Why don't you show him your salute!" Teddy is being genuinely supportive, but I could kill him for that suggestion.

"It's not quite ready—"

"Bullshit. It's great! Give him one of your earbuds like you did for me yesterday," my friend says. He doesn't seem to be deterred at all by my widened eyes that are desperately trying to convey *knock it off!* to him.

"I'd love to see what this stuff is all about." Johnny hops down from the podium again and takes his helmet with him, tucking it under his arm.

"Uhhh—" I glance to Teddy then back to Johnny, surreptitiously surveying the campus behind them for witnesses. It's one thing when the football team is busy with practice and I'm out here. Having them purposely stop and watch what I'm doing? I don't really need that.

"I swear I will stay totally silent the entire time." Johnny

crosses his chest with his taped fingers and my eyes accidentally follow his path before lingering on his exposed midriff and
ridiculously chiseled muscles. A thick scar cuts two, maybe
three inches along his right side, but I don't look at it long
enough to know for sure how bad it is. It's noticeable, but only
because his physique is so freaking perfect.

"Fine. But I'm only doing it once." My heart thumps wildly
and my palms instantly sweat. This is not my audience. And I
know in my gut this guy is not going to get what this stuff is all
about.

Nerves. That's the other thing I have trouble with. My dad
says it's what holds me back in the charisma department, and
he's right. It's definitely part of it. It's hard to push out light
when you're focused on staying in your own head.

I hand one of my earbuds to Johnny and push the other in
my left ear. Walking over to my starting point about twenty
yards away, I do my best to quell my rapid-fire pulse before
hitting play on the music file on my phone. I manage to calm
myself enough to focus on the drum cadence, and once my feet
take over to the rhythm, I run through the entire audition flaw-
lessly. With an audience. An oddly *intimidating* audience.

"Ha ha!" I breathe out a tiny triumph. Tilting to my side, I
peer down at Teddy and Johnny on the field below me. I'm a
little out of breath, which is weird, but I think it's because I
held my breath for the full three minutes of my drill. I pop my
earbud from my ear and pull my hat from my head, wiping
away the line of sweat across my forehead. It's definitely better
to have my hair up when I wear that thing.

Teddy claps, which seems to rattle Johnny to attention and
he begins to as well.

"You've got this, Brynn," Teddy says as I reach for my other
earbud from Johnny. For some reason, his lack of response—
other than the prompted clapping—irks me.

"Thanks, Ted. What do you think? Lame? I mean . . . for a football player?" My jaw tightens and my heartbeat thickens in my ears again. I've never been embarrassed by being a part of this stuff before. And I'm not now. Yet I'm oddly prepared for Johnny to burst into laughter and ridicule the last three minutes of my life.

"It was good." He shakes his head a little and blinks his eyes, glancing to Teddy and shrugging before meeting my eyes and lifting his shoulders.

"Good." I suck my lips in and nod slowly. That's a fairly benign, safe critique.

"Yeah, I mean . . . it's not like I know about any of this stuff. It was pretty cool how in sync your feet were with the drums and shit. Oh, and when you started to move your hands, I think I could tell you were counting out, like for the music or whatever."

I blink slowly at his detailed feedback then let a slight laugh eek out my lips.

"Right. Well, thanks . . . Johnny. I'm glad you could see me counting the music. That's . . . exactly what I was going for." I roll my eyes as I turn away from them both and make my way down the steps.

My level of snideness doesn't really hit me until I meet Teddy's glare.

"What?" I whisper.

"You're shitty at making friends." He grimaces.

He's right. I am. But I have all the friends I need. And how would Johnny like it if I took notes on their practice and my big reaction boiled down to *I really like the way you catch and throw the ball and stuff?*

I snag my backpack from the sideline and drop my earbuds inside alongside my wallet and the sheet music I still need to memorize by tomorrow. I zip it up and sling it over my shoulder as a tiny hint of guilt slips into my chest. I turn and am about to apologize for getting so defensive when Johnny suddenly drops his helmet to the ground and leaps back on the podium.

"It's just—"

My feet freeze about a dozen steps away from him, and my breath stills as he chews at the inside of his mouth, again squinting at something off in the distance. He waggles his head a little and Teddy mumbles *fuck* a few steps behind me.

My chest tightens.

"It was good. Don't get me wrong." He turns and holds his hands out at his sides, palms open, a move I guess is supposed to be consolatory or something. It makes my hairs stand tall on the back of my neck and down my arms.

My expression must be giving off warning shots, because Johnny swallows hard then shakes his head and utters, "You know what, never mind. I don't know shit about this."

"It's okay. I can take it."

I stiffen my stance and tighten my shoulders, physically bracing myself because no . . . I can't really take it. I don't take criticism well at all. Ever. From anyone. It's a known flaw, and one I constantly tell myself I want to work on. What better time to start?

Johnny breathes in through his nose as his mouth forms a tight line. His gaze flits to my friend briefly for approval, and I'm not sure whether Teddy grants it or not because I'm too locked in on Johnny's stupid, charming face.

"Maybe there are rules and stuff for this. Like I said, I don't know this world at all. I don't know if you have to have a certain number of steps or if you have to turn a certain way or use one hand before the other. But it seems to me . . . I don't know . . . that if I were a judge and was watching a bunch of people in feather hats take turns doing the exact same thing all damn day . . ."

"It might get boring?" He literally breathes out in relief as I finish his thought for him. His thought—my fear.

"Exactly!" Johnny bends his knees and swings his arms in the air. I've given him permission to not like my audition. Maybe deep down I knew it was boring all along. Safe. *Unremarkable.*

"It's still really good, Brynnie." Teddy is trying to ease my hurt feelings but it's too late. I'm already playing out how many times I will fail to earn the top honors at competition with that salute and band intro. Hell, at this point I'm lucky the other people auditioning aren't good at all. I could lose my shot with an audition like that. It's not only my father making the call—it's former drum majors, other teachers in the arts program, guest directors from other schools. Is safe and traditional still the way to win over that crowd? I don't really know at this point. Gah! In a matter of seconds I've begun to question everything!

"It's garbage, Ted. But thanks." I hang my head and let my backpack slide down my arm until it drops to the ground by my feet.

I'm not a crier, but there's an open wound inside my chest that wants to bleed—just a little.

Johnny's feet land with a thud on the field, and I glance up through my lashes as he strides toward me. For a moment, I half expect him to lift my chin and give me some soft, romantic pep talk. But that's just his allure and classic good looks worming their way into my imagination, drawing up fantasies in the wake of dejection.

"Maybe I can help."

I lift my head fully and meet his very serious and equally determined gaze.

I chuckle, partly from nerves.

"I know it seems like a dumb idea. I mean, I keep telling

you how I don't know anything about this stuff. But I'm creative sometimes. At least, my mom says I am. And I think what you're trying out for sounds interesting. And I don't know . . . I like music, I guess. So, what do you say?"

He holds out his palm again, another business deal just like our introduction twenty minutes ago.

This time, I glance to Teddy for his take on things. He simply laughs and waves his hand at us.

"You two are on your own with this. I thought it was fine before. And I know my place." Teddy tilts his head back and sprays the rest of his water into his mouth, his eyes conveniently closing.

He thought it was fine.

Fine.

Fine.

My eyes flit back to Johnny's. His mouth ticks up on one side as he shrugs.

"What do you have to lose?" His hand remains there for the taking, and despite my inner voice shouting at me to gracefully extricate myself from his offer, the real me dives in head first. I grip his hand and we shake once.

"What do I have to lose?"

My arm heats up as if his touch injected it with a dose of morphine—the rush climbing up my veins and into my neck, rendering my tongue numb and useless. Johnny something or another—a heartstopper in the looks department with Superman hair and a damn football jersey. I have to wonder . . . is it really losing something when you give it away so willingly?

Chapter 3
Present

I remember when this place opened. Johnny and I were seventeen, and our friend Teddy had started smoking a lot of weed. Upon reflection, he probably didn't smoke any more than other high school kids in California around the time. Didn't stop us from making fun of him for his way-too-expensive bong collection. And when Waves of the Desert opened, we constantly teased him that he needed to "catch a wave to recovery."

Some slogan. Guess it worked because at least a hundred major celebrities have done stints at this posh rehab-slash-resort over the last decade.

About to be one hundred and one.

The rain lets up for the first time in hours as I pull onto the giant circular drive flanked by twisting cypress trees that don't fit this region at all. The place looks more like a winery than a rehab, which is . . . ironic.

It's been years since Johnny and I have sat this close to one another. I wish I knew what was running through his mind right now. I'm sure it's the stuff of nightmares. Johnny was always plagued by them, awake and asleep. They've caught up to him; I guess he always kinda knew they would.

I pull to a stop under the portico as a flash lights up the sky and outlines the jagged mountain ridge to our left, a reminder that Mother Nature is simply taking a pause for the night. She'll be back in action whenever she pleases.

Johnny slumps forward, resting his forehead on my dashboard while fumbling with the seatbelt mechanism at his hip. I had to fight him to put the seat belt on in the first place. The last thing I needed to add to my horrific night was an accident on the desert highway that sent the world's favorite rock star and sex symbol through my windshield.

"It's broke. This thing . . . it's broke." Johnny slaps at the seatbelt lock. His slurred words are a little more coherent than they were back at the saloon. Of course, his inability to unclip a safety belt doesn't scream sober.

"Stop. I got it." My voice is firm, and his hand recoils into a loose fist that he buries between his thighs before I slap it. I hate seeing him like this. It's a waste of so much talent and beauty. Even if it's not completely his fault.

I unlock his belt and tell him to stay put while I get his door. Two young men in navy blue scrubs head toward us as I exit the car. One of them is pushing a wheelchair, the other is armed with a clipboard loaded with nondisclosure agreements and insurance guarantees, I'm sure. This is probably the only place where young people don't stop in their tracks when they lay eyes on Johnny Bishop. The staff maybe even expected him to roll in here at some point. I bet they didn't think it would be during the storm of the century. I sure didn't.

"I don't want the chair," Johnny coughs out, shooing it away as he attempts to plant one of his feet on the ground. His shoes look like the same ones he wore our senior year—skater slip-ons with doodles all over them. He spent most of his time in class making art on his shoes, his fingers, and his hands. And when he wasn't drawing on himself, he was writing songs. Seems he still releases nervous energy by scribbling. Of course, the markings on his fingers and arms are permanent. The designs are all his; I recognize them. Especially the hourglass filled with skulls and no sand left to count.

One of the attendants hands me the paperwork then kneels to help Johnny stand, sliding his shoulder under Johnny's arm as they make their way a few steps from the vehicle. It's clear he's going to need to sit in the damn chair if he wants to make it inside the building within an hour. Rather than let him refuse it again, I tuck the paperwork under my arm and grab the chair handles from the other attendant, jerking the chair behind Johnny's legs.

"Sit."

I slap the chair seat, then step in front of him so he can get a good look at how serious I am. He blinks up at me and I work my jaw, trying not to vocalize the rest of my frustrations and disappointments. I need to save those for a time when he can hear them. Or save them for my therapist and never step foot in this place again. I haven't thought beyond the *right now*, so no sense making plans for anything but the present. And presently, Johnny can only comprehend me barking at him and treating him like a child.

He flops back into the seat after a few seconds, but rather than tucking his chin and burying his gaze in his lap, he holds his focus on me. It's so hard to see the lost boy behind those eyes. He's still in there. I'm sure I'm the only one who sees him, though. The rest of the world only sees the version they've come to know, the small pieces of a carefully sewn together story his publicist crafted for him. Parts are true. The big things —the stuff that's hard to bury.

His father was an abusive fuck who everyone thought walked on water.

His mother was terrified and broken from years of being told she was nothing.

And some people around here think all the attention he got when his father's body was found at the bottom of Tanque Mountain Lake a week after Johnny left town is what propelled him to fame.

The truth? It made him infamous, for sure. At least for a little while. But his voice? The way he can make a human feel things they thought they were incapable of just by opening his mouth and singing his soul? That's the stuff that made him famous. That's what brought him the love he was so desperate to feel. And the untidy mystery surrounding his father's accident got swept up into his allure. All part of the tale that was spun and re-spun so many times that the root is indistinguishable from the illusion. It's a skin he wears. The bad boy with tattoos for confessions and a line of women waiting to sleep with him after every show. Famous ex-girlfriends left broken in his wake. A mother he hasn't talked to in years.

And then the rest of us here in Yucca, including me, are footnotes.

"Are you family?"

I barely note the voice at my side. My entire world is locked up in a set of bloodshot pools of blue still fighting to hold on to my gaze as the attendant wheels Johnny toward the sliding glass doors.

"Sorry, um . . ." My voice is scratchy and I cough to clear it. I'm sure the rehab worker chalks it up to my emotions, but I'm not emotional. I should be, maybe. It's sad to see someone hurting so much, to see them wreck themselves when they have the world at their fingertips. But this ending? It was written for Johnny a long time ago. I read ahead and knew the ending. And

I guess a part of me knew the promise I made out of love years ago would come full circle and force me to experience the end once it came. That's why my heart hurts. Because that ache I worked on healing for years was finally gone. Johnny Bishop was a footnote for me, too. Until he demanded one more damn chapter in my life.

This chapter.

"I can probably fill out most of it, but he has management. I'm sure his people have information ready to go. His spiral isn't really a secret." I shrug and am met with a sympathetic smile. I'm sure the employees at Waves of the Desert have every major agent and manager on speed dial.

"If you can just get things started." He nods toward the clipboard still tucked under my arm. I'd forgotten I was holding on to it.

"Right. Sure. Just give me a few minutes." I move toward my car, but the attendant brushes my elbow with his fingertips.

"You can leave your car parked here and come inside where it's more comfortable." He tilts his head to the right, toward the entrance, and I nod.

"Let me grab my purse." I lean in through the open passenger door, the smell of booze and vomit still strong from the car ride here. I roll down my window then grab my purse and shut the door, hoping the stench will dissipate enough for me to drive home without having to leave it rolled down.

I follow the worker inside and he guides me to a set of leather chairs and a dark wooden table tucked near a stone fireplace. I've gone from French country vineyards to a Tahoe lodge in a matter of steps. Soft jazz plays throughout the lobby, which looks more like a spa than a health retreat aimed at getting pampered celebrities off hardcore drugs and alcohol.

"You can call on that phone when you're done and someone will collect the paperwork from you." With a soft smile, the worker presses his badge against a card reader and slips through a heavy metal door. I do my best to glimpse the other side before it shuts, but all I'm able to see is the wooden floor planks continuing on down a hallway and stark cream-colored walls.

I fill out what I can, looking up Johnny's mother's information on Google. It surprises me I no longer know it by heart. Beth Bishop is still in Yucca, still in the small house on the hill. From what I have heard, she still works part time at the town library. I won't go in there anymore because of it. Not that anything was ever strained between her and me. It's just that Johnny left us both, and the more time that passed after her husband died and her son was gone, the harder it got to connect. Harder for me, at least. I presume she feels the same since she never once reached out or shows up for any of the school events I host. I read eBooks mostly anyhow, so giving up the brick and mortar library isn't that hard. And she seemingly gave up the coffee shop we both frequent, so it's a fair trade. Though the blown-glass fixtures she made in her home studio still hang there, making it hard not to think of her at least once when I order my coffee.

Thanks to a world of poor privacy regulation, I'm able to get most of his mother's information filled out with a few online searches, including two possible phone numbers. I find his management information online, too, and jot down the names I know they'll need. Flipping through the pages of medical history, I decide not to make any guesses there, except noting his latex allergy. His skin blows up in massive hives, and that's a fact I've seen with my own eyes so I feel comfortable writing that down. I won't be the person who writes down fodder for gossip beyond that, no matter how *secure and private* this place claims to be.

I pick up the phone near the door and press call. A woman

answers immediately and I tell her I've finished with the paper-work. She's in the lobby less than a minute later and takes the clipboard from me. Thumbing through the sheets, she stops on the list of emergency contacts and points to the second number I wrote down for Johnny's mother, Beth.

"Is this how we reach you?"

"Oh, no. That's another number for his mom. I wasn't sure which was most current," I explain.

"Right," she says, writing *Beth* #2 next to it in the margin.

I dig into my purse for my keys, ready to leave, when she hits me with a follow up.

"And your name and number?"

Pen poised on the line for a third contact, I pause with my mouth agape as my stomach drops. I'm not this person. I'm the one *he* calls. Not the one anyone calls about him.

"Oh, I'm not really . . . we aren't . . . family." I shake my head as my legs tremble with a new wave of panic. I wasn't ready to feel any of these things. I'm not ready to remember. I've come so far yet nowhere near far enough.

"Right." The woman props the clipboard against her ribs and folds her hands along the edge, the pen flattened under-neath them as she sucks in her lips and takes in a hard breath through her nose. "It's only that we need three. For lots of reasons, as I'm sure you understand."

"Not really." I shake my head and take a slight step back, debating on sprinting to my car. A tiny irrational fear invades my thoughts, though, keeping me in the room. *What if they hold me here against my will?* It's absurd, and my logical side knows it. But that small hint of skepticism just shot another dose of adrenaline through my core and I'm buzzing.

"Look, ma'am."

Shit. I'm ma'am. That sounds so formal. And older. Responsible.

I swallow down the sour taste and lick my lips as I meet her eyes.

"I've been working here for six years. We're trained to handle sensitive situations. And in my experience, a person doesn't drive someone to this place unless they want to help them. And if they want to help them, they care more than they maybe wish they did. I get it. Addiction is a thief, and it doesn't only steal from the addict. I promise you'll be the last resort. But you'll feel better knowing you're his last resort, that he *has* a last resort. At least on paper."

My mouth slopes, the corners like arrows pointing to the pit of my stomach. I take the pen she holds out, then the clipboard, and before I change my mind and write false information on the form, I fill in my real name and number under EMER-GENCY CONTACT #3.

Chapter 4
Age 17

This was a stupid idea. The only thing to come out of shaking Johnny's hand and making a deal to let him *help* me is now my self-doubt has skyrocketed out of control. I lied to Josh this morning when he asked me if I felt ready.

"Totally! I'm going to kill it."

He quirked a brow at my little add on. *Killing it* is not in my normal vernacular. It's part of my sarcasm settings, which I've mostly kept hidden from the upperclassmen at our school. I didn't want to go into my sudden freak-out with Josh, though. He'd want to help. And his help is what resulted in *fine.* I want to be better than fine. I want to be better than Josh. And to do that, I need to take some risks.

Johnny is a risk. Hell, he's a stranger with a cute smile and adorable hair and a body that makes me squirmy. I said yes to his offer for a lot of the wrong reasons, but at least some of them were right. Those are what I'm holding on to now, especially since it's the middle of the afternoon on a Saturday and Johnny is thirty-five minutes late for our meeting. The track team has already left, so at least there's nobody left on the fields to gawk at me. I've been trying to come up with my own creative salutes since Johnny's late, but the only conclusion I've come to is I lack all creativity.

I run through my last ideation one more time, a sort of chopping movement with my arms that mimics the shape of a Christmas tree until my right hand is level with my eyes. I sweep my hand into position and straighten my elbow then drop my hands to my sides and hold my posture straight. I blink a few times while I try to convince myself that I've come up with a winner, but I'm not buying what I'm selling to myself.

"Stupid," I mutter.

I walk over to the podium and take a seat, sipping from my jug of water and kicking my legs out and back, knocking the grass from my black leggings and sneakers. I wore a flowy pink tank top today, which is keeping me cool, except for the burn I'm starting to feel on my shoulders. I didn't bring the sunscreen with me, and it's definitely wearing off. I pull my hair from its tie to let it cover my skin a little. I consider bailing on this whole thing when someone on a BMX-style bike catches my gaze. The person is pedaling along the dirt road that backs up to the football stands. I squint to make out the body type, and when he cuts through the open gate and heads my way, I realize it's Johnny. I'm not sure where he lives or how long it took him to ride his bike here, but I wish he had said something when we made plans two days ago. I would have picked him up.

I don't realize how banged up the front wheel of his bike is until he's maybe a dozen feet away. It's bent, constantly jerking the bike to his right. To combat it, Johnny keeps lifting the front wheel and resetting it, like a makeshift alignment. Now I *really* feel like crap for not picking him up.

He stops next to the podium and hops from the bike, letting it land on its side in the grass. It looks like something he found in an alley. The handlebars lack pads, and the metal rods are rusted. I glance to his hands and notice he's wearing his football gloves, and the palms are stained the color of bricks.

"Sorry I'm late. My dad took the car, so I had to scramble." He un-Velcros his gloves and tosses them on the ground by his bike, then pulls the small backpack from his body and kneels as he unzips it.

"I guess we should have exchanged numbers. I would have picked you up."

My lips twist as I take in his bike, noting the missing half pedal now, too.

"Oh, yeah. No . . . it's fine. We live on the hill, and it's a pain in the ass to drive up there and back. I just haven't used this thing in—"

"Years?" I chuckle and thankfully so does Johnny. He kicks at the puckered tire.

"Yeah, I think maybe it has one more ride in its life, just enough to carry my ass back home."

"I doubt that. I'll just throw it in the trunk and take you home when we're done." I'm about to suggest we find a nice trash bin to toss the bike into when Johnny interrupts my thoughts.

"No, really. I want to give it one final send off. Sentimental. I can handle it." He pulls a water bottle from his bag and chugs half of the liquid down, turning his back to me while he drinks.

A rusty bike is a weird hill to die on, but if he insists, I guess I get karma credit for offering a ride.

"You ready to get started?" Johnny pops to his feet and runs a hand through his wavy hair before sauntering to the sideline and motioning for me to stand beside him. Wearing a loose-fitting long-sleeved white T-shirt and black shorts that show off his muscular legs, I'm both relieved that his abs aren't showing off to distract me yet cursed that it turns out his quads and calves are just as pretty to look at. I avert my gaze to his feet as I step closer to him and notice his canvas shoes are covered in random doodles and words scribbled in ball point pen. I recognize one of the lyrics from the band The National and smirk in amusement. Johnny follows my gaze to his feet and laughs.

"I take my stress out on my shoes, I guess," he says, rocking back on his heels.

"You were afraid you'd eat my brains," I say, earning a quizzical brow from him briefly before he recognizes the lyric on the top of his right shoe.

"Oh! Yeah. It's a great song. Whole album, really." His smile settles into something of fondness and he tilts his head slightly to read more of his own artistic plagiarism as he rolls his foot to the side. My chest warms and I realize I'm smiling a little too big for the moment. I dampen the curl of my mouth before he notices, but it only makes my skin buzz with nervous energy when Johnny's gaze lifts to mine.

"Definitely a top-five favorite album," I say, a thought I've never actually had about The National, but one that I could fake easily if it meant Johnny and I had something to bond over. And who knows, maybe it is on my top-five list. I have a lot of favorites, though. A burden of being a child of a music expert and growing up in a house with shelves upon shelves of vinyl.

Johnny's eyes linger on mine for a few seconds, his lips closed in a loose smirk, almost as if he wants to keep sharing favorite songs with me or something, but he eventually clears his throat and turns his attention to his phone in his hand.

"I did my homework for this. I really want to be helpful, and I figured to do that, I should probably see what this drum major stuff is all about. I found some videos and thought maybe watching a few of these might spark some ideas." He leans into me, his body radiating heat from riding his bike. Or radiating heat because hot guys like him do that.

The first video he plays is from a major drum corps based

in Texas. They have five drum majors, and I'm familiar with how spectacular their entries to the field are. They have a new routine every show, and they put on five shows a year. It's like club sports for marching band, and some of those kids go to that school for nothing but this. I let the sequence play on for about thirty seconds, letting them get to the salute part where they stagger in a row and basically do the wave, before sighing.

"They're great." I take a few steps back, feeling even less ready than I did an hour ago. "But we have *one* drum major. It's easier to do stuff like that when you have other people to play off of."

I move my hands at my sides, contemplating showing him the lame Christmas tree idea I came up with this morning, but I stop myself before things get embarrassing. *More* embarrassing.

"Okay, so what if . . ." His mouth forms a tight line as he stares at the paused video for a few long seconds then pops his head up to look me directly in the eyes.

"What if there were two?"

I narrow my eyes, not sure I heard him correctly.

"But there aren't." I blink a few times, my chest tightening for lots of reasons. The biggest of all the idea that he's suggesting he auditions for drum major with me. Him. And then me. It's . . .

"Ha." I actually let out the laugh.

"Why is that so weird? And just because there weren't two before, why can't there be now?" He shrugs and tosses his phone onto his backpack and steps toward me. He stops, arms folded over his chest.

I puff out a silent laugh and cross my own arms in defense, but the longer he stares at me with one eyebrow slightly higher than the other and a hint of a smile on his tight lips, the harder it is for me to play staring contest games. I break eye contact and shake my head.

"For starters, our band isn't big enough." That's a half truth. We have fifty members, and while that's smaller than the big schools, it's not so small that we can't pull off two drum majors. We usually do some intricate choreography on the field, so having two would mean one could handle the backfield and one the front for a few formations. Of course, my dad is a stickler for tradition.

"And even if we could sell two, my dad wouldn't go for it," I add in.

Johnny's head jerks back and his lips twist.

"My dad's the band director. He's a bit of a formal guy," I explain.

Formal.

Fine.

Boring.

Johnny nods, chewing at the inside of his mouth, and I sense him mentally weighing the pros and cons. His head waggles and his mouth clicks out a "damn."

"It doesn't mean we can't try, I guess. An audition at least, I mean." My own voice is foreign to me. That was a thought buried deep in my brain, the kind of thought meant only for my subconscious to kick around and not actually force from my mouth. It was noodling around with thoughts about Johnny's full lips, his hair, his eyes, his voice. *Shit!*

"Alright!" He claps once and before I have a chance to verbally backpedal, he takes my hand and pulls me to the center of the field. His hand is warm, fingers callused. He has tape wrapped around two of his knuckles, probably from ball. Or maybe from riding a rusty bike here to meet me.

I gulp down the onslaught of feelings choking me. The sound is audible, and it causes Johnny to let go of my hand and hunch down a little to look me in the eyes.

"You all right, Brynnie Winnie?" His lip inches up on one side. My lips get numb.

"I'm . . . good. Just, you're kind of shot out of a rocket right now. I'm trying to keep up." That's a true statement, but also—he's not the only thing I'm trying to catch up to. I'm also chasing my heartbeat, the one he seems to be driving higher with every damn adorable thing he does. *Brynnie Winnie.* Teddy's the only person who calls me Brynnie. He started that in third grade to make our names match phonetically. Sort of. I think I like Johnny's version better. I think I like Johnny better. I definitely like him *differently*.

"Sorry, I guess I'm excited. I never get to do stuff like this. It's always *football, football, football.*" He shrugs.

"You know, you'll have to stay on the field for halftime if you do this. Unless you're planning on quitting the team for band, which from what Teddy says about your arm would basically break the entire roster's collective heart."

Of course, if you don't spend the rest of today practicing with me, you'll break mine.

"Right," he says, tucking his bottom lip under his teeth and resting his hands on his hips. He glances toward the gate he rode his bike through, his nostrils widening with a deep breath that he holds in his chest for a few long seconds.

"I'll have to do both. And I'll figure it out." He nods as he speaks, and I get the sense that he's telling himself this more than me.

"People do it. I've seen lots of football players play instruments at half time at other schools, so it's not weird or anything." It's not really *that* common. Maybe one trombone player at a school way up north last year played in his jersey at halftime. But I want to set him at ease. While a tiny part of me feels protective over this gig, maybe a bit possessive over this role that I thought would be mine and mine alone, the comfort of not being alone is too overwhelming. I feel my confidence growing at the mere idea of it.

Johnny nods more forcefully, eventually uttering, "Yeah, it's not weird to do something else with football."

His word choice strikes me, but I figure he's still convincing himself this is a good idea and decide to let it go since everything seems to be leaning in my favor.

Within minutes, Johnny has come up with an entire scenario that is unlike anything I've seen before at marching competitions. It's more than out-of-the-box different. It's too-big-to-fit-in-a-box singular. I told him the music theme for this upcoming year was going to be Broadway musicals, and he immediately started painting a scene. His premise is that we're two strangers both strolling along the field from different ends. When we meet at the fifty-yard-line, our eyes connect and we slowly circle one another. He even has this idea of the band marching in two lines and circling the same way he and I do. And then, right before we're about to salute, Johnny will swirl me into his chest and dip me ballroom style. We haven't rehearsed that part yet, and my palms are sweating in anticipation. One, because I'm about as coordinated as a cardboard box, and two, I'm not confident I can stay conscious if he dips me in his arms. The butterflies in my chest are too damn overwhelming. I'll choke on them.

We both move to the podium to drink some water before our first official run-through. Johnny's talking excitedly, almost like the ideas can't stop now that he's uncorked himself. All I can think about is how I'm going to keep my head from knocking into his when he lifts me from the dip.

Johnny pulls his water bottle from his mouth with a suction sound, and my eyes jet to his face.

"You look worried," he says.

I laugh nervously.

"A little." I recap my water bottle, then take a deep breath and let my shoulders fall, though not far enough. "If you knew the wild idea I had for a salute before you got here, you'd die."

"Show me."

He tilts his head to one side, his eyes sincere. My face warms at the sheer thought of showing him any of that dumbass stuff I was coming up with before he arrived.

"Hard pass," I say through soft laughter.

His lips pucker into a tight smile and he looks at me sideways for a second.

"You're too hard on yourself."

My face puzzles. He's not wrong, but he hardly knows me.

"Not always," I counter. That's a lie, but I don't need him thinking I'm a downer with zero self-worth. A perfectionist? Yes. Type A? Oh, without a doubt. But I know I'm not totally talentless. Mine just doesn't come naturally. And I'm so jealous of people like him who can decide one second that they want to try something new and then instantly excel at it. Heck, Johnny isn't merely excelling—he's reinventing.

"Ready?" He drops his water bottle into his bag and steps toward me, holding out his hand. He offers it so easily, no hesitation. He's clearly not having the same annoying flutters I am. I see his hand and my inner pre-teen gets giggly.

"What do I have to lose?" I seem to say that a lot when it comes to him. I take his palm and hope he thinks the sheen of moisture on my hand is left over from my water bottle. He guides me out to the field and before we head in opposite directions, we each take one of my earbuds so we can listen to the drum sequence and get our timing right.

I turn to face him when there are thirty yards between us and shout ready before starting the music file. His hands dropped in his pockets, Johnny looks around and pretends to be whistling as he meanders toward me. I try to mimic his easy style, but nothing about the way I'm walking toward him is natural at all. Thankfully, he's too distracted by playing his part to notice how much I suck at this. We both stop at about five feet apart, and lock gazes in a snap. That's when things change. I can't hear the drum beat in my ear. I can't hear my own breath or my pulse that I feel taking over my chest. My fingers tingle as we circle one another, his gaze locked on mine like he means it. I know it's pretend, yet it feels so far from play-acting the way he's looking at me. When our hands meet, my lips part with a short gasp before he spins me out then back into him. I'm hanging upside down, my hair tickling the grass, my head dizzy and my heart stopped. The drums pause and Johnny jerks me up so our noses nearly touch, and for the briefest second, the world stops. My hand moves on its own, curving from around his neck down his chest, my palm flat on the center as his slowly lets go of its grip on my thigh. He blinks once before letting go, turning to face the podium and saluting with a stiff right arm that blocks my view and nearly punches me in the face.

"Oh!" I stumble back a step, and Johnny quickly grabs my arm to steady me.

"Whoa, sorry. I guess we have to work that part out." He laughs, and I join him nervously as I take a few extra steps to the side. I'm doing my best to act like we're in sync, like the last thirty seconds were the same for me as they were for him. *I don't have some stupid instant crush. I wasn't imagining a kiss. So what if his hand grabbed my thigh and it was firm and good God!*

"We should probably do it again, what do you think?" He backs away, a foot at a time until he's almost ten yards from me and I haven't moved or said a word.

"Brynnie Winnie?"

"Huh?" I shake from my stupor. He's paused.

"Trust me. I got you."

I swallow hard and I'm pretty sure he sees it. I hope he thinks it's a sign of my perfectionism, or concern about his flying elbows and such. But I know what the root of my sudden dry mouth is, and while the cuteness of his face and hotness of his body factors in, it's that *trust* word that pretty much knocked me out. If this doesn't work out for him, he'll go back to football, and the popularity and parties and homecoming and prom dates that roll up in that identity. Me on the other hand? I'll be relegated back to the horn section or worse, piccolo! A plume within a sea of plumes. A mass identity that will never be noted in the halls of this high school after I graduate.

He turns to walk the remaining distance, and I stumble back awkwardly as I stare at his freaking perfect form. His shirt is starting to stick to his shoulder blades from the heat, and I get a little dopey staring at the ripples that move the faint number 12 on the back. I bet he's going to look incredible in the game day jerseys.

"Hey, what's your last name?" I shout.

He stops right on one of the hashmarks and spins to face me.

"Bishop!" He tilts his chin up when he responds, like he's proud of his name. He should be. It's a good one. *Too* good.

"Shit, you already sound like the homecoming king. You sure you want to ruin your rep by being a band nerd?" I laugh lightly, but truthfully? I'm not kidding. He's going to confuse the hell out of people. And by people, I mean the drop-dead gorgeous girls at our school who are going to want to sleep with him.

"Why can't I be both? Band nerd and homecoming king." He flashes one open palm to the right and the other to the left, as if he's seeing his titles in lights. "What do I have to lose?"

"Ha!" I puff out.

He has no clue. I mentally flip through my sad, socially destitute post-game Friday nights and let that feeling I get—the one that's jealous and feels left out—simmer in the center of my chest.

So much, Johnny Bishop. You could literally have it all.

Chapter 5
Present

Everything is soaked. Even Johnny's travel bag, which MaryAnn managed to snag from the makeshift green room behind the main stage at Pappy & Harriet's and cram into her trunk sometime between acts.

I made it back in time for the final two to perform, and I excused myself from voting, not that my vote is the one that counts. Jade took home the grand prize, which comes with scholarship money and a whole lot of attention. Unfortunately, thanks to Johnny's surprise appearance, she won't be getting as much attention as she deserves for her incredible talent as a singer/songwriter. She's ready to be someone's opening act now, at the age of seventeen. Hell, if Johnny gets his shit together, he should make her *his* opener. He owes her one for stealing her headlines.

It didn't take long for TMZ to pick up on the dozens of social tags about Johnny showing up drunk and probably high. And where TMZ goes, pretty much everyone else follows. I've gotten good at dodging reporters looking for dirt on Johnny. People show up in Yucca Valley from time to time digging around for insight on his past. His mother had a few of them arrested for trespassing in the early years. I'm sure there are reporters hounding her this morning. I wonder if she'll be flashing that shotgun of hers.

It's peaceful outside. The roadway looks like marble fudge, streaked with a thousand mini mud rivers from the rush of water that didn't let up until the wee hours of the morning. It's muggy out, though there's a good chill in the air too. October is trying to regain its dominance after that apocalyptic storm. I prop my garage door up and slowly move items from my car to the garage to join the things MaryAnn dropped off last night. I'm hoping the dank scent filling my garage will mix with the sweet mesquite aroma left over from the rain.

Johnny's bag is tossed in the corner, out of my way. My eyes can't seem to quit jetting to it, so I may as well get this part over with. I snag it and pull out the folding chair I use to reach things on my storage shelves. Taking a seat, I unzip the top and cringe at the ruined leather from the rain. Of everything in this garage, his bag smells the worst—for lots of reasons. I open it wide and sink my hands in to feel his poorly folded sampling of T-shirts, socks, boxers and a pair of jeans. A few of his flannels are balled up near the bottom along with a Ziplock bag stuffed with toiletries, and a notebook held shut with a thick rubber band. I shake the bag in my lap, gathering a few stray items into the corner. A paperclip, three Advils, a dime, and a stick of gum. Nothing that will get me arrested for possession, thank God!

I snap the rubber band on the notebook, maybe subconsciously hoping it will break and make it easier to flip through the pages. It feels intrusive, but more than that, I'm scared to read the words he's written. Johnny always liked to scribble his lyrics in notebooks. If there's one truth about a Johnny Bishop song, it's that it bleeds honesty. Given the condition of the man I left at rehab last night, I'm not sure I'm equipped to take a look at what's happening inside. I pile his things back into the bag and take it to my laundry room where I dump the clothes into the washer and put it on a deep soak. I've always loved Johnny's style. Even when he was a teenager he had this ability to turn the simplest thing like a button-down denim shirt into the sexiest piece of clothing ever sewn. His clothes were always worn, often second-hand, and somehow smelled of every memory we made together. Now that scent is covered up with booze and weed.

I leave his bag on the counter next to the chugging washing machine and head back into the garage in time for my father's twenty-year-old Lincoln to pull into the driveway. Thankfully, it's only him. My mom tends to needle me with questions, and I'm sure she's literally ready to explode with them after last night. Dad will be subtle. Nosy, but subtle.

"You should really bring a fan out if you want that stuff to dry. The cloud cover isn't letting up until tonight," he says, letting his heavy car door clunk shut behind him. My dad is an expert in everything, especially those things he has zero expertise in—like meteorology.

"I'm not really in a hurry, so things will dry when they dry." I slowly peel apart some of the smeared music sheets that took the brunt of the rain during my last dash to the car last night. My dad's gaze sticks to them, a slight weight of disgust dragging down the corners of his mouth.

"They'll dry. I promise." My dad has always found sheet music to be a precious commodity. Probably because when he was teaching, instructors had to save their budget for printed copies to be delivered in sealed boxes and they were only guaranteed so many prints. He hasn't quite grasped the concept of cloud access and digital licensing.

"So, I read Jade Sinclair took the grand prize this year. She's one of your favorites, isn't she?" My father hasn't come to the showcase since he handed the reins over to me. He says it's because he wants it to be mine and mine alone, but I think it makes him sad to not be the one in charge. He relished the role. Prince and princess maker.

"She deserved to win. I mean, our favorites are our favorites for a reason, right?" Our eyes meet for a brief second. He knows what I mean by that. Johnny was always *his* favorite. Probably still is despite everything he's done. I was his special little girl. I always have and still do feel loved. And I am his in every single way imaginable. We are so damn similar, right down to the worry lines I'm forming around my mouth and eyes that will one day mirror the channels that circle his. Johnny is loved, too, though. Loved *differently*. When he needed someone to believe in him, my dad did.

My dad bends down and picks up one of the flashlights from the box I threw most of my household items into when I packed up. He clicks it and the light flickers, so he unscrews the back and slides out the nearly dead batteries.

"The flashlights were on almost the entire night," I explain.

"Yeah, I bet you needed them for spotlights after the rain shorted the electricity." He chuckles at his own joke and paces along the back wall of my garage, snooping through various boxes and bins for spare batteries. He should give up. I don't have any left after last night. Eventually, he sets the flashlight and battery cover down on a shelf. It will probably stay there like that for months, until I lose electricity and curse myself for not getting batteries.

"Last night was definitely a challenge." I sigh, resting both hands on my hips as I survey the music sheets, towels, and left-over certificates from the students who didn't bother to pick them up before leaving.

"I bet it was," he finally responds.

I don't lift my gaze for a few seconds, instead letting his

tone settle in. When I finally glance up, his head is askew and his mouth is a slight, sympathetic frown. I hold his stare for a few more seconds before finally exhaling and waving my hand at him.

"I'm fine. You don't have to look at me like that." My dad's pity almost hurts more than seeing Johnny again.

"Oh, I don't doubt you're fine. I know my daughter, and she'd never let someone who is such a mess rattle her for long." He walks over and pats my back with his heavy hand. I busy myself by kneeling and pulling out more dead flashlights and tools from my box.

"He's a mess. That's for sure." I don't elaborate, and I know my dad won't come out and ask for details. He's dying to know them, though. Because while Johnny might be a mess, he's still my dad's prodigy. I mean, how could he not be after publicly thanking my father during his first Grammy acceptance speech.

The two of us kick around my garage, not doing anything of consequence for another minute or two until my dad finally gives up on me sharing any more details with him. He's read the news, I'm sure. He knows where Johnny is. And he'll probably pay him a visit at some point. I'm sure of it. Maybe when I'm less irritated about the whole thing, I'll get them to switch the emergency contact name from mine to my father's and he can take over my burden.

That thought sits heavy in my gut, and I drop the unwrapped plastic ponchos back into the box as my dad waves once while backing out of my driveway. I force a smile that hurts my cheeks and wave back, letting my face drop the second I turn around.

Calling Johnny a burden doesn't feel fair. It never has. No matter how many times he made me angry, or frustrated, or . . . hurt. There was always a reason. He was easy to forgive. So goddamn easy to love. So impossible to forget.

I leave my garage door open to air out and head inside, back to the bag with the mystery notebook I can't seem to get out of my head. My inner voice is screaming at me to leave it alone, but my hands disobey. Before I blink, I've carried the bag into my kitchen and poured myself a glass of wine. I pull out a chair and plop the bag on its side so I can stare into it, my eyes glazing over at the dirty edges of the notebook. I slide it out slowly and flick the band a few more times with my thumbnail before giving myself over completely to my obsession.

The first page is instantly recognizable. It's his first big hit, the one he supposedly wrote after he got signed. But I know the truth. He wrote "Shelter" on my bedroom floor when he stayed at our house for the weekend while my parents were away. He always thought I was asleep while he wrote, my tiny nightlight on the wall the only illumination in the room. But when he wasn't looking at me, I was looking at him. I loved watching him pour out his soul. It was one of the few times he was truly fearless.

This version of "Shelter?" It's not the original. In fact, it looks like a rewrite he did recently, and there are a few tweaks to lines I know by heart. *The black and blue house on the hill* now reads *that house on the hill*. Like he's trying to erase his artistic testimony about the bruises he and his mother endured.

I flip through the first few pages, noting the familiar starts and scribbles for lyrics he either doesn't want to forget or decided to abandon. The further into his work I delve, the darker it gets. I'm not surprised. Song writing has always been his therapy, and the lines he's written more recently read like prayers and confessions. I'm about halfway through the notebook when I come upon a page with a receipt. I tilt the notebook and let it slide onto the table as my eyes scan the fading words. SACRAMENTO TROPHY SHOPPE. I can't `make out the address and the item listed, but the price is fairly hefty at $499 plus some illegible tax amount. Probably a replica of some award he threw out of a hotel window on one of his bad days.

Bad weeks.

Months.

I slip it back in its place and close the notebook, binding it again with the rubber band. I don't bother sipping my wine, instead gulping it down and reaching for the bottle to double down. I stop when the bottle's lip clanks against the rim of my glass, though, and opt to walk my glass to the sink and tuck the bottle back in my cabinet. Wine never got me anywhere good. I laugh out once, the sound pathetic as it doesn't even echo in my empty house. Wine got me here, too. Not directly, but it certainly fueled some bad decisions—including my three-month marriage to a man nobody liked and who Johnny would detest.

Wine also led to the huge rift between me and Teddy Pine, my former best friend and the third point of our supposed indestructible triangle. While Teddy never made the promise to Johnny quite like I did, the idea that he was also family was simply understood. Johnny left him, too. He'd want to know he's back, and that he came for me. Or maybe I just need someone's help, someone who gets it and whom I can trust. Even if I broke that person's heart after a careless one-night stand.

I reach for my purse and drag it toward me along the table, slipping my phone out and turning it to face me. I flip through my contacts to the grayed-out one with Teddy's name. I disabled it years ago to keep me from accidentally purse dialing him—after purse-dialing him twice in one month. I change the settings and take a deep breath before pressing call. My palms are sweating at the first ring. He picks up on the third.

"I was kind of expecting this call."

A fat tear burns its way down my cheek at the sound of his

voice. It's unexpected, and the release makes my lungs shudder as another tear chases close behind.

I sniffle and wipe them away, sure Teddy can hear my emotions. God, his voice is soothing. Even with the tinge of anger in it.

"I think I need your help, Teddy. Can you come?"

I swallow the sour pride it took to utter those words and let my chest burn with hope that he'll say yes.

"I'll be there tomorrow morning, Brynn. And you're not the one who needs my help."

My eyelids flutter with more tears as I nod and bring a fist to my mouth to hold back the blubbering. His words are short and sweet, and not for me. They're for our friend. For my love and ruin. My best worst mistake. For Johnny.

"Call me when you get in." My words are faint, exhaustion and heartbreak wearing me down.

"Yep." He ends the call at that, and I completely fall apart.

It's like it's Friday night. And I'm seventeen. All alone.

Again.

Chapter 6
Age 17

It's almost seven a.m. and Johnny isn't here.

Josh keeps giving me side eyes from the main table where he's sitting dead-center with the rest of the outgoing seniors. I'm wearing one of my mom's church dresses, a frilly thing that swings below my knees and makes my bust look like, well, like I have one. It's the only dress I could think of that seemed to match the look Johnny wanted us to go for. He kept referencing that old movie where the warring gangs dance and snap. I'm pretty sure he meant *West Side Story*. The longer I stand here fluffing the yellow skirting around my legs and ignoring the fact I'm also standing in black Mary Janes instead of the crisp white marching shoes every other student auditioning is wearing, the more my stomach churns with doubt.

"I thought you were trying out?" I jump at my friend Cori's voice at my ear, then turn to face her while attempting to fold my skirt tightly around my legs. *As if that will hide it somehow.*

"I am." Her brow dimples and her gaze falls down the length of my body. Her mouth pops open but she doesn't speak.

"I know. I know!" I whisper-shout, unfurling my skirt. My eyes dart wildly around the edge of the field to the black-slacked legs, the white button downs, and the plumes. My hair is—

"How did you get those curls to stay up like that?" Cori gently pats the bottom of one of the rolled locks of hair I have held in place with twenty-seven hairpins and a bottle of super-hold spray.

"I stayed up all night figuring out how to make pin curls." I look up, straining my eyes in an attempt to see the widow's peak I couldn't seem to avoid this morning.

"Well, you kinda nailed it," Cori says through a crooked smile. She traces the curve of the roll above my left eyebrow with her fingertip.

"Careful, it's all an illusion," I joke.

We both laugh for a few seconds, but my mouth starts to water like I might vomit and Cori must see it in my complexation because she links our arms before guiding me to the water stand next to the bleachers. Cori and I have been in band together since fourth grade, when we were allowed to pick instruments and take them home. She has never wavered from saxophone. I, however, wandered through the brass and winds and on into percussion.

"Drink," she says after filling a foam cup to the brim and handing it to me.

"Thanks." I guzzle it down and cap it off with an, "Ahh."

"So, this look you're going for . . . it was intentional?" Her jet-black left eyebrow is raised and a new wave of nausea hits me. If I weren't so freaked out that I am about to totally blow my chance at drum major, I would laugh at the irony of her question. Cori has different colored hair every month. Right now? It's a deep purple with a bright white stripe on one side. She said she was going for the *struck by lightning* look.

"It's a long story. I'll tell you the whole thing when I'm crying over a gallon of cookie dough crunch when I screw this up royally." My dad's voice is already calling over the mega-phone for everyone to take their seats by the field.

"Uh, does your long story include whoever that is?" Cori tugs on my puffy sleeve, jerking me to my right where Johnny is scaling the fence behind the scoreboard. He's wearing deep blue jeans, rolled at his ankles, and a tight white T-shirt. He slings a backpack to the ground as he lifts himself the rest of the way over the fence. He picks it up before jogging toward me, and without my permission, my body begins to sway the skirt of my dress about my legs. *Shit! I'm suddenly in character!*

"It does." I gulp and glance sideways at my friend. Cori's eyes meet mine for a second before jetting back to the hot boy pulled out of some fifties dreamboat magazine. Good lord, he even slicked his hair back, mostly.

"Sorry I'm late. I didn't have the car again." He's panting a little, and I wonder if he jogged the whole way here.

My nerves have suddenly jacked my pulse up a dozen miles per hour, and I'm not sure my lips will work when I attempt to speak. Maybe it's that he actually showed up in costume. That I did. That he was late and that Josh—and now my father—are continuously glancing my way with a majorly concerned tilt in their brows. Whatever the reason, "We don't have to do this," falls out of my mouth.

Johnny literally freezes at my words, dropping his backpack at his feet and stepping into me, placing his hands on either shoulder, pushing me back a few steps, away from ears.

"Let's talk this out." He shakes his head as his eyes light up. He wants this. Maybe more than I do, which is a lot. I grip the fringed, buttoned bodice of my dress and glance around us.

"It's just that . . . what if people don't *get it?*"

Johnny follows my gaze toward the judge's table, to my father whom he has yet to meet. Who will absolutely *not* get this. His mouth pulls into a tight line and his brow furrows.

"We'll just have to sell it." His eyes flash back to mine, his slicked-back hair slipping out of place, strands dangling over one eye. He literally just became more in-character.

I swallow hard. Again from his unbelievably handsome face and from a touch of stage fright.

"The question is—do we go first, or last?" His mouth inches up on the corner and I glance to my right shoulder, where his palm is still covering my bare skin.

"Oh, sorry." He recoils and drops his hands in his pockets while I straighten my dress. He laughs nervously and looks down at the ground between us, catching a glimpse of my shoes.

"No shit! Those are perfect!" He kicks toward them with his own perfect pair of white Vans. They look brand new, not yet covered in any of his doodles.

"We draw for order. I'm notoriously unlucky if you'd like to take this one." I'm not totally lying. I am bad at chance. I don't think I've ever shouted *Bingo!* But mostly, I don't want to walk up to the bucket and stare my father in the eyes. He won't say anything out loud to me, not out here or in front of others. But I'll get the look. Or a closer view of the look. The one that says *child, what are you doing?*

"Yeah, I got this. Here, blow on it." Johnny holds out a closed fist, and I chuckle at his quirky wish but blow on his hand for good luck. "There. Can't lose!"

Johnny files into line while I wait off to the side, avoiding meeting anyone's passing glance or stare. Cori's joined the other band members who bothered to show up early and see who comes out on top. There are strict rules about watching tryouts. Absolutely nobody is allowed to cheer or clap. It's part of the unbiased voting my dad insists on for the process, and applause has a way of influencing people. There are about thirty people in the stands, most of them from band but a few from choir. The football team and cheerleaders don't really turn out for this stuff.

Johnny jogs over to me and hands me a folded index card. I peek inside and see #7. That's next to last.

"Okay, that's . . . I think that might be good for us. Yeah?" I ask him.

He laughs silently, lifting his shoulders.

"Fuck if I know! This is *your* thing. I'm just along for the ride." He gives me a quick grin, then proceeds to stretch his arms one at a time across his chest. My eyes narrow on him as I shift my body and cross my arms. Eventually, Johnny pauses his mini-warmup routine and lifts his shoulders again.

"What?"

"Bullshit. You're all in! You want to win! And not just as a favor because we're friends. But *you* want to do this thing." I purse my lips in a smug grin while Johnny spends about three seconds wiggling his head in some lame attempt to brush off that this is a big deal for him. I shove his chest lightly and he laughs like a toddler being tickled, then holds his palms out with guilt.

"Okay, yes. Fine. I admit it. I'm competitive. And I want to win. Because we totally got this in the bag, and because you deserve this. Also . . . we're friends."

That last part, the friends part, comes out slow and quiet, and he drops his eye contact as he says it. But his lips turn up on the corners, and his cheek twitches. Friends is a big deal to him, it seems. I don't know where this boy came from, but he is going to rock the social hierarchy around this place with thoughts like that.

"Well, then," I say, holding out a fist. He looks down at it and I nod, expecting him to pound it the way Teddy does with the guys on the sidelines at the game. Instead, he timidly leans in and puckers his lips, blowing on it—for luck.

I chuckle, but drop my hand and nod, because Johnny and I have a thing now. *Our* thing. For good luck. What a weird thing.

"Let's do this." I straighten my spine and walk over to the line of chairs along the sideline, away from the judge's table. My pulse is in check, and my palms aren't nearly as sweaty as they were ten minutes ago.

Our stiffest competition, Jaqueline Mosciat, goes first. Her lines are crisp, and even though her hands are in white gloves, she somehow makes them snap when she claps together to count time and bring the fake band to attention. Johnny leans back when she shouts *hut* and he leans into me.

"Do we need to have one of those?"

I glance to my side and find his crooked, maybe slightly-worried brow. I shake my head no, and he breathes out and sinks back into his chair. What I don't say is we are so off the traditional path there's no way a *hut, hut* is going to be the thing that saves us. Either this group is going to get what we're doing or not. There won't be an in-between.

Other than Jaqueline, the remaining auditions before us are all basically the same, some form of what Josh has done for the last three years only not as good as his version. The only person left beside us is a sophomore who won't get the nod because of seniority. I applaud her for going for the experience, but at this point, it's either going to be Jaqueline or us.

"What do you say, Brynnie Winnie?" He looks at me sideways and I take in a deep breath, hoping like hell my mom's dress stays in place.

"They're going down." I don't look at him when I say it, and I think I maybe mean it. I feel a confidence that's foreign, a sureness in my feet and extra strength in my lungs. I head to the left as Johnny goes right, and we stop at the thirty-five-yard marks on either side. My body buzzes with excitement, which is normal for me before a performance, but there's something else mixed into this euphoria. My mind is racing to the little things we have planned, a full day of rehearsing and a massive sunburn to match it. I believe in this. Or maybe Johnny sold the shit out of it to me. Either way, we're about to find out.

My dad reads the small intro I wrote into the mic.

"Ladies and gents, sit back and let us entertain you. Drum majors Brynn Fisher and Johnny Bishop are going to take us all for a little walk down Broadway . . . the way only the Yucca Valley North Marching Howl can. Drum majors, is your band ready?"

I reach into the top of my dress, pulling out the bright red tube of lipstick that I had tucked in my strapless bra. I pop the cap off and color my lips slowly, my movements big enough for a stage, well, the size of a football field.

I tuck the lipstick back in place, patting it twice, then let my arms snap to my side as I nod and wink. My dad's head turns slightly to the side. He's worried. He should probably sit down for the rest of this.

Josh hits play on our walk-in music file. Everyone uses the cadence and the fight song, but late in our brainstorming Johnny came up with the idea of actually using his whistling while we stroll toward one another. He was surprisingly on tune when we recorded it into his phone, nailing "Singing in the Rain" better than our horn section has in early rehearsals. As his whistle pipes in through the field speakers, I spin around and hold my arms out as if I'm overwhelmed with joy for the nice weather. A quick glance in Johnny's direction eases my tempted nerves as he's right on time with his part, and we weave our way toward one another. My chest tightens with anticipation, as if I'm really about to run into a dreamboat on some New York avenue and go on a musical adventure with him. It isn't New York, and the desert sun is already high for the early morning. But mentally, I'm there. I feel the people around me on the sidewalk, the bright lights flashing show times on marquees above, the honking horns for a busy street and the shouts of newsies and food venders.

And then Johnny's hand grasps mine firmly, and everything falls right into place. He spins me out then back in, dipping me back and smirking when our eyes meet. Rules be damned, the entire audience cheers and whistles, and just as I'm about to utter *we did it* to my partner, he leans in and presses his lips on mine.

Oh, my tingling legs and ice cold chest being split open with fire. I can't feel my fingers. My toes are gone. I have no cheeks and my ears are oddly burning up. What is this? What is he doing? And why are his lips so strong yet soft. I can actually feel his mouth move into a smile against mine. My inner voice screams for his mouth to go back to the way it was, to open wide and show me the way, to introduce me to his tongue.

I'm completely dizzy when Johnny stands me back up. The first thing my eyes see is the bright red smeared across his mouth. There's no way I'm playing this chill. I can feel the air hitting every bit of white in my eyes. They are wide—Mississippi river wide.

"Big finish, you ready?" Johnny whispers.

"Uh, yeah," I mutter back. *That wasn't the big finish?*

I somehow remember the last few steps, taking his hand and walking around him in a circle as he kneels. I use his thigh for a step up, take the top of the podium, and turn to face the invisible band. I'm incredibly happy no one is actually in front of me to witness the bright red taking over my neck and cheeks. I might even be drooling. I don't know.

Johnny, I assume, has turned his back to our audience too and taken his place to my right on the ground. I won't look at him. I might not ever look at him again. And the longer we stand like this without any reaction or words from my father, the more I wish we did add a salute to the end to let everyone know we're finished. Then suddenly the small crowd of onlookers roars back to life with applause and feet thunder-stomping on the bleachers. I turn nervously, my hands now clutching my mother's dress as I prepare to take a curtsy. My father is applauding, his clipboard tucked under one arm. And Josh is doing the slow-clap, and not sarcastically but legiti-mately. It takes me a few more seconds to realize that literally everyone is standing. Even Jaqueline.

"That's a good sign, yeah?" Johnny says. I glance at him briefly, his crooked smile smothered in my red lipstick. My lips buzz from the memory of his on them. It was a stage kiss. More of a mouth mash. I want to do nothing but mash my mouth into Johnny Bishop's for the rest of the day. Week. *My life!*

"Yeah, Johnny. We killed it."

Chapter 7
Present

I barely slept, for a second night. I look like shit, which shouldn't matter so much but for whatever reason, it does. I'm ashamed that it does. I shouldn't care how I look when Teddy sees me. It won't matter how dressed up I get or what I do to my hair. I'm sure he'll see an ugly person standing in front of him no matter how much makeup I slather on and what clothes I decide to slip on my body.

But I feel it in my chest. The nerves. The need to prove that I'm still someone worthwhile. That even though I treated him like shit, he should be the one regretting letting me go. How crazy is that logic? Because he would have kept me forever if I only let him. He would have been perfect.

I opt for my cropped jeans, slip-on Vans, and the white T-shirt that is remarkably free of stains. I toss my hair into a ponytail and walk straight past the bathroom mirror, forbidding myself from adding extra makeup. There are more important things than my twisted sense of sudden vanity.

I get to my front door just as the Uber pulls up. Teddy texted that he was on his way. Literally three words—*on my way*. I cling to the doorknob and peer out the peep hole as he waits by the trunk for the driver to pop it open. I open the door as he's pulling out a canvas duffle. He nods a quiet *thanks* to the driver, then turns to walk up the small brick path leading to my front door. His gaze lifts to me briefly before diving back down to his feet. No pause in his step or flicker of a smile on his face. It's like we're strangers rather than two people who used to share their young and hopeful secrets with one another.

"Thank you for coming," I say, reaching out to take his bag. He steps around me, not giving it.

"I'm here for him."

I turn in my entryway after his cold greeting and take a deep breath as Teddy scans my humble home. It's still cluttered despite my early-morning attempt to clean house before he arrived. I'm too busy with school to ever get organized. Or that's the excuse I make for myself.

"So, what's first?" He drops his bag in my leather reading chair and pushes his hands into his jeans pockets, locking his arms straight as he spins around to face me. He looks good. Like a lumberjack who grooms his beard well. Teddy was always handsome, and age has taken his boyish good looks and turned him into a really attractive man. Shoulder-length hair the color of oak and honey with soft waves I would pay thousands for at a salon. His beard frames his square jaw and soft lips, the hint of red letting his green eyes take center stage. His black T-shirt hugs muscles that he clearly spends a lot of time toning, his arms filling the sleeves completely. His jeans hug his hips and gather at his black canvas shoes. I catch myself smirking at them because Teddy always thought he was taller than he was and needed to buy them extra-long.

"You want to see the guest room?" I step toward the hallway, but Teddy holds up a palm and waves it.

"Oh, no. I'm not staying here."

I fall back on my heels.

"Oh. I mean, okay. That's okay." I dart my eyes from his face to the hallway that leads to the room I spent most of the night and morning trying to make nice.

"I don't want this to be . . . I don't know, weird I guess. That's all."

What he means is he wants to do our business for Johnny then get out of here with minimal emotional casualties, from me. I get it. And maybe that's best. Yet a part of me was somehow hoping this sucky life moment might lead to some forgiveness and rekindling of our friendship. I miss him. I miss both of them.

"Yeah, I understand. Are you staying in town? Or the Springs?" It would make sense for him to stay somewhere near Johnny.

"I'm at the Diesel," he says with a nod. I flash a quick smile, but I'm glad he's staying in town. The Diesel is attached to Pappy & Harriet's, which means he'll get to take in some of the local music while he's here. Maybe if he can stand my company one night we'll have dinner. *Maybe.*

Awkward silence settles in after several seconds pass without a word between us. His presence in my house feels big —out of place. My ceilings aren't very high, which I suppose lends to the illusion that he's actually taller than six feet. He's not. He's just under. Regardless, he feels enormous in my living room. I'm fighting the urge to collapse into him and let him wrap me in his arms to make me feel safe. He always had that power.

"I like your place," Teddy says, breaking the thick quiet.

I laugh out once and move toward my kitchen table, still covered in everything from the showcase. I run my hand along a few of the small boxes still packed with random tools and papers.

"I could use more storage." I shrug.

Teddy's mouth breaks rank and he smiles on one side.

"Nah. You just need to suck it up and admit you're messy as shit." There's a hint of my old Teddy in his tone, and I squeeze my eyes shut and smile at his teasing.

"You're right," I admit.

God, I wish it could all be this easy. I know it won't be, though, so I'll take this small moment of what could have been. Teddy could have come back to the desert after college, maybe lived down the street, coached at the school with me. We'd be friends. He'd come over on weekends to watch football. I'd have a reason to root for our hometown team. Instead, he coaches in Encinitas. A hundred miles away.

Before another bout of uncomfortable silence blankets us, I shift my focus to Johnny's bag, which I've added to with more basic necessities like shaving cream, razors, shampoo, and the face moisturizer he used to steal from me when we were in high school. I zip his bag up, not wanting to look at the lotion and deal with the real reason I put something so trivial in there—so he'd think about me. Miss me. Regret how he left, and how he showed back up now.

Me. All about me.

I shake my head at myself and sling the bag over my shoulder before turning to face Teddy. He's snagged his own duffle bag from the chair.

"Time to see the patient?" His mouth forms a tight forced smile and his brows lift high.

"Time to deliver him his personal effects, at least." I shrug, then lead Teddy through my kitchen and out the garage door. He nearly steps on the sheet music I have yet to pick up, but thankfully the sunlight spills in soon enough after I open the main door and he stops himself.

"Oh, this is a whole new level of clutter, Brynnie." He high steps his way around the pages, and I tuck his slip-up into the back of my mind before it has a chance to warm my chest. *Brynnie.*

"The showcase was Friday, and I'm sure you had the same rain I did." I gather up the sheet music before I have a chance to forget it's in here again and pull my car in over it. I set the stack on the tool counter and place a hammer on top to keep it in place. My dad would cringe.

"Yeah, our place nearly flooded." His response is off-handed and easy, and I'm not even sure he realizes he said the word *our*. I won't pry about it, not yet. I'm too glad he's here to dig into his personal life, which he's been keen to cut me out of for years.

"Well, it was literal cat and dog chaos here," I say, following behind him toward my car in the driveway. I wince as soon as I tap UNLOCK on my key fob, and Teddy belly laughs at the laundry basket full of dank towels he has to remove from the passenger seat.

"Really showing off my weaknesses for you today," I say, rushing around to take the basket from him. It was the last one I had to move inside and I was simply too tired—*too lazy*—to deal with it yesterday. I leave the basket at the edge of the garage and slap the button to close it as I trot back to my car. I dump Johnny's bag in the back seat along with my purse and climb in. Teddy's kept his bag between his feet, probably because my back seat is mostly taken up with brass instrument cases. I'm embarrassed by disorder and all I can offer is a squint, a tight smile, and raised shoulders as I glance to him.

"Hey, you're an adult now. You like living in disarray, have at it." He chuckles at his critique and I take it in stride, pulling us out of my driveway.

The trip into the Springs is quicker than the same route Friday night. Probably because the sky isn't falling this time. We manage to score a few solid songs during the ride and some banter from the long-time DJs who broadcast to the desert cities. Our only conversation revolves around how Morning-Ride Becky and Monday-Mayhem Randall have been on the radio for most of our lives. They have to be close to retirement age by now. I wonder if Morning-Ride Becky is sick of the sexist jokes she endures thanks to some producer's brilliant idea to give her the *ride* moniker.

A young man dressed in black dress pants and a white button-down greets us at the top of the driveway into Waves. Both Teddy and I chuckle as he reaches for my door handle as I shift into park.

"Place seriously has valet," Teddy mutters at my right.

I suppose as college gigs go, running vehicles back and forth for visitors at a rehab isn't the worst job one could have. I'm certain my Subaru is not quite up to the caliber of wheels young Collin was expecting today, though. As well as the tip he's likely to get from me when we leave. I'll be scraping together whatever's in my purse.

Young Collin cruises up the driveway to a covered garage buried behind green vines and orange blossoms, and Teddy and I head toward the guest lobby. I let him scan his surroundings and process the shock and awe of this place's opulence while I check in with the front desk. I hand over my ID and wait while the receptionist types in some information on the computer.

"Someone will be here to take you back in a moment. You can take a seat." She gestures to the deep-cushioned sofa by the stone fireplace, and Teddy and I eye one another before opting instead for the basic leather wing-back seats near the window.

Within seconds, the security door swings open with a sharp beeping sound that is only cut off when the attendant presses his badge to the scanner on the wall.

"Brynn, I can take you back now."

I stand and Teddy hesitantly rises next to me.

"He's here to see him, too. Is that—"

"I'm afraid he'll have to wait here for you. He's not on the list, and Mr. Bishop didn't add anyone since you checked him in on Friday."

"Ah." I suck in my lips and turn to mouth *sorry* to Teddy.

"It's fine. I'll be here if you need me."

He falls back into the chair after pulling his phone from his pocket. I follow the attendant through the door with Johnny's bag in tow. We stop at a second check-point hidden behind the main reception area, where I check in my phone and they search Johnny's duffle.

"We'll have to monitor the razors," one of the attendants says.

"Oh." I didn't really think about them as dangerous. I didn't really think of Johnny as being *in danger*. From himself. Of course, isn't that why he's here in the first place?

I'm guided to a room at the end of a long, richly-appointed hallway. I'm not sure whether they've tucked him here because it's the best room in the joint or because it's far away from everything else—including the media. Nobody was parked outside when we came in, and I was prepared for it. I've seen a few photos on the socials from outside Waves. It was a matter of time.

My guide knocks softly on the door, pushing it open as I follow behind him.

"Mr. Bishop. You have company."

Johnny is sitting on the edge of the bed. It's made, which is more than I can say for my own. He looks ragged, somehow more tired than when I dropped him off here two days ago. He stands up halfway, like he's nervous to travel too far from the softness of a mattress, his fingertips touching the tufted comforter.

"Brynn. Hi . . . uh . . ." A bashful smile twists at his mouth, his chin and cheeks dusted with two days' worth of facial hair. It's sloppy, like his hair, which twists in various directions like one of those yarn mops my mom used to clean our kitchen when I was young. He's dressed in gray sweats, white socks, and a long-sleeved navy blue T-shirt. He's an utter mess, but somehow he looks a thousand times better than he did two days ago.

"I brought your things." I hold up the bag by the handles and toss it on the bed next to him.

"When your visit is over, you can just push this button and I'll escort you out." The attendant leaves the door ajar, and I get the impression that closing it is not an option.

When I turn back around, Johnny's sat back down on the bed. He's staring at me with those big blue doe eyes, the ones that could always talk me into anything. It's his apology. And back then? It was all he needed to do. There are too many things to apologize for now.

It's tempting to force small talk. However, this isn't the time or place to pretend things aren't heavy and serious. He knows it as much as I do, and I recognize that look in his eyes—the one that silently begs me to take it easy on him. I'm not sure I can do that.

"They kept your razors." I gesture to the bag and he takes my lead, dragging it close and unzipping to peek inside.

"I get the shaving cream, I see." He pulls the can out and chuckles before leaning forward and setting it on the small table across from the bed.

He returns to the duffle and pulls out his clothing, pausing at one of his flannels. His eyes flit to mine as he brings the shirt to his nose and smells it.

"Yeah, I washed everything. Ironed too," I admit. It was kind of therapeutic for me, really. And his clothes smelled terrible.

Johnny's lip ticks up a hint as he goes back to sorting his clothes. The last item is his notebook, and he doesn't shy away from acknowledging it, pulling it out and clutching it with both hands. His gaze shifts from the book to me, that amused smile from a moment before more somber now.

"You read it?"

He knows I did.

I nod and move to the large sitting chair tucked in the corner near the floor-to-ceiling window that looks out on a spiraled brick pathway lined with soft pink desert flowers.

Johnny cracks the book open and flips to the middle. His eyes scan briefly left to right as he turns page after page until his palm flattens the book open against his lap. His fingertips tap along the paper until eventually it's only his index finger tapping—pointing.

"You read this one?" He holds it up like a librarian during story time and I squint trying to make out the first few words.

I shrug.

"I don't know. Maybe. Why?"

His eyes linger on mine for a few long seconds, the light behind them so dim from the star he is. He chews at the inside of his mouth until his gaze drops back to the book and he utters, "No reason."

My chest burns, and my stomach feels as though it's twisting tightly on itself. Every last drop of common sense inside of me wants to leave, to get up from this chair and wish him luck on his recovery. Someone stronger than me would. *Someone colder, perhaps.* But I can't. Because I promised. And because there's enough of that invisible energy between us left to crackle in the quiet. It's simply tainted with pain now.

"I read a lot of them. They're good. You were always good at writing, though. You know that."

He tosses the book on the mattress.

"It's nothing but the dark shit in my head. People like that stuff, I guess. Label says I need a new album soon." He leans forward and rubs his temples, his elbows on his knees.

"I'm sure there are enough songs in that book for an album," I respond, not sure what more to say. An album is the last thing Johnny should be thinking about right now. Getting well, staying sober. Those need to be his priorities.

He flops back on the bed with his arms over his head. His long lashes kiss the tops of his cheeks as he blinks slowly while staring at the beamed ceiling above us. I tuck one leg under the other and ball my fisted hands in my lap. I want to yell at him, and maybe that's what he wants. But if I start, I don't know that I can stop.

"So . . . this is what the inside of Waves looks like?" I scope out his room, which looks more like a Tuscan resort backed by George Clooney, minus the bulky medical equipment tucked in a nook near his bed. He got the celebrity shortcut through detoxing and drying out. I'm not sure that's the best way to learn a lesson, but maybe he's all full up on lessons. Life's taught Johnny a lot of rotten things.

"You should see the menu for breakfast by the pool. He gestures toward a leather-bound folder on the same table he set his shaving cream on. I pull it into my lap and browse the offerings.

"What do you get when you order the frittata with a side of *self-discovery?*" My chest puffs with a short, quiet laugh.

"My mom has pancreatic cancer." His confession cuts through my attempt at light humor, through the resentful noise in my head, and my gaze darts to his face. His eyes remain lost on the ceiling, blinking slowly as the reflection from the pond outside plays with the sunlight on the honey-colored beams.

"Oh, Johnny. I'm . . . I'm so sorry." I slide the menu back onto the table as a million open ends fuse together in a matter of seconds. There's plenty of mystery left behind Johnny's eyes and why he's bottoming out here and now, but I'm sure his mother is at the root of a lot of it.

He pinches the bridge of his nose and squeezes his eyes shut. It's the same gesture he's been making since we first met. It's how he stops himself from crying. He's been hiding tears for years.

"It's not fixable. Her cancer. It's terminal. I guess. I don't know much because she wrote me a fucking letter and sent it to my management team and it took them two weeks to get it to me on the road." He breaths out a short, sad laugh. "So, whatever the time left is, it's two weeks shorter now."

His mom doesn't deserve this, not that anyone ever does. But Beth survived so much abuse her entire marriage. She should get to live out her years pain-free and in bliss. It's not right. It isn't fair.

I pull my knees up to my chest and hug them as I look on at the shell of Johnny Bishop lying limp on a temporary bed.

"I can't have her see me like this, Brynnie." His head rolls to the side and his gaze clings to mine with a feeling of desperation. It tugs at my insides and rips open every wound I've been trying to heal over this man.

"You're in the right place, then." My arms hug my legs tight and my chin rests on my knees. I'm trying to hold in everything else, the criticism and the hurt I have for selfish reasons. None of that is for now, and my better judgement knows it.

"I missed you."

And then he says something like that.

I breathe in slowly through my nose, literally biting my tongue. The longer our eyes remain connected without words, the harder it gets for me not to respond at all.

"I'm right here." I try to make my words sound soft and

kind, but even I hear the small bitter tinge behind them. *I've been here. I waited. You left and never looked back.*

"Teddy came," I add. Teddy was aways the neutralizer in our group. He kept the balance—and sometimes the peace. Especially when I wanted to throttle Johnny for being a dumbass.

A tiny smile tugs at Johnny's mouth.

"He came," he breathes out.

I blink as my gaze holds on to his gaze. There's a flicker in his eyes, that light trying to come back on, and damn if I don't feel jealous that Teddy sitting in the waiting room is the thing that charges it rather than me, here, in this fucking room.

"We both did." My words shoot past my filter, and they aren't as kind as I've been trying to maintain. The release feels oddly good, as though I've let some pressure out of my chest.

Johnny doesn't flinch, and his gaze doesn't shift away in shame. He takes it—the bite. And it makes me feel a little guilty about letting it out so soon.

"I have a lot of apologies to dole out when I get out of here, and most of them are to you, Brynn. We have a lot to catch up on." He lifts himself back up to sit and lets his palms lay flat on either side of him. My heart is thumping thanks to the instant dose of adrenaline at hearing him tiptoe around an *I'm sorry.*

"I should go," I say, stretching my legs out to the floor and hopping to a stand. I pause in the center of the room for a little inner self-debate. After a few seconds, I opt to leave with a nod and head toward the door to press the call button to alert the staff I'm leaving.

"Hey, Brynnie?"

I squeeze my eyes shut tightly at his voice, at the name he uses, at the sharp pain it still causes in my heart. Then I turn around.

"Yeah, Johnny?"

He's standing now. He hasn't moved from the safety of the bed, and maybe that's because he knows there's an invisible barrier I'm trying hard to maintain between us. His fingers curl and flex nervously at his sides. He's thin, and the barbed wire tattoo that circles his wrist accentuates just how narrow his arms have become. He was always so strong, built with muscles that cut in every direction.

"I really did miss you. Every day." His voice breaks on those last two words, and his Adam's apple bobs with a harsh swallow.

"I've been right here, Johnny. Right where you left me."

I step through the door to meet my escort and leave Johnny exactly the way I hoped I wouldn't—with my truth, with my pain. He doesn't need it on top of his own, not right now. But I couldn't help myself. That's how it's always been with him and me.

I simply can't help myself.

I check out and sign the exiting log before gathering my purse and phone. Teddy's eyes jet to me as soon as I push through the door. I don't wait for him to stand or ask questions, forcing him to catch up as I head through the main doors to the portico where I have to wait for my car. My body is quivering. I'm filled with enough energy to sprint up the mountainside, and if I didn't think it would lead me to a nervous breakdown and in a room down the hall from Johnny, maybe I would. Thoughts swirl in my head, leaping from one emotion to the next until Teddy rests a palm on the center of my back and jolts me back to reality.

"You all right?" His brow is low and his concern isn't simply him being polite. He's put our shit to the side for a moment, something I couldn't do with Johnny. I throw myself into his body and his arms slowly engulf me. I know hugging me—comforting me—is not easy for him. Yet it's somehow *so* easy.

"We need to put you on the visit list," I say before backing away and letting him off the hook.

"Okay."

I turn my attention to the front of my car, the reflection of the speckled clouds in the windshield until the driver passes under the covered area and eventually stops right in front of us. Without conversation, Teddy steps toward the driver's side and I get into the passenger seat. He drives me home, then calls an Uber to take him to his inn. And even though it's barely lunchtime, I crawl under my covers and bury my head from the light.

Chapter 8
Summer, Age 17

Johnny's doing his best to stay awake. My father is showing him videos of some of the performances from his first years with the program, and I can tell he is *way* more into it than Johnny is. The tapes are old as it is, and the sound quality isn't doing much for the blaring horns that really dominated the band more than a decade ago.

"You see how crisp our color guard was?" My dad is standing next to the television monitor, dragging his finger across the screen while the tape is paused. The flag line team was five people strong back then. It wasn't hard for five people to twirl a flag in sync.

"It's pretty cool, sir," Johnny says, covering his face with his hoodie sleeve as he releases a yawn.

"Hey, Johnny?" I call over. "Let's go through the third song one more time. You almost have it." He has it already, but I can tell he needs me to bail him out.

"Be right there!" He kicks off his perch on my dad's desk, and my father simply nods and then presses play to continue watching tapes from his glory days. He was so young and brand new to teaching. I think he relives those days to remind himself that he can do hard things. He did so much and set our music program on this elite path as a young man with a baby at home and a wife who, well, let's just say my mother is *a lot*. She has a catering gig today, and our home kitchen is her home office. I think that's why my dad is hanging around here so long today. When my mom cooks, the results are amazing, but the process is brutal.

"Thank you," Johnny whispers, sliding onto the piano bench next to me.

"My dad will keep you here until the sun is up or it's suddenly Tuesday, if you let him."

Johnny's quiet laugh jostles the seat. We've practiced together for two weeks straight so far this summer, and I keep waiting for him to bail or shirk the responsibility—*coast his way through this*. But he's here early every morning, and he comes back after football practice in the evenings. I think he's proven himself. I need to fully buy in to him now and trust that he's in this for real.

I flip through the music sheets to our third song and play through the melody with my right hand. Johnny places his fingers on the keys and matches my tune, accompanying me by memory. I shake my head and chuckle before stopping my playing to let him go on a few extra bars on his own.

He freezes eventually and gives me a quick sideways look. "What?"

I suck in my lips and shake my head more.

"I still don't understand how you're so good at piano."

Johnny has had a lot to learn about keeping time and the proper hand movements to match the counts for every song on the band's show list. He's a quick study, though. And apparently, a musical prodigy. He sat at the piano in the band room before the start of our first group rehearsal and his hands simply knew what to do. He banged out "Every Breath You Take" by

Sting like he wrote it himself. It's his mother's favorite song, he said. I didn't say it out loud, but I thought it was kismet—it's my mother's favorite, too. He doesn't read music great yet, but I guess it's only a matter of time since he's managed to learn most of the arrangements for the band's show by matching up the notes he hears to what's on the paper. It's like he's teaching himself backward.

"I told you, my favorite Christmas gift ever was a mini Casio keyboard." He grins, then moves his hands into a new chord, pressing out a muted tone.

"Yeah, I know. But I took four years of piano lessons with a woman who made me balance pennies on my knuckles as I played the scales, and I gotta say—the fact that you are better than me after tinkering around on a toy when you were a kid has me feeling a little—"

"Inadequate?" His hands play out a short *duh duh duhhh* mystery revelation tune as he quirks a brow at me. I lean into him with a little force and he catches me at his side in a half hug that sends a wave of heat around my stomach and chest. His fingers cling to my bicep, skin on skin, and I glance to my side to make sure I'm not imagining it. I'm not. His hand is there, his arm around me, all couple-like. My father's throat-clearing ends it. Johnny's hand falls away and he scoots to the edge of the bench, adding distance between us.

"Hey, Johnny. I'm going to need you to get this permission slip signed for our travel competitions." My father steps up to the piano with the folded form.

"I have one on file, for football. I figured that would cover . . ."

My dad chuckles.

"Yeah, no. They want one on file for every activity. You know . . . close those loopholes so nobody sues the school or district if you die in a bus crash." My father taps the edge of the folded form on the piano top a few times, then flattens it, leaving it there for Johnny.

"Right. Yeah . . . makes sense."

As my dad walks back to his office, Johnny stares at the form for a few seconds before picking it up and unfolding the top half. He scans the first few lines and his chest expands with a heavy breath.

"Everything okay?" There's an instant sadness about him, like my father poured warm glue over his head and its pulling down his features—drowning out his spirit.

"Yeah. Uh . . . sorry, I was thinking." He leans to his side and pushes the folded form in his back pocket, shooting me a forced smile.

I scoot closer to him, not quite as near as before but enough to test him. Not that I want his arm to swing back around me, or for him to scoot the rest of the way until our thighs touch—I mean, I do, but that's not why I lean in. I want him to feel safe with me, to trust me. I want us to be real, honest-to-God friends.

I play an ominous run of notes on the low keys, hitting the last note a few times until Johnny catches on and takes over, improvising with his own string of notes. We continue on for several minutes, playing this made-up game we never discussed but somehow both understand. Whatever I play, Johnny mimics in his own way, and improves on. That's the key with him—he's always got to make something better. When he fully takes over and starts to play both of our made-up parts, I rock back and fold my arms until he comes to a natural end of the song.

"Ohhh, I made her mad," he teases.

I twist and fold my legs up so I'm staring at him from the side.

"Damn right. It's not fair!" I point at the keys he just

punished, my dad's chuckle echoing from his office where he's listening in. He's known Johnny for less than a month and I can already tell that this boy will be his prized possession—his favorite student of all time. At least, I'm pretty certain those are the thoughts my dad has when Johnny does shit like this.

"I'm sorry?" He scrunches his shoulders up and holds out his palms, then juts out his bottom lip into a plump, kissable pout. It's adorable—fucking adorable. Great. He's too cute to be pissed at.

"It's fine. Hey, I'm hungry. Want to head to the market with me really quick? You can buy me chips and a soda to make up for bragging." I spin around and stand, leaning on the piano as Johnny stares at me with a half-smile open-mouthed gape.

"Why does this feel like a shakedown?" He turns to give me a sideways glance but slowly stands, his movement cautious as if he's waiting for me to attack him with tickles. Maybe I'm the only one thinking about that.

"Come on. I'll drive."

I pop into my dad's office and grab my small handbag.

"Want anything?" My dad's desk is covered with half drank bottles of water and coffee mugs. He's a habitual drink starter who doesn't know how to finish. He scans his desk, looking for this morning's cup. When he finds it, he gives it a shake, then puts it to his lips for a taste.

"Ahh, still warm. I'm good. Thanks."

I roll my eyes and head to the door where Johnny's waiting.

"You got lucky. You almost had to buy for him too." I play punch him in the arm and he rubs the spot as he looks down at me with a crooked grin.

As we walk to my car, Johnny nestles up right to my side, our shoulders an inch or two apart. He's staring at our feet, skipping his steps until our gaits sync up. I try to trick him with a few stutter steps, but he always catches on and fixes things within a step or two.

"You need to teach me how to march. I mean, like, the way you do. I basically walk through our routine, and I saw in those videos that there's a lot more to it than just walking. Even the guys who carry the drums seem to float on their feet. I look like I'm late for class but don't give a shit." He exaggerates his dragging feet the remaining steps to my car.

"You're right. It's not great," I tease.

He grimaces at me over the roof of my car.

"Watch me master this." He points a finger at me and I hit the key fob to unlock my car.

"Oh, I'm sure you will. You'll probably win an award for it by the time the season is over. You'll probably win *every* award. And I'll be over here coming in second." *Oh, that was my bitter rival coming out. I thought I was done with those feelings.*

I avert my eyes as I sink into the driver's seat then crank the engine and reach for the audio button, hoping a really good song will bail my big mouth out of trouble. Before I can press the power, Johnny grabs my hand—and holds it. Tight. I stare at his fingers, the way they are wrapped around my mine, and though my mouth is agape, I can't seem to close it.

"You're better at this, you know—don't you? Like, at all of it." His body moves with his emphatic words, at least I think it does. His arm seems to jostle—the arm attached to the hand holding mine.

I blink rapidly and shift my gaze to his serious face. I do my best to take in what he said. I quirk my lip up into a pathetic, relenting, one-sided smile and offer a *thanks* that I don't really mean. Johnny shakes my hand and twists, wrapping his other hand around both of ours so I'm trapped. Warmly, delightfully, happily trapped. And a bit mortified for my blabbermouth and weak self-esteem. Mostly, though, I'm happily trapped.

"Brynn, I know we don't know each other well, but trust me when I say this. I am so unbelievably jealous of your talent and accomplishments. I wish I had a school like this . . . no."—he looks down and swallows as he shakes his head—"I wish I had a *girl like you* in my life a long time ago. It's like I had all of these things I wanted to try but I didn't think there was a place for them. A place for me to be somebody else."

His head lifts as our eyes meet through his tussled hair. He blows at the strands and his mouth forms a sheepish grin. If I had any guts at all, I would take my other hand and clear the hair from his eyes, maybe palm his face. But since I'm a chicken, I layer my free hand on top of where we're linked, like a pom girl ready to do a cheer.

"I'm really glad I get to see you blossom." *Fuck. That was stupid.*

It takes Johnny about four seconds to bust into eye-watering laughter. He drops his hold on my hands and I quickly power on my Blink 182 playlist.

"Shut up."

Moment ruined.

We reach the gas station market and head in opposite directions. I grab a snack-sized bag of Fritos and fill up an extra-large cup with Dr. Pepper. Johnny grabs a breakfast sandwich and a bottle of some green juice that looks like one of my science experiments. I was kidding about making him pay, but he insists, blocking me from the cashier and handing over a twenty to cover our haul.

"That looks awful, by the way," I say, pointing to the juice bottle as he unscrews the cap. He holds it up to the sunlight and squints as if inspecting it.

"Not gonna lie, it's gross. But it's my way of counteracting the greasy sausage biscuit I'm about to devour." He tips the bottle back and gulps down about half the contents in one massive swallow, doing his best to mask the soured twist in his lips when he's done.

"Refreshing?"

He nods yes at first but quickly switches to a vehement head shake and laughs.

"Not at all."

To rub it in, I take a long draw from my straw and cap it off with an *ahh*. "Dr. Pepper never fails."

"Sugar is the devil, just you watch." He points a finger at me but I simply shrug and take another sip.

We climb back into my car and Johnny unwraps his sandwich but stops short of taking a bite before twisting in his seat.

"Do you think we could maybe stop by my house? It won't take long, and you can wait in the car. I just . . . I'd like to get this form thing done while I'm thinking about it." His thumbs are pressing into the soft bread of his sandwich, almost twitching.

"Sure. I'd love to see your house!" I smile because my nosy side is satisfied.

Johnny laughs nervously and sits back in his seat. He buckles up and continues to fidget with his sandwich as I pull us out of the market parking lot. I stop at the four-way intersection and flip on my signal to turn right. I know he lives on the hill, so I head that way. Johnny rewraps his sandwich as I drive, and eventually his silence gets impossible to ignore.

"I can totally wait in the car." I pull to the stoplight and glance at him. He nods and takes a deep breath, pointing ahead.

"Turn right at the second light. You'll take that road until it pretty much ends at our driveway."

"Okay." I chew at my bottom lip, splitting my attention between the still-red light and his profile. His eyes are fixed on the road ahead, and his jaw tics with what I think is the pressure he's putting on his molars. His nostrils flare and his lips part, and he turns to look at me just as the light changes and I have to pull forward.

"It's not that I'm embarrassed by our house or anything. It's just . . ."

I glance his way and give him an assuring smile.

"It's fine, Johnny. I get it."

I *kind of* get it. Some people are private, and some people my age aren't exactly anxious to show off their families. Whatever the reason, my response seems to put Johnny a little at ease and he finally takes a bite of his food. I'm starting to conjure images of his home and his parents in my mind as we wind up the road toward his house. The houses in this area of town are spread around without rhyme or reason. The land was broken up into weird patches years ago, and sold off piece by piece to people looking to put up small dwellings and escape the busy life in LA. Johnny's home is made of slump block and painted to match the desert. I figured this was the one he lived in when he mentioned where it was to me once. My mom has always loved this house, and when it went on the market she tried to talk my dad into moving there. It's about three miles from where we live now, and a completely different vibe from the cookie-cutter neighborhood street we're on. I think my dad's aversion to change—and the triple value price tag—put the kibosh on my mom's real-estate fantasy.

As we pull into the curve of the driveway, Johnny sits up tall in his seat. A slender woman with long blonde hair pulled back in a thick braid, a long white linen skirt blowing against her ankles, and a bright pink blouse with sleeves rolled up to her elbows is standing near the garage, her hands palming something on top of a folding table.

"You want to meet my mom?" Johnny's demeanor is a complete one-eighty from minutes ago. In fact, he's almost urgent with his excitement, already opening the passenger door before I pull to a complete stop.

"Uh, sure." I'm a bit baffled but the sudden shift, but I'm also excited to meet his mom. I shift into park and kill the engine, rushing to trail behind Johnny as he walks up the driveway and into his mom's waiting hug.

"What a nice surprise! I thought you were at practice all day." The woman steps back enough to look at her son, her hands palming his broad shoulders. She's tall, but Johnny is still taller. And he's much stockier. She glances over his shoulder toward me and her eyes shift back to her son as she smiles.

"Is this Brynn?"

She knows who I am.

"It's really nice to meet you, Mrs. Bishop," I say, stepping in close and reaching my hand out. She smirks at my palm and chuckles as she looks to her son before pulling me into an unexpected hug. I tentatively wrap my arms around her in return. She feels fragile and light, as if she's made of air and clouds. Her eyes are the same vivid blue as Johnny's, and I can see where he gets his defined cheekbones and wide smile.

She holds on to both of my hands as we part, her touch soft, which is a strange contrast to the rough skin of her fingertips. Her nails are nearly non-existent and two of her fingers are wrapped in bandages.

"Call me Beth, hun. I've heard you're quite the musician," she says, shaking my hands in hers before letting them fall.

"I mean, I'm in band." I shrug, unable to handle a compliment without a dose of awkward. "My dad's a music teacher, so I grew up learning. Stuck with it, I guess."

"*Mmm*, Johnny loves music. Don't you, babe?" She looks to her son, adoration coloring every feature of her gaze and smile.

"Yeah, Mom." He smiles tightly and when she looks away he raises his eyebrows at me. I think he's embarrassed of her bragging, but he shouldn't be. It's sweet. He does seem to love music. And he's the one who is quite the musician, so I'm discovering.

Johnny glances around the inside of their garage, which is stacked with boxes as if they still haven't fully moved in though it's been several months now.

"Dad is . . ."

"With the guys in the city. He swore he'd be back with the car in time to pick you up after football." Her eyes lock on Johnny's for a few long seconds. He eventually nods and sucks his lips into a tight line.

"I could always bring you home later," I offer.

"No, it's . . . it's fine. My dad doesn't answer his cell or texts so he won't know we deviated from the plan and it'll just irritate him if I'm not there." Johnny blinks rapidly as he looks down and shakes his head, clearly annoyed.

"Thank you, though, Brynn. That's nice of you," his mom pipes in.

I croak out a *sure* that I don't think either of them hear.

"So, why the special visit? Just to meet Brynn?" His mom's brow dips with what looks like concern.

"No. I mean, that was a perk, you two meeting. But I need you to sign something." Johnny reaches into his pocket and pulls out the form my father gave him. He hands it to his mom.

"It's so I can travel with the band for competitions. The one for football won't cover those trips," he explains as him mom reads through the permission slip. Her eyes flit up to meet her son's gaze and for a blip they widen.

"Well, let's get it signed, then." Her mouth forms a tight smile that pushes dimples into her cheeks. It seems forced, but she doesn't seem to be upset with her son. I'm getting a weird vibe from the entire interaction and my anxiety inches up as Beth searches through a few drawers in her garage for a pen or pencil to use. She finally finds one and quickly signs her name, folding the form into a smaller square and handing it back to her son.

"Thanks," Johnny whispers, leaning in and kissing her cheek. Her hand doesn't make it all the way up his back as she embraces him this time, and I instantly feel intrusive watching this private exchange.

I turn my attention to the table, which I can now see is covered in hundreds of tiny glass beads. I step in close and fight the urge to touch them.

"Those are beautiful," I remark.

"Thank you," Beth says, her spirited tone returning. "I think they'll melt into something pretty interesting."

She steps up next to me and runs her hand over them, glancing at me with an encouraging nod toward the tabletop.

"Go on, feel them."

I lay my right palm on top and roll the beads slowly, letting them tickle my palm.

"Thanks, I really wanted to," I laugh out quietly.

Johnny steps up to the other side of the table and picks one of the beads up, pinching it and holding it up to the sky to let the sun shine through it. He squints and I note how the ocean blue color matches his eyes.

"You're an artist?" I step back from the table not wanting to overdo my invitation to meddle in her things.

Beth nods and hums.

"I try," she says.

"She's being modest. She makes glass sculptures, and two of her pieces are in the main library garden in Long Beach," Johnny brags on her behalf. Their eyes meet and they share a mutual smile that instantly warms my insides. There's genuine love between them.

"Well, government doesn't pay like private collectors. But

yes, I do have some pieces around this state and maybe in a few galleries," she says.

Johnny tosses the bead onto the table and his mother pushes it flat into place, grimacing at him in a teasing way.

"I'd love to see your work sometime," I offer, though my nosy side truly does want to see what she can make with glass.

Johnny begins to head toward my car so I follow along with him as his mother trails behind.

"I'd love to show you . . . sometime. Maybe sometime." There's a longing to her tone, or maybe I read into it and hear it that way. Whatever my instincts are telling me, I have serious doubts that I will ever get a tour of her art. She's probably modest about it. It's clear she didn't want to brag.

"Thanks again, Mom," Johnny says, pausing at the passenger door and meeting his mom's gaze. She kisses the tips of her fingers and tosses her invisible affection toward her son, who pretends to catch it.

We get back in my car and I slowly back out of their driveway, pivoting my car to head back down the winding desert road.

"You and your mom are sweet together," I say, glancing his way. He meets my eyes for a blip but immediately turns his attention to the roadway before us.

"She's my favorite person," he finally says.

I don't bring up his father, and neither does he. We drive back with my playlist blaring and an unspoken understanding lingering in the air. Johnny won't be coming back to practice with me after football tonight. And his dad is the opposite of favorite in his heart and mind.

Chapter 9
Present

Logic tells me these visits will get easier. As with all things me and Johnny Bishop, though, logic does not apply.

I've seen him four times over the last two weeks, and Teddy's gone on his own twice. I'm jealous of Teddy's visits, at least I am the way he describes them to me. They talk and reminisce and laugh with one another. Their visits seem easy. The last time Teddy went, he stayed for game night and played dominos with Johnny and two other men who apparently lost their Hollywood producing careers on some independent movie that flopped. Teddy says he's pretty sure they blew their movie fortune on drugs, and that's why they're in there—and why the movie flopped.

It's discouraging to hear the stories from others. I know the odds. We all know the odds. For some, it's their second stay at Waves. For others, it's their third or fourth. And then there are the people like Johnny, who are on their first, at least at Waves, and teetering on making it out right. There's that heavy percentage betting against them. And in the darkness lingers the quiet fear that nobody likes to talk about—what if they don't make it at all? What if they fall completely into the abyss?

What if they die? *If Johnny . . . dies?*

Johnny invited Teddy and me to come together today. Other than our short exchanges about how each of us thinks Johnny's doing, Teddy and I haven't really talked. He prefers it that way. At least, I *think* he does. Maybe I'm simply scared to open Pandora's box and work through issues with him. It's easier to put the blame on him for the grudge, especially since I'm responsible for its origin. I suppose it's healthy in some way that I realize that, even if I don't vocalize it to the one who matters.

Teddy pulls along the curb in front of my house in his rental. It's a nice truck, one of those double-cab kind with a step on the side to get in. It's maroon with shiny chrome. It suits him.

I climb in, holding the small tin of shortbread my mom insisted I bring to Johnny. I couldn't really avoid the topic with my parents, so to keep my mom from needling me about his recovery and whatever happened between us and all of the history she loves to drudge up, I put her to work. Last week, I brought him homemade blueberry muffins that I told Mom he'd been craving. This week, it's shortbread. It makes her feel as if she's contributing.

Teddy nods toward the tin as I buckle up.

"Mom baked," I explain.

His lips twist with thought.

"Think Johnny would notice if I skimmed a little off the top?"

I eye him sideways for a second then bunch my face up.

"Nah. I already had two myself," I admit. I pop the tin open and slip out a morsel, rearranging the remaining pieces to fill in the gap. I hand it to Teddy and our hands touch on the exchange.

"Sorry." I look away, ashamed that I touched him. It's stupid; this weirdness between us has to stop.

Teddy pulls forward and I glance his way in time to see him cram the entire piece into his mouth. I smile and start to make a joke but snap my mouth shut and instead opt to see what tunes he has on his playlist. I turn the volume up and get some country hit I sort of recognize, and immediately press skip to move on to the next.

"Hey!" Teddy reaches forward and presses the back button.

I roll my eyes and breathe out a laugh.

"My ride, my tunes." He turns the volume up a notch and sings along. His voice isn't bad. It's not Johnny's, though.

I don't *love* country music, but I tolerate it through seven songs on our way to Waves. We navigate the check-in process and head back with our host to a patio lounge area where Johnny's arranged for us to visit. The more times I come here, the more the *resort* side shines through. There's a spa to our right, and to the left, a health center that roars with the thumping music from a spin class. A server passes us while carrying a tray of what looks like pineapple smoothies. He disappears behind the massive wooden doors to the spa and a rich sandalwood scent wafts in our direction as the doors close. I breathe it in, willing some of the serenity to invade my body before I step outside.

Johnny spots us as we exit through the large sliding glass door. Our host hands us a remote that we're supposed to use to page him when we're ready to leave. I've learned from observation that those paging buttons are more about being able to get assistance if the person in treatment is becoming agitated. During my last visit, a woman began slapping another woman visiting her as they sat in the lounge. One press of the remote and two attendants were calming things down within seconds.

"Hey, welcome to paradise!" Johnny opens his arms and gives Teddy a hug while I slip the lanyard with the remote over my neck and make my way to the open seat on the opposite side of the table. The two men look at me as they part, wearing different expressions. Teddy's is a tad condescending, his lips pursed and his brow pulled in. He probably thinks I'm being a baby by not hugging Johnny. Of course, he looks away after a second, likely because he realizes he's being a baby about not hugging me when we meet up. Johnny's mood is more regretful, and the sadness that weighs down the bottom of his eyes gets me this time. I should have hugged him. It wouldn't kill me.

"Compliments of Meg Fisher," I announce, cutting the mood with my mother's baked goods. I slide the tin across the table and Johnny's mouth ticks up with a hopeful grin.

"Don't worry, security cleared it. And sampled it," I say.

Johnny pulls the lid away and holds the open tin to his nose, breathing in.

"I sampled it too, *brotha,* and Meg's still got it," Teddy adds. He reaches in for another sample, but Johnny's quick to swat his hand away.

"Get your own rehab pity cookies!" He pops one in his mouth and quickly shuts the tin as we all laugh and the boys take their seats around the table.

Iced water with slices of oranges and lemons curled on the lip sit on a silver tray in the center. The sun is out, but the large umbrella offers a decent amount of shade. I'm almost chilly where I sit, which I suppose is what I get for picking the far seat.

"Big two-week anniversary tonight, huh?" Teddy says. He slaps Johnny's arm like they're two friends meeting up at a football game.

"*Mmm,* yeah. No ceremony, I'm afraid. Just another bill to

my manager." Johnny laughs lightly at his joke; Teddy and I simply smile. It's uncomfortable on my part. All of this is. Every visit I have tightens my stomach until it's hard to breathe.

"So how . . . how are you doing?" I lean in and pull one of the waters toward me, mostly so I have something to do with my hands.

Johnny blows up at his hair, then runs his hand through it, clutching the waves at the back of his head. He looks well today, better than he has in years, honestly. Not that I have in-person memories to compare it to. I'm going off the photos I have seen in magazines and on social media. He's still a far cry from the eighteen-year-old with stars in his eyes. But those stars . . . I can almost see them. They're dim ghosts trapped in his chaos.

"I feel good." He rests his elbows on the table and sits up straight, clasping his hands in front of him and meeting my eyes. I feel like his parole officer, as if he's trying to sell me on his sobriety. It's been two weeks. I'm not naïve.

"Good's a start," I say. He flinches a little. It's been a long time—maybe he forgot how honest I always was with him.

I challenge his stare as a few long seconds pass. Teddy breaks the tension by reaching forward and knocking one of the glasses over, spilling water across the table and onto my lap.

"Shit!" I leap out of the seat and run my hands down my thighs, trying to brush the beads of liquid away before they sink into my jeans.

"My bad, Brynnie," Teddy says.

I flash him a stern look, my mouth tight and eyes slits. He holds out his palms and mouths, *I swear.* My gaze drifts to Johnny, whose own focus shifts between Teddy and me. I exhale and try to get my pride back in order, knowing my temper will follow, though the thought of throwing my water in

Teddy's face does cross my mind. That would be a new low for me.

"It's fine. I'm fine." I run my palms over my thighs a few more times. "It was just really cold. It surprised me."

"Why don't you sit in the sun?" Johnny suggests.

I nod slowly, now faced with the dilemma of where to pull my chair—to Johnny's side or Teddy's. I opt for Teddy, partly to test myself, but mostly as cover to any awkwardness Johnny may have picked up on between us just now.

Johnny leans back in his chair and crosses one leg over the other, holding the bottom edge of his jeans, fidgeting with the ragged hem.

"Hey, so . . . I never asked. How did the showcase turn out?" Johnny holds his bottom lip between his teeth as his head falls to one side. His shoulders rise slowly with a long breath. I can still read his body language. At least, I think I can, and he's coming to terms with the fact he barged in on a special night when he came to town. Of all people familiar with that show-case, Johnny should be the one to know what a pivotal moment it is for those students.

"Oh, you know, there's always that one standout," I say.

His eyes lock on mine for a breath.

"You would know," he says with a soft smile.

I roll my eyes and laugh off his compliment. Some things never change, and Johnny Bishop is still smooth with a line. We both know he was the standout back then, and he's the standout now. Even from rock bottom.

"A girl name Jade won. She writes her own music. She's really talented. Actually, you would love her style. Who knows . . . maybe a collab one day?" I shrug, but I'm also being serious. Assuming Johnny really gets his shit together.

"If you believe in her, she must be something. I'll check her out," he says.

Our eyes meet again and dance as we each take a deep breath through our noses. A strange euphoria sweeps over me every time this happens. It's the connection. As broken as it is, it still flickers when our wires touch.

"You should talk to her about your idea, Johnny," Teddy prods.

Johnny shifts in his seat, planting both feet on the ground and straightening his spine. I glance to Teddy and his eyes widen for a blip as his mouth tightens. I think he's warning me to be kind about whatever Johnny's about to say.

"What idea?" My eyes shift back to Johnny. He laughs quietly, his nerves slipping out.

"I was going to work up to that. Thanks for the nice segue, Ted." Johnny leans to his right and pats Teddy's shoulder. Meanwhile, my stomach tightens even more and my teeth gnash as I force my grin to stay in place.

"Well, we're here now, so what's the big idea?" My pulse is so strong I can feel it in my cheeks.

Johnny rubs his hands together, looking down at them as he does. He bites the tip of his tongue through his smile, and in these few seconds I mentally flash through every memory I have of him making this same irresistible face. He had publicity shots done of him wearing that sexy smirk. Hell, it was his first album cover!

"I was wondering if maybe . . . when I get out and settled into my place . . ." He pauses to let out more nervous laughter, and it stuns me into a frozen state. It's rare to see this man nervous. That's one thing he's never been.

I thread my own hands together, squeezing them tight enough to cut off the circulation to my fingertips.

"Could I maybe come in and work with some of your students? Like, as an assistant or something? Or mentor, maybe?" His mouth twists and his nose crinkles as his eyes squint. Just one more of his trademark adorable expressions. It's how he always got his way.

My heart has stopped. My class is my one domain, my safe space. It's what I've done with my life. I don't have Grammys or songwriting credits or albums. I have those kids—and my passion to help them become the next Johnny Bishop. To be *better* than Johnny Bishop.

"Oh, I—"

"I know it's out of the blue. And I'm not sure if it's even a thing the school would allow, what with the attention and all that. I'm sure it would be a distraction. Though I do remember famous graduates coming back to visit other areas. Who was that one director guy?" He looks to Teddy.

"Ian Glassmeyer," Teddy pipes in.

"Right! That guy!" Johnny snaps his fingers and returns his focus to me.

"He won an academy award," I mutter.

"Right! And maybe, ya know, since I have the Grammys and all . . ."

I swallow down bile.

"Unless you think it's a bad idea."

I do.

"Umm. It's just that . . . it's a lot. To take in, I mean." I nod as I speak, my eyes not really focusing on anything. "Can I think about it?"

I shift my gaze to Johnny and am immediately rocked with guilt. His eyes are pleading, even as his mouth says *okay* and *I understand*. My gut sinks, and my heart sinks with it. Why didn't I just say yes? Of course our school wants him to visit. It's me who isn't sure.

"I'm sure it will be all right." I hear my own voice without fully being aware that I'm speaking.

"Yeah?" Johnny sits up, his mouth turning upward on the

corners. My heart thumps against my chest cavity like a racquetball.

"Yeah. I mean, let me run it up the chain of command, but—"

Johnny salutes me.

"Yes, ma'am. And you'd be the boss. My boss, I mean. Whatever you say, I do. Whatever you need—"

I wave my hand, my inner voice screaming for him to just stop. We both know how this is going to go. He is going to literally devour the oxygen in every classroom he enters. Hell, he's going to knock the power out of the entire town simply by moving back home.

Which makes me wonder . . .

"Are you going to stay with your mom?" I ask.

"Oh, boy." Teddy leans back in his chair and threads his hands behind his neck, tilting his face to the sky as he blows out heavily.

"Oh boy, what?" My head bobs between the two of them.

"About that." Johnny's lip ducks right back between his teeth.

Oh, fuck.

"Oh, yeah . . . no. That's . . . I mean, teaching with me is one thing. But Johnny." I blubber out an awkward laugh that vibrates my lips. My cheeks buzz with heat, and my arms are tingling. I'm having a panic attack.

I run my arm along my forehead, both to check for feeling and to dab away the sweat.

"I'm sure I can move in with Mom eventually, for a little while. And I have someone looking for a house. It will just be for those first few days. Maybe a week. Two tops."

Two tops?

I get up and pace around my chair, then wander back into the shade because I'm suddenly burning up.

"And hotels are not in your budget?" My brow is literally in my hairline.

Johnny looks off to the side and pulls his lips in tight before forcing his gaze back to me. His eyes crinkle, a wince to his face.

"They prefer if I'm not . . . alone."

The weight of that comment slams into me. The prospect of being my roommate made me uncomfortable, but being his caretaker or babysitter?

"You have that nice guest room, and you made it all comfortable for me, so unless you've already cluttered it up?" I flash a hard stare Teddy's way and he laughs under his breath since his back is to Johnny. *Asshole!*

"It's not about space," I explain.

It's about my space.

"Johnny, I don't know that I'm equipped—" I stop myself there, not sure how to follow that up. It's not like he's bedridden or mending a broken leg. He's rehabbing, trying to kick alcohol and get clean. I'm a teacher who likes to come home and have a glass of wine. Or two. Or three!

"I understand." He leans forward and flattens his palm on the table, a soft gesture that stops my racing mind just long enough for me to catch up.

I shake my head and move back into my chair, gripping my knee caps as my legs bob nervously.

Looking up at him, I scrunch my shoulders and squint my eyes.

"You're super famous, Johnny," I say. "And the press is already nosing around town."

I've personally had to turn away four reporters from hanging around the school parking lot looking for quotes from people who knew Johnny back in the day.

"I understand," Johnny says again.

I breathe in deeply, a smidge of tension releasing. My heart beats louder, though, and my gaze shifts to Teddy. He shrugs and purses his lips before mouthing, *your call.*

He has to get what a massively bad idea this is. Of all people, Teddy knows what a mess I was back when Johnny left. Of course, he also knows how much I loved him. He knows about the promise.

My head falls forward, my hair sliding from my shoulders and dropping down between my knees as I hang low. Ants swirl on the ground between my feet where one of the orange slices sits.

"Okay." I swallow the lump in my throat then lift my head, the blood rushing back in place.

"Okay?" Johnny quirks a brow.

"Temporary, right?" I have my doubts about so many things, about him showing up on move-in day, about him only being temporary if he does, about my ability to survive any of this.

He holds up two fingers then swipes them across his chest.

"That's not even a thing." I shake my head and look to the side, away from both of them, as Johnny laughs.

"I was never a boy scout, so I don't know."

I'll say.

Chapter 10
Age 18

I pull into the parking space closest to the back exit, by the band practice field. After dozens of practices over the summer, I feel as if we're ready to take the field today for the first day's pep rally. It's maybe the one time all year the entire student body pays attention to what we do on the field. Because they are forced to, sure, but there's also that verve of new beginnings in the air. Grudges haven't formed, breakups aren't hanging over couples' heads, and our football team has yet to lose. They have yet to actually play, but . . . *details*.

This also happens to be the first time the start of school falls on my birthday. Eighteen—legal to vote. My mom made me note-shaped pancakes for breakfast this morning, and dad got me the piano sheet music for *Hamilton*. They sang to me before everyone fled for school and work, and it was like every other birthday I've had. I don't feel any different. I don't feel special. Older? Matured? Not really. I'm honestly more excited for school and our performance than I am about turning eighteen.

I tug my heavy backpack from the passenger seat and slip

my arms into the straps as I exit my car. I unzip the side pocket and feel for my phone so I can move it to the back pocket of my jeans. I check for birthday wishes first, naively hoping for several. There's only one message, though. Teddy sent me a gross animation of some guy humping a birthday cake, so I text him back a quick *gee, thanks* then put my phone away.

"Is there a reason you park as far away as possible when literally the entire parking lot is empty?"

My gaze pops up from my phone screen to find Johnny standing several spots away with his hands hidden behind his back. He's wearing his football jersey, the bright white home one with black letters and the howling coyote on the front. His dark blue jeans end at a fresh pair of white Vans waiting to be scribbled on during his first semester.

"I like being able to get out of here first," I respond, turning my attention to the mystery he's concealing behind him.

"Whatcha got there?" I nod and step forward.

He brings his hands from behind his back, revealing a single cupcake with bright yellow frosting. My favorite color. There's a candle on top, which he lights with the device in his other hand as he closes the gap between us.

"My mom helped me make it, so I promise it won't poison you. I'm not a caterer or anything like your mom, but I think it's pretty good." He laughs lightly before blowing up at the hair that's fallen over his right eye. "You said chocolate was your favorite."

I did. Once. The first week of summer when everyone in band took turns sharing their likes and dislikes during one of my father's ice breakers. That was three months ago.

I'm still far enough away that I don't think he can see how badly I'm blushing. Johnny and I spent almost every summer morning working on the show together.

"Okay, I'd blow this out quick. I'm not sure how long that

candle's been mixed in with my mom's baking things. I know it made the move here with us, and who knows how long it sat in a drawer before that." He holds the cupcake out in his palm, cupping the flame to block the small breeze.

"This was really sweet," I say, my eyes flickering to meet his before I close them and blow. I wish for this school year to be as amazing as the summer has been. I smell the smoke before my eyes reopen, and Johnny whips the used candle from the layer of frosting and tosses it on the ground. Tiny droplets of pink wax splatter and harden on the blacktop.

"So, what part of it did you make?" I take the cake into my fingers and gently pull away the thin paper cup holding it together. I'm guessing he did the frosting because it's more of a smearing than a decorative twist, definitely the touch of a teenaged boy.

"My mom let me stir." He lifts his shoulders, then shoves his hands in his pockets. He dips his chin as his eyes take on a look of anticipation.

"And the frosting?" I quirk a brow before bringing the cake to my lips and taking a small taste of the sugary cream. It's sweet and a little gritty from sugar but delicious, as sugar usually is.

"I think that's pretty obvious," he laughs out.

I laugh too, then take a full bite of cake and frosting together. A piece crumbles off and Johnny reaches forward, catching it in his palm.

"Finders keepers," he says before popping the morsel into his mouth.

I take a few more bites as Johnny and I walk toward the band room together, and traces of frosting stick to the sides of my mouth. I lick at them, but I can tell some of it is out of reach — with my luck embarrassingly spread across my cheek.

"Do I—" I turn to face him outside the band room door and point to my face.

He chuckles, then moves his hand toward my cheek. My pulse picks up, the same way it does every time we rehearse our field entry and he takes my hand and dips me. He hasn't kissed me again since that first time, but I keep hoping. I'm too shy to ask if he wants to make that a permanent part of our routine.

"Can I?" he asks, his hand paused inches from my face.

"Please."

Please.

His gaze shifts from my eyes to my cheek as his thumb gently glides from the edge of my mouth to the curve of my cheekbone.

"You must have really liked it," he teases through soft laughter. Without pause, he puts his thumb in his mouth and sucks away the leftover frosting.

"I did," I choke out.

Johnny's smile softens as his gaze blinks back to mine. He bites his thumb when our eyes lock, that sharp crackle in the air between us. It's been like this all summer. We'd spend mornings together alone before he had to leave for football practice and weightlifting. Every time he left, he'd linger, as though he was working up the courage to tell me something. That this crush I have is not one-sided. The longer it went on, though, the more I convinced myself it was in my imagination.

But then there are these moments, like this one now. And it's hard not to think maybe . . .

"Hey! Yo, birthday girl!" The harsh interruption immediately cuts my fantasy in half as Devin steps between us to pull open the band room door. He and Johnny do that half-hug, handshake thing and I follow them inside. Devin leads the drumline. He also plays a mean set for the jazz band and writes some of his own arrangements. He wants to produce when he gets out of the Valley, and he's already got major labels looking to mentor him.

Before Johnny showed up, Devin was my favorite distraction. Drummers, man. They have a way, and Devin basically exudes every stereotype. His dad runs a tattoo joint in the Springs, so Devin's arms are covered in works of art. He got his first tat at fifteen, and it bloomed into two sleeves over three years.

"Hey, I got you something," Devin says, tossing his backpack into a corner of the room then reaching for his back pockets and pulling out a set of sticks. He hands them to me, and I blink a few times before I realize they're personalized. He's burnt my name into them, or more likely, his dad did.

"Devin!" My shocked reaction catches the attention of Cori and a few of the others who just spilled into the room, and soon, there's a small crowd of girls standing around me looking at the gift I got from the boy who *used* to be the cutest one in our program.

My stomach flutters, mostly from the instant attention. There's also a strange weight tugging at my gut, and a quick glance to Johnny confirms the cause of it. He feels out-gifted.

"I hope you like them. Eighteen's a big one. Happy birthday." Before I have a chance to ready myself, Devin engulfs me in a full-armed hug that wraps me completely and holds me to his chest, a place I would have given anything to visit a few months ago. His usual spicy cologne tickles my nose.

"I love them, Dev. Seriously, thank you," I say, holding them tightly in a fist as we part.

I leave my smile in place for him until he heads toward the back of the room where the drums are stored. I shift my focus to Johnny, hoping he's moved on and busied himself with something else by now, but I find him still looking on from the stool at the front of the room. He offers a tight-lipped smile and an approving nod, and all I can think to do is to lift my amazing gift up a little to acknowledge it. I both love and hate these sticks right now.

Chapter 11
Present

I'm furious. And I'm not sure at whom. For now, I choose to be livid with Teddy.

He knows it's a bad idea for Johnny to move in with me. I mean, what the hell? Johnny is wealthy beyond belief. Surely he could rent himself some hideaway nearby so he's close to his mom. Or use the mad hookups he probably has to get one of his tour buses stationed out in the desert.

But no. *Nooo.* He needs to stay in my spare bedroom—the place where I shove all of my dead-ends. The closet is full of failed quilting attempts. The sewing machine on the floor in there has a burnt engine because I tried to force a zipper through when all signs told me to stop. There are boxes under the guest bed filled with pictures—*photos of me and Johnny, back then!* And then there's my wine rack, with bottles I've worked to collect from the few trips I've taken to Northern California. Pretty sure I'm going to need to move those to my parents' house for a while, which means my mom will bring up the fact I still haven't gone to Paris like I planned. Or put together a musical for the stage. *It's half-written.*

We're closing in on my neighborhood, and my blood gets

hotter with every bump in the road this rental truck jostles over. When Teddy purposely drives across a huge pothole, tossing me up in my seat and slamming my head back into the head-rest, I lose it.

"Okay, you wanna do this? We're gonna do this, buddy!" I reach forward and smack the power button on the entertainment system before twisting in my seat and crossing my arms over my chest.

Teddy bursts into laughter.

"Brynn, what the hell are you talking about?" His shoulders shake with his laughing.

I narrow my eyes.

"Don't pretend. Don't . . . don't . . . I don't know, act all innocent. Like you didn't hit that pothole on purpose."

"Ha! Serious? Brynn, this is a rental and I'm not looking to turn it in with damage. And you know the roads around here are shit. Calm down." He rolls his eyes and drapes his wrist over the top of the steering wheel before making a *tssk* and glancing out his side window.

"Fine, maybe the road was an accident. But back there? With Johnny?" I point my thumb to the roadway behind us. Teddy turns my way briefly, just long enough for our eyes to meet, then he rolls his eyes again and shakes his head.

"You're being dramatic, Brynn." His tone is curt and his expression says he's getting as pissed as I am. Good. He needs to match my mood so we can finally spar and end this dumb whatever it is between us.

I shove him and he twists the wheel slightly, jerking the car.

"Hey! Do not do that! Stop playing!" He points a finger at me, which only ticks me off more.

I push him again, and this time he jerks the wheel to the side of the road. The truck pulls off into the dirt of an open lot near some of the old town businesses.

"Are you trying to get us killed?" He pushes his palm against his forehead and slowly runs his hand into his hair, his fingers digging into his scalp. His face is red. A few tourists have stopped in the restaurant parking lot a few yards away from us, and Teddy forces a smile and waves.

"Yeah, hi. We're making a scene. Sorry, but move along," he says, his tone dripping in sarcasm.

"Look at me," I demand.

His nostrils flare and he continues to stare ahead for a few long seconds, his wrists propped on the steering wheel. Finally, he lowers his head and turns to face me.

"What, Brynn? What is this about, huh?" His palms turn up but his hands remain slung over the wheel.

"It's about you and me, and a night that was—"

"A mistake. Yeah, I remember. Clearly." He blinks rapidly and blows out with frustration.

"Don't do that." I force my tone to be softer, kinder. We aren't going to get anywhere if all I do is shout at his shouting.

"Do what, Brynn?" He falls back into the seat and rolls his head so our gazes lock. I lean against my seat and force myself to look into his green eyes without saying a word. I hold his stare hostage, trying to force him to let his guard down for just one damn second. It feels like minutes pass, but I think maybe time simply slowed. His eyes get glossy and he breaks away, looking forward and pinching the bridge of his nose before sweeping the dampness from under his eyes.

"Dammit, Brynn. I just wanted to help our friend. I wanted to be here for him and maybe help him get back to the light. He's got so much, ya know? His talent and the guy he was back then? He was my friend!"

"He was friends with both of us!" I bite my tongue before I call him out and use his name . . . *Teddy*. I know that's why he's been saying my name over and over . . . to needle me. He used

123

to do that when we were young, and he knows I hate it. It makes him sound like my parent.

His eyes grow heavy and he blinks slowly as he wets his lips with his tongue.

"He was more than just your friend, Brynn." He did it again. And this time, my chest burns.

"I know." I nod slowly.

Teddy pushes at the wheel, then turns away from me as he utters, "Damn it all to hell."

I lean across the console, slowly, curling my fingers at first, afraid to extend them. Teddy breathes deeply, his body almost vibrating with his mixed emotions. I know this feeling. I *feel* this. Shutting my eyes, I lean just enough for my hand to rest on his bicep. When he doesn't jerk away, I squeeze lightly. Eventually, he covers my hand with his own and warms my skin.

"I was so pissed at you," he croaks.

I don't respond. I nod, though. Even though he's not looking at me, I nod. And I let him speak. I'll wait however long it takes for him to get this out.

"I know that night for you was just . . . acting out, I guess. You were going through your shit, and maybe I was too. But Brynn, in the back of my mind, there was always this part of me that thought you would have been better off with me. That I wouldn't have tucked and bailed on you the way he did. And when we slept together, I guess . . ." He rolls his head back and our eyes meet. He looks exhausted by this. "I got caught up in it. Started hoping maybe there was a world where you and I got together. That Johnny fucked up and it was his loss. My turn."

He spits out a short laugh and shakes his head, closing his eyes. I reach over with my other hand and cover his, urging his fingers to open and let me hold on to him, just a little.

"I'm so sorry." I suck in my quivering bottom lip and let the tear that's been building fall from my right eye. Teddy looks down at our hands and squeezes mine back.

"I know you are. And I know you mean it."

"I do," I say quickly.

I look down, the guilt crushing me, but Teddy reaches for my chin and nudges my head back up, forcing me to look him in the eyes. I stare long and hard, even when it's hard to. Those eyes haven't changed a bit. The kindness and warmth is still there, just as it was after we both graduated college and celebrated with our few remaining friends who lived in Yucca. It was a cool night and I was a sucker for a fire pit in the desert. I like to blame the wine for my impaired judgement, but I knew what I was doing. I was soothing the hurt, filling the lonely void. Being in this town after going away for four years of college was hard, and being here without Johnny was even harder. I was drowning in memories. And I used my willing friend for air.

"The sex, though . . . it was good. Right?" Teddy squints one eye and quirks his lip up.

"Oh, my God!" My eyes flutter shut and my cheeks burn. I play slap at him and he tethers me up and pulls me into a bear hug, practically dragging me over the center console into his massive body. In his arms, I finally breathe—fully. Deeply. It's cleansing and refreshing. Comforting. *Real.*

"Yeah, Teddy. The sex was good."

His body shakes with laughter and I bury my heated face in his shirt.

"I should probably tell you, then. Uh . . . so . . . well . . ."

I sit up and wipe my eyes dry, my mouth stretching into a relieved smile. I haven't felt this kind of smile on my face in ages. Months. *Years?*

"I'm engaged." He bunches his shoulders up and his eyebrows lift to his hair line.

"You dog!" I slap at him again. His grin grows so large it pushes his cheeks into apples. "Well, don't hold out on me, Teddy Pine. Show me the pics. Let me see who this girl is!"

I snap my fingers as he plucks out his phone. I nestle into the seat, pulling my legs up beneath me so I can lean toward him comfortably as he slides through several photos of him and a tall blonde girl who has muscles that might actually rival his.

"Teddy!" I widen my eyes at him and take the phone into my hand so I can zoom in on the photo of her in a bathing suit at the beach. "She's too good for you," I tease.

"Ha!" He jerks his phone back, cradling it in his palm against the steering wheel. "Don't I know it. She's a surfer."

"I was gonna say. Those are some guns on her." She really is beautiful. She's exactly who I picture him with. "She looks nice."

"She is," he coos. He looks back to me, his face full of life, his eyes bright. He's in love, and it's . . . it's beautiful. "Maybe in a couple weeks I can bring her back here. I'd like you to meet her, and she loves road trips."

"I'd really love that." I mean it. I mean it with my whole entire heart.

Teddy nods as his mouth settles into the most natural smile, his lips soft and his face relaxed. The shit wall between us— gone. I almost relax, too, and then Teddy swallows.

"I'm sorry I pushed you into taking him in. For letting him move in, I mean." He bunches his face and gives me a guilty sideways look. It brings me right back to my reality, and that rock in my stomach doubles in size.

"I would have done it anyway. I'm soft like that, and we both know it. We both know . . ." I don't say it out loud. I don't have to. We do both know, just like we knew then.

Johnny is more than just my friend. He always will be.

Chapter 12
Age 18, First Competition

The bus is practically shaking as we riffle around inside, slipping into our performance jackets and exchanging the comfy shoes we rode here in for the bright white ones for marching. Johnny wasn't able to ride with us, so his mom is dropping him off at the field and he'll meet us at the check-in table. He promised me he would text when he arrived, but I still don't have a message from him.

I stand up on my knees in my seat in the very back of the bus, craning my neck to make eye contact with my dad. I find his panicked face waiting for me, and when he raises a hopeful brow, I shake my head and shrug. He grimaces.

My dad is competitive, and he has high hopes for our first competition of the year. We're a small school compared to the others in our division, which is based on region rather than size. But what we have going for us this year, he says, is *panache*.

Panache. As in Johnny Bishop.

Our panache, however, is nowhere to be found.

"He's going to be here, right?" Devin grumps from across the aisle. He's stretched his leg across to my seat, resting his shoe on the edge so he can tie it.

"He promised he'd be here, so he will be here," I say, my voice matter-of-fact.

He puffs out a short laugh and mumbles, "Whatever."

"Stop it," I bite out. He doesn't react, though, instead grabbing his sticks and leaving through the back door of the bus.

"What's his deal?" Cori whispers.

I shrug at her question, but I have this weird feeling in my tummy. It's tight and sour every time Devin takes some sort of jab at Johnny. He's been doing it a lot the last few weeks. When Johnny had to bail last minute from our show during the first day's pep rally because the football coach wouldn't let him leave the team, Devin started calling him part-timer and spread a rumor that Johnny was only participating in band to fill in some missing credit he needs for graduation. Cori thinks it's because Devin likes me and he's jealous. I think she might be right. I never thought I would be in a place where I wished Devin Cruz wasn't into me.

I push my small duffle bag holding my hair brush, phone, spare socks and slides under the seat and slip the red wool poodle skirt up over my black leggings. One of the other band parents made the skirt for me, and my mom went out and purchased a perfectly matching red lipstick. "Bright, bold colors!" my mom said when she gave it to me. I lit up on the outside and took it exuberantly, but on the inside I thought how much less likely Johnny was to kiss me if my lips were bleeding bright red lipstick. My dad says the details will sell it to the judges, so before leaving the bus, I touch up my lips and tuck the tube of lipstick into the small pocket on my waistband.

"He's here!" Cori shouts from the front exit of the bus.

My heart hammers in my chest and I push up on the backs of the seats so I can see over my bandmates' heads. Rather than wade through the remaining people getting off the bus, I follow Devin's route and push the back door open. Our driver hates it when we do that because it makes a buzzing sound, but I don't really care if she's ticked at me.

Once my feet hit the ground, I jog to the front of the bus where a large blue SUV is idling. I can see the back of Johnny's slicked-back hair through the windshield, so I rush to the passenger door to help him gather whatever he needs. His back is to me as I step up, but his mom spots me and stretches her mouth into a face-covering smile.

"Brynn! I'm so sorry we're late. I had some trouble with the car, and—"

"It's fine, Mom. Go ahead and I'll ride back with them."

Johnny's mom's smile quivers.

"Hey," I murmur as I flatten my hand on his shoulder blade. He tenses instantly under my touch, nearly flinching before leaning his head back and blowing out a loud breath.

He looks back down, then shoves a sweatshirt into a small backpack and zips it up. Pausing for a few seconds, he eventually leans across the seats and puts a hand on his mom's shoulder. She covers it with her hand.

"I love you. Thank you for the ride. You do not have to stay and watch this time." His voice is monotone, yet not cold. It seems to be exactly what his mom needs to hear as her face shifts into a tepid, tight smile. Her eyes blink rapidly as she pats her son's hand a few times and takes in a deep breath of her own.

"Good luck, sweetheart." She leans into the wheel to meet my eyes. "Good luck, Brynn. I know you'll be great."

"Thank you," I nod as her son backs away and closes the door.

"Are you all right?" I ask as he turns into me and his mom drives away.

"I'm fine, yeah. I just . . . hate being late." He blows up at a lock of loose hair when he's fully facing me, and my eyes instantly zoom to his swollen eyebrow.

"Johnny!" I whisper shout, reaching up to dab at what looks like makeup. His brow is egged slightly and there's a purple tinge around it, what looks like glue holding a small cut closed within the small hairs.

"I know. It was a dumb football hit, and my mom tried to cover it up. Is it bad? I mean, the makeup. I know the bruise is bad." His eyes sag along with the corners of his mouth. I study the wound, then step back half a pace to take in his entire face. In a way, it almost makes him look more in character.

"You know, it's really not that bad. She blended it well. I doubt from far away anyone will notice." I reach forward and he steps back. "I just want to fix one small spot."

He nods, his eyes focusing on my hand as it approaches his face. He glances up as I run my finger lightly over his brow, smoothing the small splotches that probably got messed up with his fidgeting or trying to fix it. I smooth his hairs in the same direction, careful not to press too hard on the swollen skin.

"Okay?" I ask as my hand drops.

He nods, his gaze lingering on mine for a few seconds as his lips part slightly. My chest burns in anticipation, and I'm not even sure what I'm wishing for—a kiss, a simple thanks, or some declaration about how he wanted me to touch his face? The thoughts make me instantly feel stupid. I clear my throat and step to the side to create more space between us.

"We have to check in."

"Right." Johnny nods and turns his attention to my father, who is loudly clapping several yards away to gain everyone's attention. The drumline has harnessed their drums, and the wind instruments are already filling the air with a cacophony of sound.

Johnny jogs to my father's side and puts his fingers in his mouth, blowing out a loud whistle that stops everyone where they stand.

"Let's go get it, yeah?" he shouts.

He's like gravity, and everyone filters toward him. I straggle in the back to watch him lead, to learn from him.

To admire him.

A few of the band members pound fists with him, probably relieved he's shown up. Devin twirls one of his sticks in his hand, lifting it in the air in his own form of approval and support. My dad leans forward a step, likely inspecting Johnny's eye, but quickly turns his attention to someone tuning their clarinet.

I maneuver my way through the band to stand at Johnny's side, leaning into him before we call the band to attention.

"They are relieved you're here," I mutter.

He surprises me by bending enough to rest his head on top of mine. I glance up, only able to really see his jawline and a hint of his lashes.

"I'm relieved I'm here, too."

As if on cue, the bass drummers pound out their warmups, which thankfully drowns out the pounding in my chest. I'm sure if it weren't for their sound, everyone within a few steps of me would hear my pulse. It's rushing through my head, pumping a beat into my wrists, making my eyes see the world a little brighter with every thump.

My euphoria continues through ten minutes of warmups, and I ride the high all the way through check-in and to the end zone of the Central College football field. The stands are filled with at least a dozen bands who have already performed. At least ten more are filing into the parking lot, getting ready for their own turn. We drew a middle time slot, the brightest part of the day. It's a good draw for a band our size, my dad said, because up until this point the judges have seen a lot of the same. We're the smallest in the field, and some of the really big schools are going after us.

"We will be a pleasant surprise and break up the day," my dad said during dinner last night.

I swallow down my nerves, hoping his prediction is right. The other band is blowing out their final note and the crowd is cheering loudly. There's a brotherhood of support among us band types, and I don't want Johnny to think it means anything more than respect. Before I can tell him not to let it bother him, he steps in front of me and dips his head. My mouth goes dry as I glance up into his eyes. We're so close—secret-telling close.

"We're going to blow them out of the fucking water." His lips settle into a seductive smirk. "I hope that lipstick is smudge-proof."

He chuckles as he moves back to my side, and the only response I can get to leave my mouth is nervous laughter. I should warn him that my lipstick is untested, but I don't. I'm willing to take a gamble if he's willing to kiss me again.

The previous band exits the field and I shake my head to force my senses back into competition mode. More than a little piece of me is still hanging out, swooning with hope. As soon as the last row of marchers leaves the track, I turn and call the band to attention. Everyone snaps to a crisp stand, legs together and knees locked. Chins all at a forty-five-degree angle. Expressions . . . serious. This part always gives me chills, and my arms instantly speckle with goose bumps.

Devin clicks his sticks to set a tempo, and soon the drumline begins the cadence for us to take the field. I call out the count, and as a group we march ten steps in place before moving as one cohesive unit toward the fifty-yard line. My hands are stiff at my sides, balled into fists, and I assume Johnny is doing the same until I feel the featherlight touch of his finger against my knuckle. I know I shouldn't look down, but my body reacts automatically, and I tuck my chin to find his open palm waiting for me.

Crap! This isn't the plan. The judges won't like this. I bet they saw my head dip. This is too cutesy. It's not going to show us in sync. Point deductions! My dad is going to be pissed!

All of that falls flat in a blink as my hand swivels to link with Johnny's, and in one more beat we're taking the field —*holding hands.*

I'm not sure if my palm is the one sweating so much or his. Maybe it's both of us having a sweat apocalypse. We pivot at the fifty-yard line and head toward the crowd, everyone standing and whistling—a few people howling, I think. Probably because they saw him take my hand. We've morphed from drum corps into rom com. None of this is going the way it's supposed to. What happened to my big plan? To lead us to championships this year?

Johnny doesn't let go of my hand until we hit our mark and each pivot to stroll around the rest of the band in opposite directions. My breath is measured, nothing at all like the racket going on inside my stomach and chest. The skin where Johnny was touching me is on fire, tingly and almost itchy from the rush of blood to the surface. I hope I wasn't squeezing him too tightly.

As the band marches into their starting formation, I begin my slow walk toward Johnny. We've done this a hundred times by this point, and my feet—*thank God!*—travel along the grass out of pure habit. I glance around the field, stopping to check my reflection inside one of the trumpet bells, a clever addition the theater teacher suggested after seeing us rehearse. All I see is my bright red lips, and they swell at the thought of being kissed. Every nerve in my body feels as if it's going to overheat and leave me limp on the ground but I power through, continuing toward Johnny until finally, the hand he let go a minute before is once again locked in his.

It all happens so fast. He spins me, bringing me close to his chest, his body smelling like dryer sheets, his breath fresh with mint from the piece of gum he swallowed as soon as we entered the field. My world spins as he cradles my back and dips me, my long curls I worked so hard to shape dangling from the ponytail on top of my head down to the tips of the grass. I close my eyes, bringing time to a halt, and my body vibrates with anticipation. I can't hear a thing, and I'm not sure if I've gone deaf or if everyone has gone silent. The quiet lingers for what feels like seconds, and then it happens. Johnny kisses me. And it's still sweet, and not quite as deep as I want it to be. But it's long—and it's not just my imagination. I know it's real, because the silence gives way to an eruption of cheers from the crowd. I blink my eyes open as Johnny's lips leave mine, and somehow manage to move my arms and hands along with the rest of our routine into a formal salute.

Everyone—even the big schools who usually skip watching our performance in favor of grabbing a snack—is on their feet. We're only getting started.

I've spent the last hour trying to remember the rest of our show. It's as if my mind took a few random snapshots because I only recall single frames of our nearly fourteen-minute performance. I know that I made it up the podium without tripping. I know that the drum feature got a big round of applause from the stands. And I know that Johnny looked blissfully happy, maybe even proud, when we closed the final song. His smile, still stained slightly from my lipstick, hasn't faded once, even now as he and I wait on the field for our final results, along with the drum majors for every other band.

My smile isn't as steady, and I wish it was. This is Johnny's first competition. This is my twentieth, maybe more. I know the signs, and I have learned how to read the judges. They shouldn't have favorites, and there shouldn't be bias at these events, but there is. There always is. And the big schools love to hate on us for having so many famous graduates.

"No matter what happens, I'm so proud of you," I blurt out. I turn to face Johnny, ignoring that we're supposed to stand at attention the entire time. Screw stupid rules. If they aren't going to give us the gold, I'm not going to play along when it doesn't count.

"What?" His brow pulls in tight and his mouth pinches on one side. "Hey, didn't you say I'm supposed to stand at attention?"

"Yeah, but they're going to punish us for being good. For being . . . I don't know, *us*." My stomach sinks as I say the truth out loud. Johnny doesn't seem to believe me yet, but he will.

"Stop. You're just being hard on yourself. You do that, you know—assume the worst?" He's no longer talking to me sideways, trying to hide our conversation. He's facing me directly while everyone around us stares straight ahead.

"That's not entirely true," I defend, but hearing my voice, I can't help but relent a little. "Okay, maybe. But I could tell by the way the judges arranged the table. I heard them talk about the field coverage and the massive sound. We're good. No, we're better musicians than anyone here. But it's hard to compete with a wall of sound that's two hundred instruments strong."

Johnny laughs me off at first, but he glances around as the awards are divvied out. The golds on the table are nearly gone, every winner so far one of the large schools. The odds are not in our favor, and it has nothing to do with our performance. He turns back to face me and exhales.

"Maybe you're right, but I'm not giving up. I believe in us." It's a corny thing to say, and I don't think he meant it to be very deep at first. But something about the flicker in his eyes, the way the blue gets just a hint deeper as I meet his stare, has me stuck.

He holds his fist up and his head ticks to the side to match his crooked smirk. It takes me a second to catch on, but when I do, I blow on his knuckles. *Good luck.*

The last gold is awarded. And the winner for best drum majors isn't us. We aren't called until the last silver is awarded. Only two bands were scored lower. The scores are meaningless because I know how good we were. And while we weren't perfect, we were better than most. Probably better than all. Through it all, Johnny smiles. He shakes hands and congratulates the other drum majors. I fight against sulking, but my stomach is brewing with the need to fight. At least a good rant. I'm sure my dad is livid, too. This isn't the first time his school has been shunned at this competition.

Most of us stare at the ground as we walk through the parking lot. Other than a few freshmen flute players who giggle over cute boys from another school because they don't quite get it yet, our crew is quiet.

"That's bullshit," Devin says as he loads the drum harnesses into the bottom of the bus.

"I know, but we half expected it," Cori laments.

Nobody blames the way we took the field—the routine Johnny initiated. But my stomach knots with this nagging feeling that a lot of them are thinking it. I climb up the bus steps behind my father, Johnny behind me. The sun is setting, and the light inside is a dim orange. I want to get this wool skirt off. I wish I wore shorts instead of leggings, because I'm hot.

I shuffle my way to the back where Cori is already swapping out her shoes. I peel my skirt off and roll it into a ball to fit in my bag while my dad finishes his count to make sure we aren't missing anyone.

"Don't forget Johnny is plus one," I remind him when he finishes at me. He snaps his fingers and winks at me.

"I did forget," he says. His usual upbeat lightness feels clouded, and I know it's because he hates making this speech—the one where he tells us we'll get 'em next time. And we always do get 'em eventually. When the match-ups are even—when we're among bands our size rather than simply matched with bands that are within an hour's drive—we earn all the hardware. Our glass case is filled with plenty of proof that our program is one of the best. But damn, it sure would be nice to win at this one, just once.

"All right, guys. First thing I want to say to you—pat yourselves on the back." My dad's voice fills the bus and a few people act out his command to be funny. Nobody really laughs.

"Actually, Mr. Fisher . . . would you mind if I said something?" Johnny steps into the aisle from the seat he took across from my dad. His request seems to rattle my dad as he stammers out a *sure* after a few *uhs* and *ohs*.

The bus door squeaks shut as our driver pulls the lever, and Johnny looks over his shoulder to her.

"I promise I'll only be a minute." He turns more and places his palms together as if to beg.

"All right, go on," she says.

I sit up and rest my arms on the seat back in front of me, balancing my chin on my folded hands. The bus rumbles around me as it idles, the air inside stagnant without a breeze coming in through the windows. Despite feeling so sticky and uncomfortable, I don't complain. Nobody does. We look on and wait for this newcomer to take a stab at making us feel better.

And as jaded as I am, there's a tiny jolt stirring up my belly and making me believe he can.

"I know it sucks losing," he begins. A few of us, including me, laugh.

"It blows!" Devin shouts from the seat across from me.

"Yes, it does!" Johnny shouts back, pointing to him. They share this weird *bro* moment that somehow lightens the mood a touch more.

"At my last school, we were stripped of our playoff spot because our right tackle played in a game while he was failing biology. One guy out of forty-four of us had a bad day and didn't label the parts of a cell right on a test, and we lost an entire season of potential. That . . ." Johnny blows out so hard his lips flap, which triggers a few more laughs. "That really blows."

I don't know why I'm smiling, but the more he talks, the less my chest hurts. I glance around to see mouths inching up around me. And even though my dad's hand is covering half his mouth as he leans to the side, I can tell by the way his cheek is creased that under his palm he's smiling too.

"But you guys. I mean . . . guys!" Johnny dips his chin and levels us all with his sinister smirk and brooding eyes. Maybe I'm the only one seeing him that way, but also . . . maybe not. Someone from the middle seats lets out a *hoot!* Another person whistles.

"Am I right?" Johnny starts to nod, and Devin starts to clap. "Did you see their reaction?"

"Yeah, we saw it!" Cori shouts as she stands in her seat and claps too.

"They all fucking loved us! *Sorry, Mr. Fisher. Earmuffs.*" He cups his ears as he shrugs toward my dad, but nobody cares about his language. We fucking love it. We fucking need it!

"That crowd? Guys! We owned them!" Johnny folds his

hands over his forehead as if he's in disbelief or shock. Yet I think maybe he's not shocked by anything we did on the field at all. I think he saw it all go well in his mind. I think he orchestrated it and simply knew it would play out to perfection.

"And I don't know about you, but I really don't give a shit about some plastic note glued on top of a piece of cheap marble. Me? I'll take that reaction any day. We were *good*." Johnny shakes his head with a sense of confidence I would kill to possess. Hell, I'd take a smidgen of it for an hour.

"We *were* fucking good!" one of the drummers pipes in.

In seconds, the entire bus is swaying with our claps and cheers, and my dad is laughing. Johnny turns to him and shakes his hand, and my dad shakes his head with pleasant disbelief. Before Johnny takes his seat again, he looks over the sea of high-fives and fist pumps and meets my waiting gaze. The bus is filled with chaos—unbridled happiness—yet I don't hear a thing over the rush of blood along my eardrums. My heart pounds, and it only kicks harder when Johnny's eyes crinkle from the breadth of his smile. That face . . . it infects me.

I'll never forget this moment. I'll never forget the way I feel right now. It's not that I'm okay with losing. It's that right now will always be the first time I saw Johnny Bishop's future. He's going to be a star. And the world? They're going to love him.

Chapter 13
Present

My dad's car is in the driveway as Teddy pulls in with Johnny and me hunched down in the back. Photographers have started to pop up more often. A few camera guys were waiting outside of Waves when we showed up to take Johnny home. We left through a special exit so they didn't get their shot, which means it won't be long before they figure out he's here. I guess thirty days in rehab is some sort of magic number that the paparazzi all know about. I think it has something to do with insurance coverage. Not that Johnny can't afford to drop a boatload of cash and stay at Waves as long as he wants, but he has things to do. Bridges to mend with his mother. With a lot of people.

One person he doesn't have to worry about, though, is my dad. An unwavering fan, even when his baby girl's heart was breaking. It's still a little infuriating. Even more so as he steps out of his car and pulls one of his guitar cases from the back seat.

"I told him not to come. I'm sorry." I sigh.

"No, it's good. It will be nice to see him," Johnny says,

sitting up taller and scanning the street around my house as he wraps his hand around the door handle.

"Ha, you always did love his attention." My remark sounds snarkier than I intend it to and earns me a shaming glance from Teddy in the rearview mirror.

"Sorry," I utter. It's barely audible and frankly, Johnny doesn't seem fazed by my dig in the first place.

This is going to be a long few weeks with Johnny in my space, and I am going to need to work hard at keeping my own grudges in check. As badly as I want to wade through our shit, I need to get in line. I also have every right to be pissed about it, and it's that internal conflict inside that's making me irritable. Add in that for the last few days, Johnny has been . . . *old* Johnny. He keeps trying to relive moments, never quite crossing into the parts between us that were intimate, but always remarking on the special ones. Like our duets, and the time I taught him how to play trombone, which was basically the *only* instrument he wasn't a natural at.

Johnny exits the truck first, leaving me alone with Teddy for a few seconds, and he glares at me in the mirror as he takes his safety belt off.

"I know, I know," I respond. "It's just that I've always been triggered by the way my dad puts him on a pedestal. You know that."

"I do, but your dad isn't going to be living with you two," Teddy says.

"Ha, wanna bet?" I nod toward the windshield and Teddy glances down to catch my father giving Johnny a bear hug just before presenting him with his prized guitar.

"That's his Martin," I say flatly.

"I don't know what a Martin is, but I'm guessing by your tone that it's kinda like getting a Mustang," he responds.

I shake my head and pull my purse strap over my shoulder before nudging open my door.

"It's better than a Mustang," I say as I climb out.

My neighbor steps onto her porch and shades her eyes despite not needing to. The sun is setting, and it's behind her. This is how she spies on things, and she is *always* spying on me. I'm a renter, and Gladys is an owner, which already makes her dislike me, for baffling reasons. She's an *original* owner, too. Her husband built the small stucco Spanish-style home sixty-five years ago, and since he passed away last year, Gladys Peterson has busied herself with policing the neighborhood. She has left me notes about my trash bins at least a dozen times, even when I'm only a day late to pull them in. A man moving in with me? That's going to put her into hyperdrive. I'm sure she already has photos and video of Teddy coming and going. Hollywood paparazzi's got nothing on Gladys!

"Hi, Mrs. Peterson!" I wave boldly, but it doesn't shame her back inside. She holds up a hand and nods, not moving an inch from her stoop where she will watch every step we take until my dad's car and Teddy's truck pull away. Then she'll go inside and sit in that chair she parked right by the front window, where she'll wait to see if that famous rock star she read about in her tabloids comes out of the house.

"She's gonna be a problem," my dad grumbles.

"Yeah, I know. I'll have Johnny take her muffins or something. She'll love him after that, like everyone does." Teddy coughs at my quip, and I wave him off.

"Whatcha got there, Dad?" I know what he has. I have wanted that guitar my entire life. I've simply never asked for it, so I guess the joke's on me.

"I figure the kid probably didn't bring one with him to the hospital, and I don't really play this thing anymore, so—"

Hospital is what my dad calls the addiction rehab center. It's *cleaner* to say it that way.

"Mr. Fisher, that's so nice, but really . . ." Johnny is holding the case in his palms, like he's carrying a sheet cake. His eyes move to mine for a second, and I sense his uncertainty.

"Take it. It means more to him for you to have it." Johnny's gaze dips to the top of the case, polished and embossed with my dad's initials—C.A.F. for Craig Alan Fisher. Johnny's neck flexes as he tilts his head and winces.

"Are you sure?" He looks up at my dad, who simply nods with a fatherly smile.

I'm caught by the scene, instantly drawn back ten years to when my parents paid for Johnny's weekend music clinic. No one in my family ever spoke about it out loud, even after Johnny's dad was found dead in a lake, but my parents knew the abuse he endured by the man who was supposed to love him most. We talked *around* it, avoiding saying the hard, ugly things. I'm not certain why, either. Maybe it was just hard to admit that something so terrible could happen to good people. People we knew. And it killed my dad to see someone with Johnny's talent not get the support he deserved. It still kills him, I guess.

"Let's get inside before Gladys starts live streaming this, shall we?" I raise my brows over my wide eyes, and Teddy chuckles. Johnny glances over his shoulder to take in my neighbor, but I put my arm around him to redirect and guide him inside.

"You gotta play that one carefully," I warn. "Let's get you in and settled before you start making new fans, okay?"

His shoulders quiver with a soft laugh.

"How do you know she's not already a fan?" His charm is peeking through. He could always say the most arrogant things but somehow make them seem humble.

He turns to meet my gaze, and his smile flattens when our eyes meet. It's still there, but it's different—it's hopeful, maybe? I realize this is the first time I've touched him since I carried his drunk and high body to my car on the way to Waves. I haven't hugged him once, even when my past-self screamed for me to give in and embrace him. Even when he stood and lingered close to me before I would leave his room.

I let my hand fall from his shoulder, careful not to let my fingertips trail down his shoulder blade or back. My touch was clinical, and that's all. At least, this is what I tell myself.

"You cleaned?" Teddy says under his breath as he holds the front door open wide for all of us.

I give him a sharp look as I pass, then shrug. He doesn't need to know that I loaded most of my clutter into bins that I shoved into the crawl space. I'll sort that out later, like when I finally move out of this place. Or maybe I'll forget those things are up there and leave them for the next renter.

My dad shuts the door as he enters last, and I spin around to face the three of them from the center of my living room.

"Alright, well, quick tour. This is where the only TV is and that chair is broken so don't push the reclining lever down. It will break off." The boys laugh, though my dad knows better and keeps his tittering on mute. He's the reason that chair is broken. The most childish sixty-four-year-old in the world couldn't push the footrest down without using the handle. Turned out he was *only* using the handle.

"Moving on," I say, waving the small group to follow. "Dining table."

"Which is never this clean," my dad pipes in. Teddy tries to cover his laugh, but when I point at them both with a sharp look, they clear their throats and half-ass apologize.

"Kitchen is right there, and it's . . . a kitchen. Maybe we can run to the market later and get things you like. Microwave, stove, oven, fridge . . ." I bother to open and close each of them as if Johnny has no idea how a kitchen works. I'm starting to sweat from panic. This house feels too small with everyone in here—with Johnny here. I don't know how I got myself in this far.

"And if we all turn around," I order, and thankfully they all do and move out of the galley kitchen so I can escape. I pass them and lead them down the short hallway, pushing open the door to the spare room and the bathroom across from it.

"And voilà." I point open palms toward either side and Johnny cranes his neck into the bathroom, then steps into the spare room, setting the guitar case he's been carrying throughout on the bed.

He takes a deep breath with his back to us all, then turns around on his exhale.

"It's great, Brynn. Really, it's perfect. And I'll take care of shopping for whatever I need, and I'll leave everything super clean. Cleaner than I found it."

His promises sound like that of a teenager rather than a man closing in on thirty. I bite my tongue and don't mention the last tabloid story I read about him trashing a suite in Seattle during his last tour.

"I know it's small, but the bed is really comfortable, and—"

"It's perfect," he cuts in, his chin low as his eyes lock on mine.

I nod, desperate to turn away or come up with something else to say. This has been my struggle since I started visiting Johnny. I don't know how to end conversations. There's always this moment where we look at one another in silence. It was hard enough in the clinic, and it's hard now with people around. I have no clue how I'm going to handle it when nobody is around and we're in my home.

"Well, I should be heading out. I have to catch my flight."

Teddy must feel it because his flight leaves four hours from now, and the airport isn't that far away.

"I'll head out with you," my dad says, likely not wanting to overstay his welcome either. My father visited Johnny twice when he was at Waves, and both visits totaled to maybe ten minutes. He always says he doesn't want to crowd people, but I think when it comes to Johnny, he doesn't want to have to really see what's broken.

"Thanks, Mr. Fisher. For this," Johnny gestures to the guitar. "And for . . ." He shrugs.

"Always here for you, kid. And you're always a kid." My dad chuckles and puts his arm around Johnny, drawing him in for a short hug where they both pat each other's backs.

Teddy steps in next, lifting Johnny off his feet and showing off how much stronger he is than his old friend who used to tease him relentlessly over how easy it was for him to gain muscle.

"I'll be back soon. I'll bring Simone, and you both will love her." Teddy's eyes meet mine when he makes this claim, and it eases that tightness in my chest some. The one good thing to come of this so far is reconnecting with Teddy. I genuinely can't wait to meet his fiancée.

I walk my father and Teddy to the door and linger at it as they head down my driveway and get into their cars. I wave, knowing they aren't looking. As soon as I stop waving I'm going to have to close this door and head inside. And then things are going to get incredibly real. When Teddy fires up the truck engine, I give in and push the door closed, leaving my palm flat on it for a few seconds.

"I know this is hard. I won't stay long." Johnny's voice is softer now that we're alone. It's regretful.

I take a deep breath and turn around, resting my back on the door as I face him and shake my head.

"Stay as long as you need." I both mean that and am a liar.

Our gazes tangle in the familiar quiet for a few more seconds. Johnny is the first to break, breathing out a short laugh as his focus shifts toward the floor where he's standing at the edge of the hallway. He knows I told a truth lie just then, too.

Truth lie. That's our made up word for the way we are with one another. It started back in high school, when we both admitted our feelings for one another. We professed jealousy and dislike for one another when things got complicated, admitting to feelings that we knew were nowhere near how we really felt. Truth lies. Johnny has a song on his first album by that same name.

"You need a shower? I put clean towels in there." I nod toward the hallway bathroom.

He shakes his head.

"Maybe later." His eyes flit up to mine again, and the air crackles.

"Right, well . . . I have class tomorrow. And the principal is excited to meet you. You're still good to get there after school starts?" Our school administration practically gave me a raise for bringing Johnny Bishop to them. We decided having him come in while class was going was probably the best way to avoid absolute chaos. Eventually, when he's working with students, everyone will know he's there. But if we can keep the parking lot mob scene to a minimum, maybe we'll be able to handle the media that's bound to show up too.

"Yeah, I can get there. I have a driver coming. It's a service, but one that my publicist uses when we're at the casinos."

I can't help my chuckle that sputters out as he explains his life to me.

"What?" He tilts his head and gives me a half smile. *It's him—my old Johnny.*

I shake that feeling off and look down.

"Nothing. It's just your life is so crazy. That's all." I swallow down my words as I realize how crazy his life is in a bad way, too. I blink a few times until I meet his gaze again. "I meant with the driver and casino shows and all that."

"I know what you meant. And yeah, it's . . . it's crazy. Too crazy most of the time. I was not prepared." His smile slips into a tight line.

"Who could be prepared for hitting Billboard number-one with their first single?" I shrug and shake my head in an attempt to lighten the mood. It seems to work a little and Johnny moves into the living room, closer. He points to the broken chair and I give him a sideways look.

"At your own risk," I say.

He sits slowly, bracing his weight at first with the arm rests. It's a bit overboard, but it amuses me so I'm gonna let that one go on for a few days. I peel myself away from the door and take a seat on the sofa, perched on the edge like I'm a visitor in my own home.

"Are you hungry?" I ask.

"I could eat." Johnny nods.

Thankful for an excuse to move around, I leap back up from the couch and head into the kitchen where I start naming off items in my cabinet and fridge. We settle on spaghetti, and I pull a pot out to boil water and another to heat a can of sauce. Johnny swivels the chair carefully so he's facing the kitchen while I work. As long as I cook or clean every time I'm alone with him I'll be able to survive this.

"Hey, can I get your advice?"

I look over my shoulder to find him leaning forward in the chair, hands clasped as his elbows rest on his knees.

"Yeah. What's up?" I lift my arm to wipe the steam from my forehead. I refuse to leave this pot, so I need to weather this heat.

Johnny's brow draws in and his mouth tightens as his gaze fixes on the window near the dining table. The warm orange glow from outside is dimming. His lips mash a bit as his lashes flicker against his cheek. It's in these small moments that I see his younger self. It's when he isn't sure about himself. It's the remnants of doubt his father beat into him. That characteristic will never leave him, and I hate its origin because without the doubt and its cause, he looks so innocent this way.

He shifts his head a tick, meeting my waiting gaze, and my stomach rushes with adrenaline. I stir without looking at the pot, instead focusing on Johnny.

"How do I talk to her?" He blinks slowly, his lips quivering once. He sucks in a short breath that stops his apparent temptation to cry.

"Your mom?"

He nods.

I bite my lower lip and glance down for a beat.

"You didn't call her or anything?" I ask, looking back up to find his guilty expression.

I lean my head to one side.

"Johnny," I scold. I shouldn't, but I'm terrible at being this guarded.

"I know!" he huffs out, bringing his fists to his forehead, pressing against his skull as if he's punishing himself. "I know I should have. But I just . . ."

I turn back to the pot and give it a good stir before turning the heat down low, then move to the edge of the counter to give him more attention. More of me. I reach toward him but stop myself, glad his eyes are closed as he drops his head into his palms and pulls at his hair. It's in need of a cut, and a wash. He's a million times more together than a month ago, but seeing him break down like this, I realize how far he has to go.

"Hey, I know. It's hard. And she's your person. Your rock," I say.

He lifts his head and his eyes are glassy. He quickly runs his arm along them and wipes away the emotion before nodding and croaking out a *yeah*.

"I know you know this already, but you're famous," I say, which gets him to laugh out loud. He tears up again, but this time from amusement, or at least I think that's why.

"Yeah, I know," he finally says.

"She probably reads the paper or watches the news. She still goes to work at the library, you know?" I lift a brow at him.

"You see her often?" His question rocks my stomach with guilt. Do I see her? Yes. Do I speak to her? Never.

"It's . . . I mean. We don't visit, if that's what you mean. But I have seen her from time to time. Even recently." I think about my most recent sighting and try to recall how Beth looked. She seemed healthy to me, though I didn't spend a lot of time studying her. I wonder how she would look if I saw her through my now informed lenses.

"Well, you see her more than me. And I'm her fucking son." His mouth drops with the weight of his cheek, almost like he's going to be sick.

"It's been a long time. But you're here now." *You're here. With me. And you haven't seen me in a long time, either.*

This isn't about me.

"Grab a chair at the table. Pasta's done," I say, turning my attention back to the noodles and red sauce simmering behind me. I pour each of us a portion and leave the leftovers on low on the stove. I take the seat across from Johnny, wedging myself into the tight space where the table is pushed too close to the wall. He studies me while I work my way into the chair, and purses his lips when I glance up at him.

"I like this chair," I lie.

He chuckles, then scoots back about a foot before dragging my entire wood table toward him, giving me room on my side. He shakes his head and continues to laugh as he digs into his pasta. I will my hot cheeks to calm down, and swallow my embarrassment along with my first bite. We share dinner in silence for a few minutes—other than his few cursory compliments of my ability to boil water and heat up canned sauce.

"It's not quite five-star here. Sorry about that," I finally say.

He sucks in his last piece of spaghetti, the noodle flailing around on its trip into his mouth, flinging a few bits of sauce on his white T-shirt. He tucks his chin and pulls the shirt out a little, taking his napkin and dabbing at the spots, which only makes them bigger.

"Leave it. I'll get it out for you. What is that, like a designer shirt or something?" I roll my eyes, but before I take another bite, Johnny pulls the back of the shirt up over his head and tosses it toward my kitchen trashcan. It slides onto the floor, not quite making it all the way in, and I swallow hard before turning my attention to his naked torso.

"Goodwill," he says, lifting his chin with a smug little grin.

Mother fucker.

My knee bobs under the table and my inner voice warns me to keep my eyes on his neck and above. It's no use, though, because he gets up to take his bowl to the sink, bending over to pick up his shirt on the way.

"I can still clean a Goodwill shirt, ya know," I say, swallowing down the dry lump I'm left with. His back muscles form this perfect V, and there's a line from one of his songs tattooed along his shoulder blade. I recognize them immediately, even in cursive.

Be bolder than the storm.

It's from "Shelter." His dad was the storm.

I scooch my chair back to leave the table and take my bowl

to the sink, but before I get more than two steps away, Johnny rushes over and takes the bowl from my hands.

"You cooked. I'll wash dishes." He lowers his head as though waiting for me to agree, and I have to lick my dry lips.

"I, uh. I have a dishwasher. So that's not really a fair trade." I suck in my bottom lip and jut my hip as I hold his stare, doing my best to keep things playful. To keep my tongue in my mouth. His fucking smirk is making that really hard.

"Okay, Brynnie Winnie. I see you," he says through a chuckle, nodding his head as he backs away. My knees buckle but I lay a palm on the table to hold myself up and mask the effect he has on me.

I stay back while he rinses the dishes and loads the washer then stores the leftovers in the fridge. I finally make my way to the trash bin and fish out his shirt. The cotton is thick, and on a hunch I inspect the tag which says PRADA.

"Ha ha!" The laugh flies out uncontrollably and Johnny spins with the dishtowel in his hands to catch me in the act. I hold the shirt up as proof.

"Pretty nice Goodwill find, buddy!" I tease.

He doesn't break a sweat. Instead, he finishes drying his hands before tossing the towel to the side, walking toward me, and taking the shirt from my hands. He throws it back in the trash then looks down at me, mere inches between us.

"I know."

The air feels suddenly warmer, like ten, fifteen degrees warmer. My chest feels like it's on fire, and my dry mouth is now watering behind my numb lips. My ears ring from the rush of blood, from my lack of breathing. I lift my gaze slowly, reminding myself what his smooth chest looks like, the tiny mole that kisses his right pectoral, the way his black chain looks against his collarbone. I gave him that necklace. And he's still wearing it. I blink the rest of the way up and find his blue eyes weighed down at the edges, conflicted maybe.

"Would you like me to go with you tomorrow after school? To talk to Beth?" My hands are at my sides, my fingers flexing slowly because I don't know what to do with my hands. His must be the same because more than once, our knuckles brush against one another. Finally, I hook one finger into one of his, and the way our hands fit together is timeless. Everything falls into place below our line of sight, and both hands are soon linked while we stare at each other.

"I'd like that very much," he finally says. I squeeze his hands in mine, knowing I won't touch him any more than this.

This was for soothing purposes, for comfort.

"Then I can do that for you. With you." I hold his gaze until he nods and swallows, then I break our connection and move past him into the kitchen where I bend down to push the start button on the dishwasher. I can't feel my fingertips when I do, and I can't feel the floor beneath my feet. I'm not quite floating, but I'm definitely not grounded.

"Hey, Brynnie?" I close my eyes at the sound of my name, his way in his voice.

"Yeah, Johnny?" I straighten and face him, relieved to see him in the middle of the room.

"My mom? She's not my person."

Those words . . . they ground me. They anchor me to the floor and sink me in several inches. They break my ribs and crumble the bones until they fall at my feet. My heart swells about ten times its size and my lungs quit working. My lips part but there aren't any words ready to be said. My thoughts have stopped. My heart has stopped. My life has stopped—again. All because of Johnny Bishop and his ability to sweep me off my feet.

"Good night, Brynn," he says finally, maybe realizing that

I'm not able to respond, or not going to. Maybe he's dejected, or perhaps he's hopeful. I wait until he turns around and walks toward the spare room door before I respond.

"Good night, Johnny."

You were my person once, too.

Chapter 14
Age 18, First Football Game

M aybe I should have nosed my way on over to the football field a few times when Johnny left for practice. Teddy has always nagged me to watch a few of his scrimmages.

"It's enough I have to endure your games," I always say.

And that was because before Johnny arrived, our team was truly awful. The only games we won were against teams that were short enough players to be able to field an offense and a defense. I was convinced we won because the other team was too damn tired by the fourth quarter.

I get the hype now. The hype about Johnny coming here. Apparently, his dad was quite the quarterback in his day before a freak injury on the field left him unable to throw the ball anymore. He was one touchdown shy of winning the Super Bowl for San Diego eighteen years ago—the year Johnny was born. How I'm the person who has spent the most time with him until now yet seem to be the only one not to know his dad is Kevin Forrester baffles me. Johnny never brought it up. I never asked. He was always cagey about his dad, though, and now I understand why. He's standing in the upper right corner of the home stands, the opposite side from the band, and the line of people waiting to shake his hand and take a photo with him is ridiculous.

I'm not interested in the near legend at the other end of the bleachers, though. I'm too invested in every single step Johnny is taking on the field in front of me. Everything he does looks effortless. It's the same way he is with music and with dance, or the little bit of dance we kind of do for the show. His movements are all so sure and steady, and he seems to be impossible to knock down. He's dipped and zagged his way out of so many sacks already, and it's only the first half. With two minutes to go, we're up twenty-seven to zero, and Johnny's driving us down the field to squeeze in one more attempt at the end zone.

"You know he's totally hot, right?" Cori always saves me space on the bleachers next to her so when I'm not standing on the riser and directing the band for time-out music, I have a place to sit. Not that we've sat once this game. There's been too much to cheer about.

"I mean, I guess," I mumble back, pretending I'm not burning up with embarrassment at her remark. She's been teasing me a little more lately, in her friendly way, because it seems Devin and Johnny both might want to take me to the Fall Fest dance next weekend. Devin asked me if I had a date a few days ago, and I told him I wasn't sure, which Johnny overheard. Cori says he smiled and turned bright red when that happened, but I've been waiting, holding out hope that Johnny would ask me, for three days now. Every time we're alone, I hold my breath and subtly bring the dance up. This morning, I mentioned that I needed to buy a dress this weekend. His only response was that he was glad he didn't have to worry about finding the right dress for things. I've never gone to this dance with a date. *Any* dance with a date, actually. It's usually me and a group of people from band, and we spend the entire evening waiting out the slow songs from the edges of the room while the good-looking couples make out as they rock and spin slowly in the middle of the gym floor. It would be nice to be one of those couples, just once.

"You are so lucky, Brynn. I hope you know that." Cori pushes a finger into my side to tickle me, but she pushes hard enough that I think she also might be a touch jealous.

"Well, so far all I am is going to the dance with you and eight other girls, so we're both lucky, I guess." I step in front of her on my way to the riser step and she grimaces at my remark.

"Yeah, I'm so lucky that I get to go to the dance with Phoebe and Lilah and Meghan and oh! Maybe Desiree will come this time. Yep, I'm a lucky girl. Me and my pod of dateless losers." She sinks down to sit on the bleacher and I step down to pick up her spirits. I didn't realize how she felt, or how important something like having a date for the dance was to her. I kinda didn't realize how much it mattered to me until I was faced with the possibility.

"Hey," I say, tugging on the feather plume on her hat.

She rolls her eyes.

"It's fine. But you know what? It also sucks that you get to wear your hair all cute this year and I have to sweat under this stupid thing." She looks up as hard as she can, her lashes batting with the strain. I smirk and take the hat from her head, planting it on mine.

"How about I take this until showtime," I offer. It doesn't fit on my head perfectly because of the ponytail positioned near the top, but with the chin strap stretched out, I manage to keep it up there as I step back up at the front and count down for our fight song.

We're in the middle of playing it when the crowd erupts around us with such excitement that I ball my fists and direct the band to stop so we don't interrupt whatever amazing thing

The clock is down to about fifty seconds by the time we're done, which doesn't leave us much time to get out to the track and ready to take the field for halftime. There's a verve in our steps still lingering from this feeling of being on the winning side against a good team, and we manage to work our way down to the far sideline just as the buzzer sounds.

Per usual, half the bleachers clear out as parents take the littler kids for snacks and bathroom breaks. But enough people are staying to give me a jolt of excitement to share our show. It's one thing to unveil our performance for other bands or at the pep rally. But the first game? This one is always special. This is where we let people know we're good, and that next time? They probably want to wait and get their snacks when we're done.

The team is rushing through the open gate on the far end toward the locker room, and I catch a glimpse of Johnny's back, his helmet clutched in one hand as he jogs away. He must need to check in with coach first. He'll be here by the time we hit the field.

"Okay, warm-ups!" I turn my focus to the band, and I count out the time to start our scales. Everyone sounds a little sharp, and I think it's the extra force pushing through everyone's lungs. It happens when you overplay, and right now we have a lot of unexpected energy.

I start on one end and listen to a player at a time as they continue to work up and down the scale. My dad takes the other end, and by the time we meet in the middle, everything is in tune and ready to go.

"Johnny coming?" my dad asks, cupping his mouth as he and I walk together to the edge of the field. I squint as I stare across toward the now-closed locker room door. I shake my head.

"I'm sure he is. Yeah. It's fine. He'll be right here. He knows the timing is tight." I don't fully believe the words I'm saying, and I think my dad can tell.

"Just be ready. Simple back-up plan will be fine. And you're the lead, so everyone will know to look at you for direction." His voice is a little breathless, and maybe urgent.

"Huh?" I glance to him as my mind catches up to his advice. I nod quickly. "Yeah, right. I know. It will be fine."

"Go get 'em, kiddo." My dad tugs on the feather plume I forgot I was still wearing. I look up and chuckle, then slip Cori's hat off so I can rush it over to her. She slips it on her head again.

"I was hoping you'd forget," she says in a mused tone. Truthfully, though? I think she really was.

My dad's voice booms through the speakers after a minute, and he starts his introduction of the band. He lists our songs, and I strain my neck and stand on my toes, my eyes boring a hole through the locker room door a hundred yards away. It hasn't moved a single time since the team disappeared through it, and my stomach sinks as my father finishes out his intro.

"Marching Howl and drum major Brynn Fisher—are you ready to take the field?"

I swallow hard, my eyes stinging with utter disappointment. He isn't coming.

I snap my head up, push all of that pain down into my gut, and clap out the count. Devin takes over and the cadence begins. I'm doing this alone. It's just me leading the band in front of everyone. And yeah, this is what I originally wanted. I even envisioned it just like this. But now I know differently—I know that the version of this moment with Johnny in it is simply better. *We're* better. I'm better. The show is better. Now, everyone out there is going to get the back-up version, as my dad called it.

The cadence stops, and rather than strolling across the front of the band toward a boy who may or may not kiss me in front of everyone, I walk stiffly with rigid arms and tight shoulders until I'm in the middle alone. I keep it simple, bringing my hand up for the salute and letting it drop. I have to climb the podium steps on my own, so I'm careful not to trip. It's weird that I'm dressed like half of West Side Story alone. I lead the band through the song as Maria without her Tony. I'm so angry and hurt that I can't even fully enjoy the sound blasting back at me. The band sounds good—crisp, loud, powerful. We are all the things the judges said we needed to get better at last week. And I don't care.

Because Johnny Bishop? He's the stupid, egotistical jock I thought he was in the first place.

The team scores two more times in the second half, and Riverside only manages a single touchdown. It's an epic win for us, and for the most part, everyone in the band is thrilled. It means this season is going to be more than just waiting to get to our show then tolerating the hour of game left afterwards.

I couldn't sit by Cori in the second half. I didn't want my piss poor mood to taint her elation. But I couldn't hide my disappointment from Devin during our short break before the final minutes of the game. Probably because he wasn't hiding his, either.

"What a dick!" was the first thing he said.

And instead of defending Johnny, I said, "I know!"

My stomach is boiling, and my mouth is dry from all the silent yelling matches I've had when nobody was looking. I can't believe he bailed on me like that. I hate myself for giving in to his stupid ideas in the first place, for letting him worm his way into my dreams. The more I stew about it, the more doubt I build that his talent is really that impressive anyway. I mean, he's a great quarterback. His piano playing, though? It's all right, I guess. And his voice is nothing special. He sounds like a guy singing. *So what!*

"Hey, take it easy on him. Coach can be a jerk, and I bet they didn't want to let him out for halftime because they were afraid of messing up their good mojo." My dad's excuse makes sense, and it's kind toward Johnny. But I'm not buying it.

I shrug and purse my lips.

"Maybe," I say, turning my attention back to the bleacher rows, now emptied from the band. I walk each lane to make sure nobody left anything behind. Someone's asthma inhaler is teetering on one of the seats, so I put that in my pocket, and I find one booklet of sheet music that I tuck under my sweater to hide from my dad. He hates when people leave music behind, and if he finds out someone did, that person will be running laps during our next practice. The only one who should be running laps next week is Johnny *stupid* Bishop!

Only a few families are left lingering in the bleachers. I smile at a few of the kids and one little girl rushes over to touch my skirt.

"I like your hair," she says, shaking her hair to show off her own ponytail.

I kneel down to get on her level.

"Thank you. I like yours! Do you want to be a drum major someday?"

She shakes her head.

"Uh uh. I want to be a cheerleader!" She points out to the field where a few of the players are already carrying some of the cheerleaders around on their backs and hollering swear words for no reason. They're getting ready to party out in the hills. Drum majors don't go to those parties.

"Your choice I guess, kid," I snark, standing up and leaving the stands. Nobody heard me and that girl didn't really care, so I let myself off the hook for being a bitch. She made me mad —madder.

My body is buzzing with this frustrated vigor. I want to punch something, and I go so far as to form a tight fist at my side, my other arm trapping the music booklet under my sweater. I'm so lost in my thoughts and pretend conversations with Johnny that I don't realize he's a foot in front of me before I run into him.

"Oww! Sorry, I—"

He spins around and our eyes meet. For a moment, it feels like everyone around us is frozen, yet we're not able to speak. My brow lowers and my eyes squint, while his pull in as his pupils expand. There's a hardness to his stare. I can't quite read it, but he isn't angry. He's something else, something unpleasant and not at all at ease with himself. With this world. With this unfortunate interaction.

"Sorry, my son's a dumbass who doesn't look where he's going," a man says, jerking Johnny sideways by his shoulder pads.

My eyes scan to the right, up the tanned arm and to the Howl Football Program polo shirt that fits snugly on Kevin Forrester's torso.

"You're . . . Johnny's dad," I stammer out, moving my focus between the two of them a few times while my mind whirls through processing this information. I mentally run through telling him what a jackass his son is for leaving me high and dry, but my plan is interrupted when the man juts out his hand to shake mine.

"Sure am. This kid ain't half the player, either. He got lucky tonight. He's lazy is what he is." His firm grip only half distracts me from his disdainful words about his son. I lick my dry lips and scan back to Johnny, who is staring intently at the ground, his mouth a hard line.

"He's been busy," I say, and Johnny's gaze snaps to mine again.

"I'm sorry, but who are you?" Johnny shakes his head at me and bunches his face with this bewildered expression that he sells like a seasoned actor. I feel sick.

My hand is still locked into the death grip his dad has on it, and when his father laughs at his son's response to me, I feel lightheaded and weak.

"Oh, don't mind his mood. I'm sure you're very nice. What's your name?"

"I'm . . . I'm, Br—"

"You're pretty enough to cheer, ya know. You should think about that." He drops my hand and pats me on the back, urging me to move along. My ears feel like they are stuffed with acid and cotton. I can't feel my feet. And my mouth is watering the way it does right before I vomit.

What the fuck just happened? All of this night—what was it? Is this a dream?

I stumble my way across the parking lot to the band room where my duffle bag is stowed away in my dad's office. He's busy monitoring the room, making sure everyone puts instruments away correctly as he glad hands a few of the parents who were impressed with our performance. They must not know it was a complete disaster. That means I covered well. I did that.

I lead them, and covered for his no-show ass.

I dip into the girl's dressing room to swap out my outfit for my comfortable sweatpants and extra-large shirt from our state competition two years ago. I slip into my slide shoes and wipe the bright red lipstick from my mouth with a dozen harsh paper towels. My mouth is pink and swollen in an unflattering way by the time I'm done, but at least I'm myself again.

"I'll see you at home," I utter to my dad as I pass. He snags the strap of my bag to stop me, spinning me to look me in the eyes.

"You good?" He lifts a brow slightly.

I shrug. "Sure."

I'm not.

My mom only comes to a few of the games, usually the big ones like rivalries or homecoming. I'm glad she skipped this one. Dad and I have hyped up the routine so much, it would have been miserable to have to explain all the ways it went wrong and why she didn't get to see this Johnny boy we both talk so much about. I wouldn't be able to give her any answers. Because I have no fucking clue.

I get to my car and pop open the back, tossing my bag into it and slamming it shut. I glance to my right where Johnny is still standing next to his father, and there are a few other guys with them. One looks like Coach, and the others are probably star-struck assistants or parents wanting to reminisce about old NFL days with Johnny's dad.

Johnny and his dad have different last names, and when I found out who his father was, I was curious why. Now, though? I don't give a shit. Maybe his dad doesn't find him worthy of having his name. I get that, because I don't find him worthy of being my co-drum major anymore.

I blink a few times, a prick of regret tickling my tear ducts. I shake the feeling off, not willing to give in and be forgiving. Not tonight.

I move to my car and scan the rest of the parking lot, pausing with my door open when I see Devin dropping his gear into the back of his truck. He takes his drum home because he's obsessed with it. He practices constantly, and he's always making music of some kind. And Devin wants to take me to the Fall Fest dance.

Without another thought, I march across the few rows of parking spots to where Devin is pushing up his tailgate.

"Hey!"

He spins around when I get his attention, dropping his hands into the pockets of his loose jeans. He's wearing an Angels baseball jersey and has a red hat on backward, his wavy hair curling up from sweat along his neck. I bite my lip and remind myself how cute he's always seemed.

"What's up, Brynn. Hey, you were good tonight. That was classy. Others, not so much." He nods toward the stadium lights but I don't bother to follow his gesture. I know what he means —*who* he means.

"Yeah, it was . . . I don't know. We got through it, I guess. But hey, I wanted to talk to you about next weekend. The dance?" I'm starting to sweat, the sudden thought that he might have moved on to someone else paralyzing me. Shit, maybe he's going to take the ask back.

"Yeah, you find out if you're free to go with someone?" He lifts his brows high and shifts his eyes toward the stadium one more time. I ignore it.

"Yeah, I wasn't sure what the girls wanted to do, and we have this tradition."

"Oh, sure. I get it," he breaks in.

Ugh, he thinks I'm saying no.

"But it's fine! They're fine, I mean. Without me. So, if you'd like to go—?" My hands grasp the hem of my T-shirt so hard I may leave permanent wrinkles behind.

Devin's mouth ticks up on one side.

"Cool. Yeah. I'll pick you up at six." He nods the same way he does to everyone, like he's on a beach and scouting out massive waves.

"See ya then."

I turn around and head back to my car as he revs his motor

to life, and my lips buzz with glee. I think I'm actually giddy over the idea of going to the dance with a guy. A date! I have a date.

My butterflies stick around just long enough for me to get to the parking lot exit. They die the second I pull into the line right next to Johnny's SUV where Johnny is staring out the passenger window, at me, a sickening void behind his eyes. He looks broken, and I let the guilt creep in.

Chapter 15
Present

I t's hard to keep a secret. That fact doubles down when teenagers are involved.

I wasn't sure how to handle Johnny coming in today—whether I should tell my students and let their excitement simmer to a boil that I could put a lid on or go the out-of-the-blue surprise route. I chose surprise. Mostly because I didn't want to talk about Johnny coming in for an entire week before it actually happened. However, there's always someone around here who knows someone in the biz, as they say. That someone broke my news sometime late last night, and thanks to social media—and some dark web-type connection that the students all seem to have and us adults have no way of cracking into—literally every single one of them knew Johnny was coming to visit today. This morning when I pulled into the parking lot, they were all out front with balloons and posters and painted faces and T-shirts from his concerts. Our students don't show up like this for anything, not even the showcase.

It's hysteria.

So much for a normal class day.

"Maybe it's better this way," Principal Baker says, herself

having donned the black long-sleeve "Shelter" shirt from John-ny's first tour. She and I have been standing under the portico by the front office for about twenty minutes as we wait for Johnny to arrive.

"You think?" I pull my lips in as Gary, our seventy-one-year-old maintenance guy, forces a gaggle of students that blocks our view behind his makeshift rope system so Johnny has a direct path from the drive thru.

"Yeah. We have good kids here. So they're a little excited." She shrugs just before one of the students trips over Gary's yellow CAUTION sign that holds up warning tape he fash-ioned out of blue painter's tape.

Half of the student body is waiting in the gym, deciding that getting good seats is more important than watching Johnny step out of a town car. What nobody here knows, but I do, is that it doesn't matter where any of these students are when they meet him. He will give them all his time and attention and make every single one of them feel special. He'll stay here without sleeping for four days straight if that's what it takes to talk to, shake hands with, hug, and take photos with every Yucca High North student who wants a moment of his time. It's the one quality fame couldn't taint. Johnny is appreciative, and he was them. His love for them is genuine.

The first screams break through near the entry to the parking lot. In seconds, the few hundred students gathered out here, along with their parents, who simply couldn't help them-selves, are pulsing in a giant human wave that doesn't stop until Johnny's car pulls up right next to Gary's mop bucket and the back door of the black Lincoln swings open.

Chaos.

"Should we do something?" Principal Baker asks at my side as the mop bucket, mop, tape, and Gary are swallowed up by the throng of screaming teenaged girls and whistling boys pushing their way into the vehicle.

I chuckle.

"Nah, he's got this."

And he does. His back pressed against his ride, Johnny is all smiles as he reaches out toward the sea of hands straining for him. He grasps hand after hand, laughing and smiling as cell phones are hoisted in the air to document every minute. Somehow we got away with today without paparazzi showing up, or at least being intrusive—I'm still not sure they aren't zoom-lensing this scene from one of the hilltops or a roof somewhere. This little secret I tried to keep is not so secret anymore.

After about ten solid minutes of pressing literal flesh with his fans, Johnny emerges onto the walkway toward us, his arms linked with at least four students while others snuggle in close to him. Our eyes meet and I quirk a brow.

"You like to make an entrance," I shout so he can hear me over the screams that have not stopped since his car door opened.

"That I do," he laughs.

This is the new Johnny, without the weight of self-medication. It's been thirty-two days, and only a handful of hours under my watch. I feel in my gut I would know if he was sneaking something, if he was drinking or using pills. I cleared every possible temptation from my home before he arrived, which means it's been about six days of zero wine for me, too. Hell, I even threw away my bottle of cold medicine.

He's wearing black pants that hug his thighs enough to prove to anyone looking that he doesn't skip leg days. His white dress shirt hugs his torso, and the top two buttons are open, showing off the golden skin on his chest and the edge of the dagger tattoo that covers his right pec. Somehow, he's hotter like this than when he was shirtless in my kitchen last night.

Unwittingly, I wore my white blouse along with my wide-legged black pants today and my extra chunky heels. I wanted to look tall and confident. I look like entourage.

"You and Johnny were . . . *friends*, you said?" Principal Baker quirks a brow as he passes by us and steps into the office waiting area to shake hands with the four Yucca police officers who volunteered to handle extra security today.

"We were good friends," I answer, then abandon her before she can ask more questions. My boss has a lot in common with my mom. They must never meet. I step up on one of the office waiting chairs and cup my mouth after clearing my throat. I really wish I could do that finger whistle thing.

"Okay, guys. I know you want to walk Johnny Bishop everywhere he goes, but we need to actually get some learning done today. And if you want to hear his talk this morning, I'm gonna need you all to make your way to the gym, where you'll see him again in a matter of minutes, okay?"

I clap my hands loudly to get their attention and snap them from their collective awestruck daze. As I bring my hands down to my sides and ball them into fists, I make eye contact with Johnny, who smirks and gives me a quick salute.

You can take the drum major off the field but you can never get it out of her soul.

After few minutes, the students scurry their way through the hallways and head toward the gym. Johnny takes a few photos with the officers, one of them Travis Gentry, who was his wide out their senior year at this very school. I do the official introduction to Principal Baker next, and she manages to keep it semiprofessional despite having Johnny's face literally plastered across her chest.

"Maybe it would be best if you waited just outside the doorway until I get through the school business part of the assembly, then I'll introduce you, Ms. Fisher, and you can do the introduction of your friend?" My boss makes this suggestion with clear innuendo in her voice when she gets to the word friend. My neck turtles in reflex and my cheeks burn.

"Sounds great. Right behind you." I make sure my expression relays how unamused I am, but she laughs it off, brushing her curly brown hair from her shoulders before turning to head down the hall.

I let her get a few steps ahead before I turn to Johnny, flick the second button on his open shirt, then roll my eyes.

"What? Too much?" He buttons it because he knows it is. I mean, it's also just right. But the girls in this school are already dying over his presence. The extra glimpse of chest is only going to turn them into total zombies while he's talking.

"Uh, maybe a *skosh*." I make a pinch in front of him then urge him to walk with me down the hall.

"That is the most *your mom* thing you have ever said," he says through a chuckle.

I shoot a sideways glare at him.

"Fine, fine! It's buttoned." He waves his hand along the line of buttons as if he's modeling them. I turn my focus straight ahead and do my best to mask the heavy gulp I have to take from the massive sense of nostalgia that just blanketed me. This Johnny, the one I banter with—God, I missed him. And the new things—this scent and the somehow larger presence, broader shoulders, purposely messy yet just right hair—these things are nice additions.

"So, how do you want me to introduce you?" I pull my phone from my pocket and glance at the brief notes I made this morning from his bio. I could talk about Johnny and his rise to fame for hours without help. The notes are to keep me brief and on point.

He shrugs next to me as we pause just outside the gym doors.

"Maybe talk about how we were . . . *friends*." His subtle grin ticks me off.

"Stop that," I say, flicking my eyes to his for only a beat.

"Uh, you started it."

My teeth clench as I type in my notes: DO NOT TELL THEM HE'S AN ASSHOLE. I make sure he can see my screen and he quickly retracts his words.

"Hey, wait . . . fine, I'm sorry. The new principal, she was just funny. The way she said it. I'm guessing people don't really know we—" He waggles his head side-to-side as he points from my chest to his.

"That we were *we?*" I make the same gesture he did then shake my head.

I hold his gaze for a few long seconds, and note the burn in my chest as we barely broach the topic of us. Johnny's mouth flattens as he bends a knee and leans his foot and back against the wall with a thud.

"Oh," he says.

There is a lot of hurt in my future. Not now, though. For now, I'm going to revel in getting to be the cool teacher who brought a rock star in for show-and-tell.

"I'm going to tell them how talented you were at their age," I say as I delete the asshole bit from my notes. I don't want to deflate him entirely. I merely want to protect myself.

"I wasn't the talented one," he says in a hushed tone.

I shake with a single laugh and roll my eyes toward him.

"Flattery isn't going to make my breakfasts any better," I joke. I made waffles this morning, and half of them are still stuck to the iron, which I had to throw in the trash. My joke brings a tinge of a smile to his face, which will have to do as Principal Baker is calling me to the middle of the gym.

"You stay put," I whisper, tapping his chest and instantly regretting the touch. I curl my index finger into my fist as I head through the doors and into the gym. His chest is rock solid, and I'm not sure whether it was actually hot or if I imagined it to be warm. Or maybe I'm hot. Yeah, I'm definitely breaking a sweat.

My boss hands the microphone to me and I tap on it twice to test the volume. It sounds normal, but my simple *hi* sends a shrill ring through the speakers that reverberates off of the gym walls. Students in the front row push their fingers in their ears to be jerks, and I turn to the AV club kids sitting behind the scoring table, where we keep the equipment. I gesture for them to lower the levels and hope they do as I finally start.

"Everyone awake now?" I get a few pity laughs. I'll take them.

I clear my throat and eyeball the notes on my phone one more time, smirking at the word HOLE. Apparently I didn't erase everything. I pocket my phone and hold the mic with both hands.

"I'm not going to pretend that you all don't know who is here today. And I won't take up too much time because I know you all are tired of hearing me talk."

"Not me! I love you, Ms. Fisher. Marry me!" Cade is that one student who has to show off in every situation. He's a pain in my ass, but I've given him more breaks than a service shop. And I believe if I said yes, he really would marry me. I hold up a finger and point toward him.

"Thank you for the affirmation, Cade. Now, sit down." My handling of him gets a little more laughter, which helps me loosen up more. Public speaking is never a problem for me. Most of the teachers over on the arts side of the house rise to the occasion. I suppose we all love the spotlight. But talking about Johnny? That's a different level of public speaking.

"The man here to speak to you today was sitting on one of those exact bleacher seats nearly ten years ago to the day. I know you have seen the memorabilia put up in the case, and

I'm sure you're well versed in all things Bishopverse thanks to the endless barrage of videos and gossip streams you gobble up on your phones. But put that to the side for me—for him—for just a little while. Think of him as one of you, because he very much was. He was a football player here, and he was good. But when it came to music, he was . . ." I drift a bit, giving myself grace to smile—to admire. In the pause, a few students whistle. I decide to let that stand on its own.

"Exactly," I say. More laughs.

"Our guest did not have some special extra edge. What he did have was a fearless sense of trying. Of putting himself out there. Of letting people see his vulnerable side and letting their judgement fall on whatever side it may. That's not easy to do as an adult. It's definitely not easy to do when you're eighteen and your brain is full of all kinds of hormones and self-doubt."

When your father thinks music is for weak asses and that you giving up football is bullshit that's going to ruin your life and his legacy.

I keep those thoughts inside. That's Johnny's story to tell when and where he wishes.

"You all have dreams. Even if you think you don't, you do. Every dream is different, some a little, some by a lot. I hope after this morning, you leave this gym with a little dose of magic in your soul, and some faith in yourself. Johnny Bishop has a way of doing that for people."

I turn and swing open my arm to invite him in to the roaring cheers that don't diminish at all as he walks across the gym toward me, holding his hands up to wave to the students on his way. I hand him the mic when we meet, and his hand covers mine in the transaction. He covers the hot part and lowers our hands, leaning into me, his mouth near my ear.

"I didn't deserve any of those words, but I'll try to live up to them. Thank you." As he steps back, our gazes meet, and the glimmer of that eighteen-year-old sparkles in his eyes. My hand unravels from underneath his. I feel him even when he's gone.

"Hey."

He grabs the back of his neck and spins in a slow circle to take in the instant cheers at his frat-boy greeting. His hair has slipped out of place to cover his eyes, so he pushes it back and grips his neck again. How does he know how to move like that? How to stand just right and do these simple things that are so incredibly sexy? I shift my feet, crossing my legs as I stand several feet behind him, wishing I had a chair. I cannot pass out from infatuation and panic. I will not do that.

"Alright, alright. Take your seats," he says, patting his palm toward the floor. Unlike when I request quiet, they listen to Johnny. What he has to say matters to them. I get it. It's still annoying.

"Thanks for that really flattering introduction, Ms. Fisher. Can we all get a round of applause for your teacher? I'm sure she's your favorite, right? I mean, has to be. Come on, let's hear it."

Most of the students clap after he goads them into it, and my pits break out in a sweat. Rather than torture myself, I step to where a small section of the bleachers is clear and take a seat, leaving the principal on her own to manage the room. I've done my job, and I have a feeling I'm going to need to sit for the rest of this.

"I like what you said, Brynnie," Johnny says, using the pet name and drumming up all kinds of *oooh* noises from the students. I think I even hear a few of the teachers chiming in. I drop my forehead into my palms and rest my elbows on my knees. This is a nightmare.

"Sorry, some habits are hard to break. Ms. Fisher and I, we go way back. But what she said about ten years ago, and me sitting where you are? You know she was in these seats too, right? We were students here, and her dad was one hell of a teacher. Some big shoes to fill, but I bet she does. I bet some of you in the music department feel like maybe you can take a shot at your dream because of her. Yeah, I see those nods. I see 'em."

I'm not sure anyone is really nodding, but they are smiling. He has them rapt, and not just because of his stardom. He could always own a crowd, capture a room. It's his charisma. His personality. His fucking charm.

"I'd like to thank your principal and the faculty here for letting me be disruptive as an adult. I was plenty disruptive as a student. Yeah, I see you, Mr. Kinley." He points to the opposite side of the gym where the longtime chemistry teacher is camped out with papers to grade balanced in his lap. He looks toward Johnny and adjusts his glasses by pushing them up his nose before shaking his head with a grimace. That is one man who isn't starstruck. Johnny and chemistry didn't get each other, and he found lots of reasons to get kicked out of class. Some of them a little explosive. Kinley gave Johnny a C only because Johnny's father intimidated him into it in order for his son to stay eligible for football. Johnny just wanted to stay eligible for band competitions.

"When Ms. Fisher called to let me know I'd be talking to the entire school, not just the music kids, I did some quick but serious thinking. I kinda shifted what I wanted to talk to you all about today, and I think . . ." He pushes his tongue into his cheek and rests the mic at his chin for a second, and whether it's performance or not, it's captivating. The little things with him just are that way.

"I think maybe it's good that I changed plans. I think this talk is more important than the chasing your dreams talk. I think this talk is about the stuff that matters. The stuff that makes you, that gives you that sense of self and that courage in your belly." He pounds his fist against his gut a few times as he paces around the center of the gym, completely at ease. The room is silent, the students hanging on every word.

"There are people in this room who no doubt you think of as best friends. They're the people you maybe tell secrets to. You show them your underbelly—that means the parts of you that aren't pretty, that you aren't proud of. I have to dumb it down for you jocks, don't I?" He teases the football team, all sitting in the front row next to me, and they eat it up, laughing with him. Anyone else who poked fun of them like that would feel the social isolation and their wrath. Johnny is their god.

I'm in awe of it all the way until his sightline stops on me.

"Best friends are rare in life. People who get you, even the parts you maybe aren't quite ready to get yourself. Those people are special." His lip tugs up, so innocent and familiar. My body tingles, my arms rushed with the pattering sensation of water trickling down my skin. I blink rapidly, feeling more than Johnny's eyes on mine, yet when I scan the room, nobody is looking at me. All eyes are on him.

"What I want to get through to you today is how important it is to treat precious relationships as they should be treated —*precious.*"

My throat is a desert, and my swallow gets stuck somewhere in my esophagus. I bring my fist to my mouth to cough, but I leave it there to hide part of myself. To ground myself.

"I haven't been the person I want to be for a long time. I've done a lot of stupid things, some of which I'm more than positive you all have saved in your whatever accounts and turned into memes or whatever the hell you guys do now with your phones." He paces the gym in a wide circle as he speaks, but I know he's coming back to me. I feel it, and my eyes bore into his face, noting every single tic, each tiny tell, the signs of Johnny's heart and soul. These are the characteristics I always saw first, some of them movements and expressions nobody saw but me.

"I'm thirty-two days clean and sober." He stops where he stands and smirks at the shine on the floor, the top of the key for the basketball court. He squeaks his shoe against the foul line while the room cheers on his sobriety. He rolls his head to the side and crosses his arms over his chest, holding the mic to his chest as he takes in their support.

"Thank you," he finally says. "But I have a whole lifetime to go. Thirty-two days is like, hell . . . like a commercial."

The gym echoes with a few muted laughs. Johnny finishes his circle, coming back toward me.

"I know some of you in here are struggling. One or two . . . ten or eleven . . . fifty. I don't know. It's always more people than you think. And it's always someone suffering who you thought was completely fine. It's a mask we wear, that life at home—life away from our peers—is fine."

His gaze lifts from the floor and stops on mine. I shift my hand over my mouth and chew at my nails as his gait slows.

"My dad was a college football hero, and he almost won a Super Bowl. People in the great state of California fucking loved him." He turns to face Principal Baker briefly, holding up a hand in apology for his F bomb, but she waves him off. Language isn't really policed at this school. Never has been. And my gut tells me a four-letter word is nothing compared what he's about to share.

"I played football here my senior year. We moved here . . ." He scans the room and crosses one arm over his chest, tucking his hand under the elbow of the other as he chews at his cheek. "We didn't move here for the great music program, or for the drama classes, or the famous alumni."

He nods slowly, bringing his focus back to me. We're like parts of an atom, needing each other. I'm powering him right now, and there have been so many times—times long in our past —when he powered me.

"We moved to Yucca because my dad got asked to resign from a coaching gig at Pacific West University. You see, it was the first week of practice there and one of his players didn't hit his route. And Kevin Forrester, *ooof*, he likes it when his players hit their routes."

He sucks in his bottom lip, and I travel back in time with him in a single breath. He's eighteen and just finished the best game of his life. He fumbled once, though. We recovered that fumble on the very next play and won by four touchdowns. But it didn't matter; Johnny was less than perfect. His dad pulled him out of the line of players walking back to the locker room by his hair, pulled him into the dark corner of the parking lot— where he liked to park, away from eyes so he could drink himself stupid before games—then beat the shit out of his son. And all the while, the public—they still loved him.

"My dad choked him. It got settled and he got told to resign. And me, my mom, and that piece of . . ." He stops short and simply laughs out once to make his point.

I lived this story with Johnny. I know it by heart, and I know the details he's grazing over intimately. But I've never heard him simply speak it out loud. Not to a single person. You could hear a pin drop in this massive, crowded room.

"We ended up here. Where the football team was desperate, and where he could hide in the hills, fish on the lake, abandon my mom without a car as he took the only set of wheels we had into LA to party it up with his old pals, people who were as screwed up as he was or willing to tolerate him because he picked up the tab. We landed here. And I made some of the best friends of my entire life."

His lashes kiss the tops of his cheeks, and everyone around us disappears from my mind. It's only me and him, and the innocent boy he was before he left this place. The one he's desperate to get back to and make a man.

"But fame, ha. Oh man, you guys. That devil, fame. It will tempt you." A devious laugh filters from him, growing louder as he wanders away from me again, leaving my chest empty and my lungs sore. When he connects with me like this, I can't breathe. It's always been that way. That hasn't changed.

"I couldn't wait to get out of that house, but no matter how far you run, those demons will hunt you. And there isn't a pill or a drink or a drug that can silence them forever. Believe me, I tried." He laughs softly but nobody else does. He looks over his shoulder at me, stopping once more in the center of the gym. "The only thing that can keep the demons away are the people you love. Those friends. Those . . . more than friends. The special ones who get the ugly and love you back anyway."

His gaze drops as he draws in a heavy breath. A silent sob chokes me behind my palm but nobody is the wiser, thank God. I have to teach today. I have to host him in my classroom and turn him loose to impact my students. I'm not sure whether that's the best idea in the world or the worst right now. I just know that this hurt is going to drag on and on. And I missed him. I *miss* him. Even though he's here.

"Phew! That was heavy, right?"

Nervous laughter spills out from the crowd.

"Anyway, so yeah, don't do drugs, chase your dreams, you can be anything you want, blah blah blah."

The laughter grows.

"But none of it is worth a damn without your people. That's what I'm saying to you today. Keep your people. Hold them close. Don't let them go. And when they need you, step up. I'm lucky that mine did."

I made a promise.

Chapter 16
Age 18, The Fall Fest Dance

I feel out of sorts getting ready to go to a dance with an actual date. I usually spend the night at Cori's or with one of the other girls in band and a group of us get ready together, one of our various parents dropping us off at the school gym.

I'm alone, though. In my room. Praying my mom does not embarrass me when Devin comes to pick me up. She bought two corsages, one pink and one red, that she has tucked away in our refrigerator in case Devin doesn't bring one. I'm not even sure corsages are a thing for the Fall Fest. I didn't go to Junior Prom last year, though, and Mom feels she missed out on all of the pomp and circumstance that goes along with formals like that.

"Remember to be nice," my dad says under his breath as he stops by the bathroom's open door.

I pull out the final roller twist from my hair, I catch his gaze in the mirror and smile with tight lips and a high brow.

"Your mom is excited."

"I know," I say. It's my mantra today.

Now, steam your dress an hour before the dance.

I know, Mom.

You should try the heatless curls, they hold up in your hair longer.

I know.

And for God's sake, do not eat onions at lunch!

I know!

I didn't eat lunch because of the amount of pressure she was putting on me. Everything suddenly looked like an onion. I regret that decision some because my stomach will not quit grumbling.

In my bare feet and bronze-colored slip, I bend backward against the sink counter so I can scoop half of my now wavy hair up into a clip. It's the only hairstyle I know how to do, but it usually looks nice when I'm done pushing pins in on top of my head. I like to leave half of my hair down to cover my shoulders. To be honest, I also like the security blanket sense of having it down. Once the hair is in place, I spray it with the light apple-scented styling spritz my mom gave me. I don't really wear perfume, and I like the lightness of this even if I smell a little like an orchard.

I palm my phone and use it to examine the back of my head as I awkwardly lean against the sink. It's not a great view, but nothing seems to be jarring back there. I dab a tiny bit of gloss on my lips then shut off the lights and head into my room to slip into my dress. It's a simple black gown with a velvet heart-shaped bodice and a sheer layered A-line skirt that stops right at my knees. We bought it on sale two years ago with the hopes that by the time I got to my senior year it might fit. I think I finally have the C-cup bust required to hold it up, though I'm a little terrified about going braless.

"Here goes." I pump myself up for my final fitting as I slip my undergarment off and unzip the dress.

Our doorbell rings while I'm stepping into the dress, which jets up my pulse. Devin is early. I'm supposed to have twenty minutes left. I fidget with the zipper as I hear voices downstairs, and I'm not quite able to get the back pulled up completely, leaving about four-inches of zipper to go. I'll have to get help from my mom. I stuff my feet into the ballet flats, wincing at how childish my feet look compared to the rest of me. I don't walk well in heels, which is a goal I promise to remedy by graduation. I want to walk across the stage taller than any other girl in our class.

I creak open my door and poke my head out to see what I can hear downstairs, but it's hard to make out the conversation my dad is having. I don't hear my mother's voice either, so I hope that means she's in a different room and can help me zip up my dress. I grab the small clutch purse along with my phone and tiptoe my way down the hall. My parents' bedroom is empty, so my last hope is I'll find my mom in the kitchen—with the stupid corsages.

My footsteps are delicate on the first few steps as I make my way down, but when I reach the halfway point, my father and Johnny cross the bottom of the steps moving from our living room toward my father's study. They halt when they see me.

"Oh, my." Dad's head tilts to the side and his eyes fill with fatherly adoration. I barely register his complimenting gaze, however, because the moment I look at Johnny, I'm completely sucked into his orbit. His gaze narrows on me, somehow on *all* of me, but I can tell he's cut away every distraction. I'm all he sees as his pupils dilate and his jaw twitches. At his sides, his hands form fists that pulse as he squeezes his thumbs in his palms. I somehow feel naked.

"You're . . . uh, you're going to the dance?" His voice collapses into a breathy rasp, forcing him to clear his throat.

I lift my chin and push my chest out a hint.

"I am."

Ask me who I'm going with.

Johnny nods as his tongue peeks between his tight lips. His gaze moves from my face down my body, pausing somewhere around my knees. My legs quiver under the attention, so with the aid of the stair rail that I now clutch in a death grip, I continue my descent toward him and my father.

"You, uh. You look—"

"Beautiful!" My mom buzzes from the kitchen with the two corsage boxes in her hands. She sets them on the table by the door then takes my hands, spinning me in a half circle so she can admire my hair and dress, which she was *very involved* in the artistic direction of.

"Let me get some pictures before you go," she demands, rushing up the stairs, probably for one of her disposable cameras. She keeps a dozen of them in her closet at all times. I think she's maybe developed two.

My gaze follows my mom up the stairs, but I feel Johnny's eyes on me in my periphery. My dad has stepped into his office, leaving us here alone. The air is thick with whatever this is I'm feeling mixed with the strange vibe Johnny is giving off. I can't tell whether he's surprised to see me dressed up like this or jealous or . . . somehow offended that I think I'm good enough to go to a formal dance.

Johnny and I haven't talked at all this week. We haven't said a word to one another since he blew me off in front of his father. It rained Monday through Thursday, so our morning field practices were cancelled, and it was easy to avoid him during our first hour. He pretty much stayed glued to the piano while I worked with a different instrument group each day. Everyone was pretty angry with him for skipping out on us at halftime. Everyone but my dad. The team travelled to a school near Fresno for yesterday's game, and since the band doesn't travel out of the county for football, I made it a full seven days without having to confront him.

And now we're literally inches apart, standing in my foyer alone, without a goddamn thing to say to one another.

I turn and back into the table where my mom left the flower wristbands, knocking over the framed photo of me with my parents at Bear Lake last winter. I spin to catch it and keep it from falling on the ground.

"Shit," I mutter, my hands fumbling with the photo, righting it while still clutching my phone and small purse.

"Your zipper . . ."

I glance over my shoulder, suddenly remembering the reason I need my mom's help.

"Oh, yeah." I leave my things with the photos on the table, then stretch my arm behind my head to try again to reach the zipper pull.

"Can I?" Johnny reaches up with one hand, stopping before touching me.

"Thank you," I croak, pulling all of my hair over one shoulder, out of the way. Johnny's breath tickles my bare skin as he closes in behind me. A palm flattens against the arch of my back and his fingertips brush along my spine as he slowly pulls the zipper up the remaining few inches. The bodice feels incredibly tight, as though my lungs are struggling to gain enough air underneath the constraints.

I tuck my chin into my shoulder, still feeling him close. My eyes flit up to find his jawline near my neck. His mouth near my ear.

"Thank you," I murmur.

"I found it!" My father's voice booms from his office, breaking the sudden thickness in the air. The shuffling of boxes continues as my dad whistles one of the songs from our show and rearranges whatever it is he's looking for in there. Johnny coughs as he steps back. He's wearing a gray USC hoodie and black joggers that are pushed up on his calves. There are no socks with his white sneakers, and his hair is curlier than normal, like he ran here through rain. There isn't a storm for miles, though.

"I found my last camera," my mom professes as she descends our stairs.

"Great," I deadpan. My eyes scan to Johnny and he smirks.

"This is the one I was telling you about," my dad announces, exiting his study with one of his old guitars. I'm not sure but I think it's the one he played when he was in college. The case is dusty and held together at the hinges with silver duct tape. He pushes my phone and purse along with the photo I just saved to one side and the corsages to the other so he can set the case down flat.

"Don't mind us," my mom grunts as she scoops the flowers up and moves them to the chair at the entry to the living room.

For only four of us in the house, it feels suddenly crowded, people moving in all directions, each of us with a different purpose. I gather the pleats of my skirt into my palms and squeeze the fabric as my eyes dart from the now open guitar case to Johnny's eyes to the antique clock on the wall. Devin will be here in minutes.

"Okay, Brynn. Stand by the door where the light is brighter." My mom motions for me to move where Johnny is. We exchange places with muttered apologics for being in each other's way, but somewhere in the shuffle his hand finds the small of my back. I freeze at the sensation of his warm hand, my head swiveling to my right until our eyes meet.

His gaze dips to my mouth for the briefest of moments, and the tip of his tongue grazes his lower lip. The knock at the door scares him off, and my heart squeezes in anticipation of the next few minutes. I don't know what I want. It seemed so clear this week when we didn't speak, when I was mad at him for ditching me and the rest of the band. *Me.*

Now, though? I don't feel so angry all of a sudden. I feel sorry maybe, and other emotions are swimming in my head and making it hurt.

"Well, hello, handsome!" My mom gushes over Devin as she lets him in the door beside me. "Perfect timing, as I was just about to grab some photos."

My eyes haven't left the back of Johnny's head. Other than a quick glance, he remains steadfast in his concentration on my father's guitar. My dad explains the glitches with the tuning, the spare string coiled and tucked inside the felt compartment, and the small tube of car wax he uses to maximize the shine after a cleaning—a little trick he learned from some blues musician he met once in Memphis.

"Oh, that is lovely, Devin. Brynn, look at this!" My mom takes my wrist, tugging me into her conversation with Devin. He brought a corsage, a silver one accented with pearls. It's dark and beautiful, and exactly what I would have picked out for myself.

I wish Johnny were giving it to me.

"Thank you, Devin. It's really nice." I keep my voice low on purpose, not wanting to do any of this in front of Johnny. There was a moment this week when the fantasy of making him jealous with a scene like this amused me. I was so wrong to feel that way. Nothing about this is delightful. My gut hurts. I'm sick.

"It looked like something that would fit you." He blows up at his hair, which—minus a few loose pieces that have fallen over his brow—is slicked back. He ties the small cluster of flowers and beads around my wrist, then slips his arm around my waist as we pose for my mom's photos.

"Brynn, you look beautiful," my dad says, pausing his guitar

195

tour with Johnny to give me and my date a final look.

"Thanks, Dad." I force my embarrassed smile to look as normal as I can, and when my dad steps in to hug me, my eyes shift to Johnny's. He finally stopped trying to ignore me and Devin, and I'm not one-hundred-percent certain what my smile looks like, but I think it might match his. Forced and pained.

He nods at me as I break my embrace with my dad.

"Not going with Cori tonight, huh?" he mutters, biting the inside of his cheek as he struggles to maintain our eye contact.

"No, uh. Devin asked, and I figured . . ." I shrug.

I figured you weren't going to ask, so I might as well move on and go with him. Besides, you don't even know me, remember?

"Brynn? We should go." Devin's hand slides from my hip to my hand, linking a few of his fingers with mine. I should be over the moon to be in this position. My freshman year, I would imagine holding hands with him before I fell asleep at night, holding my own hand and pretending.

"Right. Yeah." I smile toward Devin and reach behind Johnny to snag my phone and purse from the table's edge.

"Have a good time, honey." My mom snaps the last of the pictures with her disposable as we exit.

Devin holds my hand all the way to his truck, opening the passenger door for me, and keeping my hand in his so he can help me balance as I step up into the seat.

"Phew," he whistles, his gaze running down my legs, which I quickly cross at the ankles. "That's some dress, Brynn."

My cheeks swell and I suck in my bottom lip before croaking out a quiet, "Thank you."

I've never had a boy make me feel sexy before. Words like *hot* don't really get tossed around with girls like me. I've been called cute, and maybe pretty, and it's usually by guys from other bands at other schools or band camp. This attention is new, and despite wanting it for so long, I'm not sure what I think of it.

Devin pushes my door closed, then jogs around to the driver's side. I fake a struggle with the seat belt—a few seconds' cover to look back at my front porch. I don't know why I thought Johnny might be standing there in the doorway, or maybe rushing toward the truck to beg me to go to this dance with him instead of Devin. The only one peering through the window, though, is my mom. I raise my hand to wave at her, then buckle up to begin my night out.

M usic and friends are the ideal elixir. I wasn't sure I was going to be able to fake a good time when we drove away from my house, but by the time Devin and I entered the gym and met up with our friends, the hole that was burning in my chest was beginning to subside. I can honestly say that the last hour of my evening was marked by unbridled bliss. I laughed and smiled for sixty-minutes straight as we moved from some coordinated line dance into a hip hop song that had all of us thumping on the dance floor, jumping with such vigor that we may have damaged a few of the old wooden boards.

And the slow dances. They were sweet. And Devin was a gentleman. His hands never veered from the curve of my hips. And he talked to me through every song, ignoring the *ooohs* and *ahhhs* from my friends who all stood by the drink and snack table ogling us. We talked about our senior year, and our time together at Yucca. Only once did he mention last Friday night, the one that Johnny ruined. I think he could tell it bummed me out, so he quickly changed subjects. The night with Devin was easy.

As we near my house, a small piece of me hopes for a good-night kiss. I know Devin isn't looking at me to be his girlfriend. He doesn't *do* girlfriends. But he does kiss a lot of girls. And I wouldn't mind the experience. A badge of honor among my friends, maybe?

He shuts the truck lights off before he gets close to my driveway, stopping just behind the desert sage that my dad has let grow into a wild mess of orange and green. We're out of view from the front of the house and my mom's peeping eyes. It's midnight, so I doubt she's still up. But I know she tried. Tonight was as much for her as it was for me.

"Let me get the door. Hold on." Devin flies from the driver's side and rushes around the front of his truck to open my door and take my hand to help me step down.

"Thank you," I murmur, my lips buzzing with anticipation. I don't know the protocol for nights like this. I've never really been on a date. I've seen movies with Teddy, but I usually let myself out of his car, give him the finger and shout our plans to see each other the next day as I run up my walkway.

"I had a really good time tonight." He takes my other hand in his, turning us a bit until my back is against the side of the truck bed.

"Me, too."

We stare into each other's eyes for a few long seconds until we both succumb to embarrassed laughter.

"It's weird because we've known each other for so long, ya know?" Devin's mouth forms a crooked smile and his gaze shifts to my mouth.

"Yeah. We have." I glance up at the sky, forcing my eyes to roll back as far as they'll go as my lips pucker into a tight, shy grin. I shake with my nervous laughter and Devin chuckles.

"Can I kiss you good night?"

I let my focus return to his adorable face, a thin silver hoop piercing his right eyebrow. His eyes are the same shade as the cat I grew up with, somewhere between brown and gray. His all black suit and dress shirt make him look dangerous, or maybe I simply want to think he does. My parents didn't seem to have any qualms about letting me go out with him. As far as bad boys go, Devin is pretty tame.

"You may," I finally utter, shirking my shoulders up a few inches and bunching up my face.

"Why are you being so cute?" He taps his fingertip to my nose and I look down with more nervous giggling.

"I don't know. It's just weird. And I'm embarrassed."

His hand finds my chin next and he coaxes me to look him in the eyes.

"You're cute. And I had a nice time." His smile has shifted into the one that spawned my crush on him our freshman year, that cocky one that leaves just enough space between his lips for him to breathe. His eyes haze before closing, and as his mouth nears mine, I squeeze mine shut.

His lips brush against mine lightly then take in my lower lip with a tiny suck, holding me in place for a few seconds before we part.

"Thanks for going to the dance with me, Brynn Fisher." His cocky smile remains.

"You're welcome," I say.

"Come on. Let me walk you to the door."

I nod, then reach into the truck to grab my phone and purse. We walk together up the short path to my front porch. He lets me climb the three steps on my own, and when I unzip my handbag to fish out my key, he says, "Good night."

I linger by my door, my key digging into my palm as the cute drummer boy I always liked so much gets into his truck and drives away. My chest thumps a few times as I bring my free hand to my lips and touch where he kissed me. A tiny laugh escapes me and I glance down to my feet, my lame shoes no longer feeling very important.

Turning my attention back to my front door, I work the key into its hole as my phone buzzes from inside my small purse. I dig it back out before unlocking the door, expecting some sweet text from Devin or a nosy one from Cori. It's neither of them.

> JOHNNY: Can you hang out front for a few more minutes?

I spin around and scan my front yard, chirping crickets the only sound. The landscape is lit by the soft glow of my mom's solar garden lights. They're tiny glass dragonflies that cast faint pinks and greens. The bright porch light behind me makes it hard to see much farther, so I step back onto the walkway and shade my eyes from its harsh beam.

"Hello?" My voice isn't quite a whisper, but it's not normal speaking volume. My pulse is racing. I look back at my phone and decide to answer Johnny.

> ME: I'm outside. Are you here?

I hit send and venture a few more steps until I'm near the sidewalk. I look to my right, seeing nothing but empty road and a stray cat that wanders across it. Then I look left and see Johnny's form moving closer down the middle of the street. His hands appear to be buried in the front of his hoodie, which he has pulled up over his head. I would have been frightened, unsure whether it was him, if his bright white shoes weren't glowing against the black pavement.

"Is that you?" I know it is, but my belly is flickering with nerves and it's all I can think to say.

Johnny picks up his pace, jogging the remaining distance until we're face to face. He pushes his hood back from his head, then runs his hand through his hair. The waves have loosened from earlier. His smile is faint, and he can't seem to hold eye contact for more than a fraction of a second.

"What do you want, Johnny?" My key is lodged in the door and my purse is sitting on the small bench by my mom's potted plants. I clutch my phone in both hands, a restless energy brewing in my palms and slowly working its way up my arms and down my legs.

"Yeah, sorry. I know it's late. I just . . ." He runs his hand through his hair again, gripping it at the top of his head and staring out into the street. The yellow hue from my porch outlines his profile.

"It's late. I need to get ins—"

"He kiss you?" Johnny's gaze snaps to mine, and my heart beats once, really hard, then stops.

"Devin?" *Duh. Yeah, Devin.*

He purses his lips.

I blink a few times and lower my gaze, shrugging.

"It wasn't a big deal, really. It was a goodnight kiss." Except, it was a big deal. And it had me floating until two seconds ago, when Johnny asked about it. Now, I want to diminish it. I almost wish it didn't happen at all.

I lift my chin and match Johnny's stare with my own. His nostrils flare with his inhale and my smile completely collapses. No matter how hard I try to look away, I can't. Shaking his head in slow motion, his lips part, panting out a breath full of exasperation.

"What, Johnny?" I shrug and shake my head back.

"You deserve to be kissed like it's a big deal."

My entire body buzzes with electricity, heat rushing from my toes to my fingers to my ears and down my legs again. I open my mouth to breathe, hoping some word—the perfect word—will reach my lips by the time I try to speak. But I don't

201

need to. Within a single heartbeat, Johnny's hands cup my cheeks and I'm on my toes as his mouth covers mine in a manic sense of hunger, a desperate want. My fingers fly open, my phone falling to the ground as I simply try to maintain my balance.

His lips are warm and soft, but still so strong as they move against mine. When he takes my lower lip between his, the sharp edge of his teeth grazes against me and ignites a fire in my chest that forces my hands to wrap around his wrists.

I kiss him back. My fingers splay along the backs of his hands, fingers intertwining with his then moving along his arms to his neck, and finally into his hair. My hands sink into the soft, thick hair I have been dying to touch since the first day we met.

Our lips part, leaving me panting as I sink to my flat feet, Johnny towering over me, his forehead resting against mine. I cling to the front of his sweatshirt as his nose tickles mine. My lashes flutter as I try to memorize everything from right now. The surprisingly warm autumn air. The cinnamon taste of his tongue. The way his hands holding my face makes me feel safe.

"I'm so fucking sorry that I didn't show up for you, Brynnie. I'll never let you down again."

His apology.

My heart.

Chapter 17
Present

I'm still not convinced having Johnny immerse himself into my class and our school is the best idea, but I can't deny the renewed spark his presence seems to give us. Even the math department head was inspired to get more creative with his class structure. And my students, Jade especially, were definitely boosted by him being in our classroom for the day.

My worry is that none of it will last. I suppose that's how Johnny's trained me to feel. The good times are so good, until they're gone.

The crowd lingering outside the school gates is a fraction of what it was this morning. We sent Johnny's driver home for the day, agreeing I would drive with him to visit his mom. Rather than force our way through the stragglers hanging around the exit, Johnny decides to walk ahead while I get my car so he can sign autographs and take more pictures. Two of the campus officers stick around the area to keep things orderly.

I pull up as he's posing with a group of football players and a few of their dads. The sick irony of this moment isn't lost on me, and when Johnny's eyes meet mine for a quick roll, I know

Ginger Scott

he gets it, too. Father-son relationships are hard for him, especially when football is involved.

Deciding to play back-up for him, and to be a bit nosy, I shift my car into park and let it idle under a nearby tree. The subject of his father comes up almost instantly from one of the football dads, so I hurry my steps to be there in case I have to step in to diffuse the conversation. Not that I would be any use in a confrontation between these massive gentlemen around me.

"What you said in there, about your dad . . . that was some real honest shit," one of the fathers says. Johnny nods as he finishes signing a magazine with him on the cover.

"Yeah, well, that's my promise to myself now. I'm going to be honest with everyone, even when I'm embarrassed by it. And I was embarrassed by my dad for a real long time." Johnny squints from the sun as he looks up and hands the magazine back to the dad.

"You shouldn't be. Your dad was a hell of a football player. Doesn't mean he was a great person." There's a moment between the two of them after that, their eyes connecting for a long breath as unsaid words seem to pass between them. I could be imagining it, but there are a lot of people who have stories like Johnny's. There's a kindred spirit in surviving.

"We should get going so we're not late," I interject. Johnny's feet have started to shift and shuffle nervously as he stands on the sidewalk. It's a tell he's had since we were teenagers. When he got panicked or felt pressure, he would dance in one spot almost like a toddler holding in having to pee. This is the grown-up version of that.

"Hey, if you can, Mr. Bishop. We'd love to honor you at one of our games," one of the players says as Johnny caps a pen and hands it back to him. It's Clayton Trent, our current quarterback and a pretty decent student. He's not musical the way

206

Johnny was, but he does like theater. And his dad is in the front row for every performance that kid has—on the field or the stage.

"Maybe, yeah. I . . . haven't touched a football field in a long time. Might take me a minute to work up to that, but I'll let you know. Or Ms. Fisher will. Cool?" Johnny holds out a fist and Clayton pounds it with his own.

"For sure. For sure." Clayton shrinks as he takes a few steps back.

"Hey, see you all tomorrow, though. And the next day, and the next. Wait a minute!" Johnny shifts to look at me. "How did I get myself back in high school?"

The few students still hanging around laugh.

"You volunteered, dumbass." I punch his shoulder, then nod toward my car.

Johnny holds up a palm to say goodbye and he gets a collective goodbye from the people remaining. I wait a few minutes when we get into the car, relishing the cool interior and quiet now that the doors are shut. I can tell Johnny needs it.

"Good first day?" I finally ask. We haven't had time alone in a while.

He nods slowly, his eyes fixed out into the distance and his mouth not quite a smile. My gut says he's already thinking about what's next—visiting his mom.

"You were great this morning. I mean, you could have maybe not called me Brynnie, or hey! How about you don't mention me *at all* during your speeches?" I laugh lightly as I twist to face him, crossing my arms to play mad, though I am still a little irritated by being called out in front of the school.

"I can work on the Brynnie thing. Though it's gonna be tough," he says through a soft laugh. He drops his head forward and to the side, meeting my gaze. "But not mentioning you at all? I'm not me without you, Brynn Fisher. Not even close."

The quiet is back. It's uncomfortable. I want to swoon from his kind words but I haven't gotten the other feelings out of my way. The need to shake him silly. To scream at him. Maybe throw a thing or two.

"I wasn't looking for a compliment." I shift in my seat and move the gear into drive. I can feel Johnny's eyes still on me as I pull us through the gate. I wave to my students, but they couldn't care less about *me*.

"Wave to your fans, Johnny."

He sinks back into his seat but holds up a palm. He's probably smiling, but I'll have to trust my gut on that. I'm not looking at him. If I do that, I'm going to pull us over and have things out right now before we make it to his mom's house. There's always something bigger in the way, a windmill he needs to conquer before I lay our mountain of shit at his feet.

His phone rings while I drive us through the old neighborhood, and he answers but keeps his attention fixed on everything outside our car. Not much has changed here in the ten years he's been gone, and a quick sideways glance in his direction reveals his smirk as he sees some of the old stomping grounds. The malt shop is still open by the steakhouse, and DJ's Auto Service is still run by Danny Ortega, the only honest mechanic left on this hemisphere, at least that's what my father always says. Danny's gotta be in his late sixties by now.

"Kaylee, can we pick this up again later? There's something I've gotta do real quick," he says as we make our final turn to head into the hills, toward his mom's place. He cups his phone and holds it to his side, turning toward me.

"Publicist. We should have your dad check your house," he whispers.

My eyes widen.

"Great." I swallow and do my best to pretend I'm not freaking out while he wraps up his talk with Kaylee.

I pull to a stop at end of the gravel driveway and glance up toward the house I once knew so well. I was rarely inside, but the driveway was where I learned to shoot a basketball and where I spun a thread of glass in a roll-out kiln. Those were times when Johnny's dad was out of town. The good times. The *best* times.

"Okay, sorry about that. She left me a few messages during school." He leans to his side and pushes his phone into his pocket, then meets my waiting expression.

I clear my throat.

"Check the house?" My brow lifts on one side.

Johnny breathes in slow and deep through his nose, and I can tell right away that he's serious about the suggestion.

"Apparently, the media knows where I'm staying."

A dozen scenarios flash through my mind at this revelation, most of them involving a brawl or a broken window for some reason. Maybe I have watched too much TMZ. And I'm not sure I want to send my dad into that.

"Kaylee's already en route here. She got a room at the Diesel for a couple weeks. I just meant it might be a good idea for your dad to drive by and see if anyone is camped out." My face must have told him I was concerned.

"I can ask. I'll text him now, and maybe you can . . ." I lean my head toward the driveway and the quiet house at the end. Johnny follows my sightline and sighs.

"I have no idea what to say to her."

I stop mid-text message to my father and look up at the closed garage door and dead plants that line her driveway. She hasn't taken care of them in a while it seems. Beth was always attentive to her plants.

"Just start with, 'Hi, Mom.'" I turn to look at him, his eyes still set on his history.

After a few quiet seconds, he utters *okay* and pushes open

the door. I finish my text to my father, then look on as Johnny stops just shy of the front steps to his old front door. His feet shuffle against the driveway as he kicks at the same spot, his hands stuffed in his pockets. I really hoped he would be able to do this on his own, that I could merely get him here. I'm not sure I'm ready to *watch* this reunion, much less have one of my own. I haven't exactly reached out to Beth.

Johnny spins on his feet to look at me, and I kill the engine and get out of the car to join him. This walk is hard for me, too. The last time I made the trip up this driveway, Johnny's mom answered the door to let me know her son left town. Before that, was the time I heard Johnny arguing with his dad. It was loud enough to hear every word clearly, even through his father's drunken slurs. His dad called me a useless distraction and Johnny told him he was in love with me. He never actually said those words to my face. The only time I heard him profess his feelings was colored by so much ugliness. I hate this house.

"Come on. I'll ring the bell." I slip my arm through his and urge him forward. His body vibrates with nerves, the tremors growing in intensity as we take the steps. He wipes his arm across his forehead as I press the doorbell.

I reach over and straighten his collar. "You look nice."

His gaze drops to mine, his eyelids heavy, eyes drawn inward like the young boy who was afraid to go home.

Beth opens the door only a few inches at first, her eyes matching the weight in her son's. Her breath falters as she gasps in a pained effort to fill her lungs. Johnny pulls the screen door wide and steps on the threshold, taking his mom in his arms. The two of them cry hard in their embrace. I do my best to step back and give them space. I don't know what do to with my hands, so I shove them in the pockets of my black pants as I lean against the porch support post.

After a few emotional minutes, Beth steps back, squeezing

her son's face between her palms, pushing his cheeks with enough force that his lips look fish-like. It makes him laugh a little. It makes her laugh a lot. She gives his cheek a light love pat then turns her gaze to me. Without sound, she mouths *thank you*. I simply smile. I did nothing. I did less than nothing. I should have visited her.

"Come in. Please, come in. Are you both thirsty? I have tea. And lemonade. It has honey in it because that's better for you, or I can brew coffee or—"

"We're fine, Mom. I came for you."

His mother stops in the middle of her living room and spins around, her vibrant broomstick skirt swishing around her ankles. She's barefoot, as she almost always was, and her arms seem thin in the gauzy white long-sleeved shirt she's wearing for a top. Her hair is as thick as it ever was, piled into a braided twist on top of her head with random wispy curls falling down on all sides. It's grayer than it once was, but somehow still magical. Beth Bishop always appeared magical, despite her nightmare.

"Well, then, sit. Get comfortable. Stay awhile. Please, stay." She moves a few large pillows from a giant green sofa. The furniture in this room is all different from what it was back then. It's comforting and seems more *her* than her late husband. The house is bright and full of color, the heavy masculine feel stripped away. I wondered how she could handle staying here, but being inside now reveals an almost entirely different space from the one that existed a decade ago.

Johnny plops down on one end of the sofa and I take the other, still not sure of my role here. Beth takes a seat in the yellow wingback chair across from us, folding her legs up in the seat. Her smile is soft even if her cheeks are set in from weight loss. I haven't seen her in a long time, longer than I realized.

"I would have come," Johnny finally says, breaking the peaceful but thick quiet in the room.

"*Shh.*" Beth shakes her head. Her eyes flit to me, her soft smile ticking up a tiny bit.

"I'm sorry I didn't know," I blurt out, guilt overcoming me. I wrap my arms around my stomach and squeeze.

"Oh, honey. No, no. I didn't want anyone to know, and you and I . . . Brynn, we're just fine." She levels me with a sense of certainty in her eyes, her chin dipping as her brow raises a hair.

"I still should have been by to visit." I cut myself off from the river of apologies I suddenly feel I need to offer. This isn't *my* visit. It's Johnny's. It's theirs.

"Me, too, Brynn. Me, too." Beth locks her eyes on me, her head tilted with an apologetic softness to her features. My chest floods with tingles. I think it's relief. All I can do is breathe out heavily.

"It wasn't your job, Brynn. It was mine." Johnny's voice cracks as he speaks, and he pinches the bridge of his nose, sucking in hard in an attempt to keep his own tears at bay.

His mom leans forward and flattens her hand on the small coffee table between us. Her son scoots to the edge of the sofa cushion and places his hand on top of hers. The contrast between their skin is harsh—the age difference more than the actual numbers they are. For all Johnny's done to himself, his hand should look more worn than it does. Yet he's the healthy one. His hand firm while Beth's is frail.

"You look well, my son. Very well. And that makes me so happy. To see you . . . well."

Johnny lifts his gaze to meet his mom's, his Adam's apple dropping with a hard swallow.

"I'm sorry I let you down, Mom. I was—"

"You were perfect. And you are a gift." Her words are so direct, and I wonder if she's rehearsed this moment a thousand times. She seems to have the perfect response for everything he's feeling. It's soothing to watch.

Johnny chuckles and sits back, running the back of his palm over his damp eyes with a sniffle.

"I was definitely not perfect, Mom. But you were always biased."

The two of them laugh quietly, and Johnny leans against the armrest, resting his cheek in his palm. He looks on at his mom as if he's lost and found all at once.

"Can you fight?" His question is barely audible. It's how Johnny has always asked the things he's afraid to put in the universe.

Beth shakes her head.

"That time has passed, baby boy. But I have this time. And you're here."

He shakes with quiet crying and moves his palm to cover his mouth while his eyes remain on his mother.

"Okay," he whispers.

I scan the room we're in, the shelves lined with beautiful glass sculptures. One in particular catches my eye and I move from the sofa to get a closer look. Also to rid my legs of the tension that seems to be pooling in them.

"You like those?" Beth asks.

I pick up the first in a series of a dozen. It's a pair of angel wings, the inside of the glass marred with sharp cuts and broken pieces, all a deep, blood red. With every version, the shards seem to heal until the glass in the final pair is clear with a hint of frosted blue.

"They're gorgeous," I say, carefully placing the piece back in its spot.

"They're yours. If you want them."

I jerk a little at her offer, then spin to see her looking at me over her shoulder and the top of the chair.

"Oh, no. I could never. I—"

"They're yours," she repeats.

I tuck my bottom lip in my teeth and glance to Johnny. His mouth still cupped, his eyes blink twice, and I think he's trying to tell me to accept them. I move my gaze back to Beth.

"Thank you. If it's okay, though, I'd like to leave them here . . . for a little while." *Until I must.*

She nods slowly.

Something beeps in her kitchen, startling the three of us. Beth hops to her feet and scurries toward one of her cabinets, and Johnny stretches his body into a stand, slowly following her.

"Sorry about that. I have a reminder for my meds. And Andrea should be here soon." Beth fills a glass with water and opens a container marked with today's date and time, popping what looks to be four pills in her mouth before tilting her head back to swallow.

"Who's Andrea?" Johnny glances to me, his face defensive.

His mom grabs his wrist, though, bringing his temperature down.

"Home health, honey. She's my nurse, and she'll be here more and more as I need her. I took care of things." She pats her hand along his arm then tends to putting away her medicine case and returning the glass to the sink.

"I think it's time I give you the tour. You'll be shocked when you see your old room." She urges her son to follow, and I let the two of them move about the house, Johnny holding his mom's arm. She doesn't need his help yet, but it's as if the two of them are practicing and cherishing this moment.

I take my seat on the sofa again, pulling my phone out to text with my dad, who has driven by our house four times now. He's retired, and I have a feeling has just made himself our personal security staff. Maybe he'll turn any reporters he finds onto the many stories he always wanted to write, like the lore about the singing winds up in the canyon, or how music theory should be a mandatory class taught in all high schools. Any reporter who tangles with him will be trapped, and maybe that's okay.

Johnny and his mom spend most of their time in Johnny's old room, and I hear bits and pieces of their conversation, which is often kept low and sometimes even a whisper. She asked about his sobriety and begged him to stay strong. He promised, and when he did, the weight of it landed in my chest. Promises were something he and I swore we would always take to our graves. Sure, we were idealistic teenagers in love, but those promises felt solid. Forged in forever. I've kept mine. Johnny's track record, however, is less than.

Andrea rings the bell after about twenty minutes pass, and Beth rushes into the room, light on her feet as her skirt sweeps along the floor on her way to the door. We make our introductions, and the fact that Andrea is a former military nurse somehow gives me comfort. Beth can leave a little too much in life up to chance—*to the universe* as she always said. It's a beautiful sentiment, but I'm glad to see the science backed by military time.

I hug Beth goodbye, my body quivering against her, still not quite over my own guilt. Her frail arms somehow feel strong, and we make promises to one another to visit often. Especially since she refused Johnny's pleas for him to move in with her. She didn't say it out loud, but I sense that a great part of her doesn't want his own healing journey to cross paths with hers and lose its way. Or, perhaps, she wants him to stay put in my house, where we are forced together. She was not so subtle about how good it was to see the two of us close again.

I head to my car as Johnny clings to his mother on the porch. I look at them through the windshield, and am hit with the many times I've captured this very scene in my memory. Johnny hugging his mom in that very spot, telling her he's okay, asking if she's okay, holding each other up after the storm passed through their walls. I'd bring him back to my house, where he'd stay for a few days. He always went back for her. And she never left.

Johnny gets into the passenger seat and a rush of air leaves his mouth. He doesn't cry but he also doesn't smile. He's caught in that exhausted place where emotion isn't enough anymore. I've been there.

I put the gear in reverse and glance over my shoulder to check the pathway for animals. A lot of desert wildlife ventures up this way. It's part of the charm.

As I turn back, Johnny stops me by putting his hand on my shoulder. His eyes are pools of deep blue, and he's devastatingly handsome because he's so vulnerable. His thumb moves slightly against my arm, tingles spreading from the spot. I don't dare look at it, though. I don't want to leave his eyes. There's something in them that I can't quite read.

"You made a promise to your mom," I breathe out. My heart is racing, and I regret the obvious double message in my words—that he broke his promise to me.

His thumb passes along my skin again, so soft, forming a small circle that feels like a permanent tattoo.

"I know. And I will keep it. There is nothing in my way anymore." He blinks slowly, and I hold my breath as I ruminate on his words. I suck in my lips and nod, letting him have the final word on the subject . . . for the time. I reach up and take his hand in mine, squeezing it but depositing it back in his own space. I can't think when he touches me. And right now, I need to think.

What was in your way then, Johnny? Was it your dad?
Did he really drown?

Chapter 18
Age 18, First Date

"You know, the two of you could always hang out with me and the guys tonight and jam." My dad's furry brow nearly meets his hairline as he peers over his black-rimmed glasses at the two of us in the back seat.

"We're good, Dad. You enjoy your session." His gaze hangs on mine for a beat then he sinks back into the driver's seat and faces the front of the car again.

I would have driven us to the Coachella Valley Fair myself, but parking is expensive. My dad leapt at the chance to chaperone the driving part, and I think despite me being eighteen and technically an adult, he sees me as his little girl right now. And while he loves Johnny as a student and as my friend, his feelings are less enthusiastic about the boy who kissed me in their driveway a week ago.

"Maybe next time, Mr. Fisher." Johnny's hand squeezes mine. We've remained tethered for the entire drive. In fact, I don't think I've let go of his hand once when we're together since we went public with our feelings at school on Monday.

"You can keep calling me Mr. Fisher, by the way." My dad smirks in the rearview mirror, but there's a little bite to his joke.

Johnny shifts in his seat.

"Yes, sir."

His eyes flit to mine and I hold back my laugh, spitting out air through tight lips.

My dad isn't really that intimidating. He wears a pocket protector in his polo shirts, and his idea of lifting weights is holding the trombone up for more than an hour. Still, the sentiment of protective-father is nice, and Johnny's respect for my dad is sweet.

After several minutes weaving through the dusty drop-off line, Johnny and I slide out through his side of the car at the main entrance.

"I will be here right at nine-thirty," my father says, punctuating his words with a point of his finger to his bare wrist.

"Good thing I have the watch," I joke.

His mouth falls flat, unamused.

"I'm serious, Brynn. Be careful, watch your pockets, and don't eat a bunch of crap you're only going to throw up."

"I won't, Dad," I hum, lifting my gaze to the tips of my brow.

"And I love you," he adds to his instructions.

"I love you, too." I push the door shut and wave with my free hand as my dad pulls away.

"Pockets? And throw up?" Johnny echoes the highlights of Dad's speech.

I shake my head as we head to the main entrance, our pre-purchased tickets printed out on yellow paper from the school printer.

"My dad hates the fair because the one time he took me and my friends, someone stole Cori's wallet from her pocket while we were in line waiting for Icees. We were ten."

Johnny lifts a brow.

"And the vomit?"

I sigh, then shrug.

"I threw up a lot of Icee about thirty minutes later on the Gravitron."

"Eww." His mouth twists and his nose scrunches.

"It's as bad as it sounds. I'm much more mature now."

I tug Johnny's hand toward a line with fewer people, and we zip through after our papers are scanned. We purchase ride cards at the first ticket booth we see, and rush to the funhouses near the back of the midway. The first one sends us through a rolling barrel, then a floor covered in ball bearings that make me slip and slide through a bunch of padded arches. Johnny navigates the obstacles quickly, and by the time I make it to the shifting stairs, he's waiting for me at the top, flexing his biceps in the distortion mirrors.

"How come your reflection makes you look like a power lifter and mine makes me look like a squatty mushroom," I say through a giggle. I hold my hands on my hips, making the reflection even more ridiculous.

Johnny grabs me at my waist, however, and swings me around until I fall into his arms. I look at the reflection again as my head rests on his chest and he envelopes me completely.

"I like mushrooms," he says, kissing the top of my head.

We linger here longer than we should, making odd poses in the series of mirrors and stopping to kiss between each station. Eventually, the guy in charge of the ride calls us out on a megaphone, telling us to move through the ride or get off.

We climb through the remaining levels then Johnny pulls me onto his lap when we reach the twisty slide, and we zip down onto semi-soft mats waiting at the bottom.

"One per slide," the man says through the megaphone.

We look at each other and pull our smiles in tight before giving in to fits of laughter.

I let Johnny pick the next ride, and he chooses a haunted

house with motorized cars that carry us through a series of spooky rooms all built behind the façade. The décor is cheesy, and the mechanical ghosts and ghouls don't even seem to scare the grade school kids in the car ahead of us. Despite that, this ride quickly becomes my favorite for its dark corners and slow route. As soon as we make the second turn into the glow-in-the-dark room, Johnny's hand finds my chin, and he coaxes my mouth toward his. I loop my arms around his neck and pull my leg up so I'm sitting sideways as he kisses me. His hands push my hair from my face, and his light whiskers from his barely-there mustache scratch against my lips. At one point, one of the kids in the car near us giggles and the other says *gross*. It makes me laugh against Johnny's lips, and his smile breaks free against my mouth. We leave our heads together while fake screams filter through cheap speakers and plastic bats flap above our heads. I sit back the right way just as our car pulls out into the open. And seeing there is no line for the ride, I quickly hand over our cards to swipe so Johnny and I can go again.

We spend most of our ride credits on the funhouses, saving just enough for a trip on the Ferris wheel. I give the carnival worker our cards and Johnny holds the gate open for me so I can step into the lift first. Once our gate is locked, we zip up several feet at a time while they load more riders below us. Johnny rocks our seat a little, until I clutch his thigh and squeal.

"Okay, I'll stop. Sorry, Miss Deathgrip," he says through a soft laugh before cupping my face and kissing my forehead.

"I'm not so good with the heights thing," I admit.

Johnny peels my hand from his leg and holds it in both of his, rubbing both sides to warm my knuckles. He brings my hand to his mouth and kisses the back of it before enclosing it again in his warm palms.

"We didn't have to ride," he says.

My gaze roams around his face, his hair being blown

around in the breeze, his eyes so bright as they reflect the changing colors from the ride lights around us. His dimples deepen as he blushes under my scrutiny, and he rolls his head and looks the other way.

"Am I making you uncomfortable?" I lean into him, nudging his attention back to my face.

He stares at me with his mouth paused on the verge of grinning. His head cocks just a hint so he's giving me a bit of a sideways glare.

"Maybe nervous?" he finally admits.

My mouth buzzes from the memory of our kisses in the haunted house. My gaze darts to his chest, his black Howl Football T-shirt tight over the long-sleeved white shirt. His thighs stretch the denim around them. My hair is a wild mess around me, the wind doing its best to knot my attempt at curls. My Save-the-Pandas sweatshirt is just long enough to cover my ass and hips over my black leggings.

"I feel like a little girl when I'm with you," I confess, burying my face in his shoulder.

"What?" he laughs out.

The wheel carries us to the top, and Johnny's arm squeezes me close when I flinch.

"I got you," he says.

I unbury my face and glance out to the tops of all the rides, bringing my focus back to his face. He presses the tip of my nose with his fingertip and says, "Boop." His mouth puckers a smile. "See? I'm not really a grown-up, either."

"That's not quite what I meant," I say.

His head falls to the opposite side and I sigh, a little embarrassed I brought up my feelings.

"You've kissed a lot of girls, haven't you?" My face tingles with my blush. Johnny squints with one eye.

"I mean, not like hundreds or anything, but . . ."

I shake my head.

"I mean, more than four, right? Because that's my number. I've kissed four people. And the third kiss was right before ours. You're just a lot more experienced and developed." My eyes widen as I glance down his body, stopping just below his waist. My face burns because I wasn't even thinking of *that* part of him.

Johnny chuckles and lifts my chin with his finger. The wheel begins to move again, but this time, I keep my eyes locked on his. I don't flinch at all. Possibly because I'm frozen.

"Trust me, Brynnie. You are plenty . . . developed." My chest warms as his eyes dip down to my chest and his tongue peeks out between his lips. It's a tiny slip in consistently chivalrous behavior, and I'm surprised how much I like it.

"Oh."

I shift to nestle in under his arm, incredibly aware of where his hand rests on my other shoulder. I could probably calculate mentally the exact distance his fingers are from my bra strap—and everything that's underneath my bra.

The wheel finally rotates, carrying us along the ground then up to the sky. My fear of heights is buried under the charge my body feels everywhere Johnny's body touches mine. Thigh to thigh, my cheek to his shoulder, his hand on my arm, our knees, calves and feet. I could fly like this. I feel safe.

On our last pass high above the fair lights, Johnny tucks his chin, bringing our lips close. I strain to see his face, but can only capture the sharp line of his law and flicker of his eyelashes. Our noses touch.

"I like you so much, Brynn. So very much."

"Yeah?" My mouth stretches into a bashful grin that I have zero control over.

Johnny breathes out a gentle laugh.

"Yeah," he says, closing the final inches between us and

taking my bottom lip between his. He holds our kiss frozen in time until the wheel slows and we near the ground for the last time.

We exit the ride and make our way to the game area. My dad will be here for us soon, but Johnny promised he would win me a prize before we left for the night. I'm terrible at the games, and I know they're rigged, but some people still get to win. I figure we have an edge with Johnny's throwing arm.

"What do you say—a panda for a panda?" He nods down to my sweatshirt and I smile as I spin around and see the enormous stuffed bears tacked to the top of the game booth. I look back over my shoulder and lift one brow.

"Do you think you can do it?"

"*Pfff.*" He steps around me, swinging his arm in a wide circle then stretching it across his body. It's one of those booths where you have to knock down three bottles, and my dad always told me they were glued to the bottom.

Johnny pulls a five dollar bill from his back pocket and hands it to a man with a beard so long it's braided into a fine point below his collar bone. He tucks cash into a leather zip pouch, then palms three baseballs. He sets them on the counter and explains the rules. Any bottles count. Two out of the three win a small prize, and three gets me the big bear.

"Stand back, Brynnie Winnie," he says, kissing me on my cheek.

I move to the side and make room for him to throw, but his attempt is interrupted. Devin steps up with a few of the other guys in the band and raises his hand to purchase three balls of his own.

"Hey, look who's here. Big quarterback man. What do you say, bruh. You up for going against some band nerd for the big prize?"

My body fills with lava and my mouth is rendered useless. I

probably should have said something to Devin after the dance, after my double kiss. I was too scared, though. Confrontation isn't in my skillset. And I rationalized it under the fact that Devin didn't do girlfriends and our kiss was probably nothing special to him.

Johnny's head falls to the side and he glances sideways at Devin, biting his tongue.

"Oh, I got under your skin with that. Didn't I?" Devin tosses one of the balls in his right hand a few times then throws it as hard as he can, knocking down one of the bottles. He turns back to face Johnny with an O mouth, that he covers with a fist to barely mask his arrogant laugh.

"Devin, don't be like that," I say in a hushed voice, reaching toward his arm. He jerks it away and glares at me with a scolding expression that makes me feel small.

I scan the area, feeling a bit lost and alone. Johnny's eyes haven't left Devin once.

"Devin, man. Chill," our friend Beau says. I think, thankfully, he finds this situation as awkward as I do.

"I'm so chill." Devin unleashes another throw, knocking down a bottle on the end.

The carnie shouts, "Winner!"

"Hey, Brynn. You can have the prize. I mean, seems fitting since I kissed you first that I should also get you a bear first, huh?"

I flit my gaze to him, my blood boiling at his behavior. He grips the ball tight after a short toss in the air, then throws it as hard as he can at the stand. He misses the bottles completely. It nails a corner of one of the platforms and ricochets out of the booth and down the row where a little boy picks it up and runs to his mom to brag about his treasure.

"And a pink bear for the gentleman in plaid," the game guy

says. He tugs one of the bears loose from where it's clipped to a net, handing it to Devin who holds it out for me.

"I don't want it," I say, forcing myself to look him in the eyes. He smells like weed, and his eyes are puffy and red.

He stuffs his tongue in his cheek and smirks at me for a few seconds before looking over my shoulder. "Hey, cutie. Yeah, you," he shouts. I don't turn to see who's behind me, but eventually another girl steps into our small group and Devin tosses the bear to her.

"Aww, thank you," she squeals. She has two friends with her who all coo over the kind gesture, but all I can think of is how I want to push Devin into the booth on the other side where rubber ducks float in a fake pond.

Devin drops his gaze back on me for a beat, then turns to walk the few steps over to Johnny. He lunges at him, but Johnny doesn't flinch.

"You're welcome, Bishop. I warmed her up for you." Devin's always been moody, but he's never been outright mean. I feel as if all of this is more about Johnny ditching the band than *me* and Johnny. Either way, it's childish. And it's making me uncomfortable.

"Go home, Devin," I say.

"Excuse me?" He flips around to meet my eyes, flattening a hand over his chest as if he's actually offended.

"Look," I say, emboldening myself to do the hard thing and be the bigger person. I close the distance between us and stand nearly chest to chest. "I'm sorry I didn't talk to you when it happened, and I'm sorry it went down the way it did, but I really like Johnny. I have feelings for him, and he likes me, too. I never meant to lead you on or anything."

My eyes pool with pleading emotion, and for a moment I think Devin might apologize and backtrack out of this situation he's stirred. But then he suddenly laughs hard, his breath blasting my face, the smell of weed and hard liquor swirling around me. I step back and scrunch my nose.

"I don't do girlfriends, Bishop. It's fine," he says, enough bite to his words to indicate it isn't *quite* fine.

"Then why are you acting like this?" I ask.

"Because he's pissed at me and doesn't think I belong," Johnny butts in. His eyes meet mine then shift right to Devin. He tosses one of the balls in his hands and chews at his lip. "He thinks I'm an asshole for not showing up at halftime. And he thinks you're some trophy I don't deserve."

"Fuck no, you don't deserve her!" Devin shoves Johnny's side, but he braces himself for the impact and barely moves.

"Come on. Man up!" Devin tugs the neck of Johnny's double shirt, twisting it as if he's ready to send his other fist into Johnny's face. Johnny's nostrils flare, and his hand flexes where it clutches the ball. His other hand, though, remains open, fingers flexed. It's as if he's physically forcing himself to not engage, no matter how hard Devin pushes.

As their standoff continues, Devin fidgets, glancing to me then to his friends. The reality of how this looks seems to seep into his conscience. He lets go of Johnny's shirt, taking a slow step back then dropping his focus to the gravel beneath our feet.

"I'm sorry, Devin. I let you down, and I'm sorry," Johnny says.

Devin's head snaps up and he blinks slowly, his mouth moving as if it's trying to decide what kind of words to respond with.

Johnny's eyes flit to me.

"And I like her a lot, Devin. I respect her and I like her a lot."

My chest fills and I smile on the inside, careful not to glow or gloat. But this declaration, the class of it and the maturity?

This is why I chose him. This is what I fell for and why I like this boy so much. He's full of surprises, and every page in his story draws me in to him more.

"Fuck, man," Devin says, pinching the bridge of his nose and breathing out a laugh that's colored with his high. "I'm just fucked up tonight, yo. And I know . . . we're good. I'm . . ."

Devin shakes his head and laughs more, never uttering the word sorry even though that's what we all expect. I think it's what he wants to say, but that ego inside of him holds a lot hostage, including his character.

"We're good, Devin. I'll see you Monday," Johnny says.

Devin nods a few times, the girl he gave the bear to long gone. She drifted away sometime after he tried to force Johnny into a fight. Beau punches his friend in the arm, urging them toward the back of the fair, where the fences are low and where I'm sure they parked to smoke before sneaking in. A lot of locals get in that way.

I hold my breath until they're out of hearing range, then turn my attention back to Johnny, whose eyes are set on them beyond me. I think he's making sure they really leave.

"I'm sorry about that. I should have talked to him about us," I say.

His eyes snap to mine.

"Not your job. And you should not be sorry for a thing. That's all on him. His choice to act like that. And he can own it when his head is right."

I nod lightly, sensing something more behind his words, a seriousness in his eyes that hazes them a little. It lasts for a few seconds, and he quickly tucks it behind a broad smile that I can tell isn't as genuine as he makes it seem. He didn't like what happened just now, but I'm not going to give it any more time than it's already stolen.

"One panda, coming right up."

I step back as he winds up again, this time sending the ball zinging toward a bottle in the very middle. It shatters at the neck, which lends to my dad's theory, but the game man tells us a broken one counts. Johnny snags the last two balls from the counter and proceeds to knock two more bottles down in seconds.

"Winner, winner!" the man shouts.

"Chicken dinner!" Johnny adds. The man climbs a small ladder and tugs one of the giant pandas loose, tossing it down to Johnny, who hugs it then turns to smoosh it between us.

"Joint custody," I joke.

"No, I can't take this thing to my house," he says, chuckling.

"Why, not panda friendly?" I say.

His mouth falls into a tight smile and he leaves it at that.

Johnny and I have a thing we do. We tell each other truth lies, and sometimes we don't have to utter them out loud. That look he gave me just now? That was a wordless truth lie—he's happy to make me happy, and sad about the unsaid things about his home.

I blink a few times as I take the bear fully into my arms. It's so big I can't see over it, so Johnny guides me down the midway and to the exit. My dad is waiting in the long line of cars there to pick up fairgoers. Johnny waves him down, then takes the bear for me, hoisting it over one shoulder as we jog toward my dad's car.

"I see we have an extra passenger," my dad praises.

"He knocked over three bottles," I declare. My dad gives me side eyes, always the skeptic. I set the bear in the front seat, next to my dad, and buckle him in to be funny.

"Huh. I'll be damned," my dad says, maybe softening his stance that all fair games are run by crooks.

We regale my dad with highlights from our night as he zooms down the interstate then pulls onto the highway that leads to Yucca Valley. We conveniently leave out the parts where we made out until my lips were raw from Johnny's whiskers and when Devin tried to lure Johnny into a fight. By the time we reach Johnny's house, my dad seems to be teetering on the edge of wanting to go to the fair himself next year. I'm about to suggest it to him when Johnny opens the car door and the sounds of shouting seep from his house.

"That's all you do is play around and make art, spend my money. You're like a whore, only nobody wants to fuck you!"

I gasp and flatten my back against my seat, my eyes jetting to meet my father's stare in the mirror. Johnny has one leg out of the car, one in, and his grip on the front seatback is tight enough to puncture the vinyl.

"You won't let me work!" Johnny's mother's voice sounds frantic, and I slide to the middle to grab Johnny's arm. He holds up his palm.

"Son, should we call someone for you?" My dad is leaning over the console, his focus locked on the open garage door in front of us and the shadows that periodically cast across the driveway.

Johnny's body is rigid, his hand still up to me, the other bracing his weight on the car door. His chest is working hard, pumping air in and out too fast. He's going to pass out if he keeps this up.

"Johnny?" I whisper.

After a few more seconds, Johnny slowly backs into the car again, pulling the door closed but barely latching it so it doesn't make a sound.

"We can go to the police," my dad suggests.

"No, uh . . . no," Johnny stammers. His gaze is on the open garage, too. His mouth working on invisible gum as his eyes twitch along with his upper lip as if he's mentally working through every possibility.

Ginger Scott

"Would you like to stay at our house tonight? Meg can make up the sofa bed. It's pretty comfortable. And I could always bring you back in the morning. *Early.*"

My father's gaze hits mine again in the reflection.

"Yeah, I think. Yes, sir. I'd like that." Johnny's hand feels to his left in search of the buckle. I help him by pulling it out for slack and putting it in his hand. My dad shifts into reverse and backs us out slowly, and he doesn't press the gas until we're well into the dirt road that leads from Johnny's house.

I take Johnny's hand and he squeezes tight, not letting up for the entire drive to my house. My dad turns the radio on to fill the heavy void now filling the car with a darkness. My mind hopscotches through every clue—from the scars on his side, the black eye, and the harsh introduction to his dad. His mother is so kind. Johnny seems to be so much of her.

"He wasn't supposed to be home," he utters quietly as we pull onto my street.

I cover our locked hands with my free one and his head swivels until our eyes meet. There's a blankness to his stare, almost as if he's been stripped of the ability to show feeling.

"I'm sorry," he says.

Before I can tell him not to be, my dad does it for me.

"You can stay as long as you need, whenever you need. You are welcome here, son. You're safe."

Chapter 19
Present

Johnny's ten times the guitar player I am. Still, it stings to see my father's Martin in his hands. If I really wanted it, I suppose I should have asked. I'm sure my dad would have given it to me. Maybe deep down I always knew he held on to it to give to Johnny one day.

It's his *now*. And it fits him like the perfect pair of jeans. It's an extension of him, more than any other guitar has suited him. I'm glad he has it, but I'm jealous. There has always been a thread of envy running through me when it comes to Johnny.

He spent the rest of the evening after our visit with his mom out on my patio, experimenting with new riffs. I pretended to work on lesson plans at the kitchen table while I listened. Every now and then, he would add a few words, then scribble them down in his book. His voice cut like a knife. Yet I sat there glued to that chair until he packed up and told me good night.

"You know everyone wants to transfer into this class now, don't you?" Principal Baker rarely visits my class herself, so I snort a short laugh at her observation since she's standing by the door with me.

"Big rush on musical theory, huh?" I cock a brow.

"I mean, it does boost the program even more than it already is." She glances up and waggles her head, those invisible dollar signs she's always stressed about almost visible in the air above her.

"Yeah, but the thing that makes this program good is the people in it actually do the work, and churn out music, and have talent." I nod toward Jade, one of the few students to pass through here since Johnny Bishop who might actually have more talent than he does.

"So we build another beginning class." She shrugs as if that's something I can pull out of a hat, not even flinching at the hard laugh I huff out in response.

"We'll discuss."

I lift my hand, ready to gesticulate all of the discussion points I'd like to get out right now, but she walks away before I have a chance. She takes my chair behind the desk I rarely use, leaving me to stand on my own while my assistant, MaryAnn, finishes filling out attendance forms for the day and Johnny tunes the Martin at the front of the room.

MaryAnn nods to me when she's done, so I kick the stopper out of the way and let the classroom door slam closed. The bang jolts everyone in their seats, and instead of leaning forward and staring at Johnny, all eyes in the classroom are on me. I clasp my hands and smile.

"There are my students' faces." I smirk and flit my gaze to Johnny, who shakes his head. He knows I borrowed that move from my dad. He did it at least once a week back in the day, and it scared the shit out of us every time.

"As most of you know, Mr. Bishop—"

"Call me Johnny," he sneaks in.

I tighten my mouth and glance off to the side with an

exhale. We talked about this on the way in this morning—about him undermining me.

"Or Mr. Bishop. Or Johnny Bishop. Full name, definitely. Professional." He rambles out a few more options that do nothing more than rile up the class of twenty-five into giggling fits.

I hold out my palms and he mouths *sorry*.

I push the door open and let it slam shut again, calming the chatter and making my point, albeit in a bit of a passive aggressive way. This is *my* classroom.

"You may continue to call me Ms. Fisher," I say, cutting off the quiet laughs that threaten to build again. They stop as I walk through the center of the room, down the carpeted risers to where Johnny is sitting on the practice stage. We rehearse our small-group performances in here and it's where the various instruments hold sectionals. The main band room is on the other side of the office and dressing rooms, and it works when the entire marching squad is in here. But this room has the acoustics. Johnny deserves to be heard in perfect conditions, no matter how uncertain I still am of this experiment.

"Since all of you are working on your auditions for the winter concert and your applications to various programs, I thought we could start today off with a little lesson in performance."

I pace as I talk. Usually, I do it to keep the kids engaged with my movement; today, it's totally due to nerves. My knees quiver when I stand still for too long. And I wore a dress today, a green one that flows in an uneven cut around my knees. When I shake, I basically look like a bell, my black-boots knocking against the fringed hem on either side.

"I know you all have heard Johnny's story, and you got to know him a little more when he visited yesterday, but today we get to dive a bit deeper into what makes Johnny Bishop so good."

"Because he's hot!" Kristen, who plays drum set and has the class clown role nailed down to perfection, sets off a new round of tittering.

I glance to my right where Johnny is sitting with one leg outstretched, the other propped on the middle rung of the stool. My neck warms at the sight of him, and as smooth as he is in the face of being called hot, I'm lit with embarrassment.

"The world is full of *hot* people," I respond, trying to deflect.

"Wow, way to take a compliment from a guy," Johnny quips.

I laugh with the class this time, but use Johnny's quick wit as lesson number one.

"Now *that!* There it is." I lift myself up to take a seat on one of the side tables pushed to the edge of the room, crossing one leg over the other as I wait for a few long seconds to make everyone curious. I also like the way Johnny smiles when he's not sure what's going on. His tongue pushed behind his teeth, his eyes moving around the room—to me.

"Johnny Bishop may very well be *hot,* as you say, Kristen. But looks alone aren't his *it* factor. Neither is skill. If it came down to skill, do you all think I would still be teaching high school music theory in the middle of the desert?" Half of the students blink their gazes to me, and I have a feeling my boss is looking at me, too. I've never talked about my dreams *before* Johnny Bishop. I suppose most of the students to pass through my class over the last decade assumed this was my crowning achievement, to follow in my dad's footsteps.

"The *it* factor, ladies and gentlemen, comes down to personality. It's about the performance. Let me illustrate. Err, rather . . . Johnny, will you help me illustrate?"

Johnny lifts his chin along with one side of his mouth.

"Yes, Ms. Fisher."

I give him a quick glare for being so pointed in the way he said my name, but move on because this lesson is going to make a huge difference for some of the kids in here, the ones who are right on the cusp of next level.

"Will you play the happy birthday song for me, and pretend you're giving a small-venue acoustic performance at a pre-party for the Oscars?" It's a mouthful of directions, and it takes Johnny a few moments to get into character. But eventually, he picks out a gentle riff that is reminiscent of the birthday song, his head crouched and guitar propped on his knee. He holds the body of the guitar close, almost as if his eyes are scanning for the right strings to pluck nanoseconds before he plucks them.

Everyone leans in to search the strings with him. As the volume builds and Johnny finally brings his head up, we all slowly sink back in our seats. We aren't relaxed. We're ready. Ready for whatever he wishes to do to us, wherever he cares to take us. We're hooked.

His gaze seems to be locked on Kristen, and judging from the way her eyes are frozen wide open, I'm guessing she gets the point right about now.

The tune settles into something more familiar, but still derivative. Johnny's lips part with a downright seductive breath before he begins to sing. This isn't the pop star or the rock voice that echoes in arenas. This voice is soft, intimate—the sound of secrets set to melody. My point is made by the first verse, but I let it play out because . . . well . . . he's Johnny Bishop, and even the fucking birthday song is that good when he plays it.

He carries on the trickle of strumming, his playing mimicking a gentle stream and wind chimes. And when he rests the guitar flat on his lap again, nobody makes a sound.

Ginger Scott

"Holy shit." Kristen, naturally, is the first to break the respectful quiet.

I glance to my boss, whose mouth is hung open. I think I can get away with this one in here.

"Indeed, Kristen. Holy shit," I say.

My swear loosens everyone up again, but the effect of Johnny's song lingers in the room.

"Was his voice good? Yes. Was he . . ." I clear my throat, my body temperature a tad on the flushed side. "Was he sexy? Sure, maybe."

Definitely.

"Was it just a birthday song? Yes. And we all know how simple that piece is to play, and how little skill is required. Yet a moment ago, you all were positively mesmerized. Because Johnny took all of the tools he has at his disposal, and poured them into performance, into personality. He built an entire character and painted a scene over sixty-five seconds. And that is what he is here to teach you how to tap into. That's what he will get out of each of you."

A few students clap, Kristen the most enthusiastic. She's not being funny for attention this time, though. She's jazzed to learn to be her best performing self. She is me when I was her age, the first time I saw what Johnny Bishop could do. Was he handsome? Devastatingly so. But more than being *seen* by him, I wanted to *be* him.

"Now, who is ready to take their turn and let him see what you've been working on?" I slip down from the table and pace across the front of the room, taking in my students' anxious faces. Their heads bob and swivel, each looking to another to be the first to volunteer. I'm about to pick someone at random when Johnny chooses for me.

"Why don't you show them what you can do?"

Huh? No, no, no . . . that's not how this goes.

"They've all seen me," I say, waving my hand at him.

"Sure, they've seen you teach. But have they seen what you can really do?" He's persistent. I should have remembered this. His confidence has always been one of the qualities I envied the most.

"Trust me, they aren't going to learn anything from seeing me up there . . . again." My nervous laughter is so transparent, there's no way everyone in this room doesn't read exactly how badly I don't want to do this. And since they're all seventeen and eighteen years old, they are going to want me to torture myself for their amusement. Because teenagers are all dicks.

"Who wants to see Ms. Fisher take a stab at performance?" Johnny urges them to clap with him, and of course, because he's freaking magnetic, they all do.

He's a dick too. They are all dicks.

"All right," I give in, because dragging this out is only going to make the painful attention last longer. I hold up my palms, then head to the back of the stage to grab a second stool.

You're dead, I mouth to Johnny, drawing a line across my neck. Some of the students chuckle at the way I discipline him, and at least I can make them laugh. That's something, I suppose, even if I will never be able to make them feel the way Johnny did.

I situate myself on the stool, tucking my skirt under my thigh as I cross my leg. I reach for the guitar, but Johnny twists slightly to keep it out of my reach.

"Come on, you got to use the guitar. I can't do this without a crutch." My mouth is watering and my arms tingle. I like hiding behind the guitar, and playing while I sing has always given me something to look at other than the people staring at me. Unlike Johnny, connection terrifies me. *What if I see disappointment in their faces?*

"You can't play the song, if I remember correctly." He lifts a brow.

"The birthday song? Uh, yeah. I think I can." He's starting to piss me off. More.

He shakes his head and strums, the notes all over the place at first. That's one of his favorite ways to tease people, to flirt with a key and melody for a while before settling in and revealing what's to come. It's great to watch him do it in the middle of a concert. Sitting on a wooden stool in front of my students? Not great. Not great at all.

"You aren't going to do the birthday song, Brynnie. This is about performance, remember?"

His brow lowers and his eyes lock on mine. He bites the tip of his tongue through a devious grin and the melody for "Landslide" begins to come together. My favorite song. The one I showcased our senior year, when I came in second. To him.

I shake my head but he nods. My pulse races, and my legs feel numb. I shift my position, crossing my other leg on top and running my sweaty palms down my thighs in an attempt to wake them up. I breathe out with my lips pulled into a tight O, my eyes flitting to Johnny, then to the floor. I haven't uttered the words to this song in front of anyone in a decade. And other than the safety of my car, I haven't sung with any sense of seriousness. I hum notes and maybe a short refrain so students know how something goes. I use my voice to show what key something is in, my perfect pitch a useless gift in terms of personality.

In terms of performance.

Johnny passes through the intro twice, slowing at the place where I'm supposed to jump in. I'm paralyzed, though, and I can't get air to fill my lungs let alone come back out of me to form sound.

A slight shake of my head as my eyes well with panic is as

much as I can offer before I stuff my hands under my thighs. Johnny keeps playing, though. He leans forward and looks me in the eyes, and this time, when he reaches the section meant to have words, he sings them. His voice is faint, the way a grade school teacher prompts fourth graders in a choir performance. And as embarrassed, terrified, and angry as I am, his effort tugs at the corner of my mouth, and when the third line comes up, I sit taller and join him at "snow-covered hills."

The corners of his mouth rise more, and I mirror him, pushing the words out, using my diaphragm to carry me through until I'm coasting. Johnny never stops singing along with me, but gradually, he lets me lead, his voice slipping in at the right spots, adding depth and weight to the words that mean the most.

The changing ocean tides.

The seasons.

Growing older.

We're both growing older.

Together, we sing the entire song. Whether Johnny intended it to or not, as our voices blend in that way only the two of us can, the song takes me back to the very first time our voices fell into sync. Alone in this very room. On these very stools.

This song.

It hits me like the landslide it is, and my chest shudders through the final words. My students, the ones I have kept a careful wall up for, are on their feet clapping. My boss wipes a tear away, and MaryAnn is clutching her chest. And while Johnny was good and is part of the cause of their reaction, he's not the entirety of it. He's not even half. This praise is for me. I've missed it so much.

And it breaks my fucking heart.

Chapter 20
Age 18, A Quiet Sunday Night

My family doesn't go to church, except for the three times a year that the Spirit of the Desert hosts their fundraisers. My mom always professes that we, as a family, are spiritual. But truthfully? My mom is competitive, just like my dad is. Where he likes to win with music, she likes to *take the cake*. And as long as she contributes her shortbreads and pies three times a year, the good reverend makes her feel welcome and blessed. All of this love without me and Dad having to wake up early on Sunday mornings—it's a fair trade, my father says. I think he wouldn't mind going more often but for his great distaste of the music they play. Hard to be a jazz and blues aficionado and sit through a series of hymns all performed in the key of C with very little emotion and poor-quality microphones.

These three days a year are enough for me; I actually look forward to them. While my mom handles dollar bills for six hours on the church lawn, I sit in the very center of the adobe sanctuary, smelling the wood beams above my head and the constant trail of smoke from the candles burning at the front. The building is nearly sixty years old, and there is nothing overly remarkable about it. Yet, the way the sunlight peers through the wall of windows on the east and slowly moves to the matching ones on the west is this perfect, quiet tale of time.

It's where I think. At least, since I hit puberty this has been the place where I think. When I was a kid, I maybe sat in here for a minute before running through the back doors to the playground and sand pits with the tetherballs. But by age fourteen, when I had my first heartbreaking crush on a high school boy who didn't know I existed, I realized the power of sitting in a place alone. A room meant for contemplation. I could see my way through so many troubles in here. Doing God my way.

I spent half the day in the sanctuary today, thinking about Johnny. No matter how hard I searched, I couldn't find a solution to his troubles. What we saw last weekend was in a gray area, my dad explained to me. And even though I know in my gut that Johnny's dad has done more than shout at him and his mother, I can't prove it. And Johnny doesn't want to. Or maybe, more accurately, he doesn't *want* to want to.

The rope around my chest loosened when Johnny rang our doorbell just as we sat down for dinner. And now that he's sitting with my father's guitar on our back patio, I can breathe. I think my father can too.

"Are you comfortable holding it like that?" My dad's head falls to one side as he inspects Johnny's grip and the angle he sets the guitar. It's almost childlike, the way I would hug the guitar close to my body when I was first learning and my hands weren't big enough to reach everything.

"I guess?" Johnny laughs and repeats the chord structure he's been practicing.

My dad puckers his lips and nods as the sound comes out perfect, then holds his hands up to profess that if it works for Johnny, then who cares how he holds it.

"I'm turning in, but you two stay out here and play more. I like the way the music sounds through the window. In fact, keep playing because when you stop . . ." My dad taps his finger to his temple, insinuating that he'll know we're up to something else.

"Dad!" I throw one of my mom's outdoor pillows at him and he bats it away.

"Don't think I didn't woo your mom with that same guitar." He smirks.

"Ugh, go to bed. And thanks for the nightmares," I tease. Sort of.

"Thank you, Mr. Fisher. I'll take good care of it," Johnny says to my dad.

"I know you will, son." My dad's gaze moves to me, and for a moment I wonder if he meant that as a blessing. Deciding I'm acting like a silly dreamer, I wave him away.

Johnny picks out a faint melody as my dad closes the French doors. My father makes a point to flip on various lights inside, as if I can't make out with Johnny with the lights on. Though, can I? Now I'm thinking about it, and a little stressed, which . . . *ah, that was his point.*

"That's pretty. What is it?" I pull my legs up and tuck them inside my sweatshirt where I sit on the chaise lounge across from Johnny.

"I made it up. It's been stuck in my head for a few days." He plays the melody again, this time adding a few elements.

"I thought my dad gave you that guitar already. The night of the formal?"

Johnny smirks.

"You mean the night I first kissed you?" He strums a soft chord.

"Oh, I don't know. I think you kissed me well before that. I seem to remember a tryout for drum major on May seventh." I wink at him when he lifts his head and flattens the guitar on his lap. The smirk is still glued to his face.

"At seven forty-eight in the morning," he adds.

My mouth hangs open as I lower my brow.

"You're making that up. You didn't seriously note the time of our first kiss." I wish I did, and if that's right, I will forever etch it next to the memory.

Johnny holds my stare for a few seconds then shifts his attention back to the guitar, playing a few short notes as if they're meant to lead into his punchline.

"Yeah, I made that up. But I'm pretty sure it was close." He chuckles yet my heart sinks a little. I wish he really had memorized the time.

I swing my legs around and stretch them out on the chaise, folding my hands behind my neck so I can look up at the sky. There's a thin veil of clouds over the moon and stars. Fall is setting in and the warm days turn into very cold nights. That's the secret of the desert. People assume it's hot here all the time, but as brutal as the heat is, the cold is just as bitter.

"To answer you, though, your dad did give it to me. I hope that's okay." Johnny plucks one string, then deadens it quickly.

I roll my head to find his gaze waiting.

I smile, and it's genuine. I was a little jealous at first, only because my dad seems to see so much promise in Johnny musically. But my perspective has changed. Maybe it's because I now know all I have in my life that Johnny doesn't, or perhaps it's how well I've come to know him, period. He deserves to have a guitar, because the stars deserve to hear him play.

"Of course it is. You can take it home," I encourage.

He shakes his head and whispers, "No, I can't."

Any hint of joy slips away when he utters that reality, and I can't keep my smile up, either. I hate that he has this gift that he can't nurture at home. He should be playing guitar non-stop. Every morning. Every night.

"You'll just have to come over more often," I say.

His mouth tugs up at that suggestion, and his eyes linger on mine for several quiet seconds. The intensity of it makes my upper lip twitch like Elvis. My legs tingle, and I pull them up to my chest to hug them and rub my hands over my shins.

"Cold?" Johnny sets the guitar at his side and pulls his hoodie up over his head.

"I'm fine," I lie. He laughs under his breath and proceeds to drape his sweatshirt over my legs.

"Now you're better," he says, picking up the guitar and sitting next to me on the chaise. My hip rests against his lower back, and I lean into it a little, wanting it to be more.

"I am. Thank you," I say.

Johnny glances down, his hair a floppy mess that I instantly push my hand into and ruffle. I giggle like a groupie on a date she won with her favorite poster boy, and Johnny glances up at my hand.

"Why do you like my hair so much?" His gaze falls down to me, and I twist a few strands of hair around my fingers before letting them go.

"This hair is going to make you famous. Mark my words," I say, crossing my chest.

His eyes narrow and his mouth pulls in tight, almost like he has a secret.

"What? You doubt me?" I push myself to sit up a little, still not quite to his eye level, and not enough to abandon the place where our bodies touch. There would need to be a fire or a bear coming at us for me to do that.

"Can I play something for you?" He breathes in slowly, his jaw working side to side, and I get the sense that he might actually be nervous.

"Of course. I mean, please." My eyes instantly move to his hands. I note the way they hover a fraction of a centimeter over the strings before landing in a place he seemingly knows by heart.

Johnny said he taught himself on his mother's guitar before she got rid of it, and he said he was a decent player but never really had a chance to practice. But the way his hands move, the tenderness and intention of each note he creates, indicates he must have found a way. You can't create music like Johnny is right now without knowing how. At least, I can't.

His eyes follow along with every shift in key and change in volume. It's as if he's drawing the plan out with his vision and his hands simply follow along, playing something written with his heart. The building chord structure rises in intensity and I look up at the closed windows on the second story of our house. Even though they're shut, my father must hear this. This secret audition Johnny is giving can't stay in the bottle. It's out. It should be out.

And then he stops.

"John—" My voice cracks at the start of his name, but my mouth snaps shut as he begins to sing. His playing softens to match his voice, allowing his gift to take center stage. For the first several lines, my mind is unable to decipher the words, my eyes too mesmerized by his lips. My ears too taken with the pure golden honey that seems to flow from him with ease. It's like listening to your favorite record, the scratches included, thanks to the God-gifted imperfections that are utterly perfect.

I blink a few times as he begins what sounds like the refrain.

Bolder than the storm, I must be bolder than the storm.

Quicksand starts to swarm and then the cold heart steals the warmth.

Too small to take the lightning from you, too small to see the harm.

You've lived a life half of one so I'd be bolder than the storm.

It's the start of a song. A beautiful song filled with so much of him that it's impossible not to hear the words sung in that voice and not feel the weight of being in his shoes, just for a moment. One beautiful, terrified moment. I wipe the tear falling down my cheek before he drops his chin and lowers the guitar to look at me. Not that I don't want him to see the effect, but so he doesn't hurt more than whatever it was that inspired that song.

"It's not done, and I might change some of it. But it feels like something, and—"

"It's incredible."

He sucks in his bottom lip at my interjected praise.

"You're just saying that." He shrugs. I sit up taller and wrap my hands around his bicep.

"I'm not. Johnny, you have a gift. And it's more special than I realized. I . . ." I look up to the closed windows, the lights off in my parents' room. My dad heard that. I know he did. He's probably paralyzed from it, from the magnitude of what's sitting down here on his patio playing a guitar older than I am. Johnny is a rare diamond, an interstellar miracle.

"Johnny," I lower my gaze back to his. "You have to keep going. You need to finish that and you need to showcase it."

His face bunches.

"Showcase?"

I forget sometimes he hasn't always been one of us.

I nod vehemently.

"Yeah, showcase. It's the big concert they have every year at Pappy & Harriet's." I'm already envisioning his performance and the reaction it will draw. The audience for the showcase has never been left stunned silent, but I swear if he can deliver half of what he just did for me, they will be.

"That western bar in the tourist section? That's a big show?" He silently chuckles but I move closer to him, taking the guitar from his lap and setting it on the nearby tiled table. I take both of his hands in mine, and he runs his thumbs over the tops of my hands in nervous circles.

"I don't mean to freak you out. But that bar? Yes, it's a big deal. The showcase? It's a big show. Those signed album covers and famous photos hung in the hallway by the band room? Those are all people who performed at the showcase and won. Hell, some of them came in second. And the really famous ones? They couldn't do what you just did for me right now."

My fingers thread through his and I clutch him tight, jostling his arms to force his attention. I want to will him to believe me when I express how much I believe in him.

"What did I do for you?" His gaze rests on mine, his eyes penetrating me with a hopeful intensity. If I lied, he would see right through me, and I think he knows it.

"You broke me in the best possible way, and I will never, *not ever,* be able to hear music the same again."

He blinks once, but I don't. Unflinching, I shake my head slowly to emphasize how serious I am, never once breaking our gaze.

"Never again. And I don't care, because I heard that. Even if I only hear it once, I am lucky." I'm prepared to layer it on more, to do whatever it takes to build his ego when it comes to this. But suddenly his mouth is on mine, and his hands are sliding up the base of my neck into my hair.

"I believe you," he utters against my mouth.

I smile through our kiss.

"Good," I say, my teeth tugging on his lower lip.

Johnny shifts and sweeps his hands under my thighs, lifting

me so I'm sitting on his lap, straddling him as he lays down on the chaise. My hair cascades around us, proving that even with all the lights on in the house I can still find a way to kiss him in the dark.

I can feel him growing hard underneath me, and I let my weight sink down more to enjoy the pressure of having him there between my legs. His breath picks up every time my hips rock, and eventually his hands slide into the back pockets of my shorts, gripping my ass through the denim to urge me into him more.

"Brynnie," he whispers at my ear before taking a small nibble of my earlobe. He trails kisses down my neck, then bites at the collar of my shirt.

"I wish I could take this off, but your dad would kill me," he says.

My eyes squeeze shut as I silently curse the fact that we're not *alone* alone. I don't know what one does in this position. I'm barely sure I'm kissing him right, that this is making out. But since I can feel his hard-on trying to break through the zipper of his jeans, I must be doing something right.

Pressing both of my hands on his shoulders, I push him back so he's lying flat. Before he can question whether I'm trying to bring this to a stop, I drag my palms down his arms to his wrists, and I urge his palms up my thighs, then my stomach, guiding him to the edge of my bra underneath my shirt.

"You don't have to take it off to touch me," I murmur, biting my lip because I want to seem sexy.

"Gah!" Johnny groans, sliding his hands the rest of the way until he's palming both of my breasts. His touch is practically scalding hot against my skin, and my head falls back when his thumbs slide the cups of my bra to the side, giving him access to my incredibly hard nipples. When he pinches them, I rock against him uncontrollably, which makes him groan again.

He flicks the raw tips under my shirt a few times before pressing them with his thumbs and circling them. It's like a game, and I don't care to win. Johnny sits up, sliding one of his hands behind me, down into my shorts, under my underwear. His bare hand is cupping my ass, fingers teasing with curves I didn't know could feel so alive. He pulls me against him and I move my legs so they're wrapped around him completely, bringing my throbbing center as close to his hard-on as I can through our clothes.

Johnny's hips jerk as he tugs me into him, his mouth covering mine with an urgent hunger that drives his tongue into my mouth. I like it, the way he's desperate to taste me. And when he tugs on my nipple again, rolling the bud between his finger and thumb, something builds between my legs. It's not quite a vibration, but it's as if it's trying to become one. My hands claw at his back, feeling his muscles work as he seems to chase this feeling in my core. Then I realize he's chasing his own.

I'm going to orgasm.

My nails scratch along his back, bringing fistfuls of his black T-shirt into my sweaty grip as I break our kiss and press my mouth against his neck to muffle my whimper as I fall over the edge and into bliss.

"Oh, fuck," he says, his mouth buried in the crook of my neck. He falls back with his hands now on my hips, controlling my movement with a fast, steady rock as he bucks up into me. My head falls back as my hands flatten on his belly, and I grip the fly of his jeans, wishing I had the guts to unzip them and finish things differently. Instead, I roll my hips in such a way that I think I'm stroking him with my aching parts. I do it until his eyes roll back and he thrusts up a few more times.

When his hips stop moving, I collapse against him and close my eyes, the sound of his voice and that song still imprinted in my memory as if I'm hearing it right now. Eventually, Johnny points up at something and I shift to lay at his side.

"I bet you ten bucks your dad cuts that tree tomorrow," he whispers. I stare at the thin branches that cover just enough to muddy the view of us from the upstairs windows. I giggle then twine our hands together, kissing Johnny's knuckles.

"I bet you twenty he tears up the whole goddamned patio."

Chapter 21
Present

I had forgotten how much watching him sing affected me. I'd somehow disassociated from his performances on TV. It was easy to pretend he was someone else. Most average people aren't friends with rock stars. And we weren't really friends anymore, so he was this noise that was out there, beyond me. I could choose to ignore it.

But now that he's in my classroom every morning, in my home every night, playing constantly . . . I can't pretend there isn't something deeply personal about watching Johnny Bishop sing a song. I don't think it hits Teddy the same way it does me. He drove into town this morning with his fiancée, Simone. We decided to give in to my mom's persistence for dinner, and the fall evenings are perfect for outdoor dining.

"You know she already said yes to the ring. You don't have to impress her by making your rock star friend sing her favorite songs." I wedge my way into their circle with the tray of mini burgers my dad grilled. I set them on the bricks that line the backyard fire pit, then plop into one of the open chairs as Johnny finishes up a cover of a Taylor Swift song.

"Shoot, that's not her favorite. Tay Tay is from my playlist, Brynnie." Teddy grins, then quietly applauds as Johnny strikes the final chord.

Everyone leans in and grabs a burger before my mom joins us with a second tray of food. This is how she shows love, and after running her own catering business for most of my dad's teaching career, she's gotten pretty proficient in the language. This second tray is lined with something called potato smashes, piled high with feta and fig. I make my dad eat one first because the words *smash* and *fig* aren't high on my elementary-esque palette list. When he hums, I know I'm in the clear and take one of my own.

"Johnny, honey. I made you lemonade. I can put it in one of those fancy glasses if you want so you don't feel left out." My mouth falls open and I nearly lose the food inside at my mom's ridiculous offer. My dad nearly chokes.

"Thank you, Mrs. Fisher, but I'll be fine. I'm not like a vampire. I can see beer bottles without having to go wild. I can handle a cookout." Johnny takes my mom's hand and squeezes it before kissing the back to show his appreciation for her gesture. When his gaze moves to mine from across the flickering flames, I mouth *sorry*. He shakes his head and smiles. My dad and Teddy each shift their beer bottles to the ground by their feet, seeming to take the hint from my mom's speech.

Even though Johnny says it doesn't bother him, I've seen him struggle once or twice. His legs grow restless at night when he sits on the patio, and I hear him up late most nights. I don't know that he sleeps much at all, and I'm sure there are temptations and cravings that call out to him. The first thing he said after leaving his mother's house after our first visit was how badly he needed a drink. Instead, he went to a therapy session at Waves. I drove him, then waited in the car.

"Theodore, tell us how you and Simone met." My mom's sights have firmly moved on, and both Johnny and I snicker at her use of *Theodore*.

"Well, Mamma Meg," Teddy says. My mom coos as he sweet talks her. She settles in on the chaise next to my dad, ready to listen.

"We had a beach practice for the team. They think it's a reward to get to play on the beach, but in reality, it's freaking hard to run in sand. So I get more out of the kids that way," Teddy explains. "Anyhow, I saw this beautiful woman running into the surf with her board."

"Oh, you're a surfer," my mom praises, a bit awestruck. Gee, her daughter is only a master musician. No big deal, I suppose, since she's also married to one.

"I am. Two golds in the last summer games," Simone says, not a hint of arrogance.

Okay, I might be a little smitten with her now too.

"Well, you know the move. Remember the move, Johnny?" Teddy chuckles as he swats at Johnny's arm. The two of them share a look, and I scoot to the edge of my seat, wondering what moves they were helping one another with while Johnny and I were dating.

"You two had a move?" My eyes narrow and dash between the two of them.

Johnny meets my gaze and drops his chin, making a point to single me out.

"Let's be clear . . . *Teddy* had a move. I was his wingman."

"Wing. Man." I furrow my brow, still not liking the idea that my boyfriend at the time was somehow involved in a pick-up scheme for girls. My former boyfriend. From high school. A decade ago. *This should not matter so much.*

"Yeah, so we would play catch out in the quad or at the

park or something, and if there was a girl I wanted to talk to, Johnny would throw the pass a little too deep. Ya know . . . and I'd have to sort of brush into the girl. That would strike up a conversation, and I would look cool making the catch. And voilà."

"What he's not telling you," Simone interjects, "is that this time, his quarterback hit me in the back of the fucking head."

My parents and I cup our mouths and cough out a short laugh. Johnny slaps his forehead and leaves his palm in place as he gives Teddy a sideways look.

"What can I say, man. They don't make quarterbacks like they used to," Teddy jokes. His laughter halts when he glances to his other side and finds Simone's waiting glare.

"Anyway," she continues, leaning away from Teddy and toward my mom. "Teddy felt so terrible, he carried me to his truck and drove me to the ER to get checked out for a concussion. And then he insisted on staying by my side all night to make sure I didn't have any issues. And it turns out, this immature asshat is also a really sweet guy."

"And I never went home again," Teddy adds, taking Simone's hand and bringing her attention right back to him. He mouths *I love you,* and my body rushes with envy. An injection of morphine right into my veins.

I stand to leave. "Excuse me," I say, offering a polite tight-lipped smile I drop the moment my back is to everyone.

I toss my empty water bottle into my parents' recycling bin, then duck into the powder room off the kitchen. I don't bother flipping the light on or shutting the door as I flip on the cold water and fill my palms with enough to splash my face. I pull the turkey-themed hand towel off the hook and bury my face in it.

"You okay?"

I shake with a half laugh, half cry at hearing Johnny's voice. I pull the towel away and find him filling the doorway, a face full of concern. I push my fingertips into my forehead then straighten my sweatshirt, tugging it over my hips.

"Yeah, just . . ." I shake my head with my mouth open. How do I say that I always thought we would be the ones telling the engagement story?

"Our little Teddy is growing up?"

I laugh out hard and rest my hands on my hips.

"Yeah. He really is, isn't he?"

A vision of me grabbing Johnny's collar and tugging him toward me, kicking the bathroom door closed and kissing him flashes through my mind. I blink a few times and instead look down at the floor between us. It's quiet enough to hear the various sounds of the house—the water pump kicking on, the drip in the kitchen sink my dad never manages to fix, the hum of the refrigerator motor. Johnny's feet moving closer.

His palm meets my cheek yet doesn't startle me. A part of me saw it coming, I suppose. Or I wished for it.

I look up to meet his eyes, his soft smile. His thumb runs along my cheek just below my right eye.

"I really did miss you."

I breathe out a short laugh through my nose. His words feel empty. I put a hand on his shoulder and pat.

"I missed you, too, Johnny."

As I move around him, his hand slips from my face to around my waist, and my body turns into his. My palm flattens on his chest and our noses nearly touch. My heart begins running a marathon, the pounding felt in my fingertips and I'm sure rattling against the center of his chest. I half expect to be dipped in a kiss, like we were eighteen again. His eyes search mine, and for the briefest moment, I let go of my anger. My mouth opens slightly with a faint breath. If he kisses me right now, I will kiss him back. I'll take this and enjoy it and worry about the consequences later.

"Brynn? You in here?"

We both take a step back at the sound of my mom's voice. Our gazes drop and my hand falls, fingertips grazing the center of his T-shirt. His scent swirls around me, and I breathe it in, taking what I can from a moment of poor judgement. I step into the hall and toward my mother's voice.

"Coming!"

I find my mom attempting to carry two more trays of food the six of us won't possibly be able to eat. I take one from her hands and head back to the patio, my eyes moving to the chaise lounge. My mouth quirks into a tight smile that I straighten out before anyone can see it. Some thoughts are meant to be kept to myself. This patio holds a lot of memories, though.

"You know, Simone. If you need wedding decorations or a dress maybe, we still have some of Brynn's old things."

My eyes flutter shut as I flop down into my seat. The fact that I'm no longer married—that I was married, that I'm the one who kicked him out, that I don't have grandchildren for my mom yet—is her favorite topic. It's just never been one she's brought up with company. It's usually reserved for me on the phone, or in the car when we ride together, or at Thanksgiving dinner with the three of us as she wishes there were more people at her table.

"Meg," my dad chastises her.

"What? I mean, it's perfectly good stuff. All going to waste." My mom shrugs and pops one of her potato smashes into her mouth, humming at the good taste while sporting her smug smile. I love my mother. I also hate her passive aggressive streak.

"You're kidding me! Brynnie was married?" Teddy's shock is not flattering, in many ways. He also repeats those key points just as Johnny walks up and my eyes open right on his.

"It was brief. And really? Not something I like to talk about, Mom!" I roll my head and glare at my mother sideways. She won't get it. She never does.

"Oh, I know. He wasn't *the one.*" She flits her gaze to Johnny at that comment, and I feel the blood rise to every surface of my body, painting me red.

"No, he wasn't. He was a cheater, and a thief. And about a dozen other terrible things that we have gone over plenty of times." My head falls into my open palms and my fingertips find my temples.

"You were married?" Johnny's question comes out in a gravelly near whisper. I lift my head and find him sitting back in his chair, across the pit from me. I hold his gaze and do my best to forget about the other people in our space. I lift a shoulder, as if I owe anyone an apology for an impulsive decision I regret, but one I made on my own.

My father manages to right the conversation with a story about the time he caught Teddy and Johnny trying to TP our house. The three of them gathered up the rolls of toilet paper and headed over to the cheer coach's house and did a number on hers instead. While Teddy and my father laugh about it, Johnny plays along. His gaze, however, keeps coming back to me—questions in his eyes.

Eventually, my father brings the focus back to music by heading inside and bringing out his own guitar. He and Johnny used to spend hours playing together, and I would give anything to enjoy watching the two most important men to ever grace my life make beautiful music together. But my stomach is sick, thanks to my mother. This isn't how I wanted to dole out details about my life to Johnny. I'm still wrapping my brain around the idea that he deserves to know what I've been up to for ten years. I'm grappling with the nagging need to tell him things, a feeling that is showing up more often every day he's with me. The biggest problem of all is the fact that my mom was right about one thing she said—my ex-husband was certainly not the one. He wasn't even in the same ballpark as my one. And *my one* hurt me when he left.

My mouth aches from being forced into a smile. I wish nobody noticed that I've been so quiet for the last hour, but I know most of the people here have. Teddy has questioned me with his eyes, a subtle tilt of the head and brow lift to check that I'm okay. My father has squeezed my shoulder every time he's gotten up to use the restroom, which after three beers has amounted to a half-dozen trips.

Mom is less subtle, accosting me in the kitchen as I help her clean up with a straight-to-the-point, "So, I suppose I am going to get the silent treatment now?"

And then there's Johnny. We're more alike than either of us may have ever realized. My quiet is rivaled only by his. He hasn't sung once since my mom's surgical info dump, and my dad is choosing every song they play. They used to take turns.

Johnny finally breaks his silent treatment when his phone buzzes. He takes the call on the opposite side of my parents' yard, and I literally grip the sides of my chair to keep myself from going with him.

"His mom, probably," Teddy says. My mom nods and hums a sympathetic *oh*. But I know Teddy's saying that for my benefit. Because before he decided to visit with Simone this weekend, I called him and let slip a few tiny insights into some of my frustrations. I figured listening was the least he owed me since my roommate situation was partly his fault.

Johnny has been living with me for two weeks, and we've

managed to construct a delicate shift system where he joins me for class every morning then drives himself to regular meetings with a therapist at Waves before going to his mother's house for the rest of the day. We're rarely together alone, which has made our conversations focus more on logistics for the next day rather than the past. He has a rental Jeep now, thanks to his publicist. She's cute. They spend a lot of time together at her hotel room. I don't want it to bother me.

It bothers me.

I didn't have to say it, but Teddy picked up on it rather quickly. Unlike my mom, he didn't lord it over my head. Kaylee is actually very sweet, and a bit intimidating. She's loud, which most of the people in my life are not, at least not vocally. Now, give me an instrument and I'll blast her out of the water. But I can't compete with that five-two firecracker who wears six-inch heels and can melt a cellphone with the number of F-bombs she drops at someone on the other end of the line. It's impressive, and the next time I need to buy a car, I may ask Johnny if she'd be willing to handle the negotiation for me. I wouldn't be able to ask her myself because, well, she terrifies me.

She comes to the house every morning for coffee, because apparently they don't make it strong enough in town. I brew it special for her after I make two cups for me and Johnny. Kaylee also handles the random photographers who sometimes camp out on the street. She barks at them. Literally. And they tend to run, at least far enough to have to take their photos from a block away.

MaryAnn thinks it's pretty cool that I've shown up as a blur in the tabloids. She bought the rack out from the grocery store on Monday. *Mystery girlfriend from his past?* That was her favorite headline, because she's nosy and will not let up on her instincts. I'm pretty sure everyone at the school has figured out by now that we dated. Johnny has slipped up a few times, telling stories about the past to the students. And then there was our duet of "Landslide." As much as the two minutes I sang with him freed a voice I've buried for years, it also let some of my feelings seep through the cracks in my armor. I know I looked at him a certain way. I looked at him like I was drowning from the wave of memories crushing me.

I looked at him like I loved him.

I told the students it was performance, because that was the point of the lesson. But I wasn't performing. Neither was he. And for the last few hours, we both have been under the scrutiny of the one person who could always read my feelings for Johnny like they were plastered on my forehead. And Teddy and I both know it's not Johnny's mom on the phone. It's Kaylee.

I'm jealous and really don't want to be.

"I'm sorry, something's come up and I need to deal with a PR problem. This was really nice, though, Meg. Thank you. Next time maybe I can man the grill for you, Mr. Fisher. I owe you a meal or seven hundred." Johnny holds his palm out as my dad stands to shake it. He pulls Johnny in for a hug.

"You can take me out to one of those fancy places that costs a hundred dollars a plate. And not because I want to be expensive." My dad pulls back and holds Johnny's shoulders. "Over my dead body will you ever touch my grill."

The two of them laugh. My mom, tipsy from two glasses of wine, joins in. Johnny gives her a hug, then does the same to Simone before bro-hugging Teddy. "No matter how bad his haircut, he's a great guy," Johnny says, poking Teddy in the ribs before knocking his hat from his head.

He's given a personal good-bye to everyone, and for a moment I think he may walk through the back gate and hop in his Jeep without as much as a word to me. But I'm not so lucky. Instead, he glances over his shoulder so our eyes meet.

"I'll probably be late. Don't wait up."

His eyes linger on mine for a second, and my worst self rises to the occasion. I lift my chin.

"I never do."

Thankfully, I got my jab in without any witnesses. Teddy wouldn't be proud, and he'd want to talk about it and my feelings. And as sweet as Simone is, I'm not quite ready for her to be pulled into my fucked-up circle. I hug both of them as they leave, the party naturally breaking up since the famous guy is gone. I help my dad straighten up the patio and give him a hug too, then leave before he apologizes again for my mom.

I drive home in silence. Sometimes, I like to really sit with my thoughts when I drive, and music has a way of painting the mood. Right now, mine is sour, and I don't want anything sweetening it. I need to live in this uncomfortable feeling for a while so I can figure my shit out.

By the time I turn down my street, I've moved on from being angry with my mom to indignant toward Johnny. How dare he be offended that I was married! He may have not put a ring on some girl's finger, but he's had plenty of splashy relationships over the last decade. I can't ignore every tabloid photo I come across at the market. I pull into my driveway and let the motor run for a few minutes so I can have an argument with an invisible version of Johnny, then leave it in the car and forget about it.

Unfortunately, though, Johnny had other ideas, and just as I'm ready to leave this night behind, my car lights up from a set of headlights—Jeep headlights.

I breathe in slowly through my nose, my gut telling me serenity is going to evade me no matter how many hacks I try. I do the breathing anyhow, and when I step out of my car to confront him, I prepare myself to be nothing but gracious and concerned.

"How was Kaylee?" Or maybe a bitter, jealous ex. Seems that's the route I'm taking.

"Are you serious?" Johnny laughs out as he hits the key fob to lock the Jeep. It beeps and flashes us twice before going dim.

I shake my head.

"PR trouble sounded serious to me," I say with a shrug.

Johnny's eyes narrow as he looks at me with parted lips that aren't quite smiling but seem to want to. He pushes his hand into his hair and holds on to the strands, like he did when he was eighteen and adorable. It's adorable now, but also infuriating.

"If you must know, yeah. I have some pretty serious PR shit going on. There's a reporter working on a story that might just ruin my life, Brynn. But no, I didn't run to Kaylee to talk to her about it. I told her we'd deal with it tomorrow."

"Brynn," I say.

His eyes squint and his head shakes.

"You called me Brynn. Not Brynnie." My chest hurts, and the more words we say to one another the more I regret the ones I utter, and wish for self-control. I left that in my parents' back yard, though. Hell, I left it in the parking lot of Waves the night Johnny showed up.

He steps closer, but stops just out of reach. The wind has picked up, the palm trees at the end of my driveway rustling and the chill making me shiver. I pull the sleeves of my sweatshirt over my palms and cross my arms over my chest.

"I call you Brynnie when we're being friendly, but things don't feel so friendly right now."

I laugh out and look to the side, pushing my tongue into my cheek as a self-check to keep from speaking before thinking. I squeeze my eyes shut when my mind mentally replays my mom's words from tonight. The brain is amazing the way it can buzz through memories a thousand times in less than a second. My body rushes with the same adrenaline and disgust as it did when I lived through it the first time an hour ago.

"I married a real asshole during a bad time for me. I made some stupid choices, and I'm not proud of them. For the record, you would have hated the guy." I force my gaze back to Johnny's, anticipating a smug expression. The hard jawline that flexes as he presses his molars together is far from smug. It's closer to possessive.

I shift my feet to steady my posture because if we're doing this, I might as well tear every Band-Aid off all at once.

"Yeah, you know what else you should know? I slept with Teddy." My shoulders rise as my lips twist, selling the impression that it's no big deal what I did. But the bile that creeps up my esophagus the longer Johnny's jaw works and his eyes smolder at me doesn't make my confession so easy to brush off.

"What?" I press him.

His eyes flit to the side, toward my nosy neighbor who is probably making her popcorn this very second. His gaze shifts back to me. The whites of his eyes are red, and the way it clashes with his blue irises almost makes the entire thing purple.

"You have no idea how many times I wanted to come home, to come back to you." His voice cracks mid-confession, and my chest cracks with it.

"But you didn't. You left me, Johnny! You left Teddy too. You left us all!" My voice becomes raw, the cry I've been holding back crawling up my insides. I can't hold it back for much longer.

"I didn't want to, but I had to go." His mouth tucks into itself, the kind of smile that covers a whole lot of pain breaking apart when his bottom lip quivers.

"Did you? You *had* to?" I sniffle once, but it's no use in stopping the hard sob that breaks free from my throat. I cover my mouth, ashamed of it.

Johnny's head falls forward, his fingers pinching the bridge of his nose. His perfect, stupid hair a tussled mess, his ripped-up jeans tight in the right places, and his quilted flannel jacket over his black T-shirt begging my head to rest on his chest the way it used to.

"There is so much you don't know, Brynnie."

"Because you won't tell me," I hum.

I turn my back to him and march toward my porch, opening my door then turning to find him waiting for me at the bottom of the steps. This is his house too for now, so I don't know what we do here. I don't know what we do, period.

"You know you're the only one who won't hug me?" He shoves his hands deep in his pockets and pouts his lips in some sort of *gotcha* expression.

"You want a hug, Johnny? Is that what this is all about?" I glance to my neighbor's porch the second her light flicks on. Figures.

"Yeah, Brynnie. I want a hug. From you." He lifts his chin and stares at me with challenge in his eyes.

A breathy laugh leaves my nostrils.

"I hugged you. When you accosted me in my parents' powder room," I remind him.

He shakes his head.

"That wasn't you hugging me. That was both of us running out of places to hide."

I swallow the dry lump in my throat. Damn him and his perfect words. He could always write the best lines.

"Fine, Johnny. Come here and I'll give you a hug." My gaze burrows into his as my body flickers with anger and fear. I won't let this break me. I won't forget the last ten years because of this. I won't. I refuse.

Johnny climbs the steps and pauses a few inches from me, then glances down to my dangling arms.

"Really?" His head falls to the side as he studies me. The red is clearing some, but the hurt is still there. I see it, the way his eyes slope, the weight of his lids, the heaviness underneath his eyes.

"Fine," I say, lifting my hands and moving them around his neck.

Johnny steps in closer, tucking my head under his chin and circling me in his arms. My hands link behind him and I adjust my cheek against the center of his chest. Holding my breath, I force my eyes to remain open, thinking that somehow if I can do that, I won't feel. But it's no use because all he has to do is take a deep breath. I've always fallen in sync with him this way. It was an unspoken practice between us; when one was upset, the other would breathe for the one in pain.

My lungs fill slowly as his hands rub my back and his feet nudge me backward through the doorway. My eyes are closed by the time he kicks the door shut, and within seconds he's swept my legs up and is cradling me against his body as he carries me to my favorite chair. The broken one that's not *so* broken.

"Truth lie," he murmurs against the top of my head. The feel of his lips at my crown causes my body to grow limp. He's a drug. He always has been.

"Truth lie," I respond, ready for the question I know is coming.

"Are you jealous over my publicist?"

I let his question sit in the quiet of the dark room for several seconds, opening my mouth to respond at least five times before finally speaking.

"I'm as jealous as you are over my marriage and one night with Teddy." I shift enough to look up through my lashes and

271

study his expression. His lips pucker and his eyes haze as if in thought, but eventually he nods and tucks my head back against him, blocking my view.

"I'm completely, totally, absolutely fine with it," he says.

Truth lies spoken in a perfectly broken chair.

Chapter 22
Age 18, Cross Town Rivals Game

Performing the pregame show is always hard on the ego. Nobody pays attention to the away band unless the show is something truly spectacular. I know we're special, but we're also small. So getting the Clarksville Raiders fans to pay attention to us for the next eight minutes is going to be nearly impossible. They're programmed to hate us, and the feelings are mutual. Why people have to take it out on the band kids, though, baffles me.

"I'm pretty sure a mom *and* grandmother just booed me and gave me the finger." Johnny pulls his pads off and sets them on the sideline before putting his jersey back on. I take full advantage of the strip show, and I don't even care that he catches me biting my tongue and staring at his torso.

"What? My boyfriend is hot." I shrug but also hold my breath for his reaction. This is the first time I'm testing out that word—boyfriend.

His lip ticks up and he steps in close, leaning down to kiss just below my ear.

"I seem to remember my girlfriend claiming she didn't have

sexy curves. She's such a liar." He steps back, smirking, then lets his gaze simmer on my chest for a beat before trailing down to my hips.

Girlfriend.

Johnny and I split up, each heading to a different side of the field. It's not our home field, so we have to get our show in quick to save enough time for the "Star Spangled Banner" at the end. Devin clicks off the cadence, and the rest of the band marches into place so we can start. I've been really getting into character lately, and mostly because the kiss has become a fixture of our routine. We stroll toward one another and I can't diminish the smile on my face as he dips me and stares into my eyes. Even in enemy territory, the crowd erupts when we kiss.

"You're going to expect applause every time I kiss you if they keep this up," he teases at my side right after we salute. He helps me onto the podium by giving me his hand and I step on his knee. I glance down once I'm above to find him still admiring me.

"I don't want an audience seeing what I want to do to you," I utter, instantly heating up from the massive blush that crawls up my neck and down my spine.

"Ooh oh . . . o-kay," he stammers, the smile a permanent fixture on his face as he raises his hands and waits for me to kick off our first song.

For the first time in my high school band career, I can't remember a single thing about our show. I'm sure we were good. There weren't enough people in the stands to react to much more than the kiss. The national anthem went fine. I think. I'm not sure, though, because I've been replaying the half smile and blush on Johnny's cheeks when I said what I said. That was the boldest thing I've ever done in terms of flirting. It was overt. No. It was aggressive. But ever since our major make-out session on the patio the other night, I have had these dreams that wake me up frustrated and wanting more of him. I get what boy crazy means now. I am, in fact, crazy for this boy.

Johnny snags his pads and jogs toward the visitor's locker room to join the team in prep. Coach has been really cool about him participating in the gameday performances, probably because our team isn't much of anything without him.

I look on as he heads down the track, but just before he steps through the gates to head toward the fieldhouse, a man steps in front of him and pushes him backward several steps. It's at the far end of the field, where the lights are dim and few people are around. And I'm sure anyone not in the know would think the man is one of our team's coaches. People have a way of turning a blind eye at misbehaving coaches who maybe cross that line with their players. But there's no line with this man. It's Johnny's father, and he doesn't believe in lines.

I rush to the main gate to the away stands where my dad is waving my bandmates up and into their seats.

"We have a problem," I say, grabbing my father's arm, jerking it to the side until his eyes follow and he sees what I see.

Johnny's dad has taken his conversation with his son into the parking lot between the field and buildings, and though it's impossible to hear him from this far away, there's not much mistaking his gestures. He hasn't hit Johnny yet, but he's grabbed him by the collar a few times and taken the pads from his hands and thrown them off to the side.

"I'll go," my dad says, rushing around the track and into the lot while I take over manning the gate until the rest of the band is through. Devin stops just inside, pulling his drum harness over his head and glancing toward the dark parking lot.

"Everything okay?" His eyes peel to my face after a second.

I shrug and chew at my lips. Johnny clearly doesn't want

people knowing about his situation, but he's also in trouble. And he's not the one in the wrong. My chest clenches and my lungs burn, the stress hitting me all at once. I don't know what's right here.

"I'm going to go check with my dad. Can you make sure everyone's ready with the fight song?" I ask. Devin looks over my head again, then drops his gaze to stare into my eyes, probably looking for better clues. I don't have any.

He nods.

"Thanks," I say, squeezing his arm and rushing off along the same path my dad took.

By the time I get to the parking lot, the conversation seems to have become a little more civil. Johnny's already walking away, nearly to the locker room, and my dad is holding his palms out and nodding with his words while Johnny's father runs his hand along his chin as he listens. When I step into the sliver of light cutting through the rows of vehicles, Johnny's dad shifts his eyes toward me, drops his arms, and relaxes his tense shoulders. My father turns around to meet my wide-open eyes.

"Uh, the band is ready. I wanted to see if we need to have one of the pom songs on queue or if we were going right into the fight song?" It's a bullshit question that I made up because I knew Johnny's dad wouldn't have a clue what I'm talking about. I simply needed an excuse to be here. I couldn't *not* be here. In case . . .

"Fight song is fine. I'll head back with you," my dad says. He turns back to face Johnny's father and holds out a hand. The two of them shake, though Johnny's father spills out a sloppy laugh when they do.

"Yeah, thanks for explaining to me. Kids, ya know? I didn't know he needed some art credit bullshit or whatever, but I'm glad it worked out. If you can try to get his ass in that locker room for pre-game, though? You know, because football is what he's here for. That's what's important. And that coaching staff is a fucking joke, so my son needs to be in there to lead."

My dad nods then drops his hands into his pockets. It's a move only I would recognize. It's what my dad does when he's frustrated with people. He does it at every school board meeting when he has to speak about the importance of not cutting arts funds; usually they want to cut them for football.

"I'll get with Coach Jacobs and see what we can do," my father says. "Enjoy your night."

My dad holds up a hand but promptly stuffs it back in his pocket as he turns and joins me for the walk back around the track. I let him set the pace, and the fact that he slows when we're out of earshot of anyone isn't lost on me.

"That man smells like a brewery. We have to do something to get Johnny help." His eyes flit to mine as we stroll and I swallow hard.

"Okay. What?" I ask.

My dad shakes his head and mutters, "I don't know."

My heart pounds wildly with panic. Johnny isn't going to want us to do anything. And I can't get over the overwhelming sense of doom setting up camp in my lower belly. I fear anything we say or do will only make things worse. But what *is* worse?

I hold my breath at the front of the stands, waiting for the team to come out. Everything looks dreamlike, people moving in slow motion and sound muted. The cheerleaders have formed their tunnel, and our mascot, a mangy-looking wolf, is running up and down the field waving a banner on a long pole to hype up the few of us in the away stands. The band is standing and howling behind me, Devin leading the drumline to pound out an ominous beat.

Johnny jogs out first, waiting at the start of the tunnel, bouncing on his feet as if he's nothing but hyped. I see the nuances, though. He isn't hyped. He's scared. He's pretending. No wonder he's so good at performing.

The team bursts through the tunnel and the paper banner with LET'S GO HOWL! painted in red. Johnny rushes across the center of the field to our side, arms waving in the air, mimicking the same efforts the mascot gave a minute ago. More people stand for Johnny—football parents and the few students who care enough to travel to away games. He pounds his chest a few times to prove he's ready, and I glance to the far corner of the field, behind the gate, where his father's figure looms. One of the assistant coaches for the home team has wandered over to chat with him, probably hearing through the grapevine that he's here. I wonder if he'll smell what my father smelled. I wonder if he'll care.

Johnny drops his helmet on the bench and pours water on his head from one of the green squeeze bottles. He shakes the droplets out like a golden retriever after a swim then flings his hair back before turning to look at the far end of the field. His dad is busy being charming, laughing with some other man wearing the opposite team's colors. Johnny's body swells with heavy breaths as he holds on to the collar of his shoulder pads. Eventually, he drops his chin and kicks at the grass after spitting. His gaze swivels my way and our eyes meet. I do my best to build a smile on my face, and I think he's doing the same. He pats his chest three times, leaving his palm on the center of the number 12 on his chest. I move my palm to cover my heart, and leave it there until he's forced to look away to do a job he doesn't love for a man he hates.

We ended up winning 14-0. Johnny scored both touchdowns by rushing the ball in himself. His dad left after the first one. I guess he was satisfied that his son wasn't embarrassing him based on his screwed-up sense of worth.

Johnny went home with the team, and I sat by myself on the band bus. Nobody noticed anything strange but my father and Devin, and none of us wanted to talk about it. I think Devin is still embarrassed by the way he acted at the fair. I wonder how much of this Teddy knows, if he knows any of it at all. Teddy's been all about the afterparty lately.

My dad wraps up his quick call to my mom, letting her know that Johnny will likely be spending the night so she can make up the pull-out for him. He turns to me after ending his call, and without having to ask it, I know what I need to do.

"I'm going to wait by the locker room. I won't let him go."

My father gives me a quick nod and we lock our gazes for a few seconds. I think neither of us is sure how to process this. I step into my dad and sink into his chest, wrapping my arms around his midriff as he engulfs me in his arms and presses a kiss on top of my head.

"I love you, sweetheart."

My eyes sting from the pressure of tears.

"I love you, too, Daddy."

I don't look him in the eyes again when I leave because if his expression is anything close to mine, I'll fall apart.

I pull my car into one of the spots near the locker room and wait for Johnny to come out. I've gotten used to this after home games, waiting for him in the dark. His dad usually leaves by halftime, when the attention is no longer on him.

Teddy comes out first, bumping fists with a few guys before spotting me and veering in my direction. He's shirtless, because

Teddy likes attention. His wet hair is slicked back, his jeans low, his duffel bag in his hand. He slings it over his shoulder when he reaches me, and I chuckle.

"You are such an attention whore," I tease.

He slowly runs a hand through his hair, then flexes his bicep while pretending to read an invisible watch on his wrist. I roll my eyes but laugh harder at his silliness. He lightly swings his bag into my knees.

"Hey, you're gonna bruise my beautiful ego." He drops his bag on the ground and bends at the waist to unzip it. He pulls out a T-shirt and slips it on before grimacing at me. "Fine, this better?"

"No. I have no problem objectifying you," I snap back.

He shakes his head and drops his hands in his pockets as his laughter fades. His tongue is pushed behind his teeth, his mouth half open with his uneasy smile.

"You waiting on Johnny?"

I nod. We lock eyes for a beat and eventually he sucks in his lips and glances out toward our dark field. His gaze lingers there for a few quiet breaths before he speaks.

"You see what happened with his dad?" His eyes squint, but he doesn't move his focus from the night.

"I did. My dad broke it up; diffused the situation . . . I guess." I'm not sure that's the truth. He may have simply put a pause on things. My stomach sinks.

Teddy nods then glances my way, his eyes meeting mine for a fleeting breath. I think this topic makes him uncomfortable. Teddy's parents and mine are nothing like Johnny's. I've had plenty of friends growing up who have divorced parents and blended families. But I've never had one who had a home so full of danger. At least, I don't think I have. Maybe the people in my life have just been good at hiding things.

"He's sleeping at our house," I say.

Teddy nods, his gaze not quite meeting mine again.

"That's good. He's . . . not himself right now. He was really quiet after the game. And I could tell, when he came in for pre-game. I could just . . . I could tell." His gaze finally settles on mine and I see the worry pooling in the corners of his eyes. I wonder what Teddy has seen that I haven't.

My eyes flash beyond my friend's shoulder when I spot Johnny walking through the gravel toward the parking lot. I sent him a message to look for me, so he pauses and scans the lot before shifting to head in my direction.

"I'm gonna let you two head out on your own. I think he's more comfortable with just you. You're . . . good for him. He's good for you. Whatever. You know what I mean." He lets out a nervous laugh at his own words, but I know he's trying to be supportive and sweet. I grab his hand and give it a squeeze before he heads to his truck. He lifts a hand to Johnny and gives him a, "Great game, man."

"Thanks," Johnny responds. His head is buried in his hoodie, his bag slung over one shoulder, and his hands tucked deep in the pocket at his front. It isn't that cold. He's just trying to hide. I get it.

"You're staying at our house." I don't offer it as a question, and I think that catches him a little off-guard. He opens his mouth and shakes his head at first, but when his gaze reaches my face, every tiny feature in his face that seemed defiant and strong melts.

"Okay," he relents.

He tosses his bag in the back seat and climbs in the passenger side. I turn the volume up on my stereo before buckling up but Johnny quickly turns it down. He looks at me sideways.

"It's okay. I don't need the distraction. But thank you."

I suck in my lower lip and manage to whisper, "Okay."

I'm prepared to drive us home in silence, letting him sit with his thoughts. But Johnny wasn't lying when he said he didn't need a distraction. In fact, he seems to want to shed the noise that he's been holding in for years.

"He's a real son-of-a-bitch, my dad," he says.

"Yeah?" I'm not sure what the right response is to such a confession, but I feel like that one sits right.

"And he's not one of those guys who was good until something happened and then *that thing* made him bad. He's always been bad. Rotten. A real fucker." His vile words come out with bite. I'm sure it's justified.

"Johnny, I'm so—"

"Don't be sorry. One day I will be bigger than he is. I'm already close, but there's just this . . . I don't know . . . block I have with him. I'm legally an adult, and I don't really give a shit what he thinks about me. But my mom doesn't have that luxury, and I—"

"You stay for her," I finish.

He nods silently.

The drive to my house isn't far, but we still have a block to go, and something inside me tells me this car is the place for truth. If I want to know something, now is the time to ask. I hold my mouth open for several seconds, knowing Johnny's eyes are on me. I feel his stare in my periphery. And eventually, he coaxes me to ask.

"You want to know how bad it is," he says.

"No, not really. But I can't help the worry. About you and your mom. Has he—? Has he really hurt you?" My chest shakes with my words. It seems trivial for me to struggle with a question while he has to live with the reality.

Johnny pushes his tongue into his upper lip and glances through the windshield. A light rain has started to spatter the glass with dusty drops. I flick on the wipers and they screech in front of us, leaving muddy streaks behind. Johnny chuckles at the mess, and I figure he deserves to take advantage of any out to avoid my question. I spray the window with more water to get it clean enough to see the rest of the way home, and just before I turn down my street, Johnny says, "All the fucking time."

I pull into the driveway, park, and kill the engine and lights. The sprinkle is steady, but not a full rain. It's a peaceful pattering noise, and it's soothing me. I think it might be soothing him too.

"I'm so sorry."

My words feel small.

"Thank you." He doesn't laugh or make a mockery of my response. I don't think many people know about his situation. He has a grandfather he rarely sees on his mom's side, but other than that, I don't think he has much family.

I rest my hand, palm up and open, on the center console. Johnny slides his fingers through mine, then pulls my hand to his mouth, holding his lips to my skin for several seconds. After his sweet kiss, he presses the back of my hand to his cheek and studies me with a sideways gaze.

"Goddamn are you a gift, Brynn. You're the prettiest damn girl I've ever seen, inside and out." He blinks slowly, his eyes tracing my face. I'm sure I'm blushing. As it is, I'm sucking my lips into a tight line.

"Thank you," I whisper, tucking my chin, feeling all sorts of bashful under his stare.

A car passes behind us on the street, the tires sloshing against the light water built up in the gutters. It's enough of a break in the steady sound to jar us from our sweet trance, and Johnny lets go of my hand, then opens his door. I rush to our front door to make sure my mom has unlocked it. I also want to make sure she's not spying on us through the living room window. My mom loves fiercely, but she lacks tact in all things. Thankfully, she's in the kitchen pulling sweet rolls from the oven when I step inside. Johnny is a step or two behind me, and the pull-out bed in the sitting room is already made up for him.

"Good timing. These just finished." My mom slides the hot pan onto a spare oven mitt she set on the center of the counter. This is how my mom mends wounds. She bakes.

"Thanks, Mom," I hum, taking one of the napkins from the holder, then pulling one of the rolls away from the rest. I blow on it in my hand until it's cool enough to bite then nod for Johnny to do the same.

"Maybe later," he says.

"They're even better cold, in my opinion," my mom says. I take a full breath at her response because it's against her grain not to pry and push. I'm sure deep down she wants to force him to eat his feelings. My dad must have explained.

He comes home a few minutes later, and we all sit around the kitchen and talk about the show, all the while dancing around the awkward moment nobody seems willing to bring up. After a dozen yawns, my dad finally admits to being tired. He puts a palm on Johnny's shoulder before leaving the kitchen behind my mom.

"I talked to Coach Jacobs, just to make sure our story is straight. You *need* band credit. Understand what I'm saying?" My dad dips his chin a hair and Johnny nods.

"I do, sir. Thank you."

My father's nostrils flare with a deep breath.

"I also told him I was concerned, Johnny. And I know that you maybe don't want that, but I had to." My father's eyes flash to me briefly then back to Johnny.

"It's not what you think—" Johnny stops short.

My dad tilts his head and holds Johnny's gaze before he can

finish his words. It's exactly what my dad thinks, and he doesn't want Johnny to feel he needs to lie.

"Nobody is doing anything. But if we need to—if something crosses that line and Coach sees—I need him to be aware." My dad waits silently for a few seconds until Johnny nods and once again says he understands.

We're finally alone, and I know Johnny's hungry, so I pull one of the rolls free and hand it to him. He smirks and takes it, quickly devouring nearly half.

"She's a witch or something. I swear there's voodoo magic in your mom's food." His words are muffled by chewing. I touch his cheek where a small dab of frosting was left behind after his last bite. I lick my finger and he quickly pulls my hand away from my mouth and puts my finger in his instead.

"You are not stealing my frosting, woman!" His tongue swirls around my finger before he lets go with a smack.

"My mom would have loved to hear that compliment," I say.

"Which one—the one where I called her a witch or the one where I used her frosting as an excuse to lick her daughter?"

"Shhh!" I hold my finger to my mouth and lean forward to look up the staircase.

Johnny grabs my hand again and pretends to chew his way up my arm while I try to quiet my own giggle. He finally kisses my mouth softly, tugging me away from my stool until I'm standing between his knees. His head falls against mine, and he holds me still in the quiet of our kitchen. I breathe deep and slow, feeling his body inflate with mine. It's as though I'm calming him—centering him. We can do this for one another. This is how I help.

After almost a full minute of nothing but a breath for a breath, Johnny releases his arms from around me and I step back to look him in the eyes.

"Do you think I would wake your parents if I played you something?" he asks.

My lip quirks up.

"I think my dad would happily be stirred awake by his protégé playing something on his old guitar." My dad has shown Johnny a few tricks he's picked up over years of playing with some of the best jazz and blues guitarists around. The little things he's incorporated have made his sound somehow better when I didn't think it could be.

Johnny's mouth curves into a giddy type of grin, and my body is rushed with a cooling sensation. It's probably relief that he's happy about something after such an absolutely shitty night. I follow him into the sitting room and he pulls the guitar from the coat closet where my dad keeps it for him to use anytime he wishes. I take a seat at the end of the pullout and Johnny sits opposite of me with the guitar propped on his lap.

"I finished it. The song?" He plucks a few strings and adjusts them, tuning it just right.

"The one you're going to play at showcase?" He hasn't exactly agreed to it, but I've already told my father he's signing up.

"Uh, is it?" He lifts a brow.

"Well, let's see how this goes. I mean, I guess you could have ruined a good thing."

Johnny places his fingers on the strings and picks out "Shave and a Haircut," then laughs out twice before giving me a playful glare.

"I'm kidding. But I will let you know if you suck." I wink, and he simply shakes his head and turns his attention to his guitar.

The opening is familiar, the same melody I've heard many times now. I pull my legs up onto the bed and lean forward so I can watch his hands work. I feel like he could win this year's showcase by simply playing acoustically, his finger work is so intricate and complex. Soft runs die off without warning, and unexpected notes hang in the air, leaving me to hold my breath and wait for him to pick them up again. If birds diving in and out of a field made musical sound, this would be it.

And then he sings. Suddenly, what seemed so incredible a moment before is nothing compared to now. His eyes closed, Johnny weaves through lyrics as if he's Shakespeare reciting his own sonnets by heart. His words tell painful truths yet paint hopeful dreams of a future where he isn't afraid. The song isn't direct, but if you know him as I do, as my father does, and as Teddy does, you can feel the raw truth behind every word. He speaks of shelter, of warm places to hide and of people to trust, and my heart swells knowing he's singing about me.

When weakness needs an angel, she'll come with a song . . .

Showing you how much you're worth and how much they were wrong.

Lightning strikes a thousand times, but never where you hope.

So let the shelter that she gives to you be bolder than the storm.

Bolder than the storm.

Be bolder than the storm.

His falsetto wraps around the words, dropping notes into existence like feathers in the wind. His voice nearly breaks as it fades out, and his hands still on the guitar, never hitting the final note. Or maybe that's intentional. It should be if it's not. It's an unfinished story, just like Johnny.

I bring my fist to my mouth to still my quivering lips. My dad talks about music moving him to tears, and I always believed it was possible but I never imagined it would happen to me. My mind gets too wrapped up in the technical. I fall in love with the details, the blocks that build every stanza. But I cry now. One tear, though I could easily let more fall freely down my cheeks.

"What do you think?" Johnny hugs the guitar to him and sets his gaze on my eyes, unflinching and waiting for me to give him my honest opinion.

"You are going to be so famous. I hope you remember me."

Chapter 23
Present

It's been years since I woke up in anyone's arms, but a decade since it was in the arms of someone I loved. And as hard as it is, as much as it hurts to walk through this journey, I admit to myself that I love Johnny still. More than a promise, I love him down deep. Even when I don't want to.

Sometime around midnight, I fell asleep in his arms in that chair. And it's where I am now that the sun is cresting and beginning to pour light through my front window. I can tell by the way he's breathing that he's asleep. I wonder how long he's been that way. While I don't want to bring this feeling to an end, I need to stretch my aching back, and he probably needs to work feeling back into his legs.

I shift my weight, doing my best to avoid pushing off his chest, but it's no use. His hand covers mine the moment I grip the arm of the chair.

"Hey, good morning." His voice is groggy and sweet. The timbre takes me back to those many mornings I got to wake him on my family's sofa bed.

I fall into his chest and indulge in what I know is messy, glancing up to meet his eyes. He lets go of my hand and runs his fingers through my hair, pushing pieces away from my face. He stills with his palm on my cheek and one of us quivers because I feel it. Maybe it's both of us.

"Did you sleep at all? You could have kicked me off your lap." I rub a fist into my tired eyes.

"Not a chance."

My hand falls away and I meet his stare. My heart thrums inside my hollow chest, and my stomach swirls with indecision. The more seconds that pass, the more I want him to make the choice for both of us and kiss me. To forget the last decade. Forget he ever left at all. The moment is robbed with an urgent knock at my door—the kind fueled by some kind of media crisis and a need for strong coffee.

"I'll get it," I grumble, pushing myself up from his lap. He grabs my hand before I fully walk away.

"I'll get it. Whatever it is isn't your problem; it's mine."

My eyes narrow instantly on the slight wrinkle between his eyes. It hasn't left his face since he woke up clean at Waves, and I wonder how many times it showed up between binges on the road.

"What is tearing you apart, Johnny? Tell me."

I run my thumb along the side of his hand and his eyes flit to my touch. His lips part with the kind of breath a frightened little boy might have before stepping inside an ominous house or a funeral. *A funeral.*

"I'm sorry. It's your mom. I'm . . . I'm insensitive." I feel like an asshole. *I am an asshole.*

Johnny stands and squeezes my hand harder, then moves both of his hands to cup my face.

"No, you're not insensitive. You're my angel." His eyes hold mine for a beat, then he plants a kiss on my forehead just as a second beatdown comes on my door, followed by a shrill voice calling his name.

"Coming!" He rolls his eyes to me and I head down the hallway to my room to hide. When Kaylee shows up, there's usually a press person or two lingering nearby. I've already been photographed through zoom lenses looking my absolute worst. I leave them to handle Johnny's business while I shower and get myself ready for school, even though it's still two hours from now.

The best thing I ever did as band director in Yucca was get marching band converted to a double class so the kids don't have to march in wet grass in the mornings. Granted, it's a little hot out there for the first month, but it beats them rolling out of bed at five a.m. I would know; I did it for years.

It's my favorite time of the year right now—deep into fall, the showcase over, marching winding down. As hyped as the community gets over the showcase, I like this quieter time when the serious students are working on their pieces for admission to the schools of their dreams. I remember practicing the harp for my audition into Berkeley. I sank myself into it, and I honestly think that instrument saved me from completely falling into the depths of heartache after Johnny left. I would close my eyes and just feel the strings, and even my mistakes sounded beautiful.

I decide to embrace this sudden blissful feeling and wear my favorite red dress. It's a vintage piece I got at the flea market last year on a whim, and maybe there's a part of me that wants to remind Johnny of the Broadway girl he dipped and kissed on the fifty-yard-line all those years ago. I put a few subtle waves in my hair and am hunting for my bright red lipstick when I hear Kaylee's voice raise down the hall.

"The label is going to drop you if you don't fix this, Johnny! I don't know what you think I am, but miracle worker is not on my resume."

I crack open the bedroom door and peek down the hallway.

Johnny is pacing. He pulls his flannel off and tosses it into the chair we slept in, then runs both of his hands through his hair, gripping his head. He's hurting, and Kaylee isn't helping.

Against all good judgement, I open the door completely and step into the mosh pit. Kaylee's head bops up from looking at her phone and she pushes her black-rimmed glasses down her nose. I meet her stare and take measured steps toward her.

"I'm sorry, but I don't think whatever this is"—I do my best to sound strong yet calm—"is good for him."

"It's fine, Brynn. I got it," Johnny says, but the panic in his voice says he doesn't. I glance over my shoulder and hit him with the most scolding gaze I can. *Let me do this. Let me be your supposed angel.*

"Kaylee, he might think he *has it.*" I finger quote at her, which is something she does all the time and it irks me to no end. "But maybe we need to take a beat on this and remember that two months ago, he was an addict spiraling out of control."

Her mouth flattens, but she still looks determined. She's just not getting it. I step in closer so I can lower my voice, though I know Johnny will still hear this.

"Kaylee, his mom is dying. Let's give this subject some space. That's all I'm saying." I glance over my shoulder and meet Johnny's eyes. They look so fucking broken, and I wish I was the kind of woman who would punch another woman. Not that Kaylee completely deserves it, but God, it would feel good.

When I look back to her, she seems to have softened a touch, my words perhaps getting through a touch. She blinks rapidly and glances back at her phone, scrolling through her calendar app then opening an item and writing the word DEADLINE in all caps.

"He has a week, Brynn. I'm sorry if I seem abrupt, but it's my job. And working for him is my dream job. But the label is going to drop him if he doesn't meet with this reporter. They want this story, but they want it . . . positive. Maybe you can talk to him?" She reaches into her pocket and hands me a well-worn business card.

SHAYLA MACIAS
Senior Writer
THE ELITE AFFAIR

I nod and utter, "I'll do my best."

Her gaze drifts past me to Johnny, but he's silent. I sense his movement, and imagine he's probably back to pacing. My best might not be enough, especially since I have no idea what any of this is about. I do know the *Elite Affair*, though. They write some of the best celebrity profiles I've ever read, but they are rarely done without uncovering secrets. I don't think truth lies are going to cut it with Miss Shayla Macias.

"One week," Kaylee says with a very pointed expression.

"Yeah. A week. Great. Got it." Johnny's irritable side is turning green and hairy, so I nudge Kaylee toward the door and promise I'll do my best one last time before closing it.

With a deep breath, I turn to face Johnny, flattening my back against the door. He's stopped his pacing for the moment, and is standing behind the chair with his hands squeezing the top and eyes focused somewhere on the floor between us.

"Johnny—"

"Brynn, you don't understand." He lifts his head and I'm met with wide eyes and a rigid jaw. His shoulders and neck muscles flex and I wonder if maybe my semi-broken chair is really in trouble.

"Explain it to me."

He breathes out a laugh and pushes the chair forward several inches with a frustrated shove before turning around and walking into the kitchen.

"Not sure what the chair did . . ." I sigh, moving toward it and sliding it back to its place. I follow him into the kitchen where he's flipped on the faucet to splash water on his face. I hand him a towel and he covers his face for several seconds before lowering it to look me in the eyes.

He slowly shakes his head.

"They always want to talk about *him*."

My gut told me Johnny's father was the center of this. That man is the root of most of the pain in Johnny's life, so it's not surprising that he's what's causing so much stress now, long after he died.

"So you take that off the table. I'm sure Kaylee's a pro at handling this stuff, telling reporters what is off-limits and stuff. It's not like they're writing some political investigation piece on arms trading or embezzlement."

"No, just about a famous rock star who everyone secretly thinks murdered his father."

We both freeze. I don't even breathe at hearing him say that out loud. Johnny drops the towel to the floor by his feet, but other than that, he doesn't move. He doesn't blink. His gaze holds mine hostage, and his pupils widen as the truth of his words settles into every molecule in the room.

"Nobody thinks that," I lie.

He laughs.

"You don't have to kid-glove me, Brynnie. I remember coming back to town and being questioned for hours. I remember the stories that hit the papers after he died. I know what everyone thinks, but the thing is, nobody has ever had something that makes that story carry weight . . . until now."

His shoulders slump and the color leaves his cheeks.

"Johnny." I suck in a breath, adrenaline lighting up my nerves like I was stuck with a syringe.

He glances up and holds his gaze on the ceiling for a breath, then shakes his head.

"It's not anything, or it shouldn't be, but she's going to twist it, and I can't . . ." His breath fails him and his voice dies. I step into him and pull his hands into mine, then his body. He slumps over me and I do my best to hold him up as he works to catch his breath.

"Remember how we do it—you breathe with me," I hum. He's having a panic attack, and for the last several years, he medicated them with alcohol. This is what always worked before, though. When he was with me.

"In . . . and out." I feel his chest sync with mine, our bodies expanding and shrinking together. The pounding in his chest quiets, and I no longer feel his pulse reverberating through his back.

"I'm okay," he utters into my neck. "You make me okay."

I tremble at those words. The pressure of them. The regret behind them.

"I would have helped you with all of this, through it all. If you had stayed." I bury my face in the crook of his neck and breathe him in.

"I know. And I'm so fucking sorry I didn't. I'm so sorry, Brynn. But I couldn't, and I can't tell you why, but please believe me. I couldn't. And when I could, I was so ashamed of what I'd become. I'm so sorry. Just . . ." Johnny shifts until our noses nearly touch. "So sorry. So—"

And then his mouth covers mine.

His lips are familiar yet fuller, older—better. He sucks in my bottom lip and I rise up on my toes as he straightens his spine to stand taller, his hands on my back, pulling me up with him. His tongue teases mine, and a whimper leaves my mouth at the feel of his teeth grazing against my skin. It's enough to wake me from this dream and I push back from his chest, making room between us. Space to think. To breathe.

"I'm sorry. I shouldn't have . . ."

His eyes flare as his words die off. His tongue tastes his bottom lip, where I just was. My hands ball into fists at my sides as his gaze moves down my body, stopping where the red sway of my skirt brushes below my knees.

"No, fuck that. That's a lie." His eyes flash back to mine. "I'm not sorry I did that."

I tremble enough that I grip the counter at my side.

"I should have done that a long time ago."

Our gazes locked, I swear I see our entire story in his eyes—every worry, memory, hope and regret, all in a flash.

Johnny rushes me, his hands sliding along my cheeks and into my hair. I grab his wrists to steady myself and open my mouth for him to kiss me deep and hard. I nip at his upper lip as a low growl leaves his throat and he paints me with kisses that start at my neck and move to my shoulder as he peels away my red wrap dress.

My hands move to his shoulders and he tugs the tie loose from around my waist, letting my dress fall open. He pushes the sleeves down my arms until the slinky material is pooled at my feet and I'm in nothing but a pair of white cotton panties and a lace demi bra.

"My God, did you grow up, Brynnie," he says. His gaze travels the length of my body, stopping at my navel.

"Johnny, I want you," I rasp, my hands gathering the hem of his shirt and tugging it up his chest. He pulls it over his head and tosses it behind him before sweeping me up into his grip. His hands on my ass, he lifts me up to wrap my legs around him.

We kiss as he marches us into my bedroom, my hands deep in his hair, his scratching at my thighs, clawing me with a primal need that we've clearly both fostered for years. I slide from his hold, but his hands remain on my lower back as I stand before him at the foot of my bed. He kneels, and my hands grip his hair as his tongue trails from my belly button up my rib cage until his teeth grip the lace trim of my bra. Johnny's tongue flicks at my hard nipple that's half exposed, his mouth moving the fabric out of the way until he can hold the hard peak between his teeth. A sharp ache trails through my body, down between my legs and I moan as he sucks my nipple hard. He lifts me onto the bed and lays me down gently, his mouth never leaving my body, even as he holds himself above me on his forearms.

"You are the most beautiful man I've ever seen," I say, cupping his face with my hands this time and forcing his gaze on mine. His eyes haze and his upper lip trembles. I lift my head enough to catch it between both of mine, and kiss him sweetly one last time before willing him to take more from me.

My hands move to the button on his jeans, unsnapping and lowering his zipper. He's not wearing anything underneath, and his hard cock falls into my palm the moment it's free. I wrap my fingers around his length and stroke him twice, his head falling forward as he groans.

"What happened to shy little Brynnie?" He chuckles as his mouth presses against my bare skin.

"She waited ten years to get fucked by a famous rock star."

My boldness changes him instantly. His muscles harden, and his growl comes out louder as his hand sweeps behind me, unsnapping my bra and freeing my breasts so he can taste them both and tease me until I'm crying out for relief. His tongue swirls around the edge, his mouth kissing my hard peaks softly before he flicks each nipple with his tongue. As he sits back on his knees, he drags his palms down my breasts, gripping them possessively and rolling the tips between his thumbs and fingers. I arch, completely under his control, and I'm left panting when his hands leave my skin to pull his jeans down his hips. He kicks them off completely and stands at the foot of my bed, grabbing my legs and dragging me toward him before pushing my knees open wide.

"Johnny," I breathe out before biting my knuckle and willing myself to slow down and live every moment of this.

Holding his cock in one hand, he runs his thumb over the soaking wet cotton between my legs. I writhe, bucking my hips into his touch, wanting more.

"Shhh," he hushes, bringing his fingers to his mouth and sucking two of them. He lowers his head, stroking himself with one hand as he takes his slick fingers and moves my panties to the side so he can push them inside of me.

"Gah!" I arch again, my eyes rolling back then squeezing shut as electricity pulses through my core.

"God, you're sexy. I can't wait to see my dick in you," he says, his dirty talk setting off a wave of pulses that rushes through me and leaves me numb and helpless under his touch. He presses my swollen center with his thumb, manipulating my orgasm and drawing it out until I'm bucking off the bed and grabbing his hand to make sure it doesn't leave.

Left panting and wanting so much more of him, I move my hands to my hips and lift myself enough to work my panties down my curves. Johnny takes over and yanks them down my legs, tossing them on top of his jeans before positioning himself between my legs at the foot of my bed.

"You have been making me hard for a decade, Brynn Fisher. As a horny fucking teenager; as a fucked-up rock star on the road with nothing but his memories. And now . . . you are the most beautiful woman in the world, and I'm going to fuck you enough to make up for lost years, to erase those unwelcome assholes who thought they could have what was mine, and to make sure you never want another cock inside you again. And then I'm going to taste your sweet pussy and make you come again. You're going to have to call in sick today, because you're going to be too weak to walk, but not too weak for me to fuck you again. And again."

With his cock in his hand, Johnny inches into me, my body adapting to his width as I hold my breath and wait to take in his length. He stretches me, sliding in deep and slow then pulling out completely. I gasp at the loss of him, and he quickly plunges in again. This time, I scream in ecstasy, gripping everything my hands can find around me. I ball up the sheets and pull them from the bed while Johnny holds my hips down and rocks into me, every thrust harder than the last.

I push against him, driving him deeper as he slides his hands down my thighs then hooks my legs over his arms. His hooded eyes sear into me, his singular focus on his cock plunging into me over and over again. There will be plenty of time to be gentle with one another. Right now, we're making up for lost time and pent-up desire.

His hips rock into me faster, and my second orgasm builds. I cry out his name, each syllable vibrating from my chest as I lose my breath from Johnny pounding into me. My core tightens and I clench around his cock as I fall over the edge. Johnny swells inside me. He drops my legs and collapses forward, caging me between his arms as he dives into me, on the verge of coming inside of me.

His eyes meet mine, his eyes tinged with red, his face flush.

"I can pull out," he grunts.

I shake my head and dig my fingers into his sides, holding him to me.

"I want you to finish in me. I want to feel it. I want *you* to feel it. I'm covered." I've never been more grateful for my IUD in my life.

My hands move to his face, and I coax him to keep his eyes on mine as he completely loses control. His mouth falls open and his breath spills out. I lift my head enough to catch his bottom lip between mine, sucking it in as he finishes inside of me, coating me with his warmth. His head rests against mine and his hips slow, one final push before stilling, though he continues to pulse inside me. It's like aftershocks. Powerful reminders of how potent our chemistry is.

We breathe together until it's no longer labored. Johnny lifts himself up enough to nuzzle his nose against mine then to dust my forehead, cheeks, and neck with kisses. Locked under his arms—safe, warm, and hopeful—I look him in the eyes and see all of him. I see happiness tugging at the corners of his mouth, and peace in his easy features. The tight jawline and flexed neck muscles that have framed his face for weeks are finally relaxed.

My head falls into his open palm resting beside my head, but I leave my gaze on his, afraid that if I let go, I'll somehow lose him. And I never want to lose him again. No more running away, no matter why he thinks he had to in the first place.

Chapter 24
Age 18, Showcase Night

I don't think I've ever seen Johnny Bishop nervous about performing. He's usually, well, downright cocky. But tonight is different. Tonight matters.

"Are you sure I don't look stupid?" He slouches to one side and holds out both arms.

"Yes, Johnny. You look amazing. But nobody is going to care how you look once you sing. I promise."

Johnny's mom, Beth, and I picked out his outfit for tonight, and it's maybe a little more *rocker* than he's used to. If he had his way, he would have shown up in the Niners jersey he's had since eighth grade and a pair of Levi's. That wouldn't cut it for tonight, because as much as I told him it's about his voice, it's a little about the look too. People are watching. Important people. And Johnny in a childhood jersey that's fading in most places is a whole different world from the Johnny in the tight black T-shirt and black jeans with rips on the knees. It's not a huge departure for him. Other than the jeans, everything is something from his closet. His black Vans, his mom's silver rope bracelet, his hair done his way. I gave him a black chain necklace last night for good luck, and it really tops this look off. To be honest, he's hot right now, even for Johnny Bishop, and I've had about enough of every girl in town this evening stopping by to gush on their way into the pub.

Johnny's been pacing behind Pappy & Harriet's for an hour now, and though it's October, it's unseasonably warm, especially for the evening. I'm beyond melted, and I gave up on the curls lasting in my hair a long time ago. I didn't really prepare for showcase this year anyhow. I went in the first batch of contestants and played and sang "Landslide." I know it by heart, so it didn't require much practice. My big audition will come later this year, when I apply for the music program at Berkeley.

There's no music program for what Johnny's needs. His gift isn't the kind that's taught or nurtured with books and classrooms. His gift is the kind given a break. And he needs one —*deserves* one. Anything that will take him to bigger and better places and things.

"Would you check on my mom before I go on? I don't want her to feel nervous," he says, his eyes darting all over the place. I grab his shoulders and settle his focus.

"Yes, Johnny. I will sit with your mom. I promise she has as much confidence in you as I do. The only person who needs to calm down is standing right here looking all sexy and smoldering." I bat my lashes teasingly and Johnny smirks.

"Smoldering?" He lifts a brow.

"It's the best word I could come up with."

He shifts his weight and lifts his palm to my cheek, stroking the skin under my eye with his thumb. He leans in and softly presses his lips to mine, then moves his mouth close to my ear.

"I wouldn't be here without you. I'd never believe I could do something like this." His lashes tickle against my temple, and soon his head rests against mine. I sink into him, wrapping my arms around his warm body until my ear is pressed against the center of his chest. His heart is pounding wildly, but on the outside, at least for now, he's calm.

"You're going to be incredible. They'll all see." I step back but cling to the front of his shirt for a beat so I can get one last look at the boy who is all mine. He's about to become the world's.

"Thank you, Brynnie . . . Winnie." His lips quiver into an automatic smile at his pet name for me.

"You're welcome, rock star," I say with a wink.

I lift my broomstick skirt a few inches to protect it from the dirt as I trek my way inside. I went with my Stevie Nicks look tonight, mostly for my dad. Fleetwood Mac is one of his favorite bands of all time, and he's always told me I'm his little brunette Stevie. I wish that were true when it comes to my singing. I do love her song "Landslide," and I don't think I sound so bad when I sing it.

I weave through the crowded tables toward the wall lined with photos of people who have played here over the years. Famous musicians and songwriters, many of whom still stop by. Beth is sitting at a table alone, tucked in a dark corner away from most of the other students and parents. Johnny's dad is out of town, which I've come to learn means he's off getting drunk with his buddies and gambling or spending money at a strip club. Because he won't let Beth have her own car, she's stuck at home when he runs off like that. I picked her and Johnny up for tonight, and I can tell she feels out of place being around everyone. The way she lights up when I sit at her table, though, coats my chest in warmth.

"Brynn, I saved this spot for you. Glad you found me." She reaches her hand across the table and I cover it with mine, squeezing it for good luck.

Beth and I haven't spent a lot of time together, but she did finally show me some of her art. She keeps most of it in the garage. In fact, the garage seems to be the one place where she can be herself. Her husband never parks there, probably because he's usually too drunk or too angry to see straight and line the wheels up.

When I came by today to pick out clothes for Johnny, she was making these small twists of red glass, and my eyes narrow on one of them dangling from a thin leather strap around her neck.

"Is that from today?" I gesture toward her chest.

"Oh! Yes." She lifts the necklace over her head and holds the twisted spear in her palm.

I lean forward to look at it in her hand. It's almost the color of blood, and it reminds me of a unicorn.

"It's really beautiful," I say, lifting my gaze to hers.

She tilts her head slightly to one side.

"Keep it."

My eyes flash wide.

"Oh, no. I couldn't. That's not what I meant." My heart is pounding. I'm terrible at accepting gifts, and I feel as if I bullied her into giving me this. It's too much, too . . . personal.

Beth places it in the center of my palm, then closes my hand around it with both of hers. My eyes dart to her face and my mouth hangs open. She chuckles.

"Honey, I made these out of old syrup bottle glass. It's hard to make red, so whenever we have broken glass around the house, I melt it. There wasn't a lot to the bottle so I figured I'd go the jewelry route. I'm giving the others to the ladies at the library."

"The other volunteers?" I ask, feeling the weight of the spear in my hand.

She nods, and her smile is so soft and almost pleased, I don't think I could turn her gift down now even if I wanted to.

"I love it," I say, opening my palm and pinching the glass

piece between my finger and thumb so I can hold it up to the light. "Hard to imagine this was once a bottle full of sugar."

"Mmmm. Hard to imagine indeed," she says. My eyes refocus slightly from the glass to where she's sitting beyond it, and there's a glint in her eye. I don't think the glass breaking was an accident.

I slip the leather piece over my head and let the glass dangle against my collarbone. It's cold, and though it looks sharp it's not. She's taken great care to smooth the edges.

"It goes well with your Stevie tribute." She winks at me and I lean back in my chair and flair my skirt out a little so she can get the full effect. It's a smokey fabric, just like the queen herself would wear.

"You noticed."

"Oh, I did. Rumors might be the best album ever made." She giggles and reaches over to pull my skirt out again, letting the folds shrink back up against my legs as she lets go.

"My father and you would really get along."

We smile at one another, that worry I was carrying in my tummy of being able to talk with Beth on my own completely gone thanks to some glass and some Stevie fandom.

My father taps on the mic seconds later, bringing everyone's attention back to the stage after the short break. He stresses over this night so much. I think his worries begin for the next year as soon as the current event ends. I used to love coming to watch these when I was a kid. It was like getting a free concert and permission to stay up late. Plus, the ladies in the kitchen always gave me endless refills of French fries and Coke. I may have gone home sick more than once, but it was always worth it.

There is no snacking tonight, however. I'm too nervous, though I told Johnny I wasn't. He's going to be amazing, but I hope the politics of the showcase doesn't prevent the judges from giving him the top honors. A lot of campaigning goes on before the showcase. Overzealous parents sending emails to teachers and guest judges from the district is only the tip of the corruption. I suppose that's why this event, as much as my father loves it, is also the bane of his existence. My mom doesn't even watch from out front anymore. She sits at the side of the stage, by the door to the makeshift greenroom. She doesn't like to hear the whispering among competitive parents as they disparage other peoples' kids. I think she doesn't want to hear them whisper about me and Dad, either.

"Let's all give it up for Miranda Dodge!" On the stage, my dad hands the mic over to one of the shyest girls in my class. She's going to surprise people because her specialty is opera. I lean over and warn Beth that she may want to brace herself. The volume that comes out of Miranda's tiny frame always shocks me.

The lights dim and the guest violinist and cellist begin to play Miranda's accompaniment. When Miranda's angelic soprano voice kicks in, the chatting around the pub stops. It's cool to watch people freeze in shock. I can't wait to see them do it for Johnny.

There are two more performers before him, so I whisper to his mother that I'm going to run to the restroom one last time so I'm good to go when he comes on. I slip through the rows of tables and chairs, stopping at Teddy's table so he can blow on my fist. He tells me I'm weird, but he does it anyway. I leave him bewildered then crouch by my mother near the greenroom. She's organizing coupons in her lap since she's out of view of the audience. I laugh slightly and shake my head.

"I promise I'll put these away for Johnny," she says.

"And did you put them away when I went?"

I hold her stare for a few seconds, counting her blinks—*one, two, three.*

"Do you want me to lie?" I figured she didn't, but damn. Seriously?

"It's fine," I say with a roll of my eyes.

I leave her and rush down the hall to the bathroom, then pop my head out the back door after I'm done to see if I can catch one last glimpse of Johnny. His back is to me as he sits on one of the picnic tables near the fire pits. A few people are hanging out back there smoking, and I can tell Johnny is trying to pick out his song softly so he doesn't get their attention. He stops for a moment, flattening his hands against the guitar and leaning his head back with a heavy breath. I can tell by the flutter of his lashes that he's staring at the sky, so I look up too. A thin layer of clouds covers half of it, but the crescent moon is in view straight above as is part of Orion's belt. I smile at the twinkle the stars give off and decide to leave Johnny in this peaceful place.

I hang out with my mom for a few minutes on my way back, mostly to rush her through her stupid coupon project, then dash back to the seat by Beth so I'm there in time for my dad to announce Johnny's performance. I keep telling everyone I'm not nervous for him, but right now, my hands are sweaty and my stomach is humming with butterflies.

"You know, before you, I'm the only person he ever sang for?" Beth says at my side.

I swivel my head to look her in the eyes and we both tick up the side of our mouths, like we're looking in mirrors.

The performance before Johnny's ends and my dad walks back on stage and retrieves the mic. I admire his ability to wear a straight poker face as he emcees. Nobody would ever be able to tell who he's rooting for. But I know he's been counting down the minutes for Johnny's turn.

"Playing an original song for you all tonight, which he wrote and arranged himself, please give it up for Johnny Bishop." The room buzzes with polite applause as my dad gives Johnny a reassuring look then secures the mic to the stand.

I reach over to Beth on instinct, and we clasp hands, squeezing one another to quench mutual nerves.

Johnny adjusts the stool and the height of the mic, then positions himself comfortably with the guitar resting on his thigh. Some of his hair has fallen over his eye, and when he pushes it back with his hand, someone in the room—*a female* —whistles while another screams out *wooo!* I hate how hot everyone else thinks he is. I know it's petty and unfair, but I want him to be hot only to me and for me.

"Thank you all for being here, and for being so gracious and patient tonight." His voice rasps into the mic, a texture that I've heard when he sings but that's suddenly amplified in this room. Everyone has already hushed for him, and the quiet is palpable. I can hear the pops and creaks of the building when I hold my breath.

Johnny strums the guitar a few times to make his final tuning adjustments, then he glances to his right and nods at my dad. He leans forward next, his eyes on mine, and his mouth curves just enough to dimple his cheeks.

"This song's called 'Shelter.'"

I take a deep breath, knowing I won't be able to take another one for at least two minutes. Johnny begins to play and I let my eyes fall closed, focusing on nothing but the melody that I've memorized by heart. He practiced so many times last weekend when my parents were out of town. He slept in my bed and held me all night, and when he thought I was asleep and no longer looking, he worked on his song even more, tweaking words and humming notes out in the hallway. It's been his obsession, and he's made it mine too.

This song. His voice and sound. And us. It's all one, and I don't think I will ever be able to hear it and not think of how he makes me feel. I won't be able to parse out the love I feel for him. I never want to imagine my world without him in it, and I know he feels the same.

Johnny begins to sing, and my eyes open just in time to see his fall shut. His lips caress every word as he confesses his darkest secrets to the microphone in a room full of people who are practically strangers. His falsetto lures them in, then his power holds them hostage. Johnny is everything at once, his hands creating magic on the guitar while his mouth sings poetry from his heart. And somehow, under the hot lights of a stage and in a room filled with spectators on the edges of their seats, it's as if I'm experiencing it for the very first time.

Johnny's eyes open at the second verse, his gaze drifting from me to his mom then back again. Beth and I hold hands through his entire performance, our fingers pulsing from the emotion Johnny is injecting us with. I spare a look to my side in time to catch his mother wipe away a tear. I lean in to her for comfort, and to stave off a tear of my own.

By the next verse, and as he repeats those words—*be bolder than the storm*—something magical happens in the room. The crowd begins to sing with him. His hands fall away from the guitar, again leaving everyone hanging on an unfinished note. I inhale deeply for the first time in minutes as the room erupts with whistles and applause. A few people stand on their wooden chairs and clap above their heads while others stomp on the floorboards. A chanting of *Johnny* builds, and my dad lets it roll on for nearly thirty seconds before he steps up next to Johnny on the stage.

He puts his arm around Johnny, hugging him from the side, not remotely discreet about showing where his allegiance lies. It will be impossible for anyone here tonight to doubt this year's winner. But more than Johnny blowing away the judges, it seems he's done enough to bring three men in suits to the front of the room, each of them waiting with cards in their hands, ready to pitch him on why they are the best person to make him a star.

"He was just so . . . amazing. Just . . ." Beth is crying at my side, still clapping. I circle my arms around her and we lean our heads into one another and look on as Johnny soaks up his moment. His road to fame starts here and now, and I want to be on it with him.

☘☘☘☘☘☘☘☘☘

"Are you going to hold that trophy like a teddy bear all night?" I smirk at Johnny as he clutches his prize in the passenger seat next to me.

"I don't like that it's called *teddy* bear because it makes me think of Teddy and no, I'm not going to hold Teddy all night. But this thing? Yeah, I might." He chuckles, then holds his award up, kissing the brass note affixed to the wooden base.

I laugh and shake my head. We dropped his mom off at their house. Johnny's coming back with me. My parents will be at the pub for the next few hours cleaning up and loading props and gear into volunteers' trucks and their car. I wanted time alone with my boyfriend before the rest of the world takes him over.

I pull into the driveway and we both rush to my porch and then inside. In a fit of teases and laughter, Johnny chases me up the stairs and into my room. I toss my door shut behind me in an attempt to slow him down, but it's no use. He catches me with one arm as I leap toward my bed, swinging me around at his side.

He sets his award on my desk, giving him two free hands to tickle me. I collapse into a ball on my bed as he crouches over me on his knees, needling my sides until I can't catch my breath.

"Time out! Time out!" I gasp through laughter. Johnny gives in and hooks his hand under my arm to help me sit up. I pant for several seconds, catching my breath.

"Damn you, Johnny Bishop. You messed up my hair!" I stand and run my fingers through the tangled mess around my head. My motive for standing is more than just combing out my tresses, though. I have a surprise for Johnny, something I've thought about for a long time, and I want to give it to him.

I move to my dresser and open my top drawer, reaching beneath my socks for the small box I wrapped a few days ago. I spin around and clutch it behind my back, grinning at him.

"Did you pull a cupcake out of that drawer, Brynnie?" His crooked smile is adorable.

I shake my head and scoot closer to him.

"I got you a present. You want it?" I dip my chin and squint my eyes in challenge.

He studies me for a few seconds.

"You're making me nervous. Will it bite?" He holds his hand out timidly.

"It might," I say, biting my bottom lip.

I plunk the small box wrapped in shimmery blue and purple paper in his palm. He holds my gaze for an extra breath then clutches the gift in both hands, clawing away the paper. My skin heats up in anticipation, and by the time he's holding the box of latex-free condoms clearly in his hands, I'm gnawing on my fingernail like it's a carrot.

"Oh, these are . . ."

"Yeah," I say in a meek voice.

His eyes flit up to me, his mouth parted and face painted with caution.

"Brynn, this . . . you don't have to . . ."

I suck in my lips, my pulse racing, hands sweating, forehead sweating, neck . . . sweating.

"You don't want to?" What I'm saying behind those words is *you don't want to with me?*

Johnny laughs lightly and sets the box on my bed before standing.

"God, Brynn. I want to do that with you every second of every day. And right now, alone in your room, I *really* want to. But I don't want you to think that we have to or anything like that."

"Oh. Right. Okay," I mutter, holding my breath and glancing down to my beige carpet that I vacuumed this morning for this very moment.

Johnny steps close enough to touch my chin, lifting it with the tips of his fingers until my gaze lifts with it.

"Brynn." His head tilts to his right and his eyes scan down the length of my face.

I swallow for courage as my hands gather up the gauzy gray material of my shirt, lifting it up my chest and over my head. Johnny's hand falls away and he takes a step back as he pulls his black T-shirt up and over his head. I move to my bedroom door and push it closed, turning the lock and dimming my light, just as I planned when I fantasized of this moment last night. And the night before.

"How late will your parents be?" he asks.

"Hours," I say, sliding my skirt down my hips and stepping out of it and toward Johnny. His gaze locks on my stomach then lowers to the lace trim of my black bikini panties. I bought this matching set a week ago with my birthday money. It made me feel sexy to wear something so delicate.

Johnny unsnaps his jeans and lowers his zipper, his red cotton boxers peeking out. I've felt him so many times, with my body and my hands, but it's different like this. I'm nervous, but also . . . excited. I step closer, flitting my gaze up his chest as my fingers reach him and trail up the chiseled ridges on his stomach until my palm is centered over his heart.

"It's beating so fast," I whisper.

He covers my hand with his.

"Because I'm nervous." His eyes soften as his mouth curves into his cheeks.

"You're not supposed to be nervous," I say through a soft laugh.

He shrugs slightly.

"Maybe, but I am."

His modesty emboldens me, and I move my hands to my shoulders, sliding the straps over the curves until they dangle against my biceps. I've always been a little bustier than most girls my age, and I've always been a little self-conscious about it. Tonight, though, my body's curves bolster my confidence. I reach behind my back to unhook the clasp, then catch the satin and lace against my skin before it falls away completely. Not because I'm afraid. Because I like the way Johnny's eyes burn with desire as he stares at my barely covered breasts.

"Oops," I eek out, letting the gossamer material fall to the floor. My nipples harden under his gaze and in the coolness of the air. The sensation charges my body and sends a rush of need down between my legs. I think about touching myself to quench it—to turn him on.

His eyes move to the red twisted glass that points between my breasts, down to my navel and below. I smile and clutch the gift his mom gave me, then pull it over my head and toss it on top of my shirt on the floor.

I take Johnny's hand and bring it to my breast, guiding his thumb to my hard peak and urging him to rub it with his rough skin. A sharp gasp leaves my lips when he does. While he teases my breast, I reach for his zipper, lowering it the rest of

Ginger Scott

the way then pushing his jeans to the floor. His hard-on pushes through his cotton boxers, stretching the material with his length. I draw in a deep breath and reach my hand under the band of his underwear, wrapping my hand around him and letting the heat of him warm me.

"Jesus, Brynn," he says, his voice raspy, like it was tonight on that stage. My lip curls up in a coy smile.

"I want this," I say to him, stepping in close enough to press my lips to his. His cock flexes in my hand and he deepens our kiss as he pinches my nipple so hard I whimper. That same sensation as before aches between my legs. I feel swollen and wet. Johnny slides his other hand down my stomach and under the lace of my panties, his fingers gliding against the wet skin and setting off a flurry of spasms that forces my breath away.

"Oh, gah!" My knees buckle.

"I haven't even gotten to the best part yet," he teases.

Johnny coaxes me to the bed and I lay down while he slides his boxers over his hips. I bite my knuckles as my eyes widen at the sight of him completely naked, his cock so hard and so big. I don't know how this is going to work, but my body is craving it. I squirm against the bed, pushing my ass into the mattress while my back arches to push my tits in the air. I want to be sexy for him, and I want him to touch me . . . *with that.*

He holds himself in one hand as he crawls up on the bed, sitting on his knees between my legs. His right hand begins at my knee, and he teasingly walks his fingers up my leg to my soaking wet center. He presses his palm against my middle and I push up into him, the pressure offering a little relief. His hand stills against my abdomen and his hazed eyes narrow on mine, his lips parted with heavy breath. I could watch his chest swell and release all night. He's hungry, for me.

"You are so fucking beautiful, Brynn. I want you to know that. From the moment I saw you, I thought it. And this . . ."

His eyes dip.

"This is everything," I finish for him. "I want you so bad."

A sharp breath leaves him and his fingers wrap around the top of my panties before he tugs them down. I lift my hips so he can slide the lace down my hips and calves, eventually tossing my panties into the pile of discarded clothing on the floor.

Johnny flattens his palm on the inside of my thigh and he wastes no time sliding it toward my sensitive, pulsing skin. His thumb flattens against my center and he presses then circles it. I can hear how wet I am from his touch, and rather than feel embarrassed, I open my legs to welcome him more. He pushes his thumb inside me slowly, letting me get used to the feel of him there, and after a few seconds he dips in and out. My pulse matches his rhythm. When he switches out his thumb for two fingers, I gasp at the depth. Before long, my hips rock with him, meeting his hand as he works himself in and out of me. I reach down to cover his hand with mine, to feel him as he owns me, my stomach tightening with the urge to fall over the edge. I want to come, but I also want *him*.

"I'm ready," I pant, and his gaze snaps up to meet mine.

"You're sure," he asks.

I nod and let out a breathy, "Please."

Johnny's hand leaves my body and he tears open the box of condoms, pulling out a foil packet that he rips open with his teeth. He rolls the condom over his hardness then shifts so he's hovering over me, my legs spread wide and my body waiting for him.

"We'll go slow," he promises. I nod, but I'm not sure that's what I want. My throbbing skin is begging for fast, for hard. But I'm not ready for that yet. Maybe one day, after we've done it a few times.

I writhe under his attention, turned on by my own thoughts of future us doing sexy things. Johnny teases me with his tip, running it along my wet skin a few times before putting pressure on my entrance. He nearly pushes in three times before finally, on the forth, he leans into me and slides in a few inches. It burns, but it also soothes somehow.

"Ahh," I breathe out, clutching his shoulders and squeezing my eyes shut.

"Are you okay?"

I nod and open my eyes on his heated gaze.

"You're big," I say, which lifts one side of his mouth into a cocky grin.

I play slap his shoulder, but he drops his mouth on mine before I can tell him to shut up. His kiss relaxes me, and his hips rock slowly, getting me used to his size. With each push, he slides into me more, until eventually he fills me completely. One hand rests at the side of my face while his other hand holds my hip in place so he can move in and out. Our ragged breathing is the only sound in the room other than the slap of skin against skin as his aggressiveness grows, along with my need. I hook one leg around him, pulling him into me with each thrust, the pain dissolving into a sweet pressure that builds deep inside.

Johnny takes my bottom lip between his teeth, a soft growl brewing in his chest as his hips pump. I whimper as waves of pleasure come closer and closer until I no longer have control over them. The orgasm takes me, and my leg falls limp to the side as Johnny continues to rock into me, letting out several grunts of his own. He pushes in one final time before letting his weight blanket me, our sweaty bodies sticking to one another, my room smelling of our sex.

My skin tingles everywhere, and the cool air is welcome. Johnny shifts to pull out of me before he stands and quickly discards the used condom into a tissue that he tosses in my trash. Still naked, he lays down beside me, the scar on his lower stomach pronounced. I touch it softly, then bring my fingers to my lips and press them to him again, a kiss for his pain. He grabs my hand in his and brings it to his mouth, holding my wrist to his lips and kissing it over and over again.

"I want to promise you something," he says.

"Okay," I murmur.

He rests my palm against his cheek then places his own on mine as we lay staring into one another's eyes.

"If you ever need me, for anything, no matter how big or how small, all you have to do is ask, and I will be here for you. No matter what." There's an edge to his voice, a nervous vibrato that makes me think this is something very raw for him. Needing someone to be there is important to him, probably more important than it is to most people because he has rarely had that comfort.

"Okay," I say, taking his gift and holding it in my heart before promising him the same.

"I will be there for you, too. Always. I am yours and will be your rock when you need one. No matter the trouble. Big or small. I will be there."

His eyes flicker, so I make sure he feels my words—believes them.

"I promise."

Because I love you.

Chapter 25
Present

One day of playing hooky is all I get. I'm sure my boss would be more than willing to give me more, but I feel like the reason I skipped school yesterday is all over my face. I fear I'm a walking billboard that's blasting the message: I had sex with Johnny Bishop all day yesterday!

But I did. And it was . . . everything. I've missed him so much, and yesterday was me living the fantasies I've had for ten years. But we still have work to do on us. There are questions that are unresolved, and I don't want our intense physical attraction displacing the important things—the feelings, good and bad.

The fact that he was open to my idea for the reporter today is a huge step. He's never been shy about talking to the press. Being photographed is where he excels. I can't imagine anything being more invasive than the telescopic shots I've seen of him walking around his pool deck wearing nothing. I guess fighting invasion of privacy lawsuits is easy when you sell millions of copies of a famous man's ass. I didn't buy one. But my principal did, as did MaryAnn. And at least half of the moms of my students. A few of the dads, too.

I get that *Elite Affair* is more serious than a rag at the supermarket. And though he's talked about his abusive childhood before, it's different when it's likely the main focus of the story. His polished response isn't going to cut it. This reporter is going to want to dig deeper. And Johnny keeps insisting she's going to twist things and paint him as something he's not—a murderer.

There's so much he isn't telling me. And that's what has me stuck this morning, second-guessing this plan I hatched for today. Johnny is picking up Kaylee at her hotel and meeting Shayla at our front office. My boss will bring them to my class so Shayla can observe Johnny working with the kids. I know if I were writing a story on the real Johnny Bishop, I'd want to see this. The color of his story lives here, in this classroom, on this campus, and at Pappy & Harriet's. Maybe giving her a glimpse into those things will drive the narrative more than his canned response to the mystery of his father's death.

My phone buzzes in my pocket.

JOHNNY: *We're here. Longest car ride ever.*

I sigh, letting my shoulders slump, my body basically folding into my classroom chair. Maybe this isn't a good idea at all. I should have made the drive with him. Been a distraction.

I buzz my principal's office on my classroom phone and she answers instantly. She's probably had her hand on the receiver this whole time. She's a little excited about the school being featured in a major glossy magazine. Though, given the way she dressed like she's going to a red carpet event today, maybe she's hoping to get into a photo or two as well.

The hallway outside my classroom is still quiet. No students here just yet. I prop open the door with my foot and hover at the entrance. It's about a five-minute wait before I hear voices carry down the hallway, echoing off of the concrete floors. Bless my boss for her ability to carry a conversation—her voice is the only one I hear. I'm sure Johnny is grateful.

When they round the corner, I step out and hold up a hand to say hi. Johnny's eyes flash wide and his mouth tightens. He's hating every second of this, but if it means he makes his label happy then I'm damn well going to muscle him through it. He's not losing everything because of a pushy reporter.

"Welcome to your first day of music theory." I beam and extend my hand to the beautiful Black woman in a gray pant suit standing between Johnny and my boss. She towers over all of us, even Kaylee, with the help of a set of heels that I can't imagine ever being able to balance in. Her smile is comforting, genuine, and confident. And her grip on my hand is firm. She's the female Johnny, sure and certain. This day is going to be interesting.

"You must be the famous angel in all those songs," Shayla says during our shake.

My nose twitches as I flinch. It's not that I didn't know Johnny was talking about me, it's just that hearing other people put it together feels strange. Maybe a little invasive.

"Well, I don't think I'm much of an angel, but who doesn't want to be a muse for a famous rock star from time to time." I laugh nervously and swing my hand toward my classroom to welcome everyone in.

I've arranged a few chairs off to the side, by the piano, and I guide everyone to sit there. Shayla is carrying a gear bag that she sets on the floor and immediately unzips, pulling out a recording device as well as a pretty expensive-looking camera.

"Maybe you're the one who needs a roadie," I joke. My attempt garners light laughter. Johnny's eyes flit to mine for a beat, and I'm not sure if he appreciates that attempt to lighten the mood or thinks I'm a major dork.

Shayla holds the camera up to her face and inspects the lens. She twists it off and blows inside the camera well, then snaps it back together.

"You get used to it," she says, looking through the view finder and adjusting some of the settings. "I had to carry a twenty-pound pack through the desert in Syria once for an assignment. Ever since then, everything else seems like a breeze."

"Wow. Syria." My mouth hangs open for a moment as I eye Johnny again. His mouth forms a hard line and he nods an *I told you this was going to be difficult* type of nod. I glance to Kaylee next, and she's involved in sorting through messages on her phone, which gives me some comfort. If Kaylee isn't worried, then we're doing all right. At least, I assume that's how this works. Publicists are like information bodyguards.

"Yeah. Stories about rock stars are *way* more fun than war." She chuckles as she sets her camera on top of her bag then situates herself in her chair, a slender notebook cupped in her palm, pen poised.

"Do you mind if I record?" She lifts a perfectly arched brow. Damn, I have brow envy.

"Go for it," Johnny says, clearly not as enamored with her as I am. He leans back in his chair, propping one foot up on the back of the piano and folding his hands behind his neck. He looks like he's trying too hard, but I can't really say that in front of the reporter. At least he's dressed the part—black shirt, red and black flannel, black jeans, black boots. If she doesn't leave this interview with a little bit of a crush on him, I don't understand the world at all.

I feel awkward simply sitting and watching this unfold, but Johnny really wanted me to be involved. He said it would make him less nervous having me close by, but he seems incredibly cool and I doubt I have anything to do with it. He's been through this before.

"I'd like to dive right in to the things that aren't on the bio.

Everyone knows your story on Wikipedia—musical prodigy plucked out of obscurity from the Yucca Valley desert."

Johnny's eyes squint as he smirks, his face showing a little skepticism.

"Prodigy feels a bit much, but yeah, I guess that would be my entry. I'm no Beethoven, though. To be clear."

"Ha, right. Okay," Shayla says, noting those exact words on her paper. That's a clever quote, and it makes him seem humble. I like it.

"Tell me your story in your own words, but not the one your publicist says to tell." She smirks and winks at Kaylee who winks back then rolls her eyes the moment Shayla isn't looking.

Johnny takes a deep breath and drops his foot to the floor. Leaning forward, he clasps his hands, rubbing them together as he stares at the carpet for a few seconds to gather his thoughts. He and I practiced a few responses, and I hope he's able to dig them up now. I breathe a sigh of relief when he starts talking about my classroom and how it's where he first started sharing his gift with other people. He tells her his entire story, about discovering that schools like this one had arts programs, and how it divided his time, made him realize there was more to life than football and sports.

"So, Brynn Fisher really was your angel of music." She glances to me and I feel my neck heat.

"I'm pretty sure that's the phantom of the opera, but I maybe showed him a thing or two about band," I deflect.

"She's being modest," Johnny corrects, and sweat drips down the back of my arm. I was prepared to take some of the attention for him, but I didn't promise I'd be good at accepting it.

"How so?" Shayla leads.

"Well, for starters, before I could enroll in this class, I had to learn how to read sheet music. And this one over here basically drilled me on a daily basis over the summer until I had every piece of music we were going to perform in the fall memorized."

"Wow, that's a big learning curve for someone who never read music. I took two years of piano starting when I was ten, and I don't know that I ever got beyond the basics." She laughs softly and we all seem to relax a little more. There's a kindred feeling when people share music. Band people tend to get each other. Piano lessons definitely count.

"Now, not to get too personal, but—"

"Oh, I'm sure you can't wait to get personal, Shayla." Johnny chuckles. He rubs his hands together more and sucks in his lips as his brow lifts in anticipation for her question.

"Right, well . . . it is my job. Not to beat around the bush then, did you two ever date?" She waggles her pen in the air pointing to the two of us, and I accidentally snort laugh. I'm mortified, but it cracks Johnny and Kaylee up. While I'm covering my mouth and nose with both hands, they're bending over laughing.

"Yeah, you could say we dated," Johnny says, his eyes flitting to me briefly. There's a sting in my chest, and maybe I'm just being defensive of what we had and are trying to build again. But the cavalier way he responds hurts.

"Right. I figured you don't get to be someone's angel without a little romance involved. So tell me about it. Who liked whom first? Who made the first move? And have you kept in touch?"

I remember watching my dad spray foam in the attic once. I was shocked at how quickly it could expand and fill the space with insulation. That's happening in my chest right now. Like I'm huffing on the damn stuff.

My mind is zipping through time, hopping from the first time we had sex to last night, to him showing up at Pappy &

Harriet's, to the years I spent getting over him and now, when I'm letting myself fall again.

"Oh, Shayla. Man, you go right in don't you?" Johnny's nervous laugh echoes the one happening in my head. Both my boss and Kaylee have leaned forward and are giving his response their full attention. I can't work my mouth to say anything, so the best I can do is shift in my chair and push my hands under my thighs.

"People love a good love story, what can I say." She leans back in her chair and crosses her wrists, her pen dangling from her fingers as she's prepared to wait him out.

I swallow hard and meet his eyes. They narrow on me as his smile softens, his mouth higher on one side. A deep breath lifts his chest and his head falls a little to the side.

"I would never speak for Brynn, but I can tell you this—I definitely fell first. And I was terrified to make the first move, but I guess I did. It was the single best kiss I've ever had. And no, we haven't kept in touch like we should have. Because rock stars make stupid choices sometimes. But I'm learning."

My heartbeat is a dull thud in my full chest, but the harder it beats the more room it makes inside of me. I can hardly hear anything in the room, and even Johnny's voice sounds like he's talking to me through a tin can. I'm sure I'm pale and glistening with sweat. I also want to cry with strange instant relief.

"Brynn?"

I shake my head at my name and flash my gaze to Shayla, wondering if that's the first or fifth time she's said my name. I decide to make a joke out of it.

"I'm sorry, I'm still a little rattled that the hottest guy in music thinks our teenaged kiss ranks number one."

Everyone laughs and Shayla writes down my quote.

Quite literally saved by a bell, I stand up and head to my classroom door to prop it open for the soon-to-be incoming students. Johnny and Shayla talk a little more, though she seems to have turned her recorder off, so I think that part of our morning is over. She hasn't asked about his father's death, and she seemed satisfied by his own retelling of growing up in a house with abuse. He wasn't shy about it, and he definitely gave her more detail than I think he has ever before. But he didn't go beyond him leaving and making it big. He stopped right at the line, and Shayla didn't seem to want to cross it. At least not that one. *My line, however?*

Principal Baker sent out a message to the parents of students in my class last night warning them about the media presence in my classroom today. I notice two or three of the kids opted to stay home, and I envy them a little. I wish I could have done that. The most important players are here, today. Namely, Jade, who has been working with Johnny every day to prepare her audition material. She has five schools requesting tapes, and I honestly believe she'll get into all of them. But the more she works with Johnny, the way they duet, leads me to believe someone is going to find her before she enrolls anywhere. I think she's destined for Johnny's path, albeit I hope a healthier one.

I welcome the class and introduce Shayla. A few of the students ask her questions about her job, and she lets some of them look through her camera as she gets it ready to shoot photos of Johnny at work. The next hour flies by, as Johnny and Jade work side-by-side at the piano, figuring out the perfect bridge for the song she's writing. Shayla captures shots of Johnny and Jade singing then she follows him around the room as he makes his rounds to talk with the other students. A few of them offer quotes that she jots down, sharing how inspiring it is to have someone like him in their classroom for a semester. And when class is finished, Johnny gets into how vital this work has been in helping him get clean and get back to the things that matter.

Kaylee gets a call, so she steps into the hallway as Principal Baker takes care of wrapping up my class, opening the door for the students to head to their next hour while she heads up to her office. Johnny and I are left with Shayla as my room empties, and her line of questioning from before lingers in the back of my mind. I push my hands in the pockets of my black pants and notice Johnny's done the same in his jeans. We both look guilty.

"I hope you got what you needed?" Johnny bounces on his toes, the nervous boy shining through.

"It's a good start," she responds. Johnny's feet flatten to the floor and his shoulders drop. That's not what he was hoping, but we talked about this too. Elite Affair stories are long, in-depth pieces. Shayla is going to need more material than an hour in a high school class can provide.

"I'll get with Kaylee to schedule a phone call or maybe a breakfast later this week. Does that work for you?"

She glances up from her gear bag when Johnny doesn't respond right away. My neck turtles in anticipation of what he might say.

"What's left? I mean, I can only talk about self-medicating from my past trauma so many times in so many ways." Johnny's leading her, but I know that's not what she wants to get into. My plan failed.

"I'd like to talk more about your family, beyond the trauma. You've thanked your mom in your album credits several times, for her support. And I know she's ill now . . . cancer."

My stomach sinks when I hear her utter the C word. That's something nobody should know unless Beth wants them to. And I can tell by the deepening red in Johnny's cheeks that he *definitely* doesn't want to share his mother's business.

"That's off the table." His words are curt and his mouth is a flat line.

Shayla straightens her spine and rolls her shoulders back.

"And your father's death? Is that off the table?" Her tone is colder than before. This is the war correspondent shining through.

"We're done," Johnny says. He heads toward the door, but I linger behind with Shayla. She's still not fully packed and ready to leave, and my instincts are always to try to salvage situations. I don't know why I think I can with this one, but I have to try.

"It's still raw for him," I say under my breath. My voice isn't low enough, though.

"It's going to *be* raw for a while. And it's off the table. All of it." Johnny is holding the door open, his fingers spread out wide on the wood. My body rushes with adrenaline and panic.

"Johnny, I understand wanting to keep some things private. But I wouldn't be doing my job if I didn't go there with this story, at least on some level. The world has a fascination with you, and that fame comes with great reward and some really shitty side effects. Personal space for people like you is limited. I respect how hard holding that line is, I really do. But I can't write this story without at least mentioning what most of the world knows on some level, or is going to find out thanks to the speed of social media. Some person at a grocery store will pick up on something and then share a photo with their friends, and then the Internet sleuths will put their theories together. That becomes the story. I'd rather get it on the record the right way, with the facts. I'll pull them together from every source I can. I'd really love if one of those sources was you. And about your mom, I can speak with her directly if you prefer. I think her love for you would really give the world the full picture of who Johnny Bishop is."

My legs are shaking but I fight the urge to flop down in my chair. I rest an arm on top of the piano and chew at my bottom lip while Johnny continues to glare at Shayla with a hard stare. She eventually drops her chin and shakes her head.

"That's too bad," she says, zipping up her bag.

She pulls it over her shoulder then juts a hand out for me. I shake it and croak out a polite, "Thank you for coming."

She marches toward Johnny next, pausing at the doorway with her hand out for him too. He stares at it for a few seconds then breathes a snarky laugh through his nose. He shakes it and lifts his head to meet her eyes.

"Stay away from my mom."

An uncomfortable face-off lasts about three seconds, the two of them blinking at one another before Shayla exits the room. Her heels click against the concrete and eventually fade into the rest of the noise of kids rustling around the hallway, trying to get to their next class. I have beginners coming in soon.

I meet Johnny's eyes across the room and open my mouth to take a deep breath while I search my brain for the right words. "Johnny, what if—"

"No." He points a finger at me, holding it in the air as his molars press together and he flexes his jaw.

I start to shake my head and he leaves. My eyes flutter closed as the classroom door slams shut. It opens about ten seconds later with my first student, and I turn my back on him to get myself in order. A few more of my students drift in, and their laughter over an upcoming dance sets me on edge. It's so trivial, but I know to them this dance is the most important thing in the world. It was to me once, too. I flit my gaze toward the door, waiting for it to open with more people. The next person to walk in, though, is Kaylee.

I shrug as she closes in on me, her face serious and her

phone pressed to her ear. She presses it against her hip, as if that will mute our voices for whomever is on the other line, and leans into me.

"He just busted through the back doors, and I don't know this place. I called an Uber, so if you could see whatever has him all . . ." She flits her fingers in the air to mimic fireworks, I suppose. That must be her way of saying he's freaking out.

"Shayla brought up his mom. He just needs to process it," I say, not really diving into the true root of what made him take off.

"Okay, well, help him . . . process." Her tone is unsympathetic, and she's back talking to the person on the other line before I can answer her demand of me.

I call the choir room to see if the teacher can spare Mary-Ann, who is really supposed to be *my* assistant anyhow. She sighs, because she thinks glee club is the most important thing on campus, but tells me MaryAnn will cover for my hour. She joins me at the head of the class when the last bell rings, so I show her the song the students are supposed to be working on this week. It's a simple holiday tune that they'll play for the winter recital. I know MaryAnn has a whole host of questions about why I need to leave and how this morning went, and I'm sure her Spidey senses can tell that Johnny and I have moved past the enemies to friends again line, but now's not the time. I need to fix this before it gets worse.

With second hour underway across campus, I step into the empty hallway and let my instincts guide me out to the football field. I spot his boots between the bleacher rows in the home stands. It's finally cool outside, so I wrap my sweater around my body and tuck my hands inside the sleeves. My hair blows around my neck like a scarf.

I step onto the track and catch Johnny's attention as I approach the bleacher entrance. He drops his head forward as I climb the steps until I reach his row. I take a seat in front of him, twisting so my legs are folded up on the bench and I'm tucked between his knees. He lifts his gaze and smirks when I rest my elbows on his thighs.

"You know, I bet we're not the first couple to sit like this in these bleachers."

I glare at him and let my head fall to the side.

"Sorry. I'm a boy. Even when life is shit we think about our dicks."

I close my eyes and shake my head, my laugh nearly silent.

"I'm sorry I couldn't make this completely go away," I say. His eyes settle on mine for a few seconds before he reaches for my face. His palm rests on my cheek and I lean into it.

"It's not your fault. I should have let the label drop me. I don't know why this story, of all stories, is so important. I guess I have an album coming out in a few months, assuming the music I wrote when I was drunk and high isn't total shit." He looks up at the cloudy sky and puffs his chest with a laugh.

"They call that experimental rock," I tease.

He shakes with more quiet laughter.

"Are you comparing me to Pink Floyd or the Beatles?"

I grimace and bunch my brow.

"Uh, no, Mr. Big for Your Britches. Slow down there, rock-star boy."

Johnny leans forward and presses a kiss to the top of my head.

"I'm sorry I walked out like that. It's just that things from my past seem to keep finding their way into my present. And I wish that man could just stay dead. Is that cold?" He looks into my eyes for a few seconds. "Eh, I don't even care if it's cold. He always finds a way to ruin things. And he's going to ruin me."

"I'm from your past," I say.

The skin between his eyes dents.

"You said things from your past keep finding their way into your present. I did that. And I don't know that it's so bad the second time around." I give him an impish smile that he mimics.

"You're right. Some things from my past are definitely timeless."

My chest warms at his response, but it's still hard to take a deep breath. He's still troubled, and though it's not my troubles to undo, I want to help. I need to. I promised I would—*always*.

"Can I ask something?"

His eyes blink wider and lock on mine.

"Why not. Today is interrogation day," he laughs out.

I purse my lips. "I don't want you to feel like I'm interrogating you. I want to talk. Like we always could. Is that okay?" I wait as he seems to work through my ask. His gaze softening before blinking to look down as he nods.

"How'd you get to LA? That night . . . when we were supposed to go together. You got there somehow, without me. How?" My mouth waters from the injection of anxiety simply uttering this question gives me. I have thought about this for a decade. I've pictured him hitchhiking, walking, calling someone I didn't know.

"My mom had some money saved from her art. Just stuff she sold at farmers markets and craft fairs when my dad wasn't around. She kept it as cash, hid it in the garage." He looks to his side and chuckles softly. "That damn garage was her safe space."

His eyes come back to me.

"My mom dropped me off at the bus station, and I got a twenty-four-dollar, one-way ticket. I stayed at a youth hostel for about six weeks, until luck took over."

Luck. He thinks it was all luck, still. It wasn't luck. It was destiny. But I don't know why I couldn't be the one to take him to the starting point.

"And you couldn't go with me because . . ."

My legs are numb, and I'm lightheaded. I've waited years to ask this question, to delve into the *why* and the *what*. I'm so afraid of his response, though, I almost wish I could take it back.

Johnny's eyes search mine for long, quiet seconds. His Adam's apple bobs with a desperate sense, and the corners of his mouth twitch.

"You bought a bus ticket instead of letting me take you. I have to know, Johnny. If we have any shot at all—"

"There are things that I can't come back from, Brynnie. Things *we* can't come back from. If I could tell you—if I could do *so many* things over—I would." He swallows hard and his eyes slope and get glassy.

"Time machines aren't real, Johnny. All we have left is the truth." I bundle his hands into mine. They shake and he looks down as his lips part with a ragged breath.

He's struggling, and I want to untangle him from his burdens. I just need to know what they are. I need to see all sides of him, even the things he thinks I can't handle. Maybe if he knew some of mine . . .

"I'd like to tell you about my ex. But don't look at me. I need you to keep your eyes down, because if you look at me—" My voice breaks and I squeeze my eyes shut to cut off the painful tears that threaten to fill my eyes. I've had so much therapy to overcome this part of my life. I try to remember everything I learned years ago to guide me through sharing my truth with Johnny now.

"His name was Aiden. It was also Jax, and Preston, and I think there was a Thomas in the mix."

Johnny's forehead wrinkles but he keeps his promise and remains focused on our hands.

"He was a con man. And at first, he had me believing he was a sweet, gentle man who ran a nonprofit for foster kids. We got married fast because I was trying to check off boxes in my life and maybe still trying to get over this boy who broke my heart."

He shakes his head in denial and I squeeze his hands a little.

"Stay with me. Anyhow, we dated a month before getting married. He struck me across the face with the back of his hand in our kitchen on our fifth week of marriage because I asked why he was out late the night before and not answering his phone."

Johnny draws in a sharp breath and looks up, his eyes boring into mine. I shake my head.

"You can't look at me. Even if you're angry and not blaming me. You can't look at me." I wait him out, not speaking until he finally drops his chin again. I can feel the anger radiating from his body.

"He only hit me once. But he stole from me. Drained my savings with his gambling. He broke the spire necklace your mom made me, then threw the shards in the trash. Then about a week after I questioned where he was, I saw a story on the news about a guy who was robbing beauty parlors and barber shops. Someone had caught the man on camera without his mask, and even with the blurry photo, I knew. It was him."

"I turned him in that night. He was arrested in our drive-way, and I never had to see him in person again. I identified him from a photo lineup. A lawyer handled the dissolution of marriage. It's annulled, technically. Like it never happened. But Johnny . . . it happened. And I regret every second of it."

He slowly nods but keeps to his word, not meeting my gaze.

After nearly a minute in silence, he leans forward and rests his cheek on top of our tethered hands. I give him the same respect he gave me. I let him hide.

"You know how they found my father in the lake?"

A hurricane blasts through my body and my stomach sinks.

"Yes," I croak.

Johnny lifts his head and our eyes meet.

"I took him to the lake."

Time stops. I want to gasp but somehow find the strength not to. I take a measured breath through my nose, forcing every movement my body makes to be unnoticeable. I feel as if I'm balancing a tower of champagne flutes, and the smallest wrong move will send them crashing to the ground.

"Johnny, did you—" I stop myself. He didn't. But someone did.

"He found out I wasn't in band for grade reasons. Such a stupid thing to rage about, but he raged. He was so mad. And then . . ." He pauses, his mouth open as his jaw works back and forth, as if he's calculating something. I'm not a jury, though. I'm not the cops. I'm not Shayla. He can trust me.

"His precious award broke. Man of the Year for his athletic conference in college. He loved that thing, and it . . . it broke. So when my mom dropped me off for the bus to LA, I had to wait an hour and I just kept thinking about his stupid Man of the Year trophy, so I went to this award shop I found about three blocks away and pulled up a photo for the old guy who owned the store. He said he could make one, and I gave him two hundred-dollar bills. I figured I'd be back when LA didn't work out and I'd pick it up. But then . . ." He lifts his shoulders.

"Then LA worked out," I respond.

He nods and lets out a slow, "Yeah."

My brow furrows and I piece together his disjointed story. I don't know why a trophy would matter so much, why never picking it up would matter. It's not like his dad is around to appreciate it anymore.

"Someone sent me the receipt for that award about a month before I showed up during your showcase night. A few weeks before I found out about my mom. It was in an envelope with no note. Just a ten-year-old receipt."

My eyes narrow.

"And you think Shayla sent that to you? Because . . ." I want him to finish the story for me, but he seems stuck.

"It was either Shayla or one of the many other people who still likes to drag out rumors and hearsay and conspiracy theories. Why would I order a trophy for a dead man?"

"But you didn't know he was dead," I respond.

His mouth tightens and his eyes dull, and that's when I see it.

He did know.

"Hey, y'all know they give the kids detention for that, don't you?"

I jet to my feet and hold up a hand to wave to Coach O'Brien. He took over for Coach Jacobs and never coached Johnny, but ever since his talk to the whole school a few weeks ago, our current coach has been a big fan.

Johnny stands up as well and walks a few steps down, leaving me behind him, still whirling with questions.

"I think maybe I had a detention or two like that in my day," Johnny jokes, hopping down to the track level and shaking coach's hand. The two of them banter, swapping tales of high school football then morphing into their favorite classic rock songs. I want to invite myself into their conversation, but I can't. My mind is stuck in the middle of a puzzle, and I need answers in order to get out.

The bell ending second hour blares through the speakers on the field, and I twist to look back at the school grounds where students are spilling through doors. A lot of them are coming this way for PE, which is why Coach is out here.

I make my way down to where the two men are standing and brush Johnny's arm with the back of my palm.

"Sorry to interrupt, but I need to get back to my class. Johnny, do you want me to walk you out?" My gaze begs him, and he spends a breath considering my offer.

"It's okay. I'm going to stick around for a little bit of class if that's okay with you?" He glances to Coach O'Brien, who is practically gleeful at the idea and gives him a thumbs up. He looks back to me, his eyes drawn in with what I read as apology and fear. "I'll see you later. I'm going to my mom's from here, so I can show myself to the parking lot."

My heart sinks and my stomach twists. He's freezing on me, locking everything down again. And I was just cracking him open.

Chapter 26
Age 18

ME: Hey, where RU?

Literally half of our student population was in the band room this morning waiting for Johnny to show up. A lot of people in town were at the showcase and got to see his performance, but most of the students, unless they're in the arts, only *heard* about his jaw-dropping turn on the stage. Videos were shared and texts were sent, but seeing it live is a whole different experience.

They wanted to see it live, one last time, at their school. Because we all know that soon Johnny is going to be so much bigger than this place.

But he wasn't here this morning.

I ran to his second hour classroom from mine to see if he showed up for English. And then again for government. Now, it's lunch, and I'm staring Teddy in the eyes from across the cafeteria, not sure what to do. I send Teddy a text.

ME: I don't know where he is.

I hold my phone up and waggle it, alerting him to look. He puts his slice of pizza down and shifts his weight to pull his phone from his pocket. I wait while he reads. His eyes flit up to mine and I shrug. Teddy spins in his seat and scans the cafeteria, as if Johnny would be sitting somewhere else. As if he wouldn't be surrounded by everyone in an instant, all of them begging for photos and for him to sing for them.

Teddy stands from his seat and grabs his tray. He heads my way and plops it down across from me. I'm starving because I haven't eaten yet, so I grab the rest of his pizza and take a huge bite. He eyes me.

"Sorry, I didn't get in line today."

He scowls a little then waves his hand.

"It's fine. Finish it." He slides into the seat across from me and types on his phone. I sit up tall to spy on him. He's sending Johnny a message too. When he doesn't get anything back after a minute, he calls him. I toss the slice of pizza back on his tray, way more worried than I am hungry.

"Straight to his voicemail." Teddy looks down at his lap as he waits to leave a message. "Hey, man. Brynn and I have been texting you. We're a little worried because you don't ever miss school, and people are all kinds of excited about that performance—"

"Well, maybe they can buy a ticket for the next one."

Teddy and I both jump and spin around at the sound of Johnny's voice. My body floods with instant relief, and I fly toward him, tackling him with a hug that buries my face in his chest.

"Hey," he breathes in the nook of my neck followed by a light chuckle.

"We were worried," I admit, pulling back enough to look him in the eyes. His focus moves from my left eye to my right before he reaches up and smooths wild strands of hair from my face.

"I'm okay." His expression seems peaceful, maybe even hopeful, which undoes the knot that had formed in my gut. I took Johnny back to his house late last night. He wanted to be able to celebrate his great night with his mom this morning. They must have had breakfast or done something special.

"Actually, I'm way better than okay," he says.

My face puzzles and Teddy lightly punches his friend's arm.

"Yeah? Some big record label swoop in and offer you a million dollars?" Teddy laughs at his wild prediction, but Johnny simply shrugs and lifts a brow.

"Holy shit! You're kidding!" Teddy's eyes bulge.

A few people have realized that Johnny is here now and are making their way toward us. I nod toward them to give Johnny a little warning that he's about to be more popular than anyone who has ever stepped foot in this cafeteria. He glances over his shoulder but quickly turns back to me, placing his hands on my shoulders and looking me square in the eyes.

"Owen Shephard was at the showcase. He came by the house this morning and asked me if I wanted to play a gig at this place in LA, some bar called the Train Yards."

My eyes light up.

"Johnny! That place is famous. People play there to get discovered and make it big. *Big* big! And Owen Shephard?" The lead singer of Rosco, one of the biggest bands in the world, happened to be at our showcase. It's the kind of thing my dad swears happens all the time. And I know from the stories of people who have gone on to make it big that it does happen. I just didn't think it would when I was there to see it. My stunned face is frozen with my eyes wide and mouth agape. Johnny simply laughs and says, "Yeah. Crazy, right?"

Within seconds, he's taken over by a line of our fellow students, all waiting to shake his hand and take photos with him. Some ask him to sing, and he humbly tells them he's too embarrassed. I don't think that's the case at all. He doesn't get embarrassed. But I do think maybe he's overwhelmed.

Things calm down as lunch winds to a close. Teddy and I linger behind to talk with our now famous friend, my *boyfriend*! I can't believe any of this is happening, and my mind swirls with a mix of excitement and a dose of dread. What if Johnny leaves and doesn't come back? What does this mean for us? None of those thoughts are fair because we're young and he deserves to chase this opportunity. But I'm also in love with him, and a part of me feels him somehow slipping away.

"So, what's the plan?" Teddy asks.

Johnny's eyes hover on the now-empty cafeteria seats, his mouth caught somewhere between a smile and panic. He blinks a few times before darting his gaze to me.

"My dad isn't going to let me go. I won't have a car to take." His eyes draw in and his mouth tips into a frown. "I don't know why I didn't think of it until now. Why my mom didn't think of it. I guess my mom and I were both so excited when Owen showed up at the house, and he gave me this card with a phone number to get myself on the list. I'm supposed to go Friday, but how? We have halftime. Your dad won't be okay with both of us being gone. And besides, Coach needs me, and my dad—"

"Coach will be fine. The team will be fine. It's fucking football, and while you make us better, we're still not that good, bro. This thing? This is your dream. I'll handle Coach." Teddy's reassuring tone seems to alleviate some of Johnny's worries, but his manic nodding indicates he's still on the fence.

"You guys, I can't ask Coach for this. It will become a thing, that I'm missing a game, and then someone will reach out to my dad, and—"

He cuts himself off. He doesn't have to say the ugly out loud. His dad will lose his mind, and he'll take his rage out on his son or his wife. He'd never be okay with Johnny missing a game, so what's the point of asking?

"So, don't ask." I barely recognize my own voice.

Johnny lets out a harsh chuckle at first, but when his gaze meets my dead-serious expression, he stops.

"Brynn, simply not showing? That would be worse. Even your dad would be pissed," Johnny says.

I pinch my mouth on one side and play the scenario out in my head. Yeah, he'll be pissed. But he'll also forgive me. Forgiveness later is a saying for a reason. It can be deployed for good.

"And I'll drive," I say.

I'm not sure how I'm going to accomplish this insta-promise, but he has to get to this opportunity. And I'm eighteen. He's eighteen. We're adults. Granted, my stomach is in turmoil at the thought of telling my dad we blew off a halftime show because I had to take my boyfriend for an overnight two hours away. But also, I'm a whole lot less worried about the consequences after than I am afraid to ask permission first.

"Brynn, it's a lot to ask."

"Well, you didn't ask. You could have, but you don't have to. Because I'm deciding. I'm offering. I'll drive you. What time do you go on?" I'm swaying on my feet, trying to quell my nerves, because I have a lot to sort out to make this happen. I'll need to warn someone in band, Cori maybe. Devin definitely owes both of us one, too.

Johnny pulls his phone from his pocket and slides through his messages, stopping on one he's marked as unread. "Looks like I'm on at ten."

That's late, which is good because it gives us time, but also the Train Yards is a pretty gritty bar. I'm sure Johnny will be handled on the way in and out because he's underage. I'll have to hang out with security or wait in the car. None of that matters. That's logistics. Getting him there is the goal.

"Okay. That gives us plenty of time. I'll pick you up at your house at six and we'll get there plenty early."

Johnny's eyes slit and his lips tighten.

"Earlier?" I offer.

"No, it's not that. Just . . . my dad might be home. How about we meet somewhere? Like that fish and chips place on Main. I can get there easily and it's on the way to the highway. I hate to make this request, but we'll need to come home after. I know it will be late, but I don't want my mom left to defend something I did." The crease on his forehead is deep.

"That's fine. Of course. We'll do that." I hope that letting him call the shots will give him some comfort, but his anxiety seems to have settled in for the long haul. I wish his dad would stay out of town so I could take his mom too. She'd love to see this, and I don't think he'd be half as afraid of any of it if she were along for the ride.

I step in close and press my palms on his chest as he slowly wraps me in his arms. Staring straight up at him, I meet his eyes and will myself the ability to take away his worries.

"Remember our promise?" I prompt.

He gives a slight nod, eyes still heavy.

"No matter what, I will be there. No matter what you need, even if it's that we turn around and come home at the halfway point because you don't feel right. Or we don't go at all last minute because of *him*. You have to try, and I have your back for all the rest."

"Me too, man," Teddy says, squeezing Johnny's shoulder. "Rise or fall, you're my best friend. You call, I come. That's how this works."

Johnny's eyes shift to Teddy, then back to me. I close mine

as he presses a kiss to my forehead. His heart pounds against his chest under my palms. All I can hope is that this thunder is anticipation and excitement, and not fear.

For my entire life, Friday nights in the fall have been reserved for Howl football games. As a toddler, I sat on Mom's lap at the top of the stands so I could get a good view of Dad's work and the band marching. In kindergarten, Dad let me join him for warm ups, then he brought me up to the press box with him so I could watch from up there. By the time I was in junior high, I was playing with the band for warm ups and helping out on the sidelines by organizing gear and stashing away discarded flags from the color guard.

All I ever wanted was to lead this band. To stand on that podium for a dozen Friday nights with my hands up and their sound under my control. It hurts a little to be missing it all tonight. And my stomach hasn't felt right for a week knowing how disappointed my dad is going to be when I never show up. But I don't regret this decision. Not one bit. It's the right call, and when everything is said and done, my dad, my mom, Devin, Cori, the band—they'll all see it that way.

I left my father a note on his desk in the band room. He's probably reading it right about now. I told him not to worry but I won't be coming for the game or halftime. I let him know Johnny wouldn't be there either, and then I told him why. And I begged him to understand. I alluded to Johnny's risk without putting anything down on paper that could somehow get him in trouble. My dad knows what Johnny's home is like. He'll get it once he calms down.

I'm sure I have a message from him on my phone, but I

refuse to look. I don't want anything giving me second thoughts, and if I have to call him, I would rather it be *after* Johnny goes on. Besides, my eyes need to remain on the intersection before me. I got to the restaurant early and parked by the road so I would see Johnny coming from any direction. I strain my neck to scan behind my car, squinting and shading my eyes from the bright street lights. My gaze traces the sidewalks in either direction as I slowly turn back to face the front.

No worries. It's still ten minutes until we said we'd meet. I sink down in my seat and turn the engine off to save gas. I've had Johnny's song "Shelter" stuck in my head ever since the showcase. It's one thing getting to hear him practice it piece by piece in my bedroom or in the band room, but seeing him on stage in a small venue like that brought it to life. That song is meant for a certain mood, and as much as I believe Johnny's destined to be a major headliner one day, I hope that song is saved for the right places and right times. Or maybe I'm selfish and want to keep it for myself.

I spend the next few minutes tidying my car, clearing out wrappers from various candy bars and packs of gum from my center console and collecting random coins into my palm. I count the total out twice, surprised to discover three dollars and sixteen cents in quarters, nickels, pennies and dimes. I pour them into the cupholder so they're easier to find, then lean over to the passenger seat and pop open my glovebox. I smirk at the sight of the drumstick tips. It feels like ages ago when Devin gave these to me. It feels like I've been eighteen for much longer than a few months; like I've been in love with Johnny for more than just my senior year. There's so much left to experience, and I thought I would walk this journey *with* him. But if this trip goes the way my gut says it will, I'll be doing it all without him. The state marching championship, jazz band, prom, graduation. He's not going to put stardom on pause so he can be in the highlights of the Yucca Valley North yearbook. Why would he? He'll be in a studio, recording. Joining a small tour, opening for someone. Networking and building his following. Capturing the hearts of every girl who isn't me, and there will be plenty of them.

I take the sticks out of the glovebox then snap it closed. Holding them in my hands, I patter out a rhythm on my steering wheel. They feel nice in my hands, and the swing beat I create to match the jazz song in my head is good for my nerves. I obsess over it for a few minutes, even humming the tune and doing my best to skat. I chuckle at how absurd I sound and eventually end my personal concert, dropping my sticks in my lap and giving in to the urge to check my phone.

It's five minutes past our meeting time, and I feel nauseous. As I predicted, there's a missed call and a text from my father. I open it since I don't have any messages from Johnny, and all it says is *CALL ME NOW!!!!* My arms are tingling, my skin pebbled with goose bumps as a chill travels down my spine. Something isn't right.

I prop the phone on my steering wheel and tap the edges with my fingertips, staring at the message screen, willing one to pop up from Johnny. I challenge myself to wait a full minute, and when nothing happens, I wait another. As ten minutes past our meetup time approaches, I squirm in the driver's seat. Sitting still no longer feels okay. I need to be looking for him. I turn my engine over and fire off a quick text.

ME: *I'm here. Are you close?*

I stare at the screen, willing a sign to appear that he sees my message. A response. A call. Anything.

ME: *I'm starting to worry. Did you get this?*

Another minute passes with no response. I dial his number and it goes right to voicemail. I try again and get the same result. I flip my headlights on and prop my phone in my cupholder. I pull onto the main road and make a slow pass a mile toward Johnny's house before flipping around and heading back to the restaurant.

The street is empty. Not even a car passes me heading the other way. Everyone in town is probably at the football game or at a bar. My stomach kicks with my pulse. I pass the restaurant and continue half a mile in the other direction. When that turns up nothing, I turn into the small neighborhood and weave through the nearby dark desert roads. I flip my brights on and utter *please* over and over.

There's no reason for Johnny to be on any of these roads, but he could still be at his house. I stop at a small four-way intersection and send him another message. He's now thirty minutes late.

ME: *I'm scared. I'm going to drive the route to your house. Please just call. I'll be driving.*

I turn the volume all the way up, then turn to head up the hill toward Johnny's house. About halfway there, I sit up with hope when I see what looks like a person standing by the side of the road. But when I get closer, I realize it's nothing but a piece of cardboard advertising puppies for sale taped to a road sign.

I'm legitimately scared, and my mind is creating a million different scenarios, all of them ending with Johnny being in trouble, or worse, hurt. His father's angry expression burns through my thoughts and my foot reacts by pressing the accelerator harder. I zip up the winding road and blow through a stop sign that nobody is ever around for. I pull all the way up his driveway and kick open my car door, leaving the motor running. Scanning for signs, there's nothing out of the ordinary. His house is dark and closed up, except for the porch light that glows by his front door.

My hands balled into fists that I keep squeezing then relaxing, I trek up the walkway to the front door, pausing for a breath before pressing the buzzer with my thumb. I sway on my feet as I wait for anyone to answer the door. At this point, I'd be happy to see his father. I press my face against the glass of the small window by the door. It's covered with a gauzy material, but I can see movement in the house. I'm finally able to make out Beth as she shuffles toward the door, and I step back a few feet before she opens it.

"Brynn. Hi! Why aren't you at football?"

Her greeting knocks me over mentally. Does she not know where I'm supposed to be?

"I'm looking for Johnny. Is he here?" I dig my nails into my palm as I strain to look beyond her, into the house. It's dark inside, maybe a faint light from another room spilling into the hallway. It's quiet, too. No television or music playing.

"He went to LA. He left a while ago."

My eyes flash to hers, and prickle with tears.

I shake my head.

"Were you supposed to go together? I know he's on the road. He texted me a few minutes ago." She pulls her phone from her back pocket and shows me a text.

JOHNNY: *Stopped for a snack. Call you when I get there.*

I blink at it a few times, not sure it's real. How could it be? Who is he riding with?

"Did Teddy pick him up?" It's the only solution I can think of but it's not possible. Teddy is playing a game right now.

She shakes her head and lifts a shoulder.

"I'm sorry, Brynn. I just know he left. I'm sure he'll call you, though."

All I can do is stare at her. I'm dumbstruck. I'm sick. Confused. And I think maybe I'm heartbroken. He went without me.

"I'm sorry to bother you. If he calls again, maybe . . . just tell him I hope he's amazing. Or was, if he calls after his performance. Or . . . tell him I'll be awake and he can call." I swallow down the sour taste that coats my tongue and hold up a hand for a polite wave as I backpedal to my car.

I slip inside and slam the door closed, my body shaking with every raw emotion I've ever known. My eyes zero in on the now closed door, and I replay Beth's words over and over. She was so comfortable. So calm. If Johnny had run into his dad, or if he were in trouble, she wouldn't have been able to contain it. I'd see it on her face. But she was fine.

My hands grip the steering wheel and I let my nails dig into the leather as I roar out a scream in the solace of my car. I lift up to catch my red cheeks growing more crimson in the mirror. This isn't happening. I can't handle this. If it's a joke—or if this is how he's breaking up with me—I won't be okay. I'm *not* okay.

I pull out of the driveway and turn around to head back down the hill and to the school. The football lights glow in the distance, and I will myself to make every green light that stands in my way. I pull into the parking lot near the field and park as close as I can to the gate. Sprinting through, I wave at one of the teachers who recognizes me then rush up the stands and into the announcers booth where my father is waiting to announce the band's performance. When his gaze hits me, he pushes the mic back into the holder and storms in my direction.

"Young lady, what the hell were you thinking?" His hands reach my shoulders and he squeezes them as he lowers his head to meet my eyes.

He's livid. As he should be. But all I can do is crumble into tears.

"Brynn. What is it?" He kneels as my body goes limp, and in seconds he's holding my weight up as my arms sling around his body.

"Brynn, are you okay?" His words sound as if they're piping through a tunnel.

I shake my head and struggle to breathe.

"Come here," my father says, propping my weight up with his shoulder. He helps me to a chair that one of the opposing team's coaches gives up. Someone hands me a cup of water and I take a sip then shake my head.

"Johnny left. Without me, Dad. He left without me. And I don't know where he is. And he just . . ." My body quakes with an enormous sob and tears stream down my face. "He just left."

I fall into my dad's arms again, and he scoops me into his lap, sitting on the floor as he rocks me.

"I'm sure he's all right, Brynn. We'll find out. But you're okay, right?" He pushes my tear-soaked hair away from my face, and I suck in a hard breath in an attempt to speak to him.

"I'm okay," I lie.

I'm not okay. I don't think I'm going to be for a very long time.

Chapter 27
Present

I've been staring at Beth's message to me for the last hour. I keep flip-flopping between action and inaction, my focus on her text and my phone, then on Shayla Macias's card that I've had in my purse since Kaylee handed it to me.

Beth texted me this morning, shortly after Johnny did, and asked me to facilitate a meeting between her and the reporter. Today, before it's too late. It's that *too late* part that feels ominous, maybe a touch foreboding.

Nothing is adding up. And the waiting for answers is making me more than restless. It's making me want to bully it out of people. And that would be it. I'd either get the answers I want and live with them or I wouldn't. Johnny and me, though —I'm not sure we could go back.

There are things we can't come back from.

This is what he meant. Whatever it is that I can't pinpoint, whatever truth lie is the culprit, is the key to ruining it all. I'm just not sure how deep that ruin goes. Does it ruin us? Does it ruin Beth? Johnny? His career?

To make things worse, Johnny stayed at his mother's last night. He sent me a text that he wouldn't make school today.

That news bummed some of the students out, but it disappointed me most. He had a good reason; he wants to go to a meeting. The kind that isn't sponsored by a rehab joint for rich people, but one that's held in more humble surroundings and run by people who do the work because it truly matters to them, not because they like the massive paycheck. He brought it up two days ago, and I found a group that meets at a community center in Beaumont. I sent it to him after the interview yesterday, something in my gut telling me if he was ever going to need that kind of meeting, now is the time. I'm proud of him for wanting to talk and share, for finding support outside of his small circle and beyond the program prescribed to celebrities at Waves. That circle hasn't included me for ten years, but even with me in it, it's important to have lifelines wherever necessary.

I do wish he trusted the line I offer him a little more. He's keeping secrets. He's been keeping them for years. It's ruining him from the inside out.

Then again, how could he ever trust me again if I do this favor for Beth?

Since my last hour of the day is a prep hour, I decide to let MaryAnn handle grading the quizzes from beginning music theory and for once take advantage of being the principal's favorite teacher. I don't let anyone know I'm leaving early, and manage to get my car out of the parking lot without even Carl, our security guard, noticing. Granted, Carl usually naps right about now while sitting in the golf cart he parks under the large tree by the gym.

I'm at my house in minutes, and I don't even bother changing before I barge into Johnny's room. It's sparse, and mostly still my things are in here. The straps from his bag, the one he came here with in the first place, hang from beneath the foot of the bed. I crouch and tug the bag out, feeling the weight of his notebook inside. I shake the book lightly and thumb through the pages until the receipt falls out. I remembered it the moment Johnny mentioned it.

I fall back on my ass and hold it in my hands, squinting to make out the faded print. The date is the first thing I'm able to decipher, and I have to pause to catch my breath at the sight of it. While he was buying this glass award, I was driving around in circles trying to find him. He was right there. Less than five miles away from me. The whole time.

My palm on my chin, I give myself permission to be angry at him for a minute. Damn you, Johnny Bishop. Damn you for not letting me in from the beginning.

I take the receipt into my kitchen where the light is brightest and flatten it on my counter while I pull out a pair of readers from my kitchen drawer. My sight is pretty good, but pill bottles always make me struggle. Apparently, so do clandestine receipts that might point to murder or a coverup or—*who knows!*

SACRAMENTO TROPHY SHOPPE, for some reason located in Yucca Valley, is open from eight in the morning until seven p.m. I wonder if those hours are still accurate. I could call, or I could just go. Already walking out the door with my keys, I practice my speech to whomever is working there today.

The bill is for $499, and Johnny mentioned he gave the guy two hundred dollars when he placed the order. Maybe this whole thing is simply about someone needing to collect. It's crazy what kind of fees from one's past can show up like ghosts later in life. My mom forgot to pay a dental bill for a cleaning I had done when I was in college. I had to wait for that thing to come off *my* credit report before I could get a car loan that wasn't a million percent interest.

The shop is in the very center of Old Town, blocks from the bus depot like Johnny said. I parallel park out front then smooth my hair out and touch up my lipstick before I march inside. I don't know how this receipt ended up in Johnny's presence again, so I think the best way to play this is to be confident yet vague.

A small bell rings above the door when I walk in and a young man, maybe eighteen or nineteen, comes out from a back office behind a glass-case counter. He's eating a sandwich, and seems irritated that I'm interrupting.

"Yeah," he mutters, mouth full of bread. This suddenly got easier.

"Yes, hello. I'm here on behalf of my client. He was sent this receipt for an item he purchased several years ago. Can you let me know if your store sent it?" I hold the receipt out and the kid snatches it from my hand and holds it in front of his face. His eyes are red and puffy. I'm pretty sure he's stoned.

"Let me ask my grandpa. Hold on." Curly red hair and zits all tucked under a ballcap. That's where my fate is right now. In this kid's hands.

After a few minutes, the kid comes back out carrying a box quite literally the size of a breadbox, and an old man wobbles behind him with a cane. He has two pairs of glasses on his forehead, and none on his eyes. He squints when he makes it to the counter across from me.

"You Bishop?"

I swallow the need to nervously giggle.

"I am," I answer. I mean, what's a little truth lie right now.

The man stares at me hard for a few minutes then rears back, coughing out a thundering laugh.

"Eh, I'm just messing with you. I can see fine. And I know you're a really pretty lady instead of some screwed up, head-up-his-ass rock star." The man tugs a stool close to the counter and slides half his rather wide ass on the seat. He rests an elbow on the glass top then reaches his hand out to me.

"I'm Ray. Nice to meet you."

I give his palm a skeptical half smile then decide to play this a little less deviously. We shake.

"I'm Brynn. And I'm friends with that head-up-his-ass rock star."

Ray coughs out more laughter then motions for the kid to slide the box our way. He reaches beneath the counter and pulls out a box cutter, which he uses to slice open the box. He blows away a lot of dust and I wave my hand in front of me to clear the air. My black skirt is now covered in some of it.

"I sent that receipt to that kid's people—is that what they call it? Someone's *people?*" He pulls out a few layers of tissue paper, somehow bright white and pristine. It's a strange juxtaposition against the flimsy, dirty box.

"*You* sent the receipt." I lower my chin as I peer at him.

"Yep. Kid never came back to pick this damn thing up, and I read about his dad dying and all that. I tried to find a way to get it to him for years, but then I sort of just forgot about it and put the thing in storage. We've been cleaning out for the last few months, though, and I found it again. We're modernizing—my grandson's idea." He rolls his eyes as he nods toward the pothead with red hair. I grimace and nod in commiseration.

"So you tried to reach out again," I lead, understanding this part of the story a little more.

"I might be old, but I know my way around the Internet. I found some people on that online book thing and they gave me an address to send it to."

"Ah," I nod. "And you just sent it on, in an envelope."

"Well, sure. It's pretty self-explanatory. I got your award, and you still owe me three hundred bucks, you rich asshole."

I laugh out hard at that one. I may be back on Johnny's side for most things, but he might deserve to be called a rich asshole from time to time. Especially by Ray, who I have decided I like quite a lot.

"Well, Ray. Let me take care of that for you. And I fully intend to charge that rich asshole interest for my loan." Ray chuckles and I hand him my credit card. He snaps his fingers toward his grandson, who comes over with a plug-in device he connects to Ray's phone. After a few failed attempts at connecting to Wi-Fi, they finally get things hooked up and charge my card for what Johnny owed.

"Well, you want to see it at least before you haul it away?"

I nod.

Ray slides off his stool and reaches into the box, pulling out a deep red flame-like statue with words engraved in the dead center. My eyes pass over what I assume is Kevin's name and some accolade he never deserved and instead focus on the color. Red glass. Like the red glass wings I admired in Beth's home. Red glass, which is hard to make, and so much easier to melt and reuse.

"Looks like exactly what I'm sure he ordered. Thank you." I don't know how I manage to speak coherently considering the gears spinning in my brain, all lining up at once. But I say enough to satisfy Ray, and he packs the award back up for me, taping the top closed then scooting it in my direction to take out of his hands forever.

My hands tremble when I take on the weight of the box. Not because it's heavy, though it is, but because what I'm walking out of this store with is definitely a clue. And I think maybe Beth Bishop was graced with the fortune of living in a town with a very small, incredibly unsophisticated police department.

I pull away from Ray's shop, but immediately turn a corner and stop at a gas station to process everything that just happened. My head is swirling, and the world is tilting a bit under my car. I haven't had a bout of vertigo in years, but I feel one coming on right now. Stress does this. And I'm definitely stressed.

My head swivels against my seat back and my eyes drop to the box. I don't think Beth should talk to the reporter. I don't think she should talk to anyone but the few of us she already does. Ever again. Minus any doctors. She can talk to them. Can murder be classified as a HIPPA violation?

Finally certain with my decision, I tap out a quick response to Beth's message.

> ME: I love you, Beth, but you really shouldn't talk to reporters.

I read my words over a few times and decide that my response is direct enough yet also not an implication of anything. *Jesus! I should have left this secret alone.*

I shift into drive and make it all the way to the turn lane out of the gas station when my phone vibrates against my thigh. I stop to read Beth's response.

> BETH: Too late. She's having tea with me right now.

Shit!

I waited too long. I underestimated her. Shame on me, too. I assumed she was too weak to do this on her own. I let the way her late husband treated her make that assumption for me. But Beth is a fighter. She's a survivor. She's patient and loving and would do anything for her son. *Anything.*

My eyes flutter closed for a few seconds and I consider the things Beth could have already said. She doesn't want any of this in Johnny's life. She never wanted his father in his life. It's why she insisted the both of them go by her maiden name. She used her husband's ego to give her son freedom, spinning a line about him having a hard time getting taken seriously at football because the other players and coaches constantly compare him to the great Kevin Forrester. It's the one gift Johnny got when they were forced to move to the desert after his dad was fired. He got freedom from the Forrester name. All his mom needed to do was make Kevin believe living in his shadow might affect his performance in front of scouts. And getting to relive his glory days through his son was the *only* thing Kevin Forrester cared about.

I make it to Beth's house in fifteen minutes, the entire way mentally acting out the conversation she could be having with a very astute reporter. I pull into the driveway and roll all the way up, stopping hard enough to squeal the tires. I smell the burnt rubber when I get out.

As I make my way up the walkway, I'm hit with a wave of sickening nostalgia. The last time I rushed to her house like this, I was worried about Johnny and afraid something bad had happened. Turns out, I was right.

I power through the fog from the past and don't bother with knocking or buzzing my way in. The door is unlocked, so I rush inside then slow myself to a casual walk when I reach the kitchen. Beth and Shayla sit to my right in the dining room. Shayla flips her notebook shut and tucks it into a leather satchel before zipping her attention to me.

"Brynn! Nice to see you." Her deep red lipstick reminds me of blood on a vampire's mouth. What did she get out of Beth?

"Yes, uh. Sorry, I didn't realize Beth would have company. I came over . . ."

I pause for just a breath, my stomach jolting with adrenaline and panic at my loss of words. I'm terrible at lying on the fly.

"For the wings," Beth steps in. "I promised her she could have them. I'll box them into some tissue paper for you, dear."

My eyes dart to Shayla at the mere mention of the glass sculptures. She doesn't seem fazed, so I think maybe she's unaware of what those wings really are. Or maybe she's a master at the poker face. Or interviewing murderers. What if she's interviewed so many murderers that it's basically boring to her and after learning everything she's content to yawn and call it a day?

"Beth, thank you for the tea. It was lovely getting to spend time with you and learn so much about your son. His story. *Your* story. I am grateful for your time." Shayla stands and turns to face me. She pauses with her mouth open for a moment, but snaps it shut and simply offers me a smile.

"Nice to see you again," she says as we pass.

"Likewise," I respond. That's a word I've said exactly once in my life. *Likewise?*

I scowl at her back on instinct, and as Beth walks her through the door and out to the car parked at the bottom of the driveway, I flop down in the chair she just abandoned. I glance under the table, hopeful that somehow her notebooks slipped out and got left behind. It didn't, so all that's left is hoping Beth spun a good tale for a past Pulitzer-winning reporter. I did my homework on Shayla this morning. She's the real deal.

The door clicks shut and I lift my head to make sure Beth has returned alone. She leans back on the door and folds her arms over her chest, a sure smile connecting her cheeks. She's wearing white denim overalls with daisies embroidered on the front and her hair is piled into a thousand curls on top of her head. Bright green Crocs on her feet.

"Why didn't you wait for me?" I know why, but I want her to say it.

"You were busy with school. And I know what you would

have said anyhow." She shrugs then stretches her arms over her head in a carefree manner that almost makes me laugh with hysteria.

"You don't know what I would have said," I challenge.

She lowers her chin and narrows her eyes on me.

"Honey, yes I do. You would have told me reporters aren't to be trusted, and then forbade me from talking." She strolls over to the table and gathers up the empty teacups and the kettle. She scurries them into the kitchen to rinse things off.

"Forbid feels like a strong word." I offer a sloppy, crooked smile.

She shrugs again, then finishes cleaning her tea set before coming over to join me at the table. It's been years since she and I sat like this. Back then, there was always a lingering fear in the air that her husband would come home and suck the life out of the room. He's not coming home ever again. This isn't his home anymore, either. It's hers.

"You know how much I hated not being in control of my life for most of it? I unwillingly gave up my choices. He tricked me with charm and then slowly, day by day, stole my power and my joy. I wasn't in control of anything, certainly not my own story. But Brynn? Now I am. And I was not going to let anyone, not even my sweet baby boy, tell me I couldn't."

Her perspective is a bit sobering. But I still don't think leaving her fate up to a reporter is the wisest decision. I have to ask—for my peace of mind and so I know exactly how sick Johnny is going to be.

"Did you tell her the whole story?"

"I told her my story, from beginning to end." Beth pats the table twice with her palm and sits back with ease, letting her hands fall into a comfortable pile in her lap.

"The truth?" My wide-eyed reaction makes her laugh.

"Yes, Brynn. I told that woman my truth."

She holds my stare for a few seconds, and my stomach brews with uncertainty. I'm not sure we are both talking about the same truths. There's a pretend one and the real one. I decide for clarity, I should retrieve the gift I brought in my car.

"One moment," I say, holding up a finger. I head out to my car and snag the box then carry it inside, resting it on her table. I force my thumbnail through the tape and peel open the box flaps before pulling out one very red, very obnoxious glass award.

"Look familiar?" I plunk the heavy statue down on the table and slide the box out of our way. I tap the glass with my fingernails, then glance over my shoulder toward the sets of wings.

"It melts well but it's hard to make from scratch." I turn back to face Beth, expecting horror or maybe some sort of plea to not tell anyone. Instead, I get a rather smug grin.

"It is. So thank you for bringing me more."

She pins me with the most calm, confident stare, and I let out a nervous, breathy laugh under her scrutiny. I bring my hand up to my mouth, cupping it so I can hang it open and be aghast without being rude.

"Did you tell her about the glass?" I can't imagine she walked the reporter through all the details.

"We spent our time talking about all of the ways her father was like Kevin. There's a lot of us out there, you know. So many similar stories." Beth's mouth tightens and her jaw flexes the same way her son's does when he's angry. "We both agreed that we shouldn't be afraid of being believed when we have stories like ours. We shouldn't have to think about all the ways we'll be judged and held up to an impossible standard of proof. We should get to call out abuse and get help. Instead, though, we hide in the shadows and pray to God for an out."

My heart cracks at her brutal truth. She was honest with

Shayla, from the first regret of marriage all the way to the end. I don't have to ask for transcripts. I know in my heart. She's choosing to trust that Shayla will get that story right—*just* right. I wish I had the same faith.

"Johnny told me about the lake. That he took him to the lake."

Beth blinks slowly then nods.

"He did. And that is *all* he did. His dad spent more time drinking on that lake than being a father. Johnny just put him in his natural habitat. And as far as anyone is concerned, Shayla included, Johnny was in LA when his father 'went to the lake.'"

My gaze drops because what he did was bury him under several feet of water.

"So she didn't get the *whole* story," I say.

There's a long pause as we stare at one another. Her mouth softens into a shallow smile.

"I said I told her *my* story."

My face puzzles.

"I'll tell you everything if you want, honey. But I also think this cancer and the one growing in me is mine. You and Johnny don't need to carry this weight if you hope to have a future. There are some things you just can't come back from."

My eyes flash to her face at those words. I marinate on them for a few breaths and decide, at least for now, that she and her son might be right about this. I know enough. I know that Beth did what she had to do, and then Johnny did what he had to in order to help his mom get her freedom.

Kevin Forrester supposedly hit his head on his boat propeller then the rocky floor of Tanque Mountain Lake. He was pickled with alcohol. Likely fell out of his fishing boat. Experienced blunt force trauma to the head. Case open and shut after a few cursory interviews. So what that there was lingering speculation. All that mattered was what anyone could prove. And red glass . . . it's easy to melt.

I decided it was for the best that I leave the wings at Beth's house for a little while longer. I'm not sure I really, truly want them anymore. Not now that I know.

I promised my mom that Johnny and I would come over for dinner one day this week. We had made loose plans for tonight, but after everything that's transpired over the last few days, I'm not sure we're still on. I'm also not sure Johnny will want to stay and sit next to me if we are.

One phone call right away was all it would have taken to stop his mom from calling Shayla on her own. I should have alerted him. I thought avoiding her request was buying time, but time isn't something she wastes any longer. I get that now. And I also get her right to control her own narrative.

I'm just not sure Johnny is going to see any of it that way.

I carry a glass of iced tea out to my parents' porch, the same one Johnny kissed me on when we were teenagers. I sit on the stoop and stretch my legs out while I stare at my phone. He's probably on his way back into town after his meeting. Or maybe he's at my house wondering where I am. I slide my thumb over his contact info but before a single ring sounds, his Jeep rumbles into my parents' driveway.

His swagger as he walks toward me indicates he's feeling more positive. I don't know what to do. I don't want to ruin this progress, burst his peace. But I also want us to live a life together where we don't have secrets.

"Good meeting?" I hold up my glass of tea and he bends

down to join me on the stoop before reaching for it and taking a big gulp. His mouth puckers and he hands my glass back to me.

"How do you stand it without sugar?" He makes a gagging sound.

"I am not a hummingbird. I don't drink sugar water." I shake my head and sigh out a light scoff then take another sip of my delicious tea.

"No, you drink yard clippings stirred in water," he teases.

I chuckle and choke on my sip, leaving me coughing.

I set my glass down and rest my hand, palm up and fingers stretched, on my knee. Johnny covers it with his and slides his fingers between mine one at a time.

"The meeting was good. That's the kind of group I need to lean on. The lady who runs it used to be a music teacher. She retired five years ago and started doing this in honor of her sister. You'd like her."

My gaze flits to his and I smile.

"I bet I would." Shifting my legs toward him, I cover our hands with my other one then bounce our tethered connection against his thigh.

"What's up?" He leans into me a little, his legs bumping into my knees.

My focus sticks to our hands, and I hope like hell we're still holding on to one another a few minutes from now.

"Your mom talked to Shayla." I hold my breath as my gaze zips up to his. His face reddens and his eyes flicker.

"She what? I mean . . . how?" He shakes his head, and when he tries to pull his hand away I grip him tighter. His gaze drops to my struggle then flies back to my eyes, his brow instantly three inches higher on his forehead. "*You* did this?"

I shake my head and utter, "No, no, no," as he worms his hand from mine. He jets to his feet and throws his hands into his hair as he takes long strides down the walkway.

"I didn't facilitate it. I just . . . I didn't stop it in time." I abandon my tea and walk down the pathway until I'm standing with Johnny at the front of his Jeep. His hands are threaded together on top of his head and his jaw is working side to side.

"Okay, but did you stop it before she said too much? I mean . . ." His chest heaves with a massive exhale as if someone threw a bowling ball at his chest.

"Beth texted me this morning and asked me to make the introduction, but I didn't respond until school was almost out. I figured if I didn't help, maybe she'd rethink things or enough time would pass."

"And you didn't think maybe you should tell me?" Johnny's eyes draw in, narrowing his focus on me.

"No, Johnny. And I'm sorry. I wanted you to go to your meeting, and I didn't think she would be able to find Shayla without my help."

"But she did." His chin drops to his chest as he lowers his gaze to punctuate his words.

I suck my lips into a straight line and nod.

"Johnny, your mom swore that the story will be good. She said she had a connection with Shayla—"

"A connection?" He puffs out a laugh and begins to pace again.

"She shared her story with her, and Shayla had a similar childhood to yours."

He spins around and pins me with a glare. I understand his doubt, and his distrust. But I also think it's time Beth gets to decide what she says to others.

"Brynn, you should have called me," he grumbles.

"Maybe. But would it have changed anything? You were miles away, and your mom found Shayla on her own anyhow."

Johnny leans against the side of the Jeep, letting his head

fall back on the door as his gaze drifts up to the sky. Cotton ball clouds dot the clear blue.

"I did solve one mystery for you?" I step toward him and tug on his arm, trying to connect with him and soothe his racing mind.

His head falls to the side and his eyelids lower, but he doesn't budge otherwise.

"You and Scooby and the gang?" His mouth quirks on one side, and I breathe a tiny ounce of relief that he's trying to be funny.

"The receipt and the award? The guy just wanted his money. Which I get is weird to track down three hundred bucks after ten years, but now that I've met him, I get it. He's that type of guy, and three hundred bucks is three hundred bucks." I shrug, expecting Johnny to laugh in response. Instead, his jaw hardens.

"You went to the shop?"

I give a tepid nod.

"And you *paid* him?"

I turn my head a little and look at him sideways.

"I did," I affirm.

"And I suppose the award is—"

"At your mom's." I wince, still not entirely sure what his concern is.

"Jesus Christ, Brynn!" Johnny walks away, into the street. He stops abruptly and drops his hands to his side. He looks up at the sky and begins laughing, but I can tell by the tenor he's not amused. Far from it.

I walk down the driveway toward him and he marches at me, stopping me halfway with his hands on my shoulders.

"I never should have ordered that thing. I panicked and thought I was helping, and then I changed my mind and figured I'd just let it go. It's a small shop, and why would anyone care that much about a few hundred dollars? My mom could lose what's left of her life. Brynn . . . I left town, without —" He chokes on his words as his eyes become glassy. He holds a fist to his mouth and looks to his side, his throat moving with a hard swallow.

"Your mom swears the story won't be bad." I keep repeating Beth's confident words but deep down, I don't believe her. She didn't relay exactly what she said, only that she told the truth, her truth, from beginning to end. And the only truth I know is what I've been able to piece together with receipts and random bits of glass blowing knowledge and a timeline that makes everything seem pretty grim.

"My mom . . . is the whole reason I left town without you!" His eyes pierce me, their sudden acute sadness, the way they're clouded with regret.

"Fuck, Brynn. All it's going to take is one asshole who thinks my dad walked on water to start asking questions. They'll put my mom away. For the maybe two years she has left. I missed a decade with her. A decade with you. And you and she just want to throw all of that sacrifice up into the air like confetti."

"That is not fair!" I push his chest with both palms, but he grips my wrists and stares me down. My arms relax after a few seconds. Johnny has never liked physical outbursts. He's never indulged in a fight, not even when Devin baited him when we were in high school. He doesn't want to be his father. I wish he could see all the ways he's not.

"I'm sorry. For everything, Johnny. I'm sorry I didn't call you when your mom texted me, that I didn't know I shouldn't figure out who sent you the mysterious receipt. I'm sorry I spent the last ten years of my life so angry at you for leaving me there like a fool, waiting in a fish and chips parking lot. I'm sorry I didn't just *know*. Was I supposed to? Or was I simply meant to not care enough to dwell on any of it? Because yeah, Johnny. I have spent nearly a third of my life wondering when it comes to you. Because you haven't shared. I know things but I also *don't*. I guess, and I assume, but that's not a way to be in love with someone."

His head flies up at that word—*love*.

I tremble and clench my fists against my hips, steeling myself.

"Yeah, Johnny. I'm in love with you. And ten years and a broken heart hasn't done shit to dim my feelings."

"You can't love me." He shakes his head emphatically.

I shrug and gurgle out a pathetic laugh.

"Well, sucks for me, then, because I do."

His gaze narrows even more and he shakes his head.

"You shouldn't. The memories in my head . . ." His voice trails off and his chest shudders. I reach toward him again, but he takes a step back. It's as if he fears my touch will somehow poison him. His rebuff hurts.

"Tell me, Johnny. If you're so sure your mom is wrong and that Shayla is going to write some sordid confession on her behalf, then tell me what it will say. Give me the story before I have to read it on the *Elite Affair* website." I hug myself and shift my weight, trying to make myself unmovable. If he's going to sidestep this conversation and walk away, I want him to have to literally walk around me to do it.

Our standoff lasts several seconds, the warm sun beating down on my head while the cool breeze chills my arms. It's witching season here in the desert, or so my mom has always called it. The days are warm and the nights are bone chilling. Right now, my insides are cold. So is my heart.

"You want to know why I didn't show up?"

His gaze challenges me, his expression hardened.

"Desperately," I plea.

He bites the tip of his tongue and holds my gaze hostage for a full breath.

"My father came home early. Police showed up because someone made a report. He charmed them, signed some autographs, and when they left, he wrapped his arm around my neck and squeezed until I nearly passed out. My mom stopped him."

"Johnny, oh . . ." I reach for him again, and he steps back once more.

"Do you want to know how? What that glass did to his skull? How instant it was? The blood? How heavy he was to carry to his SUV, then to his boat? How I had to swim through the water in my clothes, pushing him out toward the rocks so I could force him overboard and be sure to dent his propeller with my boot before swimming back to shore? How I ran home, soaking wet, so his stupid vehicle would be at the lake? Or maybe you want to know how my mom burned my wet clothes along with the bloody kitchen rug then gave me all the money she'd worked so hard to save and begged me to leave and never come back? How she knew those police officers would come back, and if they figured it out, she'd live with the consequences but she couldn't bear it if my life was ruined too. How I promised to stay away, to avoid contact as much as possible and make it seem as if I left both of them like some troubled teen looking for the rock star life. I muted the relentless nightmares with pills and alcohol, just like that asshole did."

His mouth goes slack, his expression sick. He runs a palm along his scruffy cheek, scratching at his whiskers as his gaze drifts to the side.

"If only you'd told me. I would have helped." I would have found a way. My father would have. Teddy. Any of us.

"No, that worry was mine to own. And fuck, Brynn. The worry. Did I clean the SUV good enough? Did I pick the right spot to dump him overboard? And then, does what I did make me like him? The fucking shame! I spent ten years blitzed out of my mind, and when I wasn't, all I could think about was what my mom did to save me, what I did to save her, and how I turned into a rotten, addict piece of shit too."

Johnny's eyes come back to mine.

"I wasn't going to ruin your life. And that's all I'd be doing, Brynn. So don't love me. The only thing people get out of doing that is a curse."

He walks around me and climbs into his Jeep without another word. His eyes don't even reach mine as he passes again while backing out. When I dial his number, he doesn't answer, though I can see him idling at the end of the driveway. It's like watching him leave all over again, only this time I actually get to see it.

I'm too empty to cry. It's a dry hurt, and it burns from the inside out. What good is getting in my car and chasing him? His demons are too deep, and his past is a waking nightmare.

"Johnny's leaving?" My dad's voice calls me back toward the house. I spin to find him strolling my way, his hands in his jeans pockets.

"Remember when you met Johnny's dad that night at the football game?" I ask my father.

"Sure do. Never forget," he says, grimacing with disdain.

"You said we needed to get Johnny help," I prompt.

My dad nods.

"Did you? Ever?"

My dad's gaze sinks into mine as he rummages through old memories.

"I did make a report with the police requesting they maybe pay a random visit or two. I thought maybe they would be able to catch on to the situation. I don't think they ever did, though."

My gut sinks.

"Yeah. That's too bad," I mutter, looking away to hide my urge to cry. My dad sent the cops to Johnny's house that day. And it was the right thing to do, though we should have done so much more. And look how it all turned out.

"He's a good man, Brynn. Despite all the shit that kid's been through, he grew up to be a good man deep down. I believe people like him can walk through their fires and come out all right." My father's palm centers on my back and I crumple inside. Because while I want to believe he's right, there's a big part of me that doesn't.

And I still love Johnny Bishop, regardless.

Chapter 28
Age 18, One Week After Johnny Left

There are so many videos.

As I knew he would, Johnny absolutely killed it in LA. His life since taking the stage in front of a bunch of screaming college girls has been a whirlwind. Apparently, he's been signed by Rosco's label and booked on one of the late night talk shows as a musical guest in the next few weeks. He's got some opening gigs set for Rosco's shows in California, Nevada, and Arizona, playing covers until his own album is done. Everyone wants to capitalize off the hype from his show, from him going viral. And it's hard to sort out what's really in the works and what's rumor, though the news coming directly from the Rosco fan page feels legit. It's impossible to avoid the news. Especially when everyone here keeps sharing it with me as if I somehow deserve credit. As if we're a couple still. As if he didn't take off without as much as a goodbye.

It's not their faults. I haven't told anyone that other than Teddy, and that's because he was left high and dry too. The videos seem to be hard for him to watch as well. It's a strange feeling, wanting to be happy and proud of someone but also hating them a little.

Is that what I feel? Do I hate Johnny?

He played "Shelter" again in LA, and my gut tells me that song will be everywhere within a month's time. That's his first single, his breakthrough hit. It's the right mix of rock and pain, which is what makes a song truly great.

There's a new round of buzz making its way through the hallways today. I've managed to avoid it for the first few hours, but Teddy is waiting for me outside the cafeteria with his phone in front of his face, which means he's going to make sure I see whatever's new. I'll watch if Teddy wants me to.

I shuffle toward him and slip one arm from my backpack so I can fish out my wallet to buy lunch. His eyes flit up to me then drop back to his phone, his brow pulled in tight and his mouth slack.

"What is it? Did he finally suck at something and someone caught it on video?" That's not possible. Johnny doesn't suck at anything. But whatever Teddy's watching is definitely not positive. He looks a little sick.

"They found his dad . . . in the lake." He hands his phone over to me and I take it in my palm.

It's a social post linking to a news story in the *Yucca News*, our local paper that spotlights football scores and bake sales. We haven't had real news to cover here in years. But that headline . . . it's big news.

BODY FOUND IN TANQUE MOUNTAIN LAKE IDENTIFIED AS FORMER FOOTBALL STAR KEVIN FORRESTER

"Holy shit," I mutter.

"Right? Holy shit," Teddy echoes.

The story offers very little detail. Someone found his body yesterday while fishing and authorities found his abandoned boat drifting in one of the coves. The lake is closed while police investigate. Then there are a few key words that pop out—*foul play* and *interviewing suspects*.

My gaze pops up to Teddy's face.

"Who are they interviewing?"

He sucks in his lips and waggles his head as he shrugs.

I give him his phone back and immediately jet to a corner table in the cafeteria so I can search for more news on my own. Teddy takes a seat across from me and does the same. The idea of actually eating at lunch is suddenly unappealing. There isn't any video news yet, so we're left piecing together tiny bits from social media.

"They've already talked to Beth, it looks like," Teddy says, showing me something he found from one of the reporters at *The Times*.

"It looks like an autopsy report is pending, but a few people have mentioned intoxication. I wonder if he crashed the boat or just fell out." Our eyes meet for a brief connection and we silently seem to agree that theory is quite possible.

"Oh shit!" Teddy bursts.

"What?" I stand from my seat and look over the top of his phone. He flattens it on the table so I can see. It's a photo someone posted of Johnny at the Yucca police station, being walked in by two officers.

"When was that?" My brow creases so deep it hurts.

"I think that's now. Like, someone just posted this," he says.

My stomach twists and my legs rush with adrenaline. *Johnny is here.*

"Teddy . . . we have to go." I stare across the table at my friend, my heart suddenly thundering in the center of my chest. My fingers teem with nervous energy and my ears are ringing with the massive rush of blood sweeping through my body. I feel sweaty and lightheaded so I flatten my hands on the tabletop.

"Are you all right?" Teddy is next to me in a flash, his shoulder under my arm as he props me up and helps me back to a seated position. He kneels in front of me while I cup my ears with my hands and bend over with my elbows on my knees.

"I think I'm going to be sick," I manage to get out about a second before vomiting on the floor.

"Oh . . . damn. Brynn, it's okay. I'll get help."

I wave him off, embarrassed and confused at the same time. It's no use, though, and he rushes across the cafeteria, coming back with our biology teacher, Mr. Gordon, along with a bucket and mop.

"Brynn, can we get you to the nurse's office?" I'm not sure who asks me this, but I shake my head and mutter, "Uh uh."

The whooshing sound won't stop, and with every pass over my ear drum, a new wave of nausea hits. It takes me several minutes to be able to sit upright again, and when I do, I'm still not able to focus on everything around me. The world is too bright and voices are too muted. Someone helps me grasp a Styrofoam cup and urges me to lift it. I open my mouth when the edge of a straw tickles my lip.

"It's water, Brynn. Drink." I think that's Teddy.

My body is cold but sweaty. I take a big gulp that nearly chokes me, and I cough it out and set the cup down on the table. My surroundings are beginning to come into focus.

"Brynn, they called me. Sweetheart, let's go home. I'll take a half day."

I force my eyes wide and stretch my jaw in an effort to pop my ears open more. My dad comes into view, and soon his hand is rubbing circles on my back.

"I'm okay," I insist, but the small group gathered around me and the smell of disinfectant being lathered on the floor says otherwise.

"Even if you are, no harm in taking a day," my dad insists.

I swivel my head to meet his sympathetic gaze.

"Okay, Dad." My mouth tastes terrible, so I pluck the cup in my hands as my father helps me to my feet. Teddy grabs my backpack and I take careful sips of the water as the three of us snake our way through campus to my father's car.

"Give me your keys, Brynn. I'll drop your car off later," Teddy says as he sets my backpack down in my lap. I unzip the top and dig my hand in, feeling around for the jagged metal edge. I pull it out by my Howl Marching Band key ring and hand it to Teddy. He squeezes his hand around mine once before softly shutting the door.

My dad starts the engine while I work the safety belt over my body and click it in place. His radio is tuned to a news station, and they're talking about the local stir and the viral teen sensation who was hauled back to his hometown today for questioning. I blink my eyes to focus and stare at the 101.7 glowing on my dad's dashboard. His hand moves to the dial to change the station, but I touch his fingers to stop him.

"I want to listen," I say. I can feel his gaze on me, but I don't look him in the eyes. My dad is pretty intuitive. He knows I'm upset. He probably knows why I'm sick.

The report doesn't offer much. It's about as in-depth as the few sentences on the post I saw. Johnny's been brought in for questioning. Beth has already talked with police. She told them her husband was gone for a few days, which was nothing abnormal at all.

We will be following this story for you and bringing you the toxicology report when it's available.

I blink at the reporter's words. That report is going to be pickled, just like the man.

"Are you going to see him?" I don't know why my father would, but I also don't know who else Johnny has. Can Beth handle all of this? What does any of it mean?

"I don't know, Brynn. This feels like something we should stay out of until—"

"Until they find out if Johnny killed him?" I manage to give my dad a quick sideways glance. My stomach clenches at my own words.

My father shakes his head then reaches a hand over to squeeze my shoulder.

"He didn't kill anyone, Brynn. We know that much. Me and you? We know that much."

I look back to the dial on the radio console. My ears muffle the rest of the news, reports about traffic on the ten and a cooling trend. My mind replaces all other sound with Johnny's voice, with his song "Shelter," and the words that secretly skewer his father and thank me for giving him light. Maybe he'll call me or come to our house when this is done. Maybe his record label will drop him or cancel the tour. It would crush him, but maybe that's what's best.

Whatever happens, I need to see him. I need to know he's okay. I need to hug him one more time. I need his heart at my ear so I can right my own rhythm, and so he can right his. Right now, everything is just wrong.

Chapter 29
Present

Johnny's things were gone from my house when I got back. I suppose deep down I knew they would be. Maybe that's why I didn't follow him after he left my parents' house. I knew he needed space; perhaps I needed it too.

It's been a week since he left. I called Beth when I found my guest room cleared out to see if he was staying with her. She said he went to LA to take care of some business. I know what LA business is like, and I've been sick with worry and visions of the trouble he's been getting into. His recovery is fragile, and I don't want him comparing himself to his father while he's surrounded by temptations. And stress.

I've also been consuming every story Shayla has ever written. I know her piece on Johnny won't come out for several weeks. I'm media savvy enough to know how deadlines work, and I'm sure there are more photo shoots to be scheduled and facts to be checked. The label pushed this story because they want it to coincide with his next album, but all I can glean from the website is that the album is dropping soon.

Soon isn't a very firm date. Perhaps it's purposely vague in case Johnny decides not to do the interview. Or maybe they are holding back in case what comes out in the story isn't very PR friendly.

God, I hope Beth's instincts are right.

He left the Martin guitar behind, and I don't have the heart to take it back to my father. It was a gift. One my dad doesn't want back. I know that in my heart. There's also a piece of me that hopes if I hold on to it—keep it here—maybe Johnny will come back for it.

It's hard to put myself in his shoes. There's so much about the version of him that he is now that is still a mystery to me. I used to think I would know everything he was thinking. We were so in tune, so similar. But now? I can't fathom the monsters in his head. I don't know where they tell him to go, or what they tell him to do. I'm sure they're the cause of his spiral over the years. They're the reason he stayed away.

Guilt. Duty. Remorse. Fear. Love.

That's their names. He holds them all inside to protect his mother, to protect me. To him, love is a monster. Love is a weakness. If he lets love out, then the other monsters will follow and hurt us.

I've been staring at Shayla's rumpled business card for at least an hour. Jade has been staying after to work on her piece, and I've been trying to fill Johnny's shoes, but I'm not what she needs. I'm theory and strategy. But Johnny . . . he's emotions and personality. I don't know how to inject that into her work, and I want her to find success. I think I see a little of my young dreams in her eyes.

"Hey, Jade?"

She pauses her fingers on the piano and pulls the pencil from her mouth. She's been writing her own piece and it's nearly done. It's down to finessing now, and it's good. But what

Jade has is so much more than all of her talent and technical skills. She's more than a songwriter. She's a performer.

"Yes, Ms. Fisher?"

I leave my desk and slide onto the piano bench next to her, pressing my hands into the keys to play a familiar chord.

"I think we should try something bold. For your audition tape, I mean."

She leans back and takes a deep breath, likely feeling a little overwhelmed given that it's due soon and she's been spending every waking hour on the work in front of us.

"I think we should send this too, don't get me wrong." I close the songbook and pull the pencil from her hand, resting it on the ledge. "But I think, maybe, what if . . . we also give them more?"

"More, like?" Her face scowls and she coils her fingers into fists that she stuffs between her knees. Shoot, I didn't mean to stress her out. But I know she has it, what Johnny has. If we could just harness it in the right way.

"Do you know Johnny's song 'Shelter?'" I play the first few notes, surprised my fingers are able to pick them out so easily. I haven't played this song in over a decade, and back then it was only to help him work out kinks. I suppose I've always been playing it in my heart, though. In my dreams. In my thoughts when I'm driving through traffic.

"Yeah, I know it pretty well. Why?"

"I do too. And what if . . . what if we did a stripped down acoustic, you singing at a mic, and I'll accompany you at the piano? Would you be willing to try?"

Jade nods her head a little and widens her eyes.

"Uhm, I mean. I guess. As long as we send them my music too." She's such a good student, bless her heart.

"Yeah. I'm thinking a package. And for this, I'm thinking

we go ahead and post it for the world and see what it does. What do you think?"

Jade studies the piano keys for a few long seconds before turning to give me a sideways look and a slight grin. I think maybe she's excited at the idea.

"All right, Ms. Fisher. When are you thinking?"

I bite my lip and raise my brows.

"Now?"

I hold up the keys to the auditorium, and Jade's eyes zip right to them.

"You got your phone handy?" I ask.

"I'm eighteen. It's practically implanted in my hand," she jokes.

I waggle my eyebrows one more time and stand from the piano, keys in hand. Jade pauses in her seat for a few seconds, clutching the bench and staring at her closed music book. Her lips pucker as she exhales a final breath and then stands.

"Let's do it."

My body is teeming with energy. I haven't felt this excited since I was her age and about to perform with the marching band and Johnny. I lead her through the empty hallways to the auditorium near the front of the school, and I prop the door open with a nearby chair while Jade runs into the sound booth to turn on lights. In seconds, the entire stage is aglow.

"Less," I instruct.

She kills half of them, leaving only a spot on the piano and the stool by the mic. They had auditions recently for the upcoming musical. The space is perfect for this. Kismet.

We settle on dim house lights then skip down the aisle to the stage. Jade positions her phone at the edge of the stage, balancing it against one of the pop-up lights that isn't on. I let her sit on the stool and wrap her hands around the mic while I adjust the framing to make sure she's well centered in the shot.

People will be able to see me in the periphery, maybe, and that's fine. I want them to know that this performance is authentic and it's really her voice filling this room.

"Okay, you want to do a few dry runs?" I climb the steps and take a seat at the piano. This one used to be in my dad's classroom. I learned how to play on these keys. I smile at them and let my fingers roam the smooth ivory surface. This piano is home.

"I don't know; I think I'm nervous. Which I know is weird. It's just me and you, but that song is big. If I can get it right once, I think that might be the only shot I have at it." Her voice wavers with her nerves.

I hold up my hands and flatten them along the top of the piano before taking a deep breath, encouraging her to follow.

"There. Now, you're right. It's a big song. But you're a big voice. A special voice. And you might be the only other person I've met who can sing this." I'm not blowing smoke. I believe what I'm telling her, and I level her with my gaze in an effort to make her believe it too.

Her bottom lip slips from the hold of her teeth; it's trembling.

"Yeah, you're ready."

I drop my attention to the piano and move my hands into position, not looking up at Jade again until I've begun the intro and am about to cross into the first verse. I slow my playing a hint, giving her a tiny sliver to gather courage. Then it happens.

Magic.

Jade's eyes flutter shut and her hand clutches the mic as if holding on to save her from falling into the deep. Her mouth opens wide for the big notes. Her voice cracks when it's meant to. Her falsetto is a whisper that scratches open wounds, and when she hits the chorus, she's crying. Not heavy sobs, just glossy eyes that feel these words written by a truly special human. She embodies his ache and projects it into the massive auditorium, minimizing the piano accompanying her. I want to pump a fist and shout, "Yes!"

We move into the next verse and she hits her stride, opening her eyes and looking straight ahead. This is more than a simple girl singing a song. This is a young woman learning to fly, spreading her wings, letting Johnny's words carry her. It's all I can do to keep up with her, and by the time she reaches the final few notes, repeating *bolder than the storm* over and over, I find my lips moving along silently with her.

I stop playing before the end, even earlier than Johnny normally does. And Jade doesn't flinch. She keeps singing, her volume hitting the ceiling, filling my chest, and sending chills down my arms. She holds the final note out longer than Johnny does, and when her voice finally gives, that note echoes for a second longer in her wake.

I clap my hands together and bring them to my mouth, tears building in the corners of my eyes. Breathless, she draws in air as if she finished a marathon. Pushing the mic into the stand, she twists to look at me, her brown eyes wide with disbelief but crinkled at the edges with her smile. Pride. There it is. That's pride.

"Yes!" I scream, sliding away from the piano and rushing toward her. She leaps at me and we hug, then part to slap hands.

"I can't believe I just did that."

"I can." I shake my head, my hands still buzzing from pounding on the piano keys.

Johnny was always meant to perform. And when I was younger, I was jealous. But now I see it. I'm meant to teach. Not just by standing at a board and repeating concepts or by graphing out forms to march to on a field. But like this. By finding that one special gift inside my students and pulling it out. By pushing them to try.

"Should we watch it?" I lean my head toward the phone.

"Oh, hell yeah," Jade says, rushing to her device. She quickly saves the video and pulls it up for us to watch together. I hold my breath, hoping the sound does her justice, and when she hears her own voice and sees what I saw, she slaps her hand over her mouth and starts to laugh, then cry.

"I can't believe that's me!"

"I can," I reassure.

We watch the video six more times before I nudge her enough to go ahead and post it online. By the time we shut down the auditorium and make it back to my classroom, it's gotten a thousand views. It gains a dozen more with every refresh. Dozens turn into hundreds, and by the time her father comes to pick her up, she's crossed a hundred thousand views.

I'm tempted to ask her and her father to join me for dinner simply to watch that number climb along with them because I know it's going to hit a million soon. And then people are going to start to reach out to her. But this is their time. I've done my job. I gave her the nudge and turned on a few spotlights. The rest is up to her. I do warn her dad about what's coming, though, and I write down Kaylee's number for lack of knowing any other expert to send them to when things blow up. And they *will* blow up.

And maybe, if she's lucky—*if I'm lucky*—a certain mega rock star who also went to this school will show up and ask her to join him on tour.

And ask me if I'm still able to love him despite his demons.

My prediction was pretty accurate, though after three days Jade's views still haven't climbed over the million mark. They will. Her phone is already ringing with offers. It's such a different world than it was when Johnny made the leap. Sure, he was captured in video and talked about in forums, but now it's really an influencers' market, driven by this grassroots, electronic word-of-mouth that I can't keep up with.

A few of my students are walking me through the new apps I should download when my phone buzzes with a text from a number I don't recognize. My first thought is that it's one of Beth's nurses. I don't have them in my phone, and maybe I should. She and I haven't talked since Johnny left. I don't know what to say other than *I hope you were right about everything.* I know he'll be back to see her. But I don't know that he'll want to see me now that I've put words to what we've both felt for a long time.

If what we have isn't love—hasn't always been love—then I don't know what is.

I shoo my students away to focus on their work, knowing fully well that everyone in this room is busy gossiping with Jade and planning her future stadium tours rather than prepping for their music theory midterms. I hope Jade can hold on to this pure innocence through all that's coming her way. A part of me felt guilty this morning when she told me that one of the entertainment shows was going to do an interview with her. A week ago, she was focusing on Berkeley and UCLA. Maybe I didn't do such a good thing after all.

I pull up the message and zero in on Shayla's name. My stomach rolls over and my neck flushes with heat. Shayla makes me nervous. She holds too much power. I've made so many missteps since she's shown up—not stopping Beth from talking to her, then picking up that award. A part of me wants to put telling Johnny I love him in the mistake category too, but I refuse. I said it, and I've been waiting to say it for years. It was never about him saying it back, though I always hoped he would.

I step into my office and push the door shut without latching it so I have some privacy. Shayla's message is short and simple. She wants to ask me a few questions, either on or off the record. I'm tempted to do this entire thing in writing, but maybe that's worse—then there's a digital trail. My mouth waters with panic, so I uncork my water bottle and gulp down half of it.

With a deep breath, I press on her contact info and hold my phone to my ear. I don't want any of this on speaker for others to hear. Just in case.

"Brynn, thank you for the quick reply," she says, her voice denoting all business. My throat closes a little.

"Sure," I croak.

I take a pen in my hand and prop my foot up on my desk. I wore casual canvas shoes today, and while they aren't Vans like Johnny's, they are a blank canvas. Seems like a good time to copy his habit. I begin to draw shapes and shade them in.

"I'm publishing this on Monday online for subscribers, but it will print in our November issue. Most people read it online, though, so I want to make sure it's right before we go live. And I can't help but feel something is missing in this narrative."

"Oh, did you want to talk to Beth more? Or I'm sure Kaylee can track down Johnny. He's in LA—"

"I already talked to Johnny again."

Oh.

I swallow a bolt of jealousy that she spoke to him more recently than I have. I instantly feel childish yet justified.

"What can I help with, then? I really don't want to be on

397

the record, I don't think." The last thing I want is to say something that makes things worse.

"Fine, that's all right. But maybe you want to. It's up to you."

"O-kay," I hum. "Let me hear the question first."

"Do you love Johnny Bishop?"

I cough out a laugh in surprise.

"I'm sorry. I'm . . . gonna need a second. That's not what I thought—"

"You thought I was going to ask if you thought he was an accessory to murder?"

Oh, fuck.

My body drains of life and I flatten on my desk, my head barely propped up enough to keep the phone to my ear.

"I don't know what . . . I . . . *what?*" I'm dizzy navigating my way through her gotcha question. I hold my tongue, still not sure what Beth said to her. She said she didn't hold back, but *exactly* how much did she reveal?

"Brynn, I'm not recording right now. And this is my personal line. Can I be straight with you for a moment?" Good grief, this woman intimidates me. I nod, then utter, "Yes," realizing she can't see me.

"I was raised by my grandmother on my mother's side. She took me in when I was seven years old, after my father went to prison for killing my mom."

There's a short pause and I feel a need to fill it, but all I can utter is a soft, "Wow."

"Yeah. Wow."

I slide my face into my palm and buckle in for more.

"I don't share this story with anyone. Not that it's hidden, because anyone with a slight inclination to do some digging could pull up the records and find out. My dad is still in prison. He will be for life. And I haven't seen him since the police hauled him away and my grandmother tucked my face into her bosom so I didn't have to watch the investigators uncover my mom from the white sheet that someone draped over her."

"Shayla, I'm so—"

"Sorry? Yeah. That's why I don't share this, ever. That's the only thing people can say, but I don't really want the pity or sympathy. My feelings about what happened, how my young life was shaped, are pretty fucked up, Brynn. I am glad my dad is in prison. And years of therapy still haven't unearthed every-thing my young brain worked to forget. I'm not sure I want to. What I do know, is that I miss my mom. She was incredible—a vibrant soul who sang loudly at church and made things with her hands. She wasn't an artist the way Beth is, but she was to me. She was to me."

Her voice fades.

"I'm sorry, again. And I know that's not the right word. But that's the only one I have," I say.

The line is silent for a moment, then I hear a slight sniffle.

"Thank you," she finally says. "I'm telling you this because, in fourteen years of being a journalist, I have never questioned the purpose of my stories. I've uncovered corrup-tion, delicately unwoven tragedies, and I've painted the scenes of war with my words. They were hard stories, but I knew what they were for. And now here I am, staring at a notebook filled with notes that feel as if they were ripped from my own life. I've listened to my interview with Beth a hundred times. And her story? That version of Johnny's story? It might be what his label wants to dangle like a carrot to up album sales, but it's not what I want to write. Because I don't think Beth is sorry. I don't think she should be. A mother saved her son and he saved her right back. So instead, I'd like to write the other story I've picked up on through all of this."

I lift my head and slouch in my chair, spinning in a slow circle.

"What story is that?" I ask.

"A love story. Specifically, *yours*."

My mouth hangs open and my breath crackles into the phone line.

"I don't know that this story is a happy one," I admit. My heart throbs, painful stabs cutting into it with every beat. Johnny doesn't want to be loved.

"Well, maybe it's not over yet. Let me tell you what I have."

I spin back around to face my door, my eyes on my students through the small window that opens into the band room. They're still huddled around various phones and giggling.

"Hit me with it," I say.

"The handsome jock meets the band nerd and falls fast and hard. His life is ugly, and hers is bright. He dives head first into her passions, partly to be close to her, partly to discover himself. And then it turns out, she's his muse. He writes a song. A few people hear it. Then a few more. And before the young lovers know what hits them, fame sweeps in and tears them apart. Ten years, plenty of groupies, a failed marriage."

How the fu—oh that's right, she's a reporter.

"A fallen star finds himself back in his humble beginnings. A second chance. Who doesn't love a second-chance romance?"

I smirk at her quick summary of our lives. I suppose we do fit the trope, though I think there were a lot of weeds and thorns along the way.

"I'd like to read a few quotes I'm including from Beth, who I am describing as a survivor who was married to an abusive, alcoholic narcissist. She told me that Johnny didn't really come back to this town for her. Yes, she's sick, and yes, it's terminal. She has two or three years according to doctors. And her son loves her very much and would have come for her eventually. But he came because of someone else. Her diagnosis made him realize how precious time is, and how much he's lost. So let me ask you, Brynn. On the record. Do you love Johnny Bishop?"

I'm shaking in my seat, tiny ripples traveling down my arms and legs.

"Yes. On the record. I love Johnny Bishop. I just wish he loved me back."

The tear I've been holding back finally falls, but I wipe it away before it has a chance to stain my cheek.

"Well, let's see if I can get you an answer to that. I'm pretty good at my job."

I laugh out hard and loud, a little manic from my emotions, but it's enough to draw laughter from Shayla, too. It humanizes her, and all of a sudden she's not as threatening.

"Well, you are a writer. Maybe you can put the right words in his mouth."

We end our call, and I sit in my chair for a few minutes longer, staring at the happy youth laughing and plotting futures on the other side of the door. When the bell rings, I step out and stop Jade before she leaves with the others. She hangs back and we hover just inside the classroom door.

"I've been thinking, Jade. We should finish your application too. I want you to know you can have both. You can ride this wave and maybe turn it into something incredible. But you can also do this." I hold up the Berkeley folder, showing my bias for the program she should choose.

"You can be both at once. You are not limited."

The public can be both cruel and kind. They'll want to read about your tragedies and your highest successes. There won't always be a Shayla there to monitor the narrative.

"I submitted it last night, Ms. Fisher." Her cheeks round

with her grin, and my lungs open up. Of course she did. My best student ever. Of course she did.

"Good. I'm glad. Now, go give autographs away to people in PE or something." We both giggle and she runs off to catch up to her friends.

I go back into my office and shut the door, skipping my lunch hour so I can dwell in the fantasy Shayla painted a few minutes ago—a world where Johnny Bishop finds the strength to let love out and damn the consequences.

Chapter 30
Present, Monday
6:48 a.m

Beth sent the link to me the moment it went live. Just as Shayla promised, she published today. And her story is exactly as she said, though she does dive deeper into Johnny's biography and family history.

She's done her homework, dissecting his music and linking it to major events in his life. There's a section on his song "Drowning," which is about the first time he tried rehab when he was twenty-one. She spends a lot of time on 'Glass Horses,' which I always figured was a tribute to his mom. Seeing her interpretations paired with Johnny's, though, with quotes I never heard him say, sinks into my chest. Horses are wild and free, but glass is fragile. It's how his mom has lived. That song is her struggle and release. And Shayla notes it as her personal favorite. Few people will understand why.

The story structure is guided by his music, working backward from his newest songs to his very first. And while she does make mention of his father's death and the many theories that sprang up surrounding it, she never once lends them any credit. She cites the final police findings, and the autopsy and toxicology reports, that all say Kevin Forrester had opioids and a large amount of alcohol in his system.

She closes her story talking about "Shelter," revealing to the world who his angel is. I read our banter from the first interview, the one in my classroom when Johnny told her, "You could say we dated."

I grimace reading those words and hearing them in his voice.

You could say a lot of things. You could say I lost my virginity to Johnny Bishop. You could say I practiced writing his last name with my first. You could say he spent many nights in my house, a few in my room, writing his biggest hit song.

I shake off my irritation and continue reading, pausing at my words that I willingly gave on the record a few days ago.

"Yes. On the record. I love Johnny Bishop. I just wish he loved me back."

I churn through the sentences faster and faster until I get to the end—and there is no resolution. No response to my declaration. It's as if I said it in an empty room. I scan the article again, looking for those answers Shayla said she would try to get, but they aren't there. No admission of loving me back. No promise of coming to Yucca to win my heart again. Beth's words allude to me being his reason for everything, but that's all there is. His mom's hope for us. It's a sweet anecdote that will probably have half the population swooning and rooting for us and the other half canceling me on social media.

"Great. Thanks, Shayla. Just . . ." I hold back the F-bomb I want to drop just for myself. There will be plenty of those to be said in my day, I fear.

I click on the link to the side of the article that says SEE HIM LIVE, and I expect to get a list of tour dates, probably taking him to Europe and South America first just so he can be farther away than LA. But that's not what I get. Instead, it's a special charity performance where it all started.

SEE JOHNNY BISHOP LIVE, TONIGHT ONLY!
8 P.M. ALL-AGES SHOW
THE BACK PATIO AT PAPPY & HARRIET'S
PROCEEDS BENEFIT THE BETH BISHOP CANCER
FOUNDATION

Pappy & Harriet's address and phone number is displayed, and I call immediately to test the line. It's busy, which means this story is getting read already. And George's bar is going to be slammed tonight.

Out of curiosity, I check the weather, flooding with relief when I see clear skies. I've had enough of the saturated parking lot at that place to last me a lifetime. Nice weather is a perk, it turns out. One I'll enjoy tonight if I bother to attend.

I pour the rest of my coffee into a tumbler and tuck it under my arm while I gather my music books for school. I toss the books in the back seat and slide behind the wheel, gulping down one more dose of the lukewarm coffee I brewed an hour ago. I pull out of my driveway and naturally begin humming "Shelter," though the version in my head is Jade's, not Johnny's. I wonder if he's heard it. And if so, I wonder what he thinks. It's weird how the brain can multitask. My mouth mumbles the words while I navigate my way to school and mentally weigh the pros and cons of showing up to what promises to be a crowd-control nightmare. There are dozens of well-thought-out reasons not to, number one among them protecting my ego and heart from being smashed yet again.

I said I loved him. He planned a fundraiser.

Of course he planned it here, where everything started. Where I pushed him to show the world his gift and told him his life would change forever. I have to go. I can't not go. But what if I look like a fool?

MaryAnn is literally waiting in front of my parking spot in the teacher's lot when I pull in. I open the door and she pounces on me, flashing her phone in her palm.

"I can't read it when you wiggle so much," I grump, capturing her wrist to stop her from moving. I notice the headline I just finished reading and let her hand go.

"Yeah, I know. I read it." I shut my door and move to my back seat to fish out my books, which have now slid in various directions.

"You said you love him!"

I squint my eyes shut and even click my heels. Nothing happens. There is no Oz. Hell, there's no Kansas for me.

"I sure did. And man, do I feel stupid," I admit.

"Why? Oh, my God, Brynn. This is incredible! It's so . . . romantic. Like that movie *Sleepless in Seattle*. Only instead of meeting him on top of some building, you're going to a bar, in the desert, on a Monday." She chuckles at the absurdity and I push past her, shoving half of my music books into her arms.

"I'm not going," I grumble. Of course, a minute ago I decided I was. But nobody heard my thoughts.

"Stop! You are too!"

I stop in my tracks and spin around to face her, but she runs into me and we drop all of my books on the ground.

"I'm sorry," she says, crouching to scoop them up. I help her and utter, "It's fine."

It's not fine, though.

"He didn't say it back," I finally admit to MaryAnn. She falls back on her butt, folding her legs up and getting her khaki pants dirty from the sidewalk. I give in and fall back on my ass too. We may as well both have dirt and scuffs on our clothes.

"What do you mean?"

My shoulders sag and I pull my phone out, the story still pulled up on the screen. I rummage through some of the key parts, reading the story out loud, and then I get to the end.

"See? That's all me loving him in there, and a little of his mom loving the idea of us. But Johnny Bishop loving a music teacher from his hometown? A nerdy girl *you could say he dated* in high school?" I huff out a heavy breath and let my head fall forward into my hands.

"Yeah, but that's not where the story ends, Brynn. That's not how this plays out. You have to show up to see. You have to be brave enough to put it out there and show up."

"Thing is, MaryAnn. I already did. And he drove away." And moved out. And went to LA. And hasn't called. Not once.

"Then you do it again," she says.

I let a tiny punch of a laugh escape as I stare at her. Realizing she's not letting up, I concede that I'll think about it and we help each other up from the ground and head to my classroom.

The deluge of the pressure campaign only picks up steam as my day goes on. Jade has been invited to play "Shelter" with Johnny. And my parents are both coming. So is Beth. And most of the student body, half of whom are already at Pappy & Harriet's tailgating to make sure they get a good space. At this point, even if I do show up, he won't be able to see me amid the throng of fans who are going to be there.

By the time school is over, I feel physically and emotionally drained. I take my temperature in the nurse's office before I walk out, a small part of me hoping for a fever or the flu. But it reads just fine. In fact, it's perfect at ninety-eight-point-six.

The school is a ghost town. The only light on near the front offices is my boss's. I dread passing her open door because I'm sure she's heading to the concert, and like MaryAnn, I would venture to guess she's swooning over the story, too. I'll give Shayla this—she sure stirred up some buzz.

I hold my breath and count down from three, my plan to race by her office and get out the door before she knows what whirled by her. I'm busted about two steps past her door.

"There you are! Going home to get ready?"

As I assumed, she is wearing a skin-tight red dress and black boots. She's a little bit country and a little bit cougar, but all I can do is whistle and look her up and down.

"I don't know that I can top that," I say.

"Aww, thanks. But seriously. You better get there soon. I heard from MaryAnn that they are parking people in the desert. Valet for a donation."

She flashes a twenty then tucks it into her cleavage. She flips the lights to her office off and shuts the door. At this point, we're walking out together.

"I've never seen them park people in the desert." I can't even fathom how this is getting handled.

"Oh, they did back in the sixties, I guess. The Beatles came through."

I draw in my brow and consider correcting her but decide to let her have that fantasy. The Beatles never played Yucca Valley, but Johnny Bishop might just be bigger right now.

"Well, I'll see you there." She presses her key fob and flashes the lights on her car. Rather than giving her a wishy-washy maybe, I simply respond with, "Yeah" and head toward my car on the other end of the lot.

I open the back door to drop the papers I have to grade on the seat and when I shut it, I notice a lifted black truck idling near the school entrance. The massive tires are the first clue, and as it pulls closer, the country music blaring from the speakers settles it. Teddy came.

My palm flies to my chest and I let out a sob before he stops in front of me. I don't know where the tears are from, but they are coming fast and hard.

"Hey, that's not usually the reaction I get," my friend says as he hops down from his enormous truck.

"It's been a day," I confess.

He chuckles and swallows me up in his arms. Rocking me back and forth, he plants a kiss on top of my head, then steps back to give me a sinister smile.

"New truck?" I point to his wheels.

"Oh, you didn't hear? It was a gift. From a rock star."

A guttural laugh flies from my chest and my jaw drops. I walk up to his new ride and run my hand over the sleek black paint and gleaming chrome. It's gorgeous.

"Teddy, I'm not gonna lie. I'm pretty jealous." I mean, I guess I'm asking for more than a set of wheels, though. I want his heart.

"Yeah, it's pretty bad-ass. Hope you like the inside. It's your ride tonight."

I chuckle and shake my head. I can be honest with Teddy.

"Yeah, I don't know." My eyes flit from his knowing stare to the small metal ladder I would need to scale to get into that thing.

"You don't know what? If you can get in, or if you *want* to."

I chew at my bottom lip for a beat.

"Both," I admit.

"Yeah, that's not in the cards. See, I dropped Simone off an hour ago and I've been sitting out here waiting on you per my instructions from Ms. Beth."

I roll my head toward my car.

"Ah, I see. Matchmaker Beth. Did you read the story? That turned out great for me. I look like an asshole." I stop before opening my door and spin around to look Teddy in the eyes. I expect sympathy on his face but instead I get a smug grin.

"Brynn, I can think of a ton of reasons to call you an asshole, but admitting you love a man who has loved you his entire life is not one of them."

I scoff at his response.

"He didn't say it back, Ted. He didn't say it, period."

"Brynn." He levels me with a stare and twists his mouth up as if he's holding back laughter. "The man wrote an entire album about you. He went to LA and spent a week fighting with his label over postponing his next tour so he could focus his time on *you*. He made his people put together this concert, for you. So he could *show* you how he feels. He's said it plenty. You just don't hear it."

I wince, wanting to believe him so badly. But also, logic says he rearranged his tour to be close to his mom. And because a tour right now, so soon after rehab, is a terrible idea. And the concert? A charity event is a great publicity stunt. And hooking it into his hometown when the *Elite Affair* story comes out is genius.

"Don't believe me still? Damn that Johnny, he said you wouldn't."

My eyes flare.

"Come here," Teddy says, waving me toward the passenger side of the massive truck. He presses a button on his fob that opens the door, then reaches into a compartment on the door and pulls out a navy blue box tied with twine. He hands it to me and I let the weight settle in my palm while attempting to guess what's inside.

"Let me guess, it's diamonds, and I'm supposed to gush and fawn that my prince came back for me."

"Just open it, you asshole."

I glare at him for a second then pull the string to undo the knot. I pull the lid off and brush tissue paper out of the way to find a pair of twisted glass spires melted together, one red and one blue. They nearly form a heart, and they're tied on a black ribbon.

"Damn it. I am an asshole," I mutter, pulling the heavy glass from the box. It's cold to the touch, but warms when I wrap my palm around it.

"He said you had one like that but it broke. He made this with Beth for you. That's why the blue looks all fucked up, he says." I run my thumb over the blue twist, a few jagged bumps along the edge. I laugh.

"It is kind of fucked up. But it's also kind of perfect." I lift my gaze to Teddy's and he leans his head to one side, his own little *told you so.*

"Want me to tie it on?" He reaches for the ribbon but I clutch it to my chest.

"If I'm going home to change for this thing, maybe you should wait and put it on after."

He grins but takes the necklace from me anyhow, then holds out a hand to assist me into his truck.

"Yeah, your outfit? That's taken care of too."

My face puzzles, but when I step up on the ladder with Teddy's help, I see the red skirt and black blouse that is almost a perfect match to the one I wore in band ten years ago.

"Oh, my God, I'm not wearing that!" I run my hand over the felt skirt, complete with a black beaded poodle.

"Well, you better. Because he looks like a greaser from *The Outsiders* right now and I think he'll feel pretty abandoned if you bail on the outfit." My jaw drops again, shock after shock pummeling me and forcing a smile on my face.

Deciding to believe in my friend, and maybe believe a little in everyone else who has sworn to it, I get in the truck and prepare to walk into the fire and see my heart's fate. I slip into the clothes while Teddy drives, trusting him not to look because his fiancée would probably throttle him if he did. I manage to pull my hair into a ponytail with a band I find in the bottom of my purse, and before I get out of the truck, Teddy ties my necklace around my neck. I hold the glass against my heart and make a silent wish for tonight not to hurt so bad.

"Ready, band nerd?" Teddy rushes around to the passenger side and helps me down. I meet his eyes when my feet hit the ground.

"Thanks, meathead."

He snort-laughs at my retort then takes my hand to lead me through the rows and rows of vehicles that have piled up around the small desert hole-in-the-wall. He must have had a space saved for him, because I realize as we hike across the road that we are closer than most people to Pappy & Harriet's. We also don't bother with going through the front door, instead slipping through the back and cutting into a roped-off area by the back patio stage.

"Well, look who went back in time," my dad gushes, pointing to the red skirt. I salute him then spin to take in the crowd. There are at least two thousand people here, maybe more. There are hundreds sitting on the tops of trucks across the street, the inside is packed, and the back patio is standing room only with barely enough room to breathe.

I start to sweat from the sheer enormity of this moment, but before I have a chance to let the panic attack fully take over my body, the outdoor lights all zoom to the stage and Johnny Bishop walks up with his guitar in one hand and a bottle of water in the other.

He's a dream. Blue jeans. Crisp white shirt, the sleeves hugging his biceps. Hair slicked back minus the one curl that hangs over his right eye. And then his shoes—the same ones he wore in high school, all scribbled with lyrics and messages and reminders to be brave. And my name. On top of everything, in thick black marker, Johnny wrote my name with a heart

414

around it. He did it to embarrass me when we were eighteen, but I always thought it was sweet. I think it's even sweeter now.

He pulls the stool out and sits with his feet propped on the bottom rung, then swings the guitar strap over his head before adjusting the mic. His eyes find me a second after, and his gaze drops to the twisted heart on my chest.

"That looks mighty good on you." His mouth curves with the words, his smile dimpling one cheek. My skin heats under his gaze and the crowd behind me catcalls.

"Thanks, everyone, for coming out. This fundraiser is my whole heart, and it means so much to see my hometown show up like this."

His love for everyone earns him more whistles and applause.

"You know, I don't really want to sing this one alone. And we make such a great duet. Don't you think?" He licks his bottom lip then bites it, his eyes hazed as he pins me to the floor with his perfect blue eyes.

I shake my head, my legs shaking just standing here. I don't know that I would be able to step foot on that stage. Not in front of all these people.

"Brynn! Brynn! Brynn!" The front row starts the chant and it quickly spreads across the street. *Oh shit, I'm going to have to do this!*

I shut my eyes and drop my face into my hands, but manage to move my feet along the front of the stage until I reach the steps. George pulls out a stool and another mic and gets it ready for me while I nervously shuffle my way toward Johnny.

"You guys don't know this, but I'm half the singer this lady is."

A few people shout out *no way* but most people cheer. I

shake my head and slide up on the stool. I grab the mic and clear my throat.

"You guys don't know this, but Johnny Bishop is trying to flatter me," I tease. My joke gets laughter, which eases my nerves some.

"I'm definitely trying to flatter her. I might also be trying to apologize for not believing her and trusting her that things . . . well, let's just say that things would work out the way they're supposed to."

My heart flutters with hope, and I don't even bother to curse it. I'm going all in with this, and I'll either be burned a third time or I'll get my wish.

"I'm gonna play the hits for you, and some new stuff too. But first, I'd like to play a classic that damn near brought tears to my eyes the first time Brynn Fisher sang it." He begins to strum out "Landslide" and I let my head fall forward against the mic in my hand.

"Come on, I know you know the words," he says.

I lift my gaze to his, my lips tingling. I want to fast forward yet slow down time.

"Oh, I know them. By heart."

He stops strumming for a second to press his fist against the center of his chest. That move earns squeals from the crowd, and the only thing that calms them is him playing the guitar again.

I breathe in through my nose and close my eyes, doing my best to convince myself that it's only me and Johnny up here. Maybe my dad. I begin to sing, and my voice quivers with nerves at first. Then Johnny joins me, and I find my groove by the third verse. My eyes open on his, and I don't look away once. He drops in to join me for the choruses, and certain words, the ones that cut and no doubt unveiled Stevie's secrets back then.

We sync in harmony by the end, and I've taken the mic with both hands and am feeling my body work to push the notes out as far and wide as they will go. Johnny stops playing by the last repeat, and my voice is the only thing lingering in the desert night.

The applause is instant, and it rattles my bones with thunder. Johnny sets his guitar down and slides from his stool, then takes the mic from my hands and slides it back in the stand. He drops his hands in his pockets and gazes at me with the sweetest of smiles.

"Goddamn."

His voice is picked up by the mics even though we aren't holding them, and the crowd begins a new roar at his compliment.

My face bunches up, a nervous tick I haven't done in years, but I also haven't been exposed to this kind of attention in a while.

"Was it good?" I whisper.

He shakes with a quiet laugh then steps in close, sliding one hand along my cheek and moving the mic stand out of the way with the other. He brings his forehead to mine, and the ovation from the crowd nearly doubles.

"I love you. And I'm sorry I left you hanging. I promised you I would never do that again, and then I did. But I love you, too, Brynn Fisher. I have loved you for a third of my life, from the day you sprayed water in Teddy's face on the football field and told me to get off your podium. I have loved you since you looked past the cuts and bruises I tried to hide, and opened your home and heart without ever making me feel ashamed. I've loved you since I put the first few words of 'Shelter' on paper, and every time that song leaves my mouth it's dedicated to you. You are my angel. My muse. My every reason for being. And I'm sorry it took me so damn long to say it. I was just—"

"You were scared," I finish for him. His lashes brush against mine as they flutter.

"I was scared," he repeats. "But you make me brave. You make me bolder than any storm I might face. And I promise I will always come around, even if it takes me a while to get there. Always. *Always.*"

I back up an inch.

"Are you going to kiss me now? I know how you like to put on a show."

Johnny's smirk is instant.

"Yes, ma'am," he says, dropping a hand behind my back as he tilts me in my seat and presses his lips to mine in front of, possibly, everyone in the world.

It's not a show kiss. It's a *mean it* kiss. A promise for me, sealed with this kiss. Witnesses are simply a bonus.

I don't come down from floating until Johnny's hand is clutching mine and we're both standing in front of his mic. I can't take my eyes off of him. I won't, not tonight. He leans in close to the mic and pauses, letting the audience build anticipation—their whistles shifting into clapping, then stomping—until they're a storm.

"This show is just getting started! To continue the trend of women who sing a whole hell of a lot better than I do, I'd like you all to meet Jade Sinclair. She's a student here in Yucca, and I maybe taught her a chord or two, but that's just me begging for credit because, like I said . . . she sings my song a whole lot better than I do. Maybe you've seen her video. If not, you can catch her on my tour next summer."

Johnny steps to the side and holds his hand out to welcome Jade to the stage. I hug her and whisper that I'm proud of her in her ear, then follow Johnny down the steps to stand with our family—*our family.* He wraps his arms around me and holds me against his chest while we both look on at the next him coming of age on the very same stage that set his dreams ablaze. I hope her journey is far easier. I know I'll be on guard for her, and so will Johnny.

"I'd like to dedicate this to my teachers, Johnny Bishop and Ms. Fisher. This is my version of 'Shelter,'" Jade says, and as she begins to play, the crowd falls into a peaceful hush.

Johnny and I simply breathe. For the first time ever, I can actually see it—our children up on some stage, our wrinkled hands holding one another, our years of anniversaries, our homes, our travels, our life together. I see it all.

I see . . . *us.*

Epilogue

Johnny Bishop

I have thousands of reasons to be thankful for becoming a band nerd back in high school. The unspoken brotherhood that comes with having marched on a field and hung out in a band room with fellow music geeks is close to the top. No matter the age difference, us band geeks? We got each other's backs. Like the way Brynn's current marching class has mine now.

I have been crouched behind a wall of bass drum, tuba and trombone players for twenty minutes, and my calves are cramping from holding this position. But not a single one of these kids has broken rank, stepped out of formation, or even as much as snickered that I'm back here whimpering in out-of-shape pain.

The football team never would have been able to pull this off.

It's senior night, and Brynn—just like her dad back when he was the music director—always takes the field for the band's final song. She waits with the mic to present each senior

421

member with a framed photo and flowers. The students get to say a little something about what band has meant to them. What she doesn't know is that I'm going to be the last senior to speak. And the flowers? They're hers.

I never officially graduated back in the day, and it's something that has always bothered me. I was a good student, I was just a better musician, and the business took me on a ride before I got to finish the high school thing. Last week, I earned my GED. And Principal Baker is letting me be an honorary graduate with this year's class. Her warm gesture comes with the expectation that I'll give a keynote speech during the ceremony this spring, but I'll worry about that when it gets here. Maybe she'll let me sing something instead. I'm a much better singer than orator.

Right now, I'm worried about crumpling on the field in a ball of cramped muscles while I wait to surprise the love of my life by getting down on one knee in front of her—and everyone we love.

In the three years Brynn and I have been *together* together, we've cobbled together a massive family. Sure, her parents are literally family to her, but everyone else in our lives is found family. Intentional family. And since my mom passed away six months ago, they have all stepped up to fill the hole left in my heart and support me beyond any expectations I could ever have.

One of my missions when my mother told me about her diagnosis was to ensure that her life left a mark on this world, because the one she made on mine was so strong and bright and determined. The world needed to know what Beth Bishop was about. That first concert, the one I planned with my label's help and the place where I finally told Brynn I loved her, was the roots. In three years, it's grown into a massive music and cultural festival that brings artists of all kinds to this desert valley. My mom's glass is on permanent display at the small museum that welcomes everyone to our community. All profits benefit the Beth Bishop Cancer Foundation.

Cultivating this event is the second best thing I could do to honor my mother's memory. The first is going to happen in about ten minutes when I propose to the woman she insisted I have in my life forever. That's assuming, again, that I don't fall over into a ball of muscle spasm that requires the training staff to haul me away on a stretcher.

God, I really hope that doesn't happen.

The band belts out their final note of the fight song and everyone snaps to attention. I scurry my way over to the tuba players so I can stand up straight, hidden by their height. One of the kids glances over his shoulder and I point forward. "Don't you dare give me away," I whisper-shout. He winks and turns back around. When a tuba moves, people notice.

Brynn's voice booms over the loud speaker, and I stifle my laugh because it's the same speech her dad always gave and the same one she recited last year. Maybe I should bring it back for graduation. Why reinvent the wheel?

There are seven seniors this year, and it takes each of them a few minutes to pull their own speeches from their pockets and ramble them into the microphone. It's sweet and I know this moment means a lot to their parents, *but dude!* I have a ring box in my back pocket and it's burning a hole in my ass!

I position myself and glance up to the press box where her dad is ready to take over announcements and make the mic in my hand hot. Finally, Brynn's on the last one.

"Travis Yanez is planning to attend the University of Nevada on an academic scholarship. He joins their jazz band for early rehearsals this summer. Congratulations, Travis."

I stretch my legs a few times during the applause and Travis's thankfully short thank you to his parents for supporting his dreams. Peering through the rounded edges of the middle tubas, I can see Brynn shake everyone's hand one more time, then a crackle sounds over the speakers and I clear my throat. I hold up a thumb, high enough that Brynn's dad can see it, and he takes over.

"Folks, I'd like to step in here for one more announcement," he says.

Brynn spins around to face the stands, shading her eyes from the stadium lights. I see one hand flare out to her right in question, wondering what her dad is up to. My tuba shield parts so I can step through and begin my trek toward her, hopefully without her noticing, though I'm sure the growing crowd noise might clue her in. Hopefully her dad can get through his short speech first.

"Many of the parents or older siblings here might remember me, but I ran this music department for about twenty-five years. It has been an honor watching my daughter not only fill my shoes but turn them into ruby slippers. Brynn, your mother and I are so proud of you. And we want you to know that you—both of you—have our complete blessing for a beautiful life together."

Practice makes perfect, and I hit my mark as soon as my hopefully future father-in-law finishes his speech. I'm on my knee as Brynn's shoulders drop and my mic goes hot.

"Brynn Fisher," I begin. Her eyes dart around, hearing my voice in the speakers and not realizing I'm literally ten feet behind her on the grass. I cover the mic with my palm and cough. She spins around and her hands fly to her mouth.

"I'm over here," I say. The stands sound with laughter.

"How? What are you—"

"Do you mind if I talk first?" More laughter cascades into the air and Brynn shakes her head, covering her mouth once again with both hands.

"I want to tell you guys our story. If you'll indulge me."

A few people shout out while others whistle.

"When I met this girl, she was sitting on top of this very podium. The one Abby, the current drum major, is on right now."

Abby holds up a hand and waves to the crowd then hops down to make space for Brynn.

"Go on, Brynn. Take the podium. You know it's yours. Seriously, guys . . . I tried to stand on the podium when I first met her and she basically tried to push me off, like king of the mountain."

"That's not true!" Brynn shouts through giggles. I nudge her to keep climbing, and she does, stopping on top of the box. Her legs are shaking, and not only because it's cold. It's adorable to see her so nervous, and I will never forget this vision of her in her black leggings and oversized red and white Howl Band sweatshirt. Her hair is in a ponytail on top of her head, and I'd swear she's that seventeen-year-old I met more than a decade ago.

"Brynn was the absolute coolest. She knew all this stuff about music and marching and performing, and here I was this dumb jock who thought maybe it would be fun to try. She didn't have to let me worm my way into her world, but she did. She opened the door and introduced me to lifelong friends, and to a community that thinks performance art is as important as a touchdown. It was like my soul woke up the moment I met you, Brynn. And no matter how many times I try to put it back to sleep, you just keep stirring it awake. And I'm grateful. I am the man I am because of you. I have the peace I have because of you. I know how to love . . . because of you. And if you will do me the honor of saying yes and being my wife, I promise I will never touch your podium again. What do you say?"

From one knee, I rest the mic on the grass and reach into

my back pocket and pull out the black velvet box. I crack it open and the light picks up the various colors my mom carefully wove together in this unique ring. I had her make it for me two years ago, after I moved back to the desert permanently, and it's the last real piece of art she created. I knew it was what Brynn would want. Something extraordinary, like her.

I lift it up higher and shrug, my heart pounding and my body dripping with sweat. I've never been more nervous in my life. Brynn lets me off the hook in seconds, though, nodding as tears stream down her face. She pulls her hands from her mouth and shouts *yes!* I rush to her and she leaps into my arms so I can kiss her and swing her around and around until we're both dizzy.

It's a full moon tonight, the kind people make wishes upon, and mine is for this to only be the beginning of moments like this. A life of moments. A life with her. The life Beth Bishop wanted for us both.

THE END

Get the Bonus Epilogue!

Can't get enough Johnny and Brynn? For an extended bonus epilogue, sign-up for my newsletter to get a free download! (If you already get my newsletter, just put your email in and it will recognize you.)

CLICK HERE to get the bonus material now!

If you enjoyed this book, you might also like:

HOLD MY BREATH

Fractions of seconds can do lots of damage. One decision can ruin lives. A blink can be tragic. And loving a Hollister...can hurt like hell.

I would know.

They say the average person can hold their breath under water for two full minutes when pushed to the extremes. Will Hollister has been holding his for years. The oldest of two elite swimming brothers, Will was always a dominant force in the water. But in life, he preferred to let his younger brother Evan be the one to shine.

Evan got the girl, and Will...he got to bury all of the secrets. A brother's burden, the weight of it all nearly left him to drown.

The daughter of two Olympians, my path was set the day my fingertips first touched water. My future was as crystal clear as the lane I dominated in the pool—swim hard, win big, love a Hollister.

My life with Evan burned bright. He gave me arms to come home to, and a smile that fooled the world into believing everything was perfect. But it was Will who pushed me. Will...who really knew me.

And when all of the pieces fell, it was Will who started to pick them up.

In the end, the only thing that matters are those few precious seconds —and what we decide to do while we still have them in our grasp.

BUY NOW

The Varsity Series

A New Adult Sports Romance Trilogy

Begin Your Binge with Varsity Heartbreaker

Lucas Fuller is a lot of things.

He's the boy next door.

He's the first crush I ever had.

He was my first kiss.

He's also the only person who has ever broken my heart.

For two years, I've wondered what happened to the us I used to know.

We were best friends, and then suddenly...we weren't.

I tried to run away from it. I even changed schools just to make the hurt disappear.

But no matter how hard I tried to not think about Lucas, I just couldn't stay away from the high school quarterback with perfect blue eyes and so many secrets.

I'm back. We're seniors now. We've grown—all of us. And Lucas Fuller might be different, but I'm different too.

This is my time to take risks, to experience life and to fall in love for real.

I want Lucas Fuller to be a part of my story, but I know for that to happen, I need to know the truth about our past.

Acknowledgments

This one is it. This is *that* book for me. It is going to have a very special place in my soul because I will never forget how I felt while dreaming up, plotting, writing, editing, designing and giving over this book. Before I say anything else about the process and the many, many people who I need to thank, I have to start by thanking you for picking it up, clicking it, carrying it around and giving it your time. I hope I filled your cup. And left you feeling whole.

As always, I could not have done this without the support of my amazing boys and my mom, Tina. My words are shaped and trimmed by the amazing Brenda Letendre. My support system completely rests on the shoulders of Autumn at Wordsmith (who also happens to be my writing whisperer, confidence captain, whip cracker and, more often than not, brains). I will also be forever grateful to my sprinting partners on this beast of a book – Rebecca Shea, Dylan Allen, Jennie Marts, Anne Eliot and Carrie Ann Ryan. Some of you finished two books during my journey lol! And finally, to Kacey Shea, who believed in this project from the moment I spit out my jumbled explanation during our road trip to the real Yucca Valley. Thank you for lifting me up. You are an amazing writer and friend.

If you enjoyed The Moon and Back, please let someone know. I would be honored if you left a review or rating, and if you feel like telling a neighbor, or all of your social media friends, that you liked it . . . I mean, I'm not stopping you. (No, really . . . I'm kindly requesting you do.) I'm so grateful for every little boost, and I'm honored that you spend your time on my words. You may have seen that I have a bonus epilogue for this story if you sign up for my newsletter. If you missed that, go back a page or two. I promise my newsletters aren't overwhelming, and I often have freebies to share. Plus, whatever I have cooking next? I'll share the news there first.

'Til next time.

XO Ginger

About the Author

Ginger Scott is a *USA Today, Wall Street Journal* and Amazon-bestselling author from Peoria, Arizona. She has also been nominated for the Goodreads Choice and RWA Rita Awards. She is the author of several young and new adult romances, including bestsellers Cry Baby, The Hard Count, A Boy Like You, This Is Falling and Wild Reckless.

A sucker for a good romance, Ginger's other passion is sports, and she often blends the two in her stories. When she's not writing, the odds are high that she's somewhere near a baseball diamond, either watching her son swing for the fences or cheering on her favorite baseball team, the Arizona Diamondbacks. Ginger lives in Arizona and is married to her college sweetheart whom she met at ASU (fork 'em, Devils).

FIND GINGER ONLINE: www.littlemisswrite.com

 facebook.com/GingerScottAuthor

 instagram.com/authorgingerscott

 tiktok.com/@authorgingerscott

Also By Ginger Scott

The Boys of Welles

Loner

Rebel

Habit

The Fuel Series

Shift

Wreck

Burn

The Varsity Series

Varsity Heartbreaker

Varsity Tiebreaker

Varsity Rule breaker

Varsity Captain

The Waiting Series

Waiting on the Sidelines

Going Long

The Hail Mary

Like Us Duet

A Boy Like You

A Girl Like Me

The Falling Series
This Is Falling
You And Everything After
The Girl I Was Before
In Your Dreams

The Harper Boys
Wild Reckless
Wicked Restless

Standalone Reads
The Moon and Back
Southpaw
Candy Colored Sky
Cowboy Villain Damsel Duel
Drummer Girl
BRED
Cry Baby
The Hard Count
Memphis
Hold My Breath
Blindness
How We Deal With Gravity

Made in the USA
Las Vegas, NV
07 July 2024

92012365R00243